INKED IN EMERALDS

INKBOUND, BOOK 3

SHANNON MAYER

Adopted by a kindly blacksmith and his horrible wife at the age of four and unaware of her royal beginnings, Harmony has spent the last 25 years in a poverty-stricken village called The Hollow. She was plagued by dreams of a dark-haired stranger, headaches due to repressed memories and magic, all while her two evil step brothers and stepmother do their best to make her life a living hell (which is a short trip given the wretched conditions they already face). But Harm is a fighter. Plus, she's got her inventions, her best friend Molly, and her trusty falcon Fetch by her side. It might not be a lot, but it's enough to bring some glimmer of happiness to her world until she can figure out a way to escape their circumstances.

As for Molly, she's got her own plans on that front. When she takes one last, forbidden trip over the golden wall that separates The Hollow from the opulence of Alabaster City in pursuit of a wealthy husband, disaster strikes. An evening in the arms of the Crown Prince turns violent, and the stiletto heel of Molly's glass slipper winds up buried in his chest. Harm comes to save the day but she's too late. Stuck on the wrong side of the wall with a maniacal king who should be dead, an evil sorcerer, and his pack of undead soldiers called "Jackals" on the hunt for the woman who fits the glass shoe, Harmony will have to rely on her wits to keep her and Molly hidden until they can plot their escape, and sometimes the best place to hide is in plain sight…

After creating disguises for them both and landing a position as the palace falconer, Harmony is forced to rely on an unlikely group of allies, including charming but secretive Second Prince Duncan and The O'Donnellys — a family of smugglers who'd just as soon sell her for parts as help her escape. But danger lurks around every corner. Whispers — those who possess some measure of magic — still exist in Alabaster, and they aren't afraid to use their powers to ferret out the woman with the missing stiletto. As the walls start closing in, Harmony uncovers the monarchy's darkest secrets: The should-be-dead King is actually being kept "alive" through black magic, and the people of both The Hollow *and* Alabaster City are puppets under the control of a sadistic sorcerer with a plan that has served him well for nearly a century…

Strip the poor of magic, leaving them too weak to resist.

Keep the rich too comfortable to bother.

Revolutionary spirit ignited, Harm realizes she can't just save her and Molly. She must figure out how to tear the whole power structure down, and to do so, she'll need an army. When Prince Duncan offers his help, she wants to trust him, but there is no question he's hiding something.

Something big.

As the two grow closer and the prince professes his love, Harmony's dreams about the dark, handsome stranger only grow more intimate. But she needs to keep her head in the game if she has any chance of protecting her and Moll. After a series of missteps almost get them caught, Harmony realizes they are on borrowed time. She and the O'Donnelly's stage a rescue of those falsely imprisoned for Moll's "crime", and they finally make a run for it. But the sorcerer's Jackals are hot on their trail. Prince Duncan comes to their aid, and we learn his secret. He is a Whisper himself with the amazing yet terrible ability to turn into a mindless fighting machine much like a Viking berserker at the cost of both his physical well-being and his sanity. He defeats the Jackals, and they escape to join forces with famed revolutionary, The Speaker. Not quite a Shout, but far more powerful than a Whisper, The Speaker's abilities are second only to the sorcerer's himself, and he's willing to give his life to tear down the gilded wall that separates the rich from the poor and bring magic back to the people.

Their group travels to a village The Speaker has built in the treetops far away, where there are hundreds of Whispers who have been waiting for Harmony's prophesied arrival to stage their coup. The Speaker gives her a magical jeweler's loupe to help her develop the true strength of her magic as a Tinker, who can see the inner workings of things and patterns that others don't.

But when she's unable to figure out how to truly connect with her Tinker magic, and a pissed off witch from the outside world named Almira starts trying to destroy the very fabric of their universe, it seems like a long shot.

Things get bleaker when they meet up with the sorcerer and his Jackals for the battle royale. As fighting reaches a fever pitch, The Speaker insists that Harmony leave so he can finish the job, and he finally reveals the whole truth. His destiny is to die here and take the evil Sorcerer down with him. Hers is to collect three magical items and learn valuable lessons on her journey that will help her defeat the enemy bent on destroying her.

She has both gained some knowledge of her circumstances as well as a magical jeweler's loupe, which allows her to see and manipulate the filaments of magic that make up the world to create even more complex inventions. She realizes she's trapped in the pages of a fairytale book, and has done all she can in Alabaster. To complete her destiny, she needs to "turn the page" and move on to the next story.

Harmony, Molly, and Fetch approach The Shadow Abyss, and she knows she has to make the leap. But to do so, she must leave both this world and Duncan behind and turn the page…literally. As The Speaker gleefully gives his life in a blaze of glory, Duncan encourages her to leap for the dog-eared edge of their flat "world" and turn the page, carrying her, Moll, and Fetch to the next tale in their adventure, leaving Duncan behind to rebuild his fractured kingdom.

Book two, Inked in Onyx opens with Harmony, Molly, and Fetch as they are flung from one world into the next and find themselves plunged into icy waters with a pirate ship looming in the distance.

Before they can swim away in terror, they are plucked from the water by a flying Peter Pan and Tinkerbell. Harmony and Molly are relieved to find that they have been rescued by the mystical pair and have already made friends in this new world. Little do they know that they've jumped from the frying pan into the fire…

Bell and Pan bring them to an island called Neverland. Here, as they get warm and dry, they meet a group of pre-teen orphans under Bell and Pan's care called The Lost Boys, one of whom is clearly a version of Cissy Petway, a little girl they knew from The Hollow. Harm and Moll begin to realize that they are trapped inside a fairytale book, and that Cissy exists in more than one story. They are still grappling with this news when Pan begins to tell them all about the evil deeds of his mortal enemy, Captain Hook. Years before, the notorious pirate stole a magical clock from Tink and Pan it's needed to ensure that Pan would stay young forever, but before he could get away, a massive crocodile named Noru snatched the clock—and Hook's hand—and took off to a nightmarish place filled with monsters called The Weeping Fen.

Now, Pan and Hook are in a never-ending battle to get to the clock. A battle Harmony must join, when a letter The Speaker slipped into her bag lets her know that it is the key to her own destiny. She must retrieve the clock before she can turn the page to the next story and save her homeland, and to do so, she and Moll will have to betray their newfound friends.

As Harm tries to figure out how to leave Neverland to begin her journey to find the clock, she walks in on Pan practicing his knife throwing skills. When she gets closer, she sees that the target is the wanted poster of a very familiar face. She is left reeling when she finds out that the dark stranger who has been plaguing her dreams for years is the notorious Captain Hook himself. This evil pirate is clearly a part of her destiny...

A week flies by in Neverland as Bell and Pan plot their next attempt at finding the massive, clock-carrying croc as he's soon due to emerge from his lair and go on his next rampage. Harm does her best to learn about this new world and make her own plans for her and Moll to leave Never-land, along with building some new inventions she hopes will help *them* track down the croc before anyone else does.

But as Moll falls more in love with the young Lost Boys, slipping into the role of a mother figure to Cissy, Caleb, and Tristan, Harm realizes there's something off about Pan and Bell, and the idyllic facade of Neverland and its inhabitants begins to slip. She holds those thoughts close to her heart to assuage her guilt as she, Fetch, and Moll escape to take their own shot at the clock in the croc, only to find themselves scooped up by Captain Hook and his crew. At first, they fear that the bloodthirsty pirates might kill them. But when Moll shows them some of Harm's inventions and they see her Whisper magic, Hook decides to keep them on as indentured servants with only one way out; Help him get the clock before the croc hibernates again, and he will let them go free with their heads still attached to their bodies.

Harmony and Moll agree, with a plan to use Hook to get the clock and steal it from him later.

As they head on their journey, we start to see that several other characters from the previous story world also exist in this one. They hire the smuggling O'Donnellys to be their guides to The Weeping Fen, and she and Hook wind up in front of a crystal ball with Gayelette, who tells of their shared future. Harm is a princess from a place called C'an Saas, and in order to get back there, she will need to get the clock and move onto the next story. Hook's destiny is also tied to the clock, but they agree to become allies despite their mutual distrust.

On the search for the crocodile, they run into several roadblocks, including a sea serpent, Pan trying to "rescue" her and Moll, and whirlpools caused by Almira's "bookworms" eating holes in their paper world. All the while, Hook and Harm are very much enemies with a common goal here, but there is an unholy attraction building, and she hates herself for it. Moll isn't faring much better as she finds herself deeply depressed and missing her Lost Boys, despite forming an attachment to First Mate, Xander.

Just when they are questioning everything, Hook finally opens up about his past with Pan. Formerly he was one of The Lost Boys who managed to escape.

Hook knows the truth about Tinkerbell. Though she pretends to be a fairy, she's actually a monster, feeding off

The Lost Boys, who are drawn in by the magically charismatic Pan. Hook also shares that the clock they're looking for is imbued with the power to alter time and was linked to Pan by Bell, allowing them to use it to stop the aging process for him, keeping him eternally youthful and effectively immortal, like her. As long as the clock isn't ticking, neither Bell or Pan will age, and they can continue their reign of terror on orphans. So far, any attempts to stop Tink from feeding on The Lost Boys have failed because Neverland is hidden by magic. The *only* way to lure Pan out into the open again is to find the clock and get it running again.

Harmony is stunned and horrified by Hook's tale, and Molly is even more so. A lover of children, she names Tinkerbell as her mortal enemy, and the two join Hook in a vow to stop her before they leave this place, no matter what.

They, along with The O'Donnellys, delve into The Weeping Fen and find Noru The Ticking Croc. The beast is a killing machine, but they manage to defeat it and get the clock. Their victory comes at a price as they lose one of Hook's crew members and beloved friend, Trick-Eyed Tom.

They leave and head toward Neverland, sending Fetch on a mission to lure Pan and Tink away from the island so they can save the kids and set an ambush for the pair. While they sail, Harm heads to Hook's chambers to console him over the loss of his life-long friend. When she gets there, he is in the grips of a nightmare. When he is tossing and turning, she sees he is covered in tattoos. Here we learn that Hook's "gift" is that he not only absorbs the magic of those he kills, he also absorbs their memories. It's a curse that haunts him, and Harm realizes that once Hook completes his revenge against Pan and Tink, he has nothing else to live for, and it chills her to the bone. After a romantic interlude, Fetch returns, and the game is afoot. Their trap worked and Pan and Tink have left Neverland, leaving it wide open for Harm and her friends to get there and save the children.

Harmony can use her magical loupe and Whisper talents to tug at the filaments of magic within and get the clock ticking again to restart Pan's aging process. The pair are forced into a showdown for the first time as they all reunite in Neverland. They are loaded for bear, attacking Hook and his crew with everything they have. We see Pan aging, his growing panic, and the breadth of Tinkerbell's true power (along with her true physical form, which is ghastly) for the first time. During a hand-to-hand battle with Hook who is acting as a human shield for Harmony and the clock, Pan tells him he never wanted to hurt him or any of the other Lost Boys. That's why he lets them go once they get too weak to handle it. Hook laughs bitterly and says, "Is that what she told you?" He lets Pan in on the truth; When Tinkerbell claims to bring the boys back to the mainland and free them, she really takes them to a cave and drains the rest of their life force before tossing them into a pile with the others.

How does he know?

Because he found the pile of bones himself years before, which was why he escaped in the first place.

Pan's allegiance is tested here, and, for a moment, he wavers. Tinkerbell flutters to his side and begs Pan to finish him before it's too late. In the end, Pan chooses love, sacrificing himself by forcing the last of his life force into Bell in hopes of giving her enough power to win the fight and live on. A fierce battle ensues but, in the end, Harmony and her friends prevail, killing both Tink and Pan and saving the kids.

In the final chapter, they bury her and Pan together. The Lost Boys are left sad, purposeless and confused about what comes next for them. Hook offers to take them to the mainland and set them up with a place to live and a caretaker. As they sail, Molly is distraught, but Harmony is too focused on her own distress to think too much of it as they are on their way to what's known to the pirates as The Edge, which is where she will again 'turn the page.' She will have to say goodbye to Hook, and she's so tired of goodbyes...

As they get closer, she goes to the other side of the ship and tries to keep her composure. She catches sight of a distraught, weeping Molly from afar. She realizes with sudden clarity that Molly's press to get married all these years wasn't just because she wanted to rise from poverty. It was because she wanted to be a mother. Harmony knows then what she has to do. As Molly disembarks to drop The Lost Boys at their new home, Harmony instructs Hook to set sail, leaving them, and Fetch, behind.

As they glide across the sea, she realizes that more holes have opened. Almira's worms are spreading, and time is short. It's only when Hook climbs the plank beside her that she realizes he intends to go with her. She asks why and he explains that no pirate has ever sailed over The Edge, and he's about to be the first to do it.

They turn the page and are flung into Oz. As they hit the ground, Harmony looks up and is stunned to find Prince Duncan Westerly along with palace falcon, Bonnie, standing over her.

The story continues...

CHAPTER 1

"*D*uncan?"

My vision went hazy as I pushed myself to my feet.

"Harmony! Thank the gods you're alright!"

My head spun as I stared at him, openmouthed. Of all the crazy things that had happened on my journey so far, seeing Prince Charming again—here, in a whole new world—was the most surreal.

I'd run into doppelgangers before. A version of little spitfire Cissy Petway had somehow existed in multiple stories at once. Same with The O'Donnelly clan. I'd recognized each of them on the spot, but other than a fleeting hint of recognition from Cissy, it was only Gayelette, the magical visitor from C'an Saas projecting herself into the book of fairytales, that recognized me back. As far as I could tell she was like me: a traveler through the realms rather than a double like Cissy and the others.

Until now.

Duncan's eyes shone with relief as he lurched toward me and yanked me into his arms, sending Bonnie the falcon swooping off with an offended *squawk*. I returned his hug, instantly warmer inside and out at the familiar embrace.

Duncan...the *real* Duncan, was actually here. But how?

"I was starting to think I fucked it up! The Earl of Munsch said I was the only stranger to come through in years."

I was stopped from replying by the fact that my face was buried in his wool-covered chest.

"Release her before I gut you like a fish."

For a moment, Duncan's muscles flexed more tightly around me, and panic crept up the base of my spine. Hook was a stab first, ask questions later kind of pirate. Luckily, Duncan let his arms fall away as he stepped back, both hands held high in mock surrender. It was only then that I saw Hook's saber pressed against Duncan's kidney.

"James, no, it's okay! He's a friend."

Duncan cocked his head, his stare burning my skin. Joy at seeing him, both alive and well, tangled with more complex feelings—guilt and confusion. Back in Alabaster, we had gotten very close, very fast. He'd risked everything, his life, his future, his people, all to help me and Moll, and there was no question I'd felt...something for him.

And if I was being completely honest with myself, I still did. But in some ways, I'd lived a whole other lifetime since then. I'd grown stronger, learned how to fight my battles without his help, including one with a dreaded pirate who haunted my dreams and made me feel things I'd never felt before.

Not even with Duncan.

Now here we were...the three of us.

Kill me now and bury me deep from the awkwardness.

Hook never took his eyes off Duncan as he slowly lowered his weapon, but he didn't return the blade to its sheath. Duncan took a step forward and thrust out his hand.

"Duncan Westerly of Alabaster. Pleasure to make your acquaintance."

Hook's lip curled in disdain at Duncan's outstretched hand. For a second, I thought he might actually take it, if only to crush every bone. Instead, he let the silence stretch before replying.

"Captain Hook." The ice in his tone was thick as ice in the winter.

"Well, that's convenient, then, isn't it?" Duncan said, tipping his head toward James's iron appendage, the corner of his lips curving into a wry smile. The flash of a familiar dimple almost made me smile back—until I remembered he was playing with fire here.

"Duncan and I met in Alabaster, before I wound up in Neverland." I cleared my throat as Bonnie circled above twice then dropping to my shoulder. Her weight was welcome and even in the short time Fetch had been gone, I'd missed it. I missed *him*.

Now that the dust had settled, she was back and nuzzling my neck, cooing softly. She'd belonged to my mentor Bertrand, who had run the palace mew in Alabaster. Bertrand had given his life for the revolution, and I'd wondered what had happened to the falcons in his care. I let out a low sigh of contentment as I scratched at Bonnie's downy chest, the load on my heart lightening just a little.

"This here is Bonnie. She's a love, but she's also got a bit of an attitude. Don't expect her to be as easygoing as Fetch." No falcon was as good as Fetch, not even Bonnie despite the beauty that she was.

The thought of my own falcon was like a stab straight to the core of me, and I sucked in a breath. He'd been my loyal sidekick since I was four years old, and his absence was a hole inside me. Right next to the gaping void that Molly used to fill…

Nope. Not going there. Not yet. Just pretend they're on a holiday somewhere together for now.

"Speaking of Fetch, where is the little fellow?" Duncan asked, doing a quick scan of the sky before returning his gaze to me.

"This wasn't the story I came to after I left Alabaster," I explained. "There was a place before here, and…" I trailed off. Now wasn't the time to explain. "Anyway, I had a stop to make before coming here. I left Fetch there with Molly to keep her safe. We'll get to the rest of all that later. First, I need to know…how are things in Alabaster?"

When James had shown me his fairytale book—very like the one I'd had for a short while as a child, only with black-edged pages and ever-changing text, shifting and rewriting itself as new choices were made—I'd read how things had been going since we'd battled—and bested—Relyk. Still, it hadn't been long since I'd left Alabaster.

"Fantastic, although I've been away for a week now. Took a bit of time to make my way back to The Shadow Abyss and then trying to work up the nerve to jump off." He grinned and winked at me, ignoring James' glower. "That said, the rebellion was a total success, and the kingdom is now in the hands of a council elected by the people. The walls between Little Alabaster and The Hollow have come down. The shroud hiding The Smudge is no more. People are still wary, but the start is all there. The chance to re-write the future."

My jaw dropped. "All that since I left? I've only been gone a couple of weeks…"

"Weeks?" His dark brows caved into a frown. "Harmony, you've been gone for over a year."

A year…

It seemed impossible, but there it was. So how much time had passed for Molly since I'd left her back in Neverland? Six months? More?

My stomach clenched.

Her life could be completely different now… Maybe she even made a new best friend. And what of Fetch? Would he even remember me?

It was clear that Duncan did, and cared enough to risk life and limb to find me. That meant something.

I could feel James' eyes on me and I cleared my throat as I focused on nitty gritty of what Duncan was saying. "Time doesn't pass the same way in all the stories."

Was that why I needed Pan's clock, then?

More to chew on once we'd settled in, but one thing I was learning through my travels; getting the lay of the land was crucial to our success. Somehow, whether it was the fates, Gayelette, my own instincts, or a combination of all three, I needed to find the tools and the means to accomplish whatever task came my way. That's how it had gone in the last two stories.

I needed to trust the process more.

"And The Speaker's village of Whispers?" I asked, refocusing my attention on Duncan.

"They're back in Alabaster. Magic is beginning to thrive, and the land and people will prosper, the new shoots of it are already there. I'm still dealing with some minor resistance from the nobles, but all in all, things are better than I could have hoped for. We did it, Harmony. *You* did it." He made to reach for me again, stepping closer, but a low growl from James stopped him in his tracks.

My cheeks went hot, and no doubt were bright red. I cleared my throat. "How did you manage to find me?"

"I went to The Smudge to talk with the people there, that woman with the flower cart—"

"Gayelette," I cut in, nodding eagerly. "What did she say?"

"She told me that we were living inside a book of fairytales, and you had turned the page to get to the next story.

She said that you needed me." His voice rang with sincerity, his expression solemn as he spread his hands wide. "When I went back to the Shadow Abyss to follow you, I wasn't able to grab the single dog-eared page anymore. I had to take two. I just got here a few days ago and was about to leave Munsch Kin Land in search of you. But then, there you were, falling out of the sky like a shooting star."

James muttered something under his breath from behind me that sounded suspiciously like, "Bloody wanker," and I ground the toe of my boot into his instep.

"Well, I'm really glad we got here before you left. I'm so happy to see you. A friendly face, belonging to someone who actually knows who I am."

"You have no idea…" he said, his affection plain as day.

That was the thing about Duncan. Aside from hiding his Whisper when we'd first met—which gave him the ability to go berserk and fight with the strength of five men—he was an open book. You knew exactly where you stood with a man like that, as opposed to—

A slow clap broke my train of thought, and I turned to see James smacking his hand against his forearm in applause.

"Wonderful. Come to save the damsel in distress…Aren't you just a fucking hero?"

Duncan cocked his head and leveled Hook with a long stare. "Funny, at first I wondered if that heavy hook on one side versus the hand on the other would leave you off balance and an easy knock down in a fight, but now I'm realizing that chip on your shoulder probably evens things out, eh?" Duncan's smile didn't quite reach his eyes, and a bolt of fear sizzled through me as Hook took a step forward.

His voice was low and lethal when he finally spoke. "Tell you what. Why don't you test your theory and knock me down, pretty boy?"

The two men glared daggers at each other, and I saw the

moment Duncan's eye began shifting from gray to silver, his pupils elongating into diamonds…

Not good.

"Okay! Let's all take a breath here and calm down." I stepped neatly between them with a shrill chuckle. "I'm sure it's been a long day for everyone, what with us hopping worlds, and you trying to find me. Guys…we're on the same team here. No need for all this."

"You're right, as usual." Duncan was the first to step back, which was no surprise. "I'm just happy to have found you in one piece." He spared a glance at the setting sun and his brow furrowed. "We really should get indoors now, though. We don't want to be out here in the dark."

I swiveled my head, taking in my surroundings for the first time. I'd been so thrown off by seeing Duncan, I hadn't even noticed anything else.

This new world…it was a feast for the eyes—totally different from the tropical paradise of Neverland but just as beautiful. White, fluffy clouds dotted the blue sky, and the sun shone bright, but the air was cool and dry. It was the landscape that caught my attention most, though. Trees and bushes surrounded us—dark trunks exploding into a riot of stunning colors at the top—reds, purples, greens, and yellows —like a few of Molly's most outrageous wigs. The bushes were short and squat, teeming with plump fruits and berries with more colors even than the tree tops.

In spite of the idyllic scenery, I'd experienced enough horrors—from flying mantises to ticking crocs—to know one thing for sure;

If Duncan said we shouldn't be outside at night, then we shouldn't be outside at night.

"Where do we go? Where have *you* been staying?" There was no evidence of a nearby village or people.

"I've been staying in Munsch Kin Land. The townsfolk

there have been nothing but kind to me. They'll be glad to take in a couple more visitors." He turned and gestured for us to follow. "This way."

The journey was short and almost eerily silent, which gave me some much-needed time to think. I spent the precious few minutes trying to reconcile my two lives...the one I'd been living, and the one I'd left behind. Duncan and James. James and Duncan. Me and...who?

So far?

It wasn't going great.

Oddly, it felt like a year had passed for me too since I'd left Alabaster, given the countless life-changing experiences I'd gone through since I'd leapt across the pages. But when Duncan had put his arms around me, I couldn't deny...it felt so easy, so natural to burrow closer and return that hug.

I glanced at James from beneath my lashes and winced. The tension poured off him in waves—from the lines around his mouth, the narrowed eyes, the slight flare to his nostril. All as his long, no-nonsense strides threatened to put him ahead of Duncan despite the fact that he had no idea where we were going or how to get there...

Strange. When we'd jumped off the plank of the Jolly Roger, I'd been afraid of so many things:

Dying before we reached the next story. Dying *when* we reached the next story. Failing to find the item we would need to find, and never getting to return to my true home of C'an Saas. I worried about how Molly and the kids were doing, and feared we'd never be together again. And what would become of James and me after—?

I bit back a groan as my brain instantly conjured up a replay of the other night, in his cabin. His mouth on mine... his fingers playing over my heated flesh...

"Do you need to stop and consult a map?" Hook asked as Duncan paused and looked around in confusion.

"Nope, all set on that front, but thanks buddy."

That sealed it. Every other worry needed to be set to the side for the moment. The only thing I could afford to focus on right now was de-escalating the cock fight brewing between these two…

Before they wound up killing each other.

Men.

CHAPTER 2

By the time we reached the massive wall made of colored glass in every shade of the rainbow, I was ready to jump out of my skin and see if Bonnie could fly me the fuck out of here.

Glad for something to break the tension, I'd spent ten minutes of our walk filling Duncan in on all that had happened in Neverland—about Pan and Tink. About doppelganger O'Donnellys and Cissy Petway, about Noru the Ticking Croc. Then, I'd spent the last ten in tense silence, treated to a feast of barely concealed contempt and testosterone as the two men did their best to dig at one another with not-so-veiled jabs—verbal only, thank whatever gods were watching this melodrama unfold.

Fun stuff.

And now we were here...

Too bad I didn't know exactly where "here" was. I wanted to kick myself yet again for being too much of a chickenshit to let my Pawpaw read the scarier looking stories in my book of fairytales. Maybe then I'd have some idea of what we were getting into...

"This is it. Munsch Kin Land," Duncan said with a sweep of his hand.

The rainbow wall was a real feat of architecture, and I couldn't stop myself from tracing the smooth surface in wonder, my fingers pressing against the cool exterior. "I'm not a big fan of walls, as I'm sure you can imagine, but this one really is gorgeous."

The setting sun blazed through the glass, sending little twinkles of light onto the grass below like so many tiny jewels scattered at our feet. Still, a prison was a prison, no matter how fancy the bars were. I looked the length of it, trying to see an end but not finding anything definitive.

"Meant to keep danger out, or keep people in?"

"The first, it seems, although I haven't been here long enough to say for sure," Duncan replied.

"Where's the door? Assuming we go through this?" Hook asked, less impressed by the huge rainbow wall than I was.

"It's—" Before Duncan could finish his sentence, the glass in front of us trembled and shifted, a wide panel slowly sliding to one side.

"Sir Duncan, you're back!" A man with a waxed, red mustache and a bright purple suit stepped into view.

Duncan smiled and turned to me. "This is The Earl of Munsch. As the earl tells it, his father's father's father's father's father founded Munsch Kin Land centuries ago." He faced the earl again and gestured toward James and me. "I hope it's alright that I've brought some guests?"

He let out a crow of delight, slapping his barrel chest. "Most excellent, indeed. Please, come in. Friends of Sir Duncan are friends of ours!" He stepped to the side and bowed dramatically before gesturing for us to enter.

I stepped through the entrance with a gasp.

"This is the Yellow Brick Road." Duncan led the way onto a wide, golden path made of gleaming, neatly hewn bricks that seemed to give off a warmth unlike anything I'd ever felt. On either side of us, tiny homes lined the walkway, each more adorable than the last. One looked like a giant mush-room, painted white with red spots, and had flower boxes bursting with wildflowers beneath each window. The next was shaped like a pink, sugar-dusted gum-drop, with a white wraparound porch, and a little garden on the side.

"It looks like something out of a child's dream," James murmured as he looked around. I glanced at him.

"Do you recognize it from the book?"

James shook his head. "You?"

"No."

Which meant we were running blind. Again.

We turned toward the voices to see streams of people heading our way—some from a group of shops down the road, others emerging from their homes.

The people were as colorful as the village itself. None of the clothing matched—as if every person had chosen to pull pieces from their closets at random, with their eyes closed. Blues, pinks, greens, yellows, oranges, purples.

In the lead was a tall woman, wearing a top hat that added another foot to her already six-foot frame. She swept toward us, a monocle perched over one eye and a strange creature that looked like a mint green weasel snoring in her arms. Her eyes flicked over our guide.

"Ah, the earl has finally done it. You've made Munsch Kin Land the mecca of class and sophistication that everyone wants to visit—even more so than the Emerald City. And now, it's going to be the toast of Oz, as it always deserved to be. Huzzah!" she cried, shooting him a broad wink.

The man with the waxed mustache grinned, his cheeks flushing as he puffed out his chest.

"Yes, well, we all do what we can, don't we?" he said. "This means a feast, right? A feast, a feast!"

The word skittered through the growing crowd, blooming from an excited whisper into a rising chant.

"Feast! Feast! Feast! Feast!"

James grunted, his hand twitching toward his blade. I stepped closer and touched his forearm. These people didn't mean us any harm.

The tension in his arm eased, and I let myself breathe a little easier. We'd be careful, but food and a place to get a bit of rest was too good to pass up.

"It seems the people have spoken," The earl said, raising both hands in a call for silence. "Who am I to deny them? On this, the fourth day of Inezuary, I, The Earl of Munsch, declare today to be a Traveler's Feast."

He shot a glance at the woman in the top hat, and she shrugged. "That'll do."

The earl clapped his hands together three times. "We don't have much time if we're going to pull this off by supper. Go, go! We'll meet in the Great Hall when the cuckoo cuckoos seven!"

The townsfolk broke into cheers again, and scattered in all directions, some nearly colliding in their excitement to begin preparations, like a rainbow exploding, dissipating before my eyes. A man in a white apron smeared with what was either blood or jam (I hoped the latter) fought his way through the crowd until he reached us, cheeks as bright red as the stuff on his apron.

"My Lord, I know both the Lollipop Guild and the Lullaby League were heartbroken that they didn't get to perform for Sir Duncan when he first arrived. I think another slight might crush them. Is it alright if I let them know their services are welcome this time?"

The Earl of Munsch frowned and sucked in a deep breath like he was preparing to blow out a denial, along with a lot of hot air, when the tall woman interrupted.

"Ooh! I love a good Lollipop Guild performance!"

The earl let out all that hot air with one tiny squeak as his lips spread into a benevolent grin.

"Yes! I was just about to say the exact same thing. Love a good performance from the Lollipop Guild. Absolutely, Crumpet!" He patted the aproned man on the shoulder. "Let them know we'd love for them to perform. I assume you'll be making more of those potato puffs with the leeks and cheese curds?" he asked, rubbing his round belly, eyes gleaming with hope.

"Can do, My Lord. Can do. See you at seven, then!" Crumpet gave us a nod before turning and heading off himself.

The earl turned to us once more. "Now then, Sir Duncan, introduce me to your friends proper-like, if you please."

"This here is Miss Harmony, also of Alabaster," Duncan said, gesturing toward me, "and her friend James—"

"Hook," James interjected with a clipped nod.

"Pleased to make your acquaintances. Will you be staying long, I hope?" the earl asked. "We've loved listening to Sir Duncan's stories about his home of Alabaster," he said, pronouncing it with the emphasis on the wrong syllable so it came out like 'ah-LA-bister'. "We don't get out of Munsch Kin Land much since—" he broke off, shaking his head. "Never mind. In any case, please know you're welcome to stay as long as you like. We enjoy hosting, and I'm very much looking forward to tonight. Why don't you come with me, and I'll show you to your rooms? You'll be staying in the earl's mansion with me."

We followed him along the winding brick road as he played the role of charming host, pointing out everything Munsch Kin Land had to offer. From the whipped cream shop—which, according to several hand-drawn signs, apparently offered the treat made with both types of milk:

graze-horn, *and* mooligan—to a woman's hair salon that had me pining for Molly. She would've gone absolutely nuts for that shop. Wigs, hairpieces, and hats of every color and shape imaginable lined the walls. I nearly tripped over my own feet watching as one stylist sprayed some kind of shellac over her latest creation, that looked like a giant eagle's nest made from the woman's tawny hair, complete with three lacquered eggs tucked inside, pastel blue, pink, and yellow.

Bonnie's talons dug into my shoulder, and I could feel her thoughts loud and clear—those would make a tasty treat.

No, miss, those are not for you! Be a good girl. We're guests here.

I could tell she was still considering it—sassy bird that she was—until I made her a silent promise to bring her a plate of the best morsels from the party later, if she behaved. She settled back on my shoulder with a soft chortle as we continued toward the mansion.

"Perfume for the lovely lady!" a woman called as we passed by the last of the shops.

She leaned in and squeezed the ball of a diffuser, sending a mist that smelled like cotton candy straight into my face. I sneezed instantly.

"Maxime!" The earl huffed. "It won't do for you to accost our guests like that. Ask before you spritz next time."

She apologized under her breath, looking cowed.

"Don't worry," I called over my shoulder, rubbing my itchy nose. "It's…lovely!"

James gave me a surreptitious sniff. "You smell like burnt sugar."

A few minutes later, we stood in front of the earl's mansion. Given the size of the other homes, I'd expected something more modest. Instead, the sprawling structure looked like it had been plucked straight out of Little

Alabaster. Not as grand or ornate, but large enough to house twenty people or more—each with their own bedroom.

"Celia!" the earl bellowed the moment we stepped through the front door and into the foyer.

A young maid with a lime-green bonnet and a cheery yellow uniform came scampering down the stairs, her face lit with excitement.

"More company?"

The earl clapped his hands again. "Indeed. And another feast, in short order. Let's find them a place to lay their heads, then get to work."

"This has been a banner week," she marveled, her pansy-colored eyes wide. "Luckily, I just finished my monthly deep-cleaning of even the empty rooms, so we've got plenty of space for you. This way! Come, come!"

Duncan motioned for me to go ahead of him, as she led James and me up the spiral staircase and down a long hall-way. Bonnie left my shoulder and flew back to Duncan, leaving me feeling bereft. The constant absence of Fetch had for a moment been eased with her weight on my shoulder.

"That's where Sir Duncan has been sleeping," Celia said, jerking a thumb at the first closed door on the right. "And this one will be perfect for you, Miss." She opened the next door wide to reveal a room done up in every possible shade of purple, and again, I found myself thinking of Molly again, the twinge of grief at having left her behind expanding to a near-physical pain.

It hadn't been long since I'd seen her, but not knowing when—or if—I'd see her again was weighing heavy on me.

I swallowed the ball in my throat and managed a smile. "This is perfect. Thank you so much."

"And you, sir," she said, turning to James, who couldn't hide his horrified expression, "can take the next one down the hall. Don't worry, though. That room is nothing like this one," she said with a wink. That seemed to ease him some, until she added, "Nope. That room is done entirely in pink."

Hook met my gaze over her head, his dark eyes filled with something like fear, and I nearly let out a snort of laughter. Served him right, the cranky bastard.

"Feel free to take your time, have a wash up if you like, and I'll come get you when it's time for the party. Would you like me to bring you something to wear, miss?"

A bath and a clean set of clothes sounded blissful, and I nodded with a grateful smile. "That would be appreciated."

She left me in the room, closing the door between us, chattering away to Hook as they continued down the hall to his pink room.

I glanced around and wrinkled my nose. Lavender covers lay atop a heart-shaped bed shrouded by a sheer canopy the color of fresh lilacs. Amethyst walls and a fluffy royal purple rug completed the look. This place was a lot, even for me. For a man like Hook, it was surely something akin to torture. Munsch Kin Land and it's over the top colors and joyous people were like a rainbow, opposite the darkness that was Hook.

Who knew, maybe it'd do him some good?

I, for one, was thrilled that this place was loud, busy, and a little chaotic. It had taken the attention away from one very messy problem, at least for a short while.

A problem that came back in a nauseating rush as I crossed the room toward the violet, claw-footed tub…

There were two men, each with a bedroom on either side of mine.

One with a death wish and a chip on his shoulder a mile wide…that I still dreamed about, despite knowing the truth about him.

The other, a Prince Charming come to life, who had

turned everything I believed about wealthy men in power on its head.

Both owned a piece of my heart. Both had played a key part in my journey to this point, and as far as I could tell?

Both still wanted *me*…

The question was, what did *I* want?

Fucked if I knew, but for now, I'd settle with not dying in the next week or so.

Because, like Pawpaw always said, *"Shoot for the stars, Ella, but make sure to carry a ladder—just in case."*

I let out a groan and tugged off my shirt.

"From your lips to the fates' ears, Pawpaw. From your lips to the fates' ears…I just hope I don't need a ladder."

CHAPTER 3

"*Harmony!*"

I whipped my head around, my hand going for my whip coiled at my side, not recognizing the voice at first.

Duncan stood behind me at the entrance to the great room, a crooked smile tugging at his lips. That easy grin—and the oh-so-charming dimple—warmed me after so much death and carnage.

The Fen. Noru. Pan and Tink. Losing Trick-Eyed Tom. Part of me just wanted to lean forward and lay my head on Duncan's shoulder…

A shoulder that was oddly empty, I noted with a frown.

"Where's your little sidekick?"

His hand lifted as if he'd forgotten she wasn't there. "I sent Bonnie back to check on Alabaster. It seems that the falcons can go back and forth. It's going well back home, but these things can be tenuous…"

And you should be there leading the people through this difficult transition instead of here helping me, I added mentally with a wince.

"The bigger question of the day, though…" He waggled his eyebrows. "What color did you get?"

It took a second before I realized what he meant, and I let him distract me. "Purple. How about you?"

"Yellow. And I mean, they go all the way with it. If I've got to choose between an evil wizard on a quest for unchecked power, and sleeping in a room that looks like a tub of pastel paint exploded inside it, I'm going to choose the second one all day. Although…" He cocked his head like he was considering it, and a laugh bubbled from my lips.

"The bed is comfortable and the water is hot, so it's no contest for me. Plus, paint choices aside, they seem like good people, if a bit strange." I turned my attention back to the center of the great room, where dozens of round tables had been spread out for seating. Two long banquet tables had been filled to the point of bowing at the center with food. A band played a lively reel in the corner, and some of the partygoers had already begun dancing. "So what's the catch?" I crossed my arms.

There always was one. No way this place was as idyllic as it seemed.

His gaze drifted lower, to where I'd unconsciously propped up my chest, creating a tiny swell of cleavage. My cheeks went hot, and I uncrossed my arms instantly. Celia, the maid, had brought me a dress, so I was no longer wearing pants and a button-down like I had for days on end. Now I was in a white cotton frock, with sprigs of blue and green flowers along the sweetheart neckline. It was the least feminine of the three options she'd offered, and the only one in a color that didn't look like it had been inspired by something from a sweets shop. I'd accepted the fussy shoes that went with it, but had drawn the line at leaving off my belt that held my whip, despite her wrinkled nose.

Apparently, Duncan didn't find it nearly as offensive,

because his cheeks were ruddy and his gray eyes were dilated like he was hunting…something.

"I'm sorry." He scrubbed a hand over his face before meeting my gaze again. "I know things are different here, and I promise I'll catch you up. But it's hard… seeing you and not—"

"How long are we staying here?" a low voice growled.

My heart knocked against my ribs as I turned to see Hook standing behind me. His black curls were damp, brushing his collar, and the spicy scent of soap washed over me in a rush. I tried to formulate a reply, but then his gaze trailed down to my neck and lower, taking in every inch of me before returning to my face, and what remained of my thoughts fled.

"We were just discussing Munsch Kin Land, actually. Harmony was asking what the catch was," Duncan said, a tightness in his voice that hadn't been there a moment before.

"And?" Hook pressed, his inky brow arching in question.

Duncan sighed. "Apparently, there's—"

"Hear ye, hear ye! Munsch Kinfolk and guests alike!"

The three of us swung our heads toward the booming voice echoing from the stage where the band had been. The Earl of Munsch stood there with a funnel-shaped device held to his mouth to help him project his voice.

"We'll start with supper! And of course, our honored guests will sit with me and the Widow Codswallow up here on the dais. Once we've had our fill of food and drink, we have a special performance by our very own Lollipop Guild!"

Three bug-eyed young men with scowls on their faces and pipes clenched between their lips ran past, clasping both hands above their heads and shaking them like winning prizefighters. The crowd roared with excitement.

"…Followed by the Lullaby League!" the earl added, just as

three giggling young women skipped out, dressed in peach-colored tutus. They paused in the middle of the floor and did three rapid twirls before scampering away again, much to the delight of the townsfolk.

As we took our seats along with the earl and other hand-picked guests on a raised dais, I found myself wishing, *hoping*, I was wrong. That, so long as we stayed indoors at night, things in Munsch Kin Land were as perfect as they seemed.

At least in The Hollow, you knew what you were getting. You were getting shit, no matter what angle you looked at it from. Little Alabaster was different. To an outsider, it looked like paradise. But hidden behind a magical wall was the truth. Poverty, oppression, and the stain of The Smudge.

I preferred my poison marked with a skull and cross-bones over one disguised in a glass of delicious mead with a decorative flower floating on top.

Neverland had been much the same. Crystalline blue waters. Gentle weather. But at the farthest point of the island was a cave filled with the bones of Tink's victims—all The Lost Boys whose souls she had fed upon.

Deep down, I knew Munsch Kin Land would be no different. It was only a question of what kind of horror show we were dealing with.

Still, there was no point borrowing trouble. It was our first day here, and we had food, drink, and a roof over our heads. Not to mention, Duncan as an ally once more. I risked another glance his way and a sense of relief settled over me, pushing aside the last of my reservations. Having friends when it felt like the whole universe conspired against me meant everything.

I could trust Duncan. He'd proven it time and time again. Strong, dependable, like a sunrise after a long night.

The sense that someone was watching me gave me pause,

but it only took a half a heartbeat to identify the culprit, because my skin tingled.

Hook.

I tried to keep my gaze averted, but his onyx eyes drew mine like a magnet. And when I finally looked, they held me, pinned in place, as surely as chains. His expression was blank...or it would've been to the casual onlooker. Only I could see the riot of emotions roiling inside him.

Rage.

Grief.

Lust.

Fucking hell. If Duncan was a sunrise of warmth and comfort, Hook was a hurricane. And if I wasn't careful, he would obliterate me.

Dragging my eyes from his, I struggled to find something to say. Anything.

"What do we have to drink around here?" I shot the earl a half-hearted smile as low-level panic clawed at my chest.

"Oh, just wait until you see!" he crowed.

He wasn't kidding. After downing four cups of something called "thistle-grog," my body felt loose and my brain a bit fuzzy in the best way. Even Hook was looking more relaxed than usual.

The next hour flew by in a haze of laughter, gluttony, and drink.

"This is delicious," I mumbled around a mouthful of something brown and chewy, soaked in a peppery mush-room sauce. "Is this steak?" I asked, pointing my two-pronged fork in the earl's direction.

"Steak?" he asked, confused.

"Yeah, like from a cow type creature. A...mooligan, maybe?" A guess based off the sign I'd seen in the whipped cream shop window.

The earl drew back with a gasp and laid a hand over his heart. "As in the flesh of an *animal?*"

Duncan leaned in from where he was seated to my left and murmured just loud enough for me to hear. "They're vegetarians."

Whoops.

"Heavens, no. Not that. Never." The earl went a little green around the gills. "That's pawelea root." He leaned in closer, eyes narrowed. "Do they eat...steak where you're from?"

Hook and I exchanged a glance. He shook his head, reaching for his half-empty mug.

"Nope."

"Yeah, nope. Definitely not." I stuffed another bite in my mouth to keep from asking any more questions that might make an enemy out of our new allies.

The earl nodded, but didn't seem entirely convinced as he took a long pull from his cup.

"Make sure you leave some room for dessert," Duncan said, changing the subject as he set his own fork down. "The guy who met us in the white apron when we first got here?"

"Crumpet?" I thought back to the little man with the jam-smeared apron.

"Yep, that's him. He's the village baker. He makes these pastries filled with chocolate and Bavarian cream. Drizzles them with honey. Rolls them in almonds. Slice of paradise."

Even the world ending, and it very well might be, wouldn't stop me from getting one of those in my belly tonight.

Molly would have loved it. My heart twisted a little at the thoughts of my friend. I'd just have to eat one of those treats for her.

I shoved one more bite of pawelea root into my mouth and dropped my fork on the plate.

"Lead me to it." I set my hands on the arms of the chair and pushed away from the table with a groan.

A sure sign I should skip dessert, no matter how much I wanted it. Along the same lines, I should probably bypass the rest of my intoxicating drink and get a good night's sleep, so I could start doing what I'd come here to do. When I thought about the witch Almira and how fast her attacks had escalated from one story to the next, it was obvious that dilly-dallying could be the kiss of death—literally. But another part of me, the human part, knew something else, too.

Witnessing sacrifice, death, and tragedy…it took a huge toll, body, mind, and spirit. None of us would be good to anyone if we didn't take care of ourselves and refuel. Tonight, after the music quieted, the lights dimmed, and we all went to our rooms, we each had to grapple with some heavy stuff.

Duncan had left a land in flux on the tail of a coup to come for me, only to find I wasn't here alone.

It had been two days since Hook and I had left everyone we cared about behind. Three since we'd lost Trick-Eyed Tom. That wasn't even considering the complex emotions that came along with the deaths of Pan and Tink. Hook had it even worse, as he was now saddled with all *three* of their memories.

Yes, tonight, when our heads hit the pillow, they would be heavy. I'd learned this lesson with Molly, both in Little Alabaster, and again in Neverland, and it had stuck with me.

It was best to grab whatever fistfuls of joy we could, because you never knew when the next opportunity would come.

Or if it would come...

I kept my voice at a level only for the men next to me. "First thing tomorrow, we need to start figuring out exactly what we're here to do. Agreed?"

Duncan nodded.

I turned to Hook, who drained his glass and set it down. "Agreed."

"Perfect. On that note, if anyone goes up to get another drink, grab me one too." I stood, wobbling momentarily before righting myself and letting out a hiccup. "I'm going to the powder room and then the dessert table."

I could feel both sets of eyes on me as I crossed the dance floor, so I made a special effort not to swerve or stumble. The last time I'd worn a dress and shoes with a heel was when I'd gone to the Alabaster Palace Jubilee to get Molly and found her standing over Heinrich with her glass stiletto buried in his chest. Since then, I'd been in britches and the red shitkickers Duncan had given me. Now, with a belly full of thistle-grog and a buzzy head, I was feeling every centimeter of the three-inch heels I was wearing.

One foot in front of the other.

I made it without falling on my face and even managed to use the bathroom without stabbing myself with the dagger I had strapped to my thigh in the process.

"You're killing it tonight, Harm. Almira should watch her back."

Another loud hiccup bubbled from my lips as I stepped through the bathroom door, straight into a brick wall.

"*Oof!* What the—?"

A strong hand steadied me, and I craned my neck to stare up into Hook's scowling face.

"I apologize. I didn't mean to scare you," he muttered, relaxing his grip and taking a step back.

"Well, you probably shouldn't walk around making that face all the time, then." The sudden urge to boop his nose was too strong to fight, so I did it. "Boop."

He couldn't have looked more shocked than if I kicked him right in the dick, and for some reason that sent me into peals of laughter that had me bent at the waist, nearly hyper-ventilating.

"You should s-s-see your face right now!" I managed to straighten and pointed at him, still near hysterical.

He rolled his eyes toward the ceiling and let out a sigh. "Gods save me from a lightweight. What kind of pirate are you?"

"I'm the kind that isn't a pirate at all, remember?" I shot back, wiping away the tears streaming down my face with a sniff. "Phew, that felt good, though. Things have been so tense lately, and I think I needed a release." The words hung between us, and I tried to fix them in a bumbling rush. "Not *that* kind of release. I just meant, like, I needed..." I trailed off, cheeks flaming, feeling like an idiot.

"Harmony...what happened on the Jolly Roger the other night—" he broke off and scrubbed a hand over his face. "That was a mistake."

Oof again. Only this second blow was way worse than the first. I could feel the blood draining from my cheeks and I stared hard at the floor. "Yeah. Yup. I agree. Big mistake." I bit the inside of my cheek until the coppery taste of blood filled my mouth.

"Don't do that," he shot back, reaching for my arm again, which I wrenched away. "Fine, I won't touch you but at least hear me out."

I kept my eyes pinned to his shoulder, crossing my arms over my chest.

"I want you like I've never wanted another woman. I've spent a lifetime dreaming of touching you that way...of seeing your face when—"

"Stop it," I snapped, wishing the floor would swallow me whole. "You're only making it worse."

"Exactly." He reached for my chin and tipped my head up, forcing me to meet his gaze. "That's what I do, Princess. I bring the suffering. Where I go trouble follows, and I refuse to take you down with me. No matter what I want."

Pain and regret swirled in the endless night of his eyes, and the anger gripping me drained away, leaving only despair in its wake.

A hurricane of suffering.

"You don't have to be the dreaded Captain Hook anymore. People can change." My voice was barely a whisper. "You did what you set out to do…you defeated Pan and Tinkerbell. Now you can finally let yourself just be James."

"It's too late for that." He shook his head slowly. "My sins are too many to be forgiven, and I've accepted that. But I know you never will."

He was right about that, even if I wouldn't admit it out loud.

"I vow to see this to the end with you, Princess. My sword is yours. But you need to worry about saving your kingdom and your people, and you can't do that if you're busy trying to save me."

I wanted so badly to argue. To punch him right in the gut and tell him what a stupid, wrongheaded ass he was being. But I couldn't, because as much as it gutted me to hear it, he was right.

I'd spent countless sleepless nights with him haunting my dreams. And since we'd met for real, it had been nothing but an emotional whirlwind. The highest of highs and the lowest of lows. His kisses, his touch, his pain, his guilt—James Tyler Hook stood at the forefront of my mind…

Exactly where fulfilling my destiny should be.

Confused, exhausted tears pricked my eyelids, and I blinked them back. "If that's what you want, then—"

"Ah! There you two are!" Mrs. Codswallow stood a short way down the corridor and beckoned us toward her. "We have the most amazing jugglers about to do one last performance. You mustn't miss it!"

Hook held my gaze and, for a second, I was afraid he was going to put her off and try to continue this excruciating conversation, but he must've sensed my desperation to be done with it because he turned to the older woman with a tight smile.

"Lead the way."

I kept my eyes on the floor, as careful as I had been on the way to the bathroom. Although the happy little drunk in me was dead, the effects of the local booze were strong, and I didn't need to add insult to injury by face planting in front of the guy who just dumped me.

Another loud hiccup ripped from my mouth, and I swallowed a groan.

Lovely.

"What was that sound?" Hook demanded, stopping in his tracks just as we stepped back into the great room.

Cripes on a cracker, could this man give me a break?

"I hiccupped, okay? Geez, can't a girl—"

Another low rumble sounded, and the chatter all around fell into silence. I searched frantically for the source, the hair on my arms standing on end. A second later, the lights flickered and the crystal chandelier that hung from the fifty-foot-high ceiling began to shift and morph. The blush-colored glass turned molten and swirled until it formed a massive, translucent sphere.

I stared in slack-jawed shock as it floated, down, down— as if it weren't made of glass at all, but of some weightless, otherworldly material I'd never seen before.

It wasn't until it drifted ten feet closer that I realized there was something…or someone inside of it. Every nerve-ending blared in warning as I closed my fingers over the handle of my whip.

"Steady," Hook muttered. Somehow, he'd wound up just behind me. I tensed as he lifted a hand, freeing his sword from its scabbard even as Duncan unsheathed the dagger at his hip.

Cries erupted around the room as the people of Munsch Kin Land cowered, not a weapon in sight.

My skin went ice-cold and clammy as I returned my attention to the woman behind the glass. Because this was not the Gayelette I knew. This was some wretched creature who barely resembled the flower seller or the fortune teller I'd met in the previous worlds. This Gayelette was a shade of her former self. Her arms were forcibly wrapped around her torso and fastened behind her with some sort of jacket that made it impossible to move. Gray hair hung in tangled snarls around her wrinkled face that had lost all hint of color, leaving it lifeless and ashy. In fact, the only thing about her that had any life at all was her eyes, and they were wild with something close to madness.

I barely recognized her.

"We can't risk waiting to find out what it is," Hook muttered. "I'm taking the shot." He lifted his hand toward the orb.

"No!" I grabbed his arm and gripped it tightly. "We can't! Gayelette is inside."

The sphere stopped and hovered five feet off the ground as the townspeople picked up their heads and inched close enough to see while still giving the orb a wide berth.

I probably should have done the same. Instead, I found my legs propelling me forward. Hook and Duncan spoke at the same time.

"Careful."

"Watch..." Hook murmured from just behind me.

I stopped a few yards from the glass sphere and stared

into Gayelette's eyes, hoping the horror didn't show on my face.

"What's happened to you?" I whispered in a hoarse voice.

"My sister...Almira," she managed through chapped, bloody lips that looked like they hadn't seen water in days. "When her whirlpool failed in Neverland, she went into a rage. She knows I've found a way to help you. No more free to roam in my 5 by 5 cell. I'm now truly trapped with my hands bound, cast in icy darkness. I mustered all I had left to come to you this last time."

Had she truly said, *'My sister Almira'?*

If so, that was news to me, although now wasn't the time to press her on the issue. Every word was a struggle. She sucked in a breath and her lungs rattled, setting off a fit of coughing that doubled her over.

The towns folk were murmuring to one another in low, terrified whispers, and I didn't blame them. This was some scary shit. But my friend's suffering overshadowed my fear, and I stepped closer.

"How can I help you?"

I winced as she turned her head back sharply, exposing a jutting collarbone that told me it wasn't just water and sunlight she was being deprived of.

"It is I who must help you, one last time, Princess. Time passes differently here, and things have taken a terrible turn. Almira has given up any guise of diplomacy and is killing our people with reckless abandon. You must make it back to C'an Saas before there *is* no C'an Saas, so listen closely." She took a deep labored breath. "When I put you into the book, I placed a spell around each story, shielding them from her influence as best I could. She caught me before I was able to complete the task in Oz. I knew you'd come here to Munsch Kin Land first, and was able to shield this place, but until you reach The

Emerald City and your mother's protection spell, you'll be vulnerable. Almira has created an army here in Oz, and, although the process is draining, she can come and go as she chooses. Staying until her power begins to wane, then returning home until she grows strong again. Although they don't call her Almira here. They call her The Wicked Witch of the West."

The collective gasp that echoed through the room told me that the people of Munsch Kin Land were well acquainted with that moniker.

"That's all well and good but first tell me how to help you. We need to get you out of there, Gayelette." I took a step closer, and James sheathed his sword, grabbing my wrist.

"Tread carefully. Almira could be controlling her right now. This could all be a trap."

I paused, my brain stuttering in confusion as fear and thistle-grog warred for control. He wasn't wrong. As much as it made me sick to see her like this, I had no idea if this was a trick conceived by the most cunning, powerful being I'd ever encountered.

"So we do nothing?" I whispered, frozen with indecision.

He ignored me, fixing his gaze on Gayelette. "If what you say is true, why are you still alive at all? Why didn't she just kill you once she got the answers she wanted?"

"She cannot." The old woman let out a low gasp. "We were three of a coven, and as such, we are bound. Should one of us take the life of our coven sister, it would be so painful, we ourselves would likely die, too."

The words beat against my temples like a drum.

"Three...?" I asked, already sensing what would come next.

"Me, Almira, and Marin. I'm not the clairvoyant, Princess. Your mother, Marin, was. I've just been leading you to the prophecies she left behind for you to find. The final one lies in the heart of Emerald City. You need to get it before it's too late. Almira has already found a way to damage the pages, and it won't be long before she succeeds in destroying them completely."

"But what about you? I can't leave you like this. Can't I come home now? I'm strong, and my powers have been—"

"If you did, you would fail. You still don't have all you need to defeat her." She jerked her head again, and this time, sheer terror clouded her features. "Dear gods…she's back! Find The Wizard of Oz. He's the keeper of the final prophecy and has the last item you need to—"

"You stupid, stubborn cow! Did I sense you using your magic again?" The snarl seemed as if it came from within the orb, but it did not come from Gayelette. And I knew, in that moment, it was Almira's voice…I remembered it from when I'd leapt into the Shadow Abyss…

"I'll get you, my pretty, and your little bird, too."

It was no less chilling this time.

"I might not be able to kill you," Almira continued, closer, yet somewhere behind Gayelette, still out of view, "But that doesn't mean we can't have a little fun, does it?"

Gayelette let out an unholy scream as what looked like thin fingers of black lightning pelted her body from behind. Her back arched like she'd been stuck through from heel to head with an iron rod, every muscle standing out in sharp relief against her paper-thin skin.

"No more fucking magic, sister!" Almira screeched.

A distorted shape stepped up behind Gayelette and began to move closer.

"Are you with her?" Almira demanded, her voice dropping to a menacing whisper. "Are you talking to Marin and Alistair's useless little whelp right now?"

Gayelette's body contorted in jerky movements as Almira used the lightning like the strings of a marionette to move her to the side and a new face filled the orb. I stopped breathing as our gazes collided.

I didn't know what I'd expected her to look like, but this wasn't it. Long silver hair flowed around a face that could've been on the front of a coin. Regal, with high cheekbones, a strong nose, and one, ice blue eye that gleamed with hatred. The other, its match but unseeing, as if it was made of glass.

"There she is," she muttered. "So pretty, just like your mother. I'll see you soon, Harmony. And what I plan to do to you after all the trouble you've caused me will make what I did to your father look like child's play!"

Almira backed away until she was in full view, and then lowered her hands, sending Gayelette bouncing off the glass and hurtling toward the ground down face first, arms bound.

"No!" I lunged toward the sphere, tugging my whip free and flicking it at the sphere in a desperate attempt to use my magic and catch Gayelette before her face smashed into the floor. Sparks showered along the glass, and catch her I did. I used every ounce of control I had to lower her down gently.

"Just as I thought. A weak heart, just like your silly mother," Almira cackled.

"Harmony!" Hook and Duncan shouted my name in unison, but it was too late. The witch was already turning those oily tendrils of lightning on me, striking through the glass.

My body felt like it was moving in slow motion as I tried to dodge. Her magic was too fast, and one single finger of lightning licked at my face. A helplessness so complete...a despair so deep slammed into me, I screamed.

"Get the fuck down!" Hook bellowed.

Something hit me from behind, sending me to the wooden floor in a heap and knocking the breath from my lungs. I managed to open my eyes in time to see the orb tremble for a second before shattering into a billion pieces, exploding outward in a rain of glass.

I covered my head, expecting to hear screams of pain and the tinkling of glass hitting the floor. But all was quiet except for the harsh breathing and terrified gasps of the party goers. When I lifted my head, it was to find Hook standing in front of me. His body blocking mine, hand raised, using magic to keep the glass suspended in the air.

He whipped his head around to scan me up and down, his jaw clenched tight. Then he balled his hand up in a fist and dropped it to his side. The torrent of glass hung for a moment and then fell to the floor.

The room was eerily quiet for a long moment before filling with wild applause.

"Great Scott!" The Earl of Munsch ambled down from the dais, wringing his hands. "That was astonishing. Huzzah for Captain James Hook! Thank you, sir."

Duncan was pushing himself to stand a couple yards from where he'd knocked me down, and even his brows were raised in reluctant awe of the stunning display of Hook's magic.

"It was hard to see her like that, but at least we have a path laid out for us now." Hook ignored the applause as he helped me to my feet. "If what Gayelette says is true, we need to get on the road as soon as possible. Surely there's nothing out there more dangerous than what we just witnessed."

"I wouldn't be so sure about that," Duncan said, closing the distance between us.

"What do you mean?"

The Earl of Munsch let out a weary sigh and made his way over to a large rope with a decorative tassel at the end, which hung from the wall at the back of the room. He gave it a tug, and the ceiling high above our heads split open to reveal a window.

For a second, we just stared up at the starry sky, and I was about to ask what the problem was, when suddenly a screech echoed through the great hall, followed by dozens of others that grew louder and more frenzied. And then, one thud.

Another.

Another.

It wasn't until the entire ceiling had opened up that, by the light of the moon, we could actually see what was happening. And there it was…

The catch.

Dozens—no, hundreds—of flying monkeys hurled themselves against the glass, over and over again, trying to get in. Their sharpened teeth bared and dripping with saliva as they battered at it with wings and fists, doing anything they could to get through.

"*That's* why we don't go out at night," the Widow Codswallow said as she sidled up to the earl.

"What the fuck *are* those things?" Hook snarled, looking like he was seriously considering heading out to take them on all by himself.

A memory flooded my brain…the illustration inside one of the fairytales in my book, later drawn on the walls of the amphitheater in Little Alabaster by Gayelette herself. Hints of the story to come, and somehow, I'd buried it in the back of my mind until now. But I knew exactly what those creatures were.

"Winged Monkeys. Minions of a witch with green skin."

I shivered as the earl eyed me suspiciously and then nodded.

Widow Codswallow fluttered her hand against her chest. "Exactly as you say, Harmony. The army of The Wicked Witch of the West herself. They're nocturnal, so aside from the occasional scout she's given the power to withstand the sun so they can spy on her behalf, they only give us trouble at night. But many have died at their hands, including my beloved husband."

The earl's jowls trembled as he let out a harumph. "Terrible, they are. The bane of our existence. Many of us have family in The Emerald City we haven't seen in years. It's several-days' journey, and to even attempt it would be a suicide mission. As lovely as Munsch Kin Land is, we're essentially in a painted prison. The woman in the glass orb—she says you're to kill The Wicked Witch of the West or… whatever she calls herself now. She said that your mother was part of her coven, which means you're a witch, too, and while I'd love to assume you've got our best interests at heart, I've seen magic abused enough times in my day that I have a question I must ask you, Harmony of Alabaster…and a place called C'an Saas."

He turned to me, his expression solemn.

"Are you a good witch or a bad witch?"

Hell…up until about three minutes ago, I didn't know I was a witch at all, and the question rocked me down to my crimson boots. Or as the case currently was, my three inch heels.

I swayed on my feet and tried to form a reply. "I—"

The room spun into a blur, and I stumbled backward, the weight of the task before me suddenly too heavy upon my shoulders as the despair I'd felt when Almira's black lightning had touched me came back in a rush.

"It's okay. I got you."

I let myself go slack as strong arms caught me. A low, familiar rumble hummed in my ear, assuring me that everything would be alright, and I was lifted into the air like I weighed no more than a child.

Something was wrong with me.

Very wrong.

I didn't think about arguing, or what the party guests—or

even Hook—might think in that moment. I just pressed my face close to Duncan's chest.

Dimly, I could hear voices behind us.

"Why didn't she answer me?"

"Because she's half-dead with exhaustion," Hook shot back. "It's been a long, trying few days. She needs some rest, and I intend to ensure that she gets it. You have my word that she has the purest of intentions."

If only I had as much faith in me as he did…

Because once Hook's voice faded in the distance, and I forced myself to focus on the even, steady beat of Duncan's heart, it had taken on a cadence of the question I just couldn't shake.

Good witch. Bad witch. Good witch. Bad witch.

The part that scared me the most, though?

I didn't know the answer.

CHAPTER 4

We started out the next morning at the crack of dawn, weighed down by some sacks filled with bread, fruit, and little tartlets that Crumpet the baker had made for us. The towns folk had seen us off with songs and cheers, but the last words that had left my lips were a promise to the earl that we would rid Oz of the scourge of Almira.

I only hoped I could keep it.

I'd spent the first leg of our journey in silence as the night before replayed in my mind on a loop. So much had happened so fast, but despite being in a different land, with enemies new and old, one thing had followed me through every story.

Doubt.

It had been eating me up inside ever since The Speaker had sacrificed himself and through all that had happened since, right up to seeing Gayelette's agony.

I'd caused so much pain in my quest to fulfill this prophecy…cost so many people their lives.

What if I *wasn't* the good guy in this story like I thought I was?

Even Almira probably didn't think of herself as a *bad* witch. As much as I wanted to save the people of C'an Saas, my desire to see my true home...to know where I'd come from and learn about my parents was just as big of a driver for me. Was I fooling myself to think I'd done all this for some "greater good"? And what made me qualified to be the judge of what "good" was "greater?"

The earl had just said out loud what I'd been wondering in one way or another for weeks. Once Duncan had set me into my bed, though, it had been more than that keeping me awake...

I swallowed hard and laid a tentative hand on the handle of my whip. No crackling, no pulse of awareness that connected me to my weapon. Same as earlier that morning when I'd tried to touch the consciousness of a swallow-tailed kite swooping through the trees.

Nothing.

Not that I was expecting to feel anything. Whatever Almira had done to me last night had left me feeling dead inside. Not numb, exactly—that would've been better. But the despair was still there. It was just overshadowed by the fact that the sensation of life—of heat and snapping energy that had grown inside me along with my magic—was gone. Left in its place was a lump of cold stone, weighing me down, draining me dry.

I hadn't even processed it myself yet, never mind mentioning it to James or Duncan. How to work up the nerve to tell them that they'd followed me here and risked everything only to find out that even weakened, at a distance, in another fucking realm, Almira's magic was so strong that the mere brush of it had blasted mine to smithereens?

Fucking hell.

"We should find a stream and fill up our waterskins," Duncan murmured.

Hook didn't slow or glance his way. "It's not hot out. We'll have plenty of time to get water once we set up camp."

The guys had picked up on my mood or were grappling with their own shit, because that was the first peep from either of them in hours.

Either way, I was going to have to come clean soon. I'd be a liability in almost any situation, and, while I had no choice but to follow this path to the bitter end, I needed to give them the chance to bow out before things went any further.

I peered under my lashes at James, sensing the tension in him. When we'd gotten up this morning to pack, he'd been quieter than usual. Seeing the familiarity between me and Duncan was already an issue, and that was *before* Duncan had scooped me up and put me to bed. I'd been too flattened to tell him to put me down even if I'd wanted to.

Which I hadn't. Not that it mattered to James anyway, right? He didn't want to want me. So what was I worried about?

Because there was something about Duncan that made him easy to sink into. To let him carry the burden for a while. And with Hook? It always felt fraught. Loaded. Thick with anticipation and turmoil and need, even now, after he'd crushed any hope of us being together.

He chose that moment to turn his head ever so slightly, his gaze colliding with mine before ricocheting away again. At this rate, I didn't need to worry about being a liability. This man was going to burst a vein from a combination of rage and misery and drop dead all on his own, no enemy needed.

Surprisingly, a glance at the usually easy-going Duncan told me he wasn't faring much better.

In a word? Morale was low, and I didn't have a clue or the energy to find one that might help me pick it up.

As we walked, the vibrant blues and pinks gradually gave way. The oaks and shrubbery that lined the yellow path grew thicker with each passing mile, and, by mid-day, we found ourselves in a dense forest. It was lusher than any I'd seen in Alabaster, and somehow more vivid, as if all of the colors had somehow been amped up a notch.

"Wonder what type of stone this is," I murmured, suddenly desperate to break the tension.

Despite being the only road leading to The Emerald City, the gleaming, golden bricks were almost entirely free of wear and tear.

"I've been trying to figure that out for a while now." Duncan scratched at his stubbly chin. "Heinrich and Relyk would've killed for the stuff."

"They would've killed for a lot of things," I pointed out with a frown. "They weren't exactly choosy when it came to murder."

He flashed a half-smile, "Fair enough. But this time, it would've been over something useful. Imagine having roads that never need to be repaired. It could be used for all sorts of things. Buildings, wells, the list goes on and on."

I nodded, thinking back to the dirt packed, hole laden streets of The Hollow. "You should take a brick back with you when we leave. Or…when you leave…" One day, I hoped to go back to that world and see what New Alabaster looked like, but who knew if that was even possible once I returned to C'an Saas?

I absently flexed my useless fingers. *If* I returned to C'an Saas.

"Strange that there are all these trees, but not a squirrel or chipmunk in sight," Hook muttered, his expression dark as he looked off into the distance.

"Maybe the monkeys keep the population in check? Or maybe they don't even have those particular critters here."

Hook grunted.

"We can afford to go a few days without catching anything, at least." I felt my pouch, which was stuffed full with Munsch Kin Land goodies.

"Food isn't the concern. I'm more worried about the monkeys. The sheer number of them is an issue if they catch us out in the open," Hook said.

"The earl said that we should find a place to hole up, but it's hard to imagine hiding from that many of them." It didn't take much to recall the horror I'd felt when that black cloud of monsters had descended on us the night before, and I suppressed a shudder. "And I'm sure they'll be looking for us. Almira knows we're here now."

Duncan nodded, grim-faced. "We'll want to give ourselves a bit of extra time to prep for this first night until we establish a good routine."

Hook scowled at him, but I breathed a sigh of relief as he refrained from snapping back with "no shit" or another sharp reply. The friction had been awkward, but so far they'd held back from being openly hostile, aside from the whole pesky saber to the kidney thing when we first got here.

The trees were getting taller as we moved, tendrils of shadow creeping onto the shining road. It only got darker up ahead, with a canopy shielding the road from the sky above. "Going to be hard to see us if they're flying over, assuming it stays like this," I said.

A flash of red caught my eye, and I skidded to a halt, peering over at it. "Is that—?" I broke off, striding to the edge of the yellow brick road that cut a path through the thick trees. "Apples," I confirmed, reaching out to yank one free of the nearest branch. The glossy crimson fruit looked so good it made my mouth water. "We should stockpile some. We'll thank ourselves later if we run out of—*oof!*"

A jolt of pain arced through me as something hit me square in the solar plexus, hard. My hand was halfway to my whip by the time I saw the apple rolling down the golden path. "What the fuck?"

I reeled around, half expecting to see Cissy Petway hiding behind a bush with her slingshot, but I had no time to consider it further as apples rained down from the trees in a barrage of fruit fire.

I threw my arms over my head, but Hook's firm grip settled on my wrist, tugging me onward, batting apples away like he'd been doing it his whole life.

"Move, move!" Duncan shouted, sword drawn.

"Is it the monkeys?" I flinched as another apple came hurtling my way, but there was no dodging this one.

A soft twang cut through the air, and my heart skipped a beat as the apple shot sideways just inches from my throat, smacking right into a tree with an arrow through its core. A low rumble rolled through the surrounding trees, and I stared in shock as their branches moved and then stilled.

"Someone else is out here!"

I unfurled my whip with a flick of the wrist, mourning the absence of magic tingling on the surface of my skin as I searched for the unseen archer.

Hook and Duncan had already moved in front of me, so I barely caught sight of the shadowy figure that leapt from what looked like a platform high in one of the trees. Both men extended their swords as she sidled towards us, bow in hand. She was dressed in well-worn brown leather from head to toe, except for a camouflage scarf that covered most of her dark hair.

"I'm guessing you all aren't from around here," she scoffed.

That voice. Hoarser, and less animated, but that lilting brogue was definitely recognizable.

"B-Billy?" I asked, shoving my way through the two-man wall of muscle blocking my view.

Tawny curls, bright blue eyes…She might look a bit different—leaner, less curvy, more rangy muscle—but it was definitely this world's version of Billy O'Donnelly.

I stared at her, cocking an eyebrow. The differences were more than skin deep, and the deep sadness reflected in her sky blue gaze was hard to handle.

Those eyes narrowed to flat chips as she slowed to a stop. "How do you know my name?"

Duncan bumped my hand with his in a subtle warning, and I nearly laughed. He recognized her as surely as I did. Did he seriously think I was going to blurt out the real reason I knew her name?

"The Munsch Kinfolk mentioned you while we were staying with them," I said smoothly, a sour taste filling my mouth at how easily the lie came. "We're friends of theirs."

She nodded cautiously, rubbing at her lower back. "They're an alright lot, if a bit loud. What brings you all the way out here, then?"

"We're just passing through, on our way to The Emerald City."

My body was still buzzing with adrenaline as I stooped to grab one of the apples, as much for something to do with my hands as anything. She let out a snort as I brought it to my lips, and I stopped short of taking a bite.

"What?"

"Wouldn't recommend it. They're full of worms."

The nearest tree rumbled at that, and my eyes flicked up to the branches as I let the apple fall to the ground with a thud. "Are…are they actually alive?"

"Yup. And they don't like it when people pick their

apples." Billy strode over to the one she'd pierced with an arrow and yanked it free, none too gently. The tree let out a hiss and shook its leaves violently before settling again when Billy didn't budge. "The fuckers scare off all the game, though, and sometimes you just need to remind 'em who's boss."

"Thanks for helping us. Is it just you out here or…?" I peered around at the now-still trees and saw no other movement. I had to admit, I was hoping to see Paddy or even Scotty step out from behind a tree even though it might mean getting robbed by The O'Donnelly brothers in broad daylight.

"Just me." She shrugged. "Been a while since I've seen other people out this far from one of the settlements."

"Is the road not very busy?" Duncan asked.

"As busy as any road this deep in the wilds." She eyed him long and hard, then Hook, then me, before seeming to come to a decision. "Let's go somewhere where we can talk. If you're going to The Emerald City there are some things you should know, and I don't like being out in the open exposed like this for long. My hut isn't far."

"You live out here?" I asked, my eyes drifting to her ears. They were slightly off somehow, pointed a bit at the end in a way that the Billys from the other two worlds hadn't been. And there was something different about her face, too, though I couldn't quite put my finger on it.

She turned away, still holding her bow as she led us off the path and into the woods itself. Low bushes and brambles lined the edges of the makeshift trail, with a thin enough gap between them that we had to walk single file. She wove her way through the forest gracefully, weaving between tree and rock, to the point that I was nearly jogging just to keep up. She glanced back at us every few seconds but did nothing to slow her pace.

Alabaster Billy had been a bawdy riot, even when she'd been locked in a dungeon. And Neverland Billy had rode up to us on the back of a saber-toothed tiger in The Weeping Fen.

This one was a badass too, no question, but also a whole different beast at the same time. Every movement was measured and precise, like a soldier. It was like Billy minus the underpinnings of joy that took the edge off her. Maybe she was in some sort of trouble like both times before, and needed her brothers' help?

I sucked in a ragged breath, shoving down the urge to flat out ask if she had any siblings. She'd been placed in my path three times now, our destinies tied. I needed to have a little patience if I wanted to find out how and why, because other-wise this twitchier version of Billy would surely get spooked.

"This is it." She was already at the door of a small, tidy hut which sat in the center of a clearing by the time I jogged out from the tree line with the guys now flanking me.

She watched impassively, hand resting on her low back again as we trudged up to her. "I don't have much room, as you can see," she said, pushing the door open as she spoke, "but feel free to have a seat."

Five knotty pine stools sat on one side of the meager space, with a makeshift bed—really just a pile of blankets strewn across a wooden frame that could've doubled as a torture device—on the other.

No wonder her back was sore.

She ducked to avoid hitting her head on the sloped roof as she made her way to the stools. "I'd offer you something to eat, but I don't think you'd want anything I have."

I understood. Shrimp puffs and daintiques weren't an option when living a life this rugged.

I took one of the stools and Billy and Duncan followed

suit while Hook stood over us like a perpetually pissed off gargoyle.

"Why the Emerald City?" she asked, her gaze probing my face like she was some sort of human lie detector.

I tried not to fidget and considered my words carefully just in case she was. Whispers, Tideblessed, witches...who knew what magic this particular Billy might possess?

It was pure gut instinct that had the truth tumbling from my lips. "We've put together a team to go see The Wizard of Oz about a prophecy that will help us kill The Wicked Witch of the West."

The air crackled and it took everything I had not to keep blathering. Short, simple, to the point. Over-explaining would only show weakness.

And still...

"I'm not sure why, exactly, but something tells me you're supposed to join us and maybe be our guide? That probably sounds weird. It sounds really weird, right? I'm not going to try to convince you if you don't want to come, but—"

"Zip it, chatterbox." For the first time, her lips quirked into some semblance of that familiar, Billy O'Donnelly smirk. "You had me at killing the Wicked Witch of the West. I'm in."

I blinked. "Oh. Okay, then." Had we finally caught a break here?

Duncan caught my gaze and shrugged.

"What were you doing in the trees out there?" Hook had both arms crossed over his chest, making no bones that this was no casual question. Duncan and I might be team Billy, but Hook wasn't sold yet.

She sized him up long and hard before replying. "Let's just say I'm a hunter, but I have no intention of hunting you. Anything else I want you to know about me, I'll tell you. I'm willing to help, but I value my privacy. Understood?"

She aimed the sharp question at me, and I nodded. "Understood."

Hook might not be sold, but her caveat only made me more certain I was right. If I didn't get to ask her questions, that meant the same held true vice versa. Convincing someone to help was a whole lot easier when you didn't have to lead with, *"We're living inside a book right now, and oh yeah, there are more than one of you depending on what page you land on."*

When she spoke again, there was no trace of emotion in her voice. "Give me a minute to pack my things, and we can be on our way. If we leave now, we should be able to get some miles in and reach Skunk's place by nightfall. It'll be easier to stay there than make camp in the open."

She rolled to her feet and then got to work, stuffing random odds and ends into her large, leather bag. Her bow came last, and she kept it in hand as she tossed the sack over her shoulder.

"Alright, good to go."

We headed to the door, and I stepped out to a view of the lush forest. As rough as it was to live the way she did, there was something peaceful about it, too. Being in nature all day long, hearing the birds singing overhead—

A sick feeling rolled through me as I cocked my head.

Why had the birds stopped singing?

A black feather drifted down from the sky above and Billy let out a snarl.

"Gods damn it, we've got scouts! Get down!"

CHAPTER 5

Someone yanked me back, and the door slammed shut, but not before I caught sight of a dark shape overhead—

Thunk.

A spear punched through the wood, its iron tip jutting from right around where my face had been a second before. My hands went clammy as splinters peppered my cheeks.

"You okay?" Hook stood behind me, sealed against my back, arm wrapped around my chest like a steel band.

Billy was already pushing past us, nocking an arrow as she went.

"I'll take care of this." Her face was a mask of icy cold rage as she kicked the door open and launched into a full sprint before dropping to her knees. Chunks of grassy dirt sprayed into the air as she slid, loosing her first shot before skidding to a stop.

Her hand blurred back to her quiver as Hook headed out behind her, magic already flooding to his fingertips. Duncan pulled up the rear, his body seeming to swell, muscles bulging against the fabric of his shirt as he called back to me over his shoulder.

"Stay back."

Another twang sounded, followed by a muttered curse from Billy.

"Don't let him get away—Oh, shit!"

Screw this.

I launched myself out the door, yanking my whip free as a second flying monkey dive-bombed Billy with zero regard for its own safety. It landed, whipping twin swords around in a tornado of steel and fur, but she was a half-step too fast, dancing around its strikes with preternatural speed.

Duncan sprinted to her side, tearing his great sword from its sheath as Hook faced the spear handling-monkey who had nearly skewered me. I dashed toward him, heart in my throat. Up close, these things were even more horrifying than before. The creature's eyes were blinded by bloodlust, its long canines dropping saliva as it screeched and snarled.

Hook blasted a gust of gale-force wind its way that should've knocked it clean out of the sky, but with a single beat of its massive wings, the beast lunged toward us in a burst of unfathomable speed. I struck on instinct; my whip cracked empty air. The monkey was on me before the sound reached my ears.

I threw my weight sideways, seeing my life flash before my eyes as he adjusted, mid-thrust, to track my movement. A burst of uncontrolled magic roared up from within me like I'd never felt before as I hit the ground, shooting wildly in all directions in a desperate, instinctive attempt to survive—or at least take this ugly bastard with me if I didn't. The beast came to an abrupt halt, freezing in place as his spear hovered just inches from my chest.

My head roared with relief, and I sucked in a breath.

Got 'em.

It wasn't until a drop of hot blood spattered my cheek that I saw the iron hook poking from its matted, black fur. Hook yanked the monkey back, his saber ripping through the air to decapitate him before he could hit the ground.

He turned, his eyes flitting down to look at me. And, seeing that I hadn't been hurt, he strode toward Billy and Duncan before stopping in his tracks.

"Well, fuck me."

I rolled onto all fours, the scent of moss and blood swamping me as fingers of panic teased at the base of my neck. Instead of the two dead bodies I feared, I found Duncan in full berserker mode, holding the monkey scout by the leg as he swung it head-first against the ground. And, judging by the streaks of blood and pulverized bone surrounding him in all directions, it was far from the first swing.

He slammed it down a final time for good measure, then whirled in my direction. He let out a breath as he saw me, his eyes flickering from silver back to gray. "Bloody hell, those bastards are stronger than they look."

Billy emerged from behind him, giving him a wide berth as she approached the fallen corpse, her muscles still tense and on high alert.

She tore the arrow from its chest and stuffed it back in her quiver before kneeling beside the creature.

"All good?" Hook muttered, reaching down for my arm and hoisting me to my feet.

"Yeah," I said, gulping hard.

Just peachy.

"Hate to agree with prince pretty boy, but you should've stayed in the fucking hut like he told you. Until you've regained your strength, you're going to get yourself into trouble against enemies like that. Too much power and speed."

If I regained my strength. But I couldn't dwell on that right now. "I've never seen anything move that quickly."

"They're scary fast," Billy agreed, still hunched over the fallen monkey.

"What're you doing?" Duncan asked, glancing over at her. She stood, eyeing him for a long moment before answering.

"Just...checking him for valuables." She lifted her head and shot us a grim smile. "Sometimes they steal jewelry and such from people they've killed. Nothing on these, though."

"Are they all that strong?" I asked, rolling up my whip. "We saw thousands of them when we were in Munsch Kin Land through the skylight. I don't see how anyone could survive that if the shield protecting them failed."

"None of them are a walk in the park, but scouts—the ones that come out during the day like these did—are the elite. Faster, stronger, and daylight-proof. They're out collecting intel and usually don't attack unless provoked, though."

Eh.

"About that...uh, so one other thing you should probably know." I shuffled my feet, staring down at the tips of my red boots. "The whole Wicked Witch thing goes both ways. I'm hunting her, but she's hunting me, too. In fact, my guess is that she sent those scouts out specifically to find me. I'm sorry I led her to you, and I understand if that changes things..."

Apparently, I didn't need to finish my thought because she was already shaking her head.

"Doesn't change nothing. Let her come." Billy's eyes flashed blue fire, and she lifted a hand to the simple silver locket around her neck. "I've been waiting."

I wanted to ask why...and for how long? Something told me this grudge ran deep, but that same thing told me that now wasn't the time to ask. She'd tell me if and when she was ready. It was enough that she'd agreed to come along.

She glanced back at the monkey corpses and then turned to Duncan, who winced in pain...I hoped only from the aftermath of using his power.

"Thanks for your help. Just to be clear, though. I would've had him. The sword ones blow their load too fast, use up all their energy in a single combo. I was just waiting him out, is all."

The comment would've come off like a cocky joke coming from either of the old Billys' mouths, but from this one, I found myself believing it. Her movements had been incredible, keeping pace with a beast I'd been completely unable to manage.

"Well, I saved you the trouble, and that leather of yours from a whole lot of mess." Duncan glanced down at his blood-soaked clothes.

She strode over to the second of the two dead monkeys, taking a long look at the decapitated head before standing. When she turned back to us, her expression had regained a fraction of the humor I'd grown used to in the other worlds. She spared a pointed glance at a pale-faced Duncan.

"Yeah, I look great. You, on the other hand my friend, look like you got off a long shift at the butcher's shop. In fact, all of you could use a bath for yourselves and your clothes, yeah? I'll show you to the stream and then take care of these bodies—I need to burn them, before we go—then I'll come get you."

"I can help," Duncan cut in, but she held up a hand.

"My land, my job. I won't have you interfering as I'm particular about certain things, but thanks anyway."

The stream wasn't far—only a few-minutes walk downhill through brush and knee-high fern. But it was like stepping into another world. Sunlight spilled through the canopy of trees, turning the water to liquid gold. Dragonflies skated across the surface, their wings flashing sapphire and green.

If Oz needed an image to bring in visitors, this would be it.

As if by some unspoken agreement, Duncan waded upstream while Hook stalked a few yards in the opposite direction. I took a second to yank off my boots and then went straight ahead until the water lapped at my waist before sinking to my knees into the gravel.

The lazy stream was just cool enough to be refreshing, and I let out a sigh as it washed away the blood and grit. Shame it couldn't do the same with the thoughts clouding my mind.

Billy's grudge, Duncan's pain, Hook's anger, my own failing magic. And underneath it all pulsed a new worry…

Why had my magic surged, only to drain away again, leaving me hollow inside once more?

I scooped up some water and lifted it to my face, pausing as a crimson droplet splashed my wrist. Pausing, I pressed the heel of my palm against my nose and then pulled it away.

Nosebleed.

Fuck.

I stood and tipped my head back to stop the flow. Had Almira broken me for real? Was that wild, uncontrollable burst of magic like one of my flash-bangs right before it exploded into a useless pile of paper and charred sawdust?

I was so focused on the blood and what it might mean that I didn't realize someone had come up behind me until a shadow fell over me.

"Can I fix it for you?"

Hook's voice, low and as rough as the gravel under my feet.

I turned to face him and froze. His soaked linen shirt clung to his chest and shoulders, his Tideblessing tattoos peeking through. Permanent reminders of every life he'd taken, every blessing he'd absorbed, and there were dozens.

Even knowing all that, what did it say about me that he was still the most beautiful thing I'd ever seen?

"I'm fine," I lied, pinching the bridge of my nose.

He ignored my words and bent closer. "Hold still." His hooked hand hovered in the air an inch from my face and magic hissed against my skin. Tom's Mend blessing. I didn't need to swipe to know that the bleeding had stopped.

"Thanks," I whispered, my throat aching as I pictured the deck hand's smiling face.

Hook's expression softened as he lowered his hand. "Yeah, well, he'd give me hell if I let you walk around dripping blood all over Oz. He always said blood belonged in bodies, not on boots." He reached out to brush a stray lock of hair from my cheek.

Damn him for being so sweet now, when I was barely holding it together.

"I think my magic is gone." Saying it aloud felt like dropping a rock into a pool of water. No take-backsies once it sank.

His brows drew together into a fierce frown. "Almira?"

I nodded miserably. "Like she just ripped the spark right out. I had that one, wild burst back at the hut, but I couldn't control it, and I can't call on it."

"It's still there. I can see it in you even now, alive and humming. You just have to find your way back to it."

"You really think it's that simple?"

"Nothing about you is simple, Princess. But magic wants to live, and even Almira doesn't have the strength to kill the kind of magic that lives in you. She just tangled things up a bit, so we'll untangle it."

We.

Apparently, that meant we were…what? Friends again? If we'd ever been that.

I was about to open my mouth to ask, but he beat me to the punch.

"Prince pretty boy threw me for a loop. He means something to you, and I'm still wrestling with gutting him like a pig, even though I have no right. That's not your fault, though. I know I've been acting like a bastard, and I'm sorry for it."

"Well that's not *your* fault. You're only acting like a bastard because you *are* one," I reasoned with a shrug.

His lips twitched and he very nearly smiled, sending a wave of heat curling low in my belly. I opened my mouth to say I don't know what, but water splashed upstream, and we both turned to find Duncan heading toward us.

He was bare-chested, wet shirt clutched in one hand, the lion tattoo on his shoulder flexing with each step.

"Hate to break up the heart to heart, but I smell smoke. Billy's likely done with the monkey pyre."

Hook's jaw tightened, mask back in place as he nodded, the moment between us shattering like Gayelette's glass ball.

The three of us trudged back to shore in silence.

"Time to go, kids!" Billy emerged from between the trees in a fresh set of leathers with a pile of threadbare towels in hand, not a speck of gore on her. "Bodies are ash. You three look marginally less disgusting."

Her gaze snagged on Duncan a beat too long as she held out the towels.

"No need." Hook flicked his fingers; a dry wind spiraled around us, whisking the moisture from our clothes and hair. In less than twenty seconds, we were dry.

"That's a neat trick, I'll give you that." Billy gave a grudging nod of approval. "I just hope you've got plenty more of those rattling around in that big body of yours."

"Why is that?" Hook asked, one inky brow arched.

She let out a harsh laugh.

"Because if you think those monkeys were tough, wait until you get a load of The Wicked Witch of the West in the flesh." She slowed to a stop and sighed. "Look, I hate to be the bad guy—Actually, scratch that. I don't care whether I'm the bad guy or not. I'm going to give it to you honest-like. I'm here because I want that bitch dead, same as you, but that doesn't mean I think we're going to succeed. Odds are, even if we get to her, we're all gonna die. Starting with this one." She jerked her chin my way. "That's just the facts. Fortunately for you all, it's a risk I'm willing to take. You just have to decide if it's a risk *you're* willing to take."

With that, she strode away and didn't look back.

That was one thing you could count on with Billy O'Donnelly. Doppelganger or not, she was a straight shooter in every single story.

But I couldn't stop myself from wishing that her aim was a little less true for once...

CHAPTER 6

*L*unch was eaten on the go; Crumpet's tartlets, a couple of apples Billy swore weren't the wormy kind, and a shared loaf of brown bread. The weather was mild, and the scent of flowers filled the air until the breeze shifted, carrying the faint stench of burning fur and flesh, a reminder of how close to death we had come.

Even then, nobody brought up Billy's chilling prediction about our chances.

Instead, we chatted like new friends getting to know one another. She pointed out claw marks high on a tree trunk— "winged bastards roost there sometimes." Duncan told a ridiculous story about teaching palace guards to march in unison, complete with impressions that actually coaxed a laugh from Billy.

Hook shared no stories, and I found myself…less vocal than usual, consumed by thoughts of my missing magic, missing Fetch, missing Molly. Wondering what we would face down this new road.

By late afternoon, the forest had thinned, and my legs were growing heavy.

I glanced up and frowned. Another hour until sunset, tops. I turned to Billy, my thoughts shifting back to the flying monkeys.

"Skunk's Bunks is just ahead," Billy said, reading my mind. "Hoping to sleep there for the night."

"Skunk's Bunks?" Hook asked, his gravelly voice sending a tingle down my spine.

"An inn…of sorts." She didn't bother to turn around.

Duncan chuckled. "Let's hope it's nicer than it sounds."

"I promise you, it's not. But it beats sleeping out here."

"You sure we'll make it in time? How far is it?"

She rubbed at her chin for a long moment as she glanced around, looking for what, I didn't know.

"Half mile…maybe less?"

"We can't be working off of maybes," Hook said. "If we start setting up camp too late, we could find ourselves—"

He cut off as Billy let out a snarl and broke into a full-on sprint, charging right off the road.

"That motherfucker! No he did not just do that."

I stared after her, blood humming. "What the…Should we be running, too?"

She didn't answer, instead coming to a skidding stop next to a massive, half-dead maple tree.

Maybe she decided we should set up camp for the night, after all?

That idea died a swift death as she brought her foot up halfway to her waist, then slammed it back down once, and then again onto what looked like a flat piece of wood laying in the middle of the grass.

"Open up, Skunk! The sun hasn't even set yet, you lily-livered bastard."

She thrust her leg down a final time, nearly toppling backward when a trapdoor opened where she'd been stomping.

"What d'ya want, Billy?" a rusty voice from below called.

"You know damn well what we want; a place to sleep, and a hot meal. Now move out of the way and let us down, you old fool."

"We're pretty full as is." A bald, liver-spotted head poked up from the trapdoor and a pair of rheumy eyes flickered around. "Four?" He scratched his chin with a dirty fingernail that made me think his scent would live up to his nickname. "Not sure I can do it. It'd be cutting it close…"

I crept closer to the opening. I might be weak as a lamb compared to the others right now, but this I could help with. "We have coin," I assured him, throwing out my arm in front of Hook, who was stalking closer and guaranteed not to ask so nicely.

Skunk let out a sniff. "How much?"

Billy waved a dismissive hand, cutting me off before I could say more. "You let us in, or this mean fella here will blast you in the face with his murder magic and we come down and take over the whole joint. Up to you—in fact, I'm kinda hoping you pick the latter—but either way, you better hurry." She pointed to the horizon, where the fat, orange sun had already begun to fall off the edge of the horizon.

"Blech. That's why I miss seein' Paddy. Your mudder used up all the charm on making him, she did." Skunk scowled, then waved us in, disappearing from view. "Don't forget to close it behind youse, you fucking harpy," he called, his voice echoing up a chute from far below.

Okay, so at least Paddy O'Donnelly existed here in Oz. The tight feeling in my chest loosened a little as Billy stepped down into the hole and set her foot on the first rung of the ladder.

She looked up at me, face tight. "If we're going to work as a team, you need to stop with that whole catching more flies with honey shite. It's vinegar or nothing around these parts. And don't you forget it."

She disappeared from view as the ladder turned into a chute and disappeared into the shadowy depths before I could reply.

"Go ahead." Duncan was scanning the sky for potential threats as he waved me on. "We're right behind you."

I climbed down, doing my best to ignore the rush of anxiety that was setting in. No matter what it was like down there, I wasn't exactly excited at the prospect of spending the whole night locked underground like a mole-person, hiding from an army of superhuman monkeys.

"Twenty silver," Billy said, sparing a quick glance at me as I strode up next to her. "Don't give that codger a whisper more."

The room was enormous, easily as big as the great room in Munsch Kin Land with twenty-foot-high ceilings supported by wooden columns. It didn't smell of skunk, so much as poorly ventilated tobacco mixed with two parts perspiration, one part desperation. A long bar stretched across the back wall, and clusters of tables were spread throughout, with rowdy pockets of patrons drinking at all, eating at some, and gambling at others.

A roar bounced off the walls as one man shoved a pair of dice aside to scoop up a pile of money at the center of the table.

"I can give you two rooms," Skunk said, drawing my attention again. "Which is two more than you deserve. 23 and 25." He grunted as he slid a pair of keys across the counter, keeping his hand over them until I fished out the coins and set them down. "Now excuse me while I go lock up tight like I shoulda done a couple minutes ago instead of letting you in."

Two rooms?

As much as part of me would've liked if Hook and I could pick up where we left off at the stream, I knew it would only make things worse between us—and between him and Duncan…

Not to mention, staying with either of the men meant there was a fair chance they'd hear me in the midst of a dream.

"Boys in one room, girls in the other?" I blurted, cheeks flaming.

Hook scowled, but Ducan nabbed one of the keys off the counter with a wink. "Sure thing."

"We're going to stow our stuff away and then come back down for a bite to eat. Try not to kill each other in the meantime." Billy snatched the second key and disappeared down a hallway to the right of the counter, leaving us behind in a swirl of pipe-smoke.

I could feel Hook's molten gaze on me, but I kept my head low as I scurried after her. "Wait up, I'm right behind you!"

Our room looked like it had been decorated by a far-sighted junk dealer with a grudge. Two narrow beds squatted on either side of a warped dresser that bowed in the middle. A kerosene lamp hissed on a wall hook, throwing off more smoke than light. By Hollow standards, this place was middling at worst, and I shrugged.

"Good enough for me."

"Same." Billy dropped her satchel on the nearest bed and gave the lumpy mattress a whack. "Skunk must've come into money. Last time I stayed here, it was cots only."

"Moving up in the world." I tossed my own pack onto the second bed, and the rickety frame creaked ominously.

While Billy rummaged for a clean shirt, I took a quick inventory of the rest of our amenities: one cracked wash-basin, a spiderweb the size of a small child draped in the corner, and a three-legged stool tucked beside the dresser.

A low groan had me turning back to face my new-old friend. She was bent into a pretzel at the waist, rolling one shoulder, face twisted into a scowl.

I thought back to right around the monkey fight, when she'd been pressing a hand to her tailbone. "Your back giving you trouble?"

She snorted. "Never doesn't. Old injury. It's fine."

The finality in her voice told me to drop it, so I did.

For the moment.

We unpacked in silence. Aside from my bag which I left as it was, with my inventions, the magical clock and jeweler's loupe inside, I had two changes of clothes, a bit of food, and not much else. Billy had little more. A shirt and pants, her bow and a spare string, a tiny tin of some sort of salve, and that plain iron locket on a leather thong, which she set gently on the dresser.

She tugged off her camouflage scarf and her springy curls burst out in all directions. It was so at odds with her serious expression that I did a double-take.

"What?" she snapped, her brows caving into a frown as she lifted a hand to her hair. "Crazy, right? I usually keep it shorter, but I've been busy and—"

"Sorry, no, it's fine! Really cute on you, actually," I added, taken aback by the idea that she would give a rat's crack what her hair looked like. Good reminder that, at the end of the day, no matter how tough a person seemed on the outside, they still had feelings and insecurities. "Makes me think of my bestie, Moll." My throat went tight, and I cleared it before continuing. "She's always messing with my hair, trying to get me to make it pretty. She's good with all that stuff."

"Guessing you haven't seen her in a while?" Billy quipped, eyeing my hair with a dubious squint.

A snort-laugh exploded from my lips as I lifted a hand to my own hair, just now remembering my recent make-under into Moll's brother and want-to-be-pirate, Harmon.

"We had to make some changes on the fly, and she didn't have a lot to work with."

"I get it. I've hacked this mop with a hunting knife more times than I can count. How come this Moll isn't with you and your crew? Jealous all the boys picked you, is she?"

I'd been hoping she hadn't sniffed out the reason Duncan and Hook were at odds, but she didn't miss a trick.

"No. We needed to…part ways for a while." I lowered myself to the threadbare blanket that was about as welcoming as sandpaper.

I'd seen Moll less than two days ago—my time, anyway. But it felt like months, and the thought that I might never—

"Once we're done with everything we need to do, I'll see her again," I added in a rush. "She's the sister I never had. Despite your prediction, I have a lot of reasons to live, and Moll is one of them."

Billy's eyes probed my face, in search of truth. "She is like family to you, then?"

My eyes stung but I forced the rush of hot tears back with a blink. "More than any family I've ever had."

If anyone knew about the bond between family, it was Billy O'Donnelly. Again, I found myself wanting to ask about her siblings—Paddy, Andrew, Scotty and Jacob…

"Okay, then," she said, interrupting my thought. "Let's do our best to make sure you see her again, shall we? At least for long enough to fix that gods-awful hairdo."

I grinned, ready with a smartass reply when something at her feet caught my eye and had the words dying on my lips. The corner of a leatherbound book sticking out of a gap in her satchel, with the page edges dusted in green.

I got so lightheaded, I had to put both hands on the mattress to keep from keeling sideways.

Not possible.

But I already knew in my gut that it was more than possible. It was a stone-cold fact. Billy O'Donnelly of this world was in possession of a third fairytale book just like the one I had. Just like the one Hook had. Only instead of golden edges like mine, or black like Hook's, hers were dusted in emerald green.

Destiny had not come to fuck around this time. She was renting a room and staying awhile.

Before I could form words, Billy shook out her clean shirt and eyed me expectantly. "We better go eat before Skunk sells out of the only edible thing in this shithole—mire-boar stew."

"Yep," I said, voice a bit too shrill. "Sounds good. I'm starving."

"Just eat around the hooves, if you can help it."

I tipped my head. "Can do."

She stared at me expectantly, and I stared back.

"What?"

She gestured toward the door, shaking her head. "Can you go on down now, so I can change without you getting a peak at my titties?"

"Oh! Yeah, of course." I stood and grabbed my bag before backing toward the door. "See you down there. In a few. No rush. Come whenever…" I wheeled around and yanked at the knob, willing myself to stop babbling. "Bye!"

I'd barely gotten three steps down the hall when the locks tumbled behind me.

Shit.

I should've said I wasn't hungry at all. Now, if I wanted a chance to do some snooping, I was going to have to make an excuse to come back to the room before she did. As exhausted as I was, begging off due to exhaustion wouldn't even be a lie, which was good. My stomach for subterfuge was getting weaker by the day.

I took the stairs two at a time, and headed down the corridor, following the new smell of rich, peppery broth mingling with the rest of the scents.

But food was the last thing on my mind, hooves or no. As I stepped into the roar of the tavern, only one thought rang in my head;

Billy O'Donnelly had secrets. And I needed to find out what they were before I could share mine. Which meant I had to get my hands on that book, and I had to do it tonight.

CHAPTER 7

he tavern had only grown louder since I'd left. Dice rattled like the tail of a snake, and a man in the back corner of the room was sawing away at a fiddle like it owed him money.

Duncan and Hook were easy to spot—mostly because they'd claimed the same long table, managing to leave five empty chairs between them. I didn't roll my eyes, but I wanted to.

I threaded my way through the crush of bodies and slid into the middle chair, planting myself between them like a white flag no one had asked for.

"Room all right?" Duncan asked, voice pitched above the din. He had a near-full mug of ale and the beginnings of a relaxed smile that told me it likely wasn't his first.

"Fine. Yours?"

Duncan shrugged.

I raised a brow at Hook. His mug looked untouched, and he flicked me a glance before turning his attention back to the crowd at large, no doubt in search of any potential threats.

I swallowed a sigh and let my tired, gritty eyes drift shut for a second. I'd been dying to tell them what I'd seen in Billy's bag, but I couldn't very well shout it across the table. I was an instant from laying into them both when a saucy barmaid with waist-length platinum hair sidled up to the table. She wore a scarlet bodice that left nothing to the imagination, and what she had underneath was pretty outstanding, if I did say so myself.

"Hellooo, strangers." Her gaze landed on Duncan first, flicking over his broad shoulders and then back up to his wide smile. She twirled a ringlet around her finger. "Aren't you a hunk of fresh meat?" She let out a low purr and then stopped short as she caught sight of Hook. "Well, hello to you as well, sir…I gotta tell you, milk is good," she said before moving his way and running a fingernail along the rim of his mug, "but cheddar is better. I like 'em smiling and respectful —most days. But every now and then I like it when they aren't. If you catch my meaning."

Oh, I caught her meaning and I hated to agree almost as much as I hated her.

Hook's lip twitched, but whether in amusement or annoyance, I couldn't tell.

"Fucking hell, Patrice, we got mouths to feed here!" Skunk hollered from behind the bar where he stood juggling three mugs full of foamy ale.

Her eyes narrowed and she turned, shouting back at the top of her lungs. "Shut up, you weasely, pox-riddled bastard!" She turned back, a beatific smile on her lips like it had never left. "As I was saying, boys…what'll it be?"

"You guys should get the stew," I piped in, acid churning in my gut. "Billy says it's great."

That much was true, so I only felt slightly guilty. They deserved a few hooves in their stew for acting like a couple of babies. It had nothing to do with this waitress.

Nothing at all…

"Another stew for Billy, and I'll have the potatoes and cabbage," I added, putting in the rest of our order before the woman could climb into Hook's lap.

Patrice nodded and turned to go but then paused, cocking her head as she stared at me. "Why do you look so familiar, sweetheart?"

"Must have a generic face," I deadpanned.

She shrugged and then sashayed off with a promise to be back soon.

Hook turned his attention to studying the two exits, but was quickly interrupted as Billy sauntered toward us, sizing up the seating arrangement with a snort. She dropped between Duncan and me and lifted her hand for an ale.

"Well, isn't this cozy."

If you consider a lion's den cozy…

"Got room for one more?" A wiry man with iron-gray hair and mutton chops that looked like two dead squirrels pasted to his cheeks slid into one of the last two chairs without waiting for an answer. He wheezed as though he'd run a mile, slapping the table with a grin.

"Evening, folks." He offered a hand to Billy. "Name's Jack."

Billy's eyes narrowed as she shook his hand. "Seen you around once or twice, old-timer."

"Old-timer, ay?" he chuckled. "Flattery'll get you everywhere."

She rolled her eyes but didn't shove him off the bench for the silly quip. Our food arrived before long, but it wasn't Patrice delivering it, which was fine by me. Stew for the others, a shallow bowl of buttery potatoes and wilted cabbage for me, more ale for everyone. Jack produced a wooden spoon from his coat pocket and dug in.

"So," he said through a mouthful, "where's the road taking you?"

I stayed silent, choosing to let Billy take the lead. She would know what would and wouldn't be suspicious in these parts, after all.

"The Emerald City."

The truth was easiest, so long as it didn't cause any trouble, but Hook still glared at her.

"Have fun," Jack muttered. "Wouldn't catch me there on my deathbed. They won't let you wipe your own backside without a decree. Me, I like my freedom." He raised his spoon in salute.

"Freedom comes with a price, too." Billy took a long swallow from her mug before swiping the foam off her top lip. "Sometimes that price is lousy stew and a lumpy bed that smells like goats instead of a city made of emeralds."

"I always did like goats." Jack chuckled, his eyes twinkling. "Hey, how about we have some fun? Maybe even earn you enough money to buy a couple emeralds of your own." He pulled a pair of dice from his pants pocket.

Billy's whole face brightened. There was the hustler I knew and remembered.

"What are the stakes?"

"Silver, of course. Or stories, if you're broke, I suppose."

Duncan's brows rose. "Mind if I join you?"

"The more the merrier." Jack shoved the mostly empty bowls aside to make space, and then they started rolling.

The game was simple; Roll for high score. Ties went again.

The first round went to Billy with double sixes on her first roll. Jack groaned as he slid a silver piece her way, but Duncan just grinned as he paid the piper. Second round, Duncan won with eight. It took Jack another three before logging a win, and it didn't take long before he was talking shit about "beginner's luck wearing off."

As laughter erupted around me, it almost felt like a

normal night at a tavern instead of a pit stop on our way to kill a witch and her legions of flying monkeys.

Between rolls Billy and Jack gossiped about supply prices, common acquaintances, and the best way to cook possum. He was smart, I had to give him that. The man knew every bend between here and The Emerald City, plus where to get the best blackberry mead.

They were so engrossed in their conversation, I realized it was time to make my move.

Now or never.

"I'm going to the ladies'. Be right back." I spared a glance at Hook, who nodded absently, his attention still on the entrance as I slipped away, heart thudding. Halfway up the staircase I risked a glance over my shoulder to make sure no one was tailing me. I slipped into our room a minute later and let out a relieved sigh when I saw that Billy's satchel still sat where she'd left it, flap loosely buckled.

Quick in, quick out.

Mouth dry with nerves, I knelt beside the bag and lifted the flap, focused on one thing and one thing only. I'd barely set my eyes on the familiar leather cover when a rustle in the hall had me freezing in place. Footsteps, slow and deliberate, moved down the hall, closer.

Closer.

I yanked the flap shut, heart in my throat, straightening just as the knob turned.

Hook slipped inside, closing the door with a soft snick. He raised a brow as I stared up at him like a raccoon caught raiding the compost heap.

"Why do I feel like half the time I see you, you're breaking and entering?"

"I'm not breaking. Just entering," I corrected him. "This is my room…I have a key, remember?"

"That's picking nits." He folded his arms. "Want to fill me in?"

"I've been wanting to all night, but you guys were being weird sitting twenty feet away from each other and—" I broke off and waved a hand. "Whatever, doesn't matter. Bottom line is I think Billy's tied to all this in ways we don't understand. She has a fairytale book, too. Like mine. Like yours. I saw it sticking out of her bag before we went downstairs."

He let out a low whistle. "Well, that complicates things." He stepped forward, voice low. "Did you open it?"

"I was just about to." I gestured at the satchel, the guilt hitting hard and fast at touching her personal stuff. She was so guarded…so private. It felt like a violation.

Because it is.

"I was going to ask her about it outright, but what if she didn't come by it honestly?" We had to take into account that Billy here in Oz might be just as much of a hustler as she was in every other story. Had she stolen it from someone? Or was she given the book by Gayelette, and had come to help?

I rubbed my temples, wishing Gayelette were here now, and feeling bad for even thinking it, given her current situation. For all I knew, the woman was being tortured on some kind of medieval rack for her last visit at this very second.

I shoved that thought away and focused on the now.

"If Billy is still down there fleecing old Jack, we should still have time to—"

The door handle rattled and even Hook startled. I made a dive toward the bed, and was pretending to fluff my lumpy pillow when Billy strode in a second later, cheeks flushed from ale, victory, or both.

"Had to fetch more coins," she announced, oblivious. "Old geezer's had a turn of fortune, but it doesn't matter how much you lose while the game's afoot. It only matters what you walk away with."

Hook nodded, casual. "Truth."

"We were just…discussing strategy," I added.

"For dice?" She snorted. "Only strategy is roll high." She grabbed her satchel and then paused, eyes narrowing between us. "Everything alright with you two?"

"Yup, good," I said, forcing a smile.

"I know we haven't spent loads of time together, but it'd go a lot easier between you if you just, you know…fucked it out."

I blinked. Hook stared.

She rolled her hands. "You know…all that anger and such. Be good for the team on the whole, because right now, it's a lot. Think about it, is all I'm saying. But not tonight. Tonight, you have to come back downstairs with me." She slapped Hook's arm on the way back toward the door. "I'm going to need some more muscle to help me haul up my winnings."

Turned out, she wasn't wrong. By the time the night was winding down a while later, Billy had a small mountain of silver in front of her, and Jack looked one lost roll away from tears.

I sat pushing lukewarm potatoes around on my plate and tried not to stare at Billy's satchel slung over her chair.

Maybe it was for the best.

Maybe betrayal was a skill better off left back in Neverland.

I drained my glass and ordered another, not even caring that it was Patrice delivering it this time. I needed a dreamless night of sleep more than I needed a clear head right now. Reality between me and Hook was more than enough.

Sneaking a glance at him from below my lashes, I couldn't help but think about our night—our *almost* night—together on the Jolly Roger. The way he touched me...as if he knew exactly what to do to make me—

He chose that moment to turn his head my way and I stilled, those black as night eyes drawing me in like a magic spell. Billy's words rolled over me, leaving chills in their wake.

It wasn't the worst idea, a little voice in my head whispered.

We'd get it out of our system, at least. And who knew? It might even be terrible, which would make this whole existential crisis about it needless.

You might not be magic anymore, but that doesn't mean you're stupid, a second, meaner voice piped in.

Something told me, mean or not, that was the voice to listen to. Because the short time I'd spent in Hook's arms had been the furthest thing from terrible. If we did as Billy said? If we fucked it out?

It would rock my world. And my world was already plenty rocked.

I looked away, suddenly interested in the dice game. Some tension and awkwardness were manageable. Making big moves when the stakes were this high would be the mistake, no matter what Billy said. Because even though it hurt, Hook had it right. Keeping our distance and focusing on the mission needed to be priority one.

Which would be a whole lot easier if he stopped looking at me like he was a starving man, and I was the meal he was dreaming of devouring...

Fucking hell.

CHAPTER 8

*E*ither the ale had worked or, when Almira had broken my magic, she'd also broken my brain, because it was a dreamless night. Funny, it should've been a relief. But like my loss of magical spark, it wound up leaving me feeling empty inside.

The trapdoor screeched open, and a gust of brisk morning air washed over my cheeks, smelling of grass and of wet earth. The sudden chill made the skin on my arms pebble after a night in the underground sauna of a bunker and I sucked in a deep breath.

"Crazy," I arched my back until it popped, "that a place that big can still make you feel claustrophobic."

I hauled myself onto solid ground and offered Billy a hand as she appeared behind me.

She ignored it, launching herself in the air and landing like a cat, headscarf fluttering in the breeze.

The Billy from Alabaster had been far from slow, but this one moved like she'd traded her bones for springs. I already knew a person could be ordinary in one world and have magic in the next, like Cissy Petway, but watching Billy move scrambled my brain.

As she looked around, the morning sun caught on the ridges of her pointed ears, and I wondered how much of her had adapted to survive here.

Hook and Duncan came out behind us and Hook's eyes flicked to mine, a reminder of last night's loaded looks at the tavern and Billy's unbidden advice.

I turned away only to find myself locking eyes with Duncan, who shot me a half-smile that carried its own unspoken questions.

Too many loaded looks and zero energy or time to deal with them. We had to get on the road. If C'an Saas was falling as quickly as Gayelette said, every day we took to get to The Emerald City could be costing lives.

Including Gayelette's.

"Bye, now!" Skunk's voice drifted up the shaft, sounding something close to courteous. "Don't forget to shut it on yer way out—and thanks for stayin' at Skunk's Bunks. Hope to see you back soon."

Billy ran over and shoved her head back through the opening. "Get fucked, Skunk!" Laughter echoed from below and Billy slammed the door with a thud. "Crazy old bastard acts like he didn't seriously consider letting the monkeys get us last night."

I should have been angry at the innkeeper too, probably. But I'd left his place alive, somewhat rested, and with a full belly after a hearty breakfast of eggs, crispy potatoes, and some spice-rubbed meat without a single hoof in sight. I could hardly complain.

Billy shaded her eyes and scanned the horizon. "We're still a good two days out from the city, even if we keep to the Yellow Road. We'll be camping tonight for sure."

A chill skittered up my spine at the thought of open sky

and monkey scouts, but I kept quiet. If she thought we'd be alright outdoors, who was I to argue? Better to leave it to the expert.

"Do most around here live underground like that?" Duncan asked.

"Nah." Billy flicked a dismissive hand. "Just rangers. That's what the townies call us folks who choose to live outside normal society and roam some. There are outposts and then the bigger, protected hubs like Munsch Kin Land and The Emerald City. The Witch leaves most folks alone if they pay their tithes and keep their mouths shut. It's travel and defiance that gets you in the shit."

"Why travel?" I asked.

"Divide and conquer. Keep a relatively small group of people isolated in one spot, they're easy to control. If we all came together…"

The words felt all too familiar. I shared a glance with Duncan. Relyk had used different methods to keep us apart, but the endgame was the same.

My thoughts drifted to The Speaker and his village of revolutionaries.

"Is there any organized resistance here in Oz?"

"You're lookin' at it," Billy answered, voice flat as slate. "That's about as organized as it gets these days, unless you count the Munsch Kin Land. Which I don't. They might not be under her thumb, so to speak, but that's easy enough to stick to when they have a magical barrier protecting them."

I shrugged, hoisting my bag higher on my shoulder. "Well, to be fair, it's not perfect for them either. They're stuck there, if they want to live. And according to the earl, many have family in The Emerald City that they're separated from…"

"Boo fucking hoo. They and the people they love are nestled away in the two safest places in Oz. The rest of us either hide underground or roll the dice every single day we stay topside." She adjusted her scarf and put her head down. "Moral of the story? That bitch needs to die for what she's done. At first, people tried to rebel, but she's too damn strong. Now most folks toe the line. You probably met half the fools who won't last night. We trade safety for freedom, and make the best of it."

Which meant no folks to rally to our cause aside from a few dozen upstarts who, if the clientele at Skunk's Bunks was any indicator, were half off their rockers.

The idea that our rag-tag foursome patched together from three different worlds might be the only hope for Oz made my stomach twist into a knot.

Duncan pulled up closer to us as we followed the winding road. "If you know it's a losing battle, it must be hard to keep fighting. How do you do it?"

Billy glanced over, meeting his earnest gaze. When I searched her face, there was an ache there, something old but still raw. I wasn't surprised at all when she shook her head and waved him off.

"No more chatter for now, I've got to concentrate and keep my ears open for any more scouts." She lengthened her stride leaving the rest of us trailing a few yards behind her.

As the day passed, the forest changed from pine trees to towering oaks, with leaves the size of dinner plates.

My stomach rumbled at the thought, and I was about to suggest a quick lunch break when we rounded a corner and caught sight of a broken-down wagon. Its front wheel lay splintered, spokes splayed like the ribs of a dead animal. An old man beside it waved while his horse stamped its hooves and tossed its head.

"Hey! You folks helpin' or just gawkin'?" the man called.

Hook's eyes narrowed. "Is that Jack?"

"Sure is." Billy cupped her hands around her mouth. "You hurt or just the wagon?"

"I'm fine but the wheel snapped clean off." He patted the stocky mare's neck, calming her as we moved closer. "If you could help haul my goods home, I'd be obliged. Can't pay you, as I'm sure you know, since this one emptied my coin purse." His lips twisted into a wry smile as he jerked his chin at Billy.

Duncan crouched to inspect the axle, but Hook didn't budge.

"I don't like it," he muttered under his breath, watching as Jack showed Duncan where it had broken.

Billy shrugged. "No issues with him last night, he paid his debt and all, but you don't have to convince me to walk away. I'm easy like that. Besides, we rangers are a resilient lot. He'll figure it out."

I knew in my head that there was a logic to what they were saying. The Hollow worked in the same way. You always had to watch your back. There were a lot of good people there, but when life was hard, it was easy to justify being bad if that's what it took to survive.

And still, I couldn't quite bring myself to nod along with them. The earl's voice echoed in my mind: *Are you a good witch, or a bad witch?* I nibbled at the inside of my cheek and then shook my head.

"We can't leave him."

I lifted a burlap sack from the wagon bed. The contents—jars, from what it sounded like—clinked together, and the faint smell of fruit and booze rose up to tickle my nose.

"I can take two bags for you."

Jack's eyes widened with gratitude. "Much obliged, little lady. I knew you were a good egg the second I met you." He flicked a glance to my companions, and Duncan stepped forward and hefted five bags from the wagon without a word.

Hook muttered a curse but grabbed a massive crate,

muscles flexing beneath his rolled up sleeves. "Fine. Quick detour."

"Thank you! And you all can stay for lunch to show my gratitude. The wife makes the best stews and soups in all of Oz."

"Let's move," Billy grumbled, hefting a bag of empty sacks herself, looking less than thrilled.

I remembered with a twinge that she had back trouble, but I knew arguing with her would be a waste of time. I made a mental note to mention it to Hook later. Maybe he'd be willing to help with Tom's blessing.

Thankfully, Jack's "house" was only minutes away. I slowed when I saw it, taken aback by the elaborate setup, although it made sense. The place was built directly into the side of a cliff, half hidden by shrubs and the rest covered in iron doors. Each looked sturdy enough to deflect a cannonball. No surprise that the witch's minions hadn't gotten to them here.

Jack unlocked the largest door and led his horse into a stable. "Started as a rabbit tunnel," he said, puffing his chest out. "Dug it out and added rooms every year."

What had to be thousands of pounds of dirt and clay overhead in order to make the space, hung over us in an impressive feat of engineering. Past the stable, several tunnels branched out, each framed by wooden beams.

"Comin' in for lunch?" Jack asked, gesturing toward a side passage that smelled like baking bread.

"I could eat," I blurted.

Billy shrugged. "I'm not one to pass up a free meal. Especially now that I smell it."

It was only Hook who hesitated, lips curled into a frown. I met his gaze, and, after a brief pause, he gave a curt nod.

Jack opened a second door and called inside. "Andrea?"

"I thought you'd be back at sunrise," a woman called back. "I was getting worried!"

"Got caught up at Skunk's," he said, clearing his throat. "We, uh, have some company."

"Company!" A squat woman bustled from a side room, cheeks pink, hair pinned under a kerchief embroidered with tiny, red poppies. "Well, aren't you folks a sight for bored, lonely eyes! Lunch'll be ready in two shakes of a squaddle-jacks's tail."

She waved us into a cozy dining nook where the smell of onions along with something gamey wafted our way.

Once we set our bags and crates down as directed, I slid into a chair beside Hook. My cheeks flushed with heat as his elbow brushed mine.

Pathetic.

I dug my fingernails into my palms, refusing to look his way.

"This is a beautiful place you have," I offered, mostly to fill the silence while Andrea served up the thick broth into wooden bowls.

But what the hell was that strange hook hanging from the ceiling in the far corner of the room? It was caked with blood...

They were homesteader types. They had to hang their game *somewhere*, and outside wasn't an option.

"Hmm?" Jack's gaze lingered on the front door and a low, clacking sound caught my ear.

"I was just saying how nice your house is."

Jack still didn't reply and Duncan stared at him, eyes narrowed. "Something wrong?"

Jack raked a hand through his wispy hair, smile brittle. "Nah, thought I heard something. Just tired I suppose."

A louder rustle by the entrance had my muscles tense but before I could stand, all hell broke loose.

"Watch yourselves!" Hook's chair screeched; he shoved mine backward and drew his saber in one fluid motion, lunging toward something behind me. I spun as metal clanged and Andrea staggered back, the out-thrust kitchen knife knocked from her hand by Hook's blade just before she'd gotten in range to stab me.

"What the f—" I yanked my whip free, heart lurching.

Billy and Duncan both dove for Jack, but he wheeled away, flinging open the door. Five armed men swarmed inside, three with rusty spears, two with sabers, their boot heels clacking against the floor.

My pulse hammered in my ears.

We'd walked straight into a fucking ambush.

"Just give us the girl, and the rest of you can go," Jack snarled, taking aim in our general direction with a crossbow I hadn't seen him grab.

Andrea's plump, kind face was a mask of disgust as she shook her head grimly, backing away from Hook to stand closer to her husband. "I knew I should've drugged the soup."

Hook had planted himself directly between me and the intruders, sword raised.

"This is how you treat people who try to help you?" Billy's bow snapped to attention, arrow nocked and aimed straight at Jack's chest.

"Easy, now, Billy. Let's not be hasty here. The Witch is offering good coin for that one. No reason for this to result in a whole pile of bodies. Use your heads."

Duncan's muscles bulged, berserker strength simmering under his skin like lava. "You work for her?" he demanded.

"We work for whoever pays the most," he shot back, no sign of the easygoing old man we'd met the night before. "Step forward, girl, unless you want to be the reason your friends all die here."

Billy's voice was like a blade scraping ice. "Last chance to stop this, Jack."

"Nah." He shook his head, sweat beading on his upper lip. "You might've done a job on me at dice, but seven against four? Odds are mine."

She cocked her head at him. And then, she laughed. It sounded rusty and a little unhinged in the tight space.

"You really are a terrible gambler, Jack."

CHAPTER 9

"Get down!" James growled, shoving my shoulder.

I dropped. A spear hissed passed me as he answered with a thrust of his hook. Air coiled, compressed, then tore loose in a bullet of wind that punched clean through the attacker's skull. The man toppled without a sound, painting the wall behind him in blood.

Across the table Duncan roared, the glow of his berserker magic crackling over his skin. He caught a charging attacker by the collar, hauled him forward, and rammed his great sword through to the hilt.

More men poured through the doorway, knives and cudgels raised. One hurled a cleaver, but Hook batted it aside in another burst of wind, not breaking stride.

I squeezed the handle of my whip, clawing for magic that danced just out of reach. The little wisps of energy seemed to retreat just before I could latch onto them, like a forgotten word on the tip of my tongue.

"Kitchen's closed," Billy barked. She loosed an arrow, then rolled directly into the first two men, wielding her bow like a short staff. She parried a dagger swipe, then smashed the brass grip into one man's nose with a crunch. He let out a shriek, hands flying to his face, and she took the chance to plant her boot right into his knee. Bone cracked, and he folded like a wet noodle.

The second lunged with a rusty saber. Billy ducked, skipping right past him as Duncan lurched forward to cleave him in half.

A wave of revulsion rolled over me, but I shoved it aside as Andrea lunged forward yet again, tearing a knife from her belt. I scrambled to my feet as she made a beeline for me, but Billy appeared between us in the blink of an eye, deflecting the blow. Hook stepped up beside her, but she waved him off.

"You and pretty boy handle the others. I got this."

"Don't leave her side," he grunted, sparing a quick glance at me before turning his attention toward the men by the door.

"You invite us for soup and then sell us out?" Billy hissed.

Andrea brandished the knife out in front of her and shrugged, eyes gleaming with menace. "Ten thousand gold buys a lot of soup."

Billy leapt forward, dropping her bow to smash her palm right into the older woman's sternum. The knife fell, and Billy kicked her backward, straight toward that bloody butcher's hook hanging from the ceiling.

I cringed as Andrea flailed, trying to stop herself, but momentum won. The hook caught her right under the ribs, lifting her off the floor. She shrieked once and then sagged.

There was no time to celebrate as a crossbow bolt whizzed past Billy's ear, embedding in the wall behind us. We both wheeled around to find Jack, standing in the pantry doorway, hands shaking as he cranked a new one into place.

His eyes darted toward his wife's lifeless body with a wince. "Ah, you didn't have to go and do that. Bounty's nothing personal, girl."

"Feels very personal right now." Hook flicked his hand, and the wind gusted again, toppling shelves and sending jars crashing. Jack's eyes went wild with fear as he fired, but his bolt missed by feet instead of inches this time.

Jack fumbled for a cleaver hanging close by as Billy charged at him, but he was too slow. She kicked him square in the chest. He stumbled back into the second hanging hook, the iron tip ripped through him, impaling him center mass. His scream was short-lived.

An eerie silence fell over the kitchen, broken only by the wet, sucking sound of Jack's breathing and the simmering of soup still on the stove.

Hook wiped gore from his blade with a dish towel, pinning Jack with an icy stare. "How many more?"

"Just us," Jack gasped, trying to lever himself off the hook, which only drove it deeper.

Billy stepped close, face carved from stone as she lifted her bow and pointed it straight at his balls. "Time to tell us about this bounty. Talk fast."

His eyes rolled into the back of his head as he tried to wriggle away.

"Wanted posters on every tavern wall west of here. I saw them on my travels back home, but they hadn't made it as far as Skunk's yet," he wheezed. "Ten thousand for the dark-haired girl. Imagine my surprise when I walked in and saw you there. Figured I only had a day or so before every single ranger in the area was looking for her. Decided to leave early morning and wait to make my move."

My throat tightened. "Where were you supposed to bring me?"

"Old watch-tower, five kilometers east. We were offered safe passage to hand you over to the monkey scouts." He let out a gurgle and then coughed in a spray of bright red blood before he continued. "We needed the money."

"The Scouts…are they always there at the watch-tower, then?"

He shuddered, eyes going in and out of focus as his head began to loll to one side. "Not… sure."

Billy dropped her bow and lurched forward, grabbing a fistful of his hair and yanking his head back.

"Are they waiting there now?"

Jack spasmed, legs churning as if he was running the world's slowest race. "I can't…please…free my mare. She'll find her way to Skunk's place and he'll take care of her. Don't leave her here to starve."

My stomach gave a squeeze. "Billy…"

But Duncan was already stepping forward, laying a hand on her shoulder. Billy released Jack's hair with a snarl and stood back as Duncan slid a dagger across Jack's throat in one, smooth motion. Mercy even after he tried to take us.

Billy met Duncan's gaze, and he shook his head. "He had nothing more to tell us, and I couldn't leave him there to suffer."

She nodded and wordlessly picked up her bow as Hook rifled through a drawer and emerged with a stack of papers.

He slapped one on the table. It featured a fair likeness of me, whip raised, face twisted in anger. Above my image loomed bold words;

WANTED Thief and murderer. 10,000 GOLD, ALIVE. 5,000 DEAD.

I swallowed hard. "That's not good."

"We travel quieter from now on," Hook murmured.

"Which means no more stops for supplies." Billy was already raiding cupboards, and she tossed me a sack of dried beans.

Despite the logic of it, looting the house of the dead definitely didn't feel like a very good-witch thing to do. I glanced around at the fallen bodies, barely holding back the urge to vomit. They had tried to kill me, so maybe what we'd done hadn't been strictly *bad*.

Standing here in the midst of the carnage, though, I couldn't exactly call it good, either.

More like a murky shade of gray that had me asking myself what I would have chosen to do if Hook, Billy and Duncan hadn't been here and made the decision to kill everyone?

I shuddered. The truth was, I'd have died long before I got the chance to consider the morality of it. I'd been all but useless in the fight once again. A weakness rather than an asset.

My fingernails bit into my palm. Once I got my magic back, I'd be stronger, but that wasn't good enough. What if I lost my magic again, or found myself in a situation where it wasn't enough? Was I supposed to play the damsel and leave it to the others to protect me?

I traced my finger along the handle of my whip.

Never again.

Until I got my magic back, I'd have to find a way to compensate. At the very least, the goal would give me something to focus on, rather than just sitting around waiting and hoping.

I let out a breath as Billy handed me another sack of food.

"I'll go release the horse." Duncan's eyes lingered on Jack's slack face before turning away.

"Wait up," Hook grunted. "There could still be others outside."

Not exactly cordial, but better than the hostility he'd shown at the start. It was one, tiny pearl glimmer of good in an endless sea of manure.

I helped Billy load a small wheel of cheese, a sack of jerky, and some jars of pickled roots into a burlap sack. Then, she bent over Andrea's body, stripping the woman's belt-pouch, before tossing it to me. A handful of coins clinked inside.

Literal blood money.

"I don't want it."

"Suit yourself. Just know that she'd have happily gutted you for that reward." Billy slung the hefty sack of food over her shoulder. Then, she straightened and stalked off without another word.

Outside a few minutes later, the sun hung high in the sky, and I watched as the mare cantered away. I tried to speak with her mentally, searching for a spark of connection with the animal, but there was nothing.

"You okay? Not hurt anywhere?" Hook stared down at me, his expression unreadable.

"Nope. Ready to go," I said, adding in a thumb's up for good measure.

"Let's move, then," Billy said. "Ranger trail south'll keep us off the Yellow Road but moving in the same direction."

We headed down the slope, leaving Jack's cliffside home behind us as I did my best to forget those meat hooks inside.

Duncan and Hook both grabbed a sack of food from my hand, but I still felt heavier than ever. Somewhere, not too far away, an evil Witch lurked. One who was willing to pay a princely sum for my head.

And with each passing mile, I grew less and less sure I had the power to stop her from taking it…

Along with anything and everything else she wanted.

CHAPTER 10

The sun dipped slowly as we cut through the dense forest. We'd left Jack's cliff behind at around noon and had been pushing hard ever since. To avoid a repeat of that morning's near-disaster, we pulled off the Yellow Road, using Billy's ranger trails instead. They were less "trails" and more "a bunch of poorly marked deer paths trampled through thatches of bramble", but I was in no position to argue.

Still, the further we got, the tougher the terrain, and I found myself missing the easy walk down the brick road. The only positive was that we were pretty much single file, and I didn't have to bother with small talk, if there was any to be had.

Nope, just me and my swirling thoughts.

Every so often I tried coaxing a bit of magic to my finger-tips…trying to picture the thread and then tugging on it, but the moment I reached for it, it unraveled. A nagging ache had settled between my ribs. I was so desperate to get back what I'd lost, I hadn't realized until Jack's place that I still had some issues to deal with. If Almira could shut my magic off at will, she could do it again and I'd be back to dead weight the others had to drag along behind them.

"No fucking way," I mumbled under my breath. I stared at the brush below, Xander's old lessons replaying in my head.

Wrists loose, elbow drives the snap, feel the whip breathe. I'd practice tonight. But skill alone wouldn't bridge the gap between me and the mercenaries or flying death-monkeys. I needed to be faster, sharper. Like Duncan with his berserker reflexes, or Billy with her preternatural agility.

"Halt." Up ahead, Billy raised a hand. The trail dipped into a valley where a babbling stream glittered in the late afternoon sun. "We'll camp here."

I nearly groaned out loud. My calves felt like they'd taken a turn under the blacksmith's clipping hammer.

Duncan squinted at the sky. "Early stop?"

"We have to let the terrain call the shots. Rivers and streams keep the monkeys wary," Billy said, hopping down the bank. "They can't swim and hate flying over water. Gives us a buffer."

"Good enough for me," Hook muttered, rolling his shoulders.

"Might as well lean into our strengths." Billy clapped her hands together. "The ox here can haul that giant fallen pine over. We can use it for framing poles. Harmony, go with him and gather as many lighter branches as you can for bedding and for weaving."

Duncan's eyes sparkled, and I had the sense that her total lack of reverence charmed him in some way. "Am I the ox, then?"

"You've got the shoulders. You know what they say, if the yolk fits, wear it." She pointed her bow at Hook. "Tall, dark, and cranky...I'm gonna need a trench right in front of that oak tree. Dig deep, down to the roots."

Hook arched a brow.

"You've got a built-in spade," she said, tapping his hook. "Leaning into our strengths, yeah?"

He gave her a long, dead-eyed stare before popping off a salute that somehow made his hook look more like a middle finger, then strode toward the riverbank as directed.

I also did as directed and leaned into my strength…which was apparently picking up a bunch of twigs, and watched as Duncan hefted the massive tree onto his back with a wince.

"Shit, I forgot. Your Whisper makes you really sore afterward, doesn't it? Did you bring any of that salve from Alabaster?"

"All out. I'm fine," he said, wiping the wince from his face and flashing a dimple. "It's nothing a good night's sleep won't fix."

Still, I made one trip with my sticks and branches, and then went back to help him haul his cargo. We dragged the pine tree into the clearing a short while later.

"How about you…You holding up alright?" he asked, voice low as we set down our load.

"Physically, yes." I shrugged and tried to keep the sadness from peeking through. "Magic's still… mush."

"It'll come back."

"Right." I nodded. "And if it doesn't?"

"Then we'll adapt. You're more than just magic. You're also brilliant, Harm. You're going to figure it out, like you've done this whole time to even get us this far. Like you did with the lockpick and the loupe."

Warmth fluttered through me, part gratitude, part something I couldn't label. "Thanks."

For the next while, we did our best to collect as much fallen debris and wood for kindling as we could, piling it near where Hook had already started his excavating. He stood, hook extended, the wind blessing he'd taken from

Davy the pirate king scooping up dirt as easily as water from a bucket.

Billy's brows climbed high enough to touch her headscarf. "Look at you two…an ox *and* a shovel. We've got all the tools here at Casa De Billy."

"Don't get used to it," Hook grumbled, but when she marked a wider outline with her boot, he sighed and doubled the trench, sending soil spraying everywhere.

By the time the sun was touching the treetops, Hook was knee-deep in the ditch he'd dug. Billy wedged the pine trunk Duncan had brought against the tree and lashed them together with rope.

"Smart design."

Duncan started laying branches crossways as I scattered the softer switches we'd collected on the floor. Soon enough, we had ourselves a pretty decent shelter.

Billy eyeballed our humble abode and tipped her head in a nod of satisfaction. "Everyone inside. With these two big lugs, we better test the fit."

"Feel free," Hook said, not moving from his spot at the entrance.

The rest of us ducked under the slanted roof and settled in like we were bunking down for the night. The ditch was deep enough for us to sit up, and the boughs that lined the floor made it sort of comfortable. Billy had woven leafy branches so that only little patches of the setting sun shone through the roof, so I suspected we were even semi-rain-proof. Plus, from outside looking down, it probably made us look like a tangle of brush to any monkeys.

"Not bad." She took a hasty swipe at the beads of sweat on her forehead. "And we still have enough time to make something decent for dinner by the fire before we have to put it out for the night."

"I'll go grab some firewood," Duncan said.

Hook nodded, trudging toward the entrance to join him.

"See if you can flatten that section down in the corner a little more." Billy glanced over at me as she followed them out, carrying our empty waterskins. "I'm gonna top us off."

The instant the three of them were out of sight, I shot a glance over to Billy's spot near the back corner of the shelter where her satchel had been.

Gone.

Son of a bitch.

Of course she'd taken it with her. Sooner or later, I was going to have to take the bull by the horns and just ask her about it. Was there a chance it could spook her? Absolutely. Humor aside, she was one of the most guarded people I'd ever met—for sure the most guarded of the three versions I'd met. But the showdown with Almira was coming. When it did, I needed to be surrounded by people I could trust with my life, and vice versa.

For the moment though, I needed to set the thoughts of the book aside and figure out how to stop the bleeding as it were.

Was I still losing magic? No. It was all gone, so there was nothing left to lose. But my confidence was taking hit after hit, and it was hard to imagine me winning a battle against a fruit fly, never mind Almira.

I was lacking on all fronts.

With a growl, I snatched my whip from the ground and stood. Billy was right about one thing; unless I wanted to die, I needed to figure out where the fuck to go from here, magic or no. I strode a few yards from the shelter, took a deep breath, and closed my eyes.

Come on, magic. One tiny spark.

But as I searched and poked, squinted and prodded, all I got back was silence.

"Dammit," I muttered. "Fine. We'll do it the old-fashioned way."

I flicked my wrist, and the whip let out a satisfying crack.

It felt good…sounded good, too, echoing in the quiet clearing, so I did it again. I kept at it, striking anything in my path. Rocks, a dead log, an unlucky patch of mushrooms. It was good, but not great and I knew Xander would've said that my strikes lacked focus and were sloppier than they should be.

"I hear you, my friend."

I was adjusting my grip and about to try again when footsteps approached, crunching against dried leaves and brush. A second later, Duncan stepped out from the trees, an armload of firewood pressed to his chest.

"I thought I heard a whip cracking." He set the firewood down in a neat stack before stepping closer, a hint of his dimple peeking through. "Want some help?"

"Honestly? Yes." I slumped, letting the whip fall to my side. "I hate feeling helpless. It's driving me insane."

If he pitied me, he didn't show it. Instead, he rolled up his sleeves and waved me toward a patch of flat ground, clear of roots and stones. "Let's start with some solid counter maneuvers since you can't practice those on your own." He drew his sword, flipping it so the flat side faced me. "We'll start easy. Block my blade, wrap the whip around my wrist, and disarm me."

It was easier said than done, and I failed the first three times. But we drilled it again and again, my confidence slowly building. Duncan was a good teacher, patient, but not easy. He pushed me, and I liked it. Soon enough, my hair was damp with sweat and my muscles burned.

"Better." He gave me an approving grin after a particularly clean disarm. "Now, let's add movement. And remember, it's all about being aware of my footwork. Anyone can feint with their sword, but their feet will always show you their true intentions."

He demonstrated as I went at him, and I realized with a start that, while he *was* fast, the more important part was being ready…Watching the person in front of you—the way their shoulders were turned, the position of their feet, the angle of their hips—and making a choice based on what that information told you.

I was good at that. Seeing patterns, noticing details, and the realization gave me a little sliver of hope.

"Ready?"

I nodded, sucking in a breath. "Yup."

Duncan swung high; I blocked, sidestepped, and attempted to wrench his sword from his hand. I wanted to crow with glee when I could feel his grip loosening but it came out as a strangled yelp when the toe of my boot caught on a root. My feet flew out from under me, and I was prepping myself for a hard fall when Duncan dropped his sword and grabbed me, dipping me back in his arms.

He stared down at me, chest heaving as his eyes flicked to my lips.

"Sorry about that," he breathed, but didn't move.

I opened my mouth but before either of us could speak, a loud rustling broke the silence.

Hook stepped into the clearing, firewood stacked high in his arms, expression thunderous as he took in the scene. Duncan straightened immediately, stepping back and clearing his throat.

"Training," Duncan muttered.

Hook's eyes narrowed, jaw tight. "Right."

Billy appeared seconds later, water skins filled. Her eyes darted between the three of us, lips curled as she soaked in the scene.

"Sounded like you guys were having fun. If Hook isn't planning a murder right now, I'd love a turn sparring."

Hook turned away to dump his wood onto the pile. "No murder today. Carry on."

"Show me what you've got, Princess." Billy handed me a waterskin with a grin.

I froze and blinked at her. "Wh-what did you call me?"

For a second, it was silent but for the croaking of bull-frogs from the nearby stream.

Then, she shrugged. "Princess. That's what he calls you, isn't it?" she added, jerked a thumb at Hook. "Hell, if I knew it was a super-secret love name, I wouldn't have used it."

My mouth felt like it was stuffed with cotton, so I took a long swig of water before setting down the waterskin.

Sure, that *might've* been why she said it. Or, the inside of her book had told my story. The words on the page, alive... ever changing as we lived it, just like Hook's had done, and she'd known who I was all along.

As much as I wanted to have it out and get all our cards on the table, it didn't feel like the time was right for a big talk about trust. Not after I'd literally just led my whole team straight into an ambush.

Instead, I dropped low and prepared to spar instead. "Come on, then. Let's do this."

None of it was easier than it had been with Duncan, despite the two of us being much closer to the same size. Billy was fluid and quick as a thought, eyes gleaming with mischief as she pressed me harder and harder. Duncan shouted occasional pointers as Hook sat by the makeshift fire pit he'd built, onyx gaze locked on our battle.

Eventually, breathless and sweating, I finally managed a move Duncan taught me, blocking Billy's blade hand by anticipating her strike, and pulling my hidden calf-dagger free to press the flat of the blade against her ribs.

Billy froze, then chuckled. "Nice."

I grinned, victory buzzing through me…right up until I saw Billy exchange a glance with Duncan.

She'd let me win. *Son of a bitch.*

"Good student." She clapped me on the shoulder. "I'm impressed."

I tried to hold the words of praise close as I prepared a pot of soup for us to share. I *had* done well, considering. It wasn't going to happen overnight, though.

I made a mental note to get some alone time ASAP. I might still have a few tricks up my sleeve that I hadn't tapped because I wasn't sure how much to share around Billy. On the slim chance I could access the power of the clock or even the jeweler's loupe without my own magic, I could still be a force in battle…

With that thought fresh in my mind, I stayed up when Billy and Duncan went to bed right after dinner. I sat staring into the dying coals of the fire as Hook stood on guard duty no one had assigned him to.

"You really should try to sleep," Hook murmured, not looking at me.

"I doubt sleep is possible with those monkeys making all that racket," I whispered back. They were far away, but those terrifying howls carried. "How about you?"

"I'm fine without much sleep."

Not sure if it was because I was over *tired,* or just plain over *it,* but something about the total disregard for his own comfort made something inside me snap.

"You're *not* fine, James. Sleep, no sleep…you're never fine. Why is that okay with you? Why do you insist on suffering when you don't have to?"

His jaw flexed. "Because that's what I deserve, Princess." His gaze stayed locked on the night sky. "I've caused too much pain to claim peace for myself."

The words hit like arrows, straight to my heart. "You're so wrong. You deserve some happiness more than anyone after what you've been through."

He finally turned and for a second, yearning flared in his eyes as he leaned closer. "I—"

Billy groaned, shifting in her sleep. "Turn down the bloody music, Paddy. You're going to wake the wee one."

He drew back, and I could see the invisible wall already rebuilding between us. I fucking hated it but wasn't sure I had the energy to break it down again.

It was one step forward, two steps back, and this dance was exhausting me to my core.

"You're right. I guess I'll try to get some rest, then." I pushed myself to my feet, and had just turned around when I heard him mutter behind me.

"For the record…The problem isn't your lack of muscle or magic. It's that soft fucking heart of yours. It's your Achilles heel, and it scares the hell out of me. If you actually want me to sleep? You'll get it in check."

Well, fuck you very much.

Without another word, I picked my way over the sleeping bodies to my little pallet and hunkered down with a bitter sigh. Just because he was right didn't mean I couldn't be pissed at him.

Especially when I was way more pissed at myself. I'd overridden both his and Billy's concerns and nearly got us all killed. He had every right to call me on it. But he had to know that I was doing my best here. Trying to grapple between what was right and wrong…

And somehow managing to miss, every single time.

I'd never felt so confused and out of sorts in my life.

I lay back, staring at the ceiling, wishing with everything I had that Molly was here. She'd have set me straight, and fast.

My gut ached as I pictured her face in my mind, and I forced myself to think of something happy.

Me, her, and the Lost Boys—including Cissy—fishing, and playing on the beach. She'd been so happy there.

I hoped she was still happy, now. Surrounded by the kids she'd longed for, Fetch looking out for her…

When I finally closed my eyes, it was to stop the hot tears from flowing. I never expected to fall asleep.

Sun warmed my skin and I blinked, smiling as I realized with a start that I was sprawled out on the deck of the Jolly Roger. Hook stood at the wheel, shirtless, relaxed, his Tideblessings glowing with magic, more handsome than any man deserved to be.

"You're awake." He padded over to lower himself beside me to cup my cheek. "How'd you sleep?"

"Better than I have in ages." I stared at him and frowned. "Is this real or is this a dream?"

"It's real to me." He leaned in and pressed his lips to mine. I sighed, melting into his mouth, feeling safe for the first time since I didn't know when.

He pulled me up to sit, wrapping an arm around my waist. Together we looked out at the endless, blue sea, and joy threatened to swallow me whole.

"I wish we could stay like this forever." His smile was tinged with sadness and something cold prickled my spine. Dark clouds rolled in from the horizon, and Hook's grip tightened around my shoulder.

"It's coming," he whispered, voice edged with resignation.

"What is?"

"My destiny. I'm sorry, Harmony."

A figure materialized on deck, as if made from shadow itself. The darkness writhed and shifted until it began to take shape. A moment later, Almira stood before us, silver hair whipping in the rising wind, her single, blue eye glittering.

"It's time." She unsheathed a wicked sword made of glass and magic.

Hook stepped in front of me. "Do what you will to me but leave her alone."

"No! What are you saying?" I grabbed his arm. "Fight, James!"

He turned to face me as Almira let out a snarl and thrust her sword forward, blade piercing Hook from behind, emerging scarlet-tipped through his chest.

He sagged forward and I wrapped both arms around him.

"No no no no no..." Frantic, I tried to wedge my hand between us, pressing it against the wound. It was so hot. So wet..."James—stay with me," I begged as panic closed over me like a fist.

His voice was barely a whisper. "It's alright, love. You need to let me go."

Tears blurred my vision as his heartbeat faltered beneath my fingertips, slipping away. Almira's voice was a sickening murmur near my ear.

"Being queen requires sacrifice, Harmony. That was something your mother never understood."

Hook went limp, all the breath leaving him in one, final exhale and grief tore through me, sharper than Almira's blade.

"No!"

I jerked awake, my cheeks wet with fresh tears. The shelter was quiet except for the low snores of Billy and Duncan nearby. Hook sat exactly as before, alive and well, by the entrance.

Relief slammed into me, so powerful my vision blurred. But it was replaced by a chilling realization. I'd felt Hook's emotions as he died, and they were unmistakable.

Death had been a relief.

I stared at his silhouette, feeling like I was being hacked in two. As much as I wanted to save him, he didn't want to be saved. He'd warned me more than once, and diving further down this rabbit-hole of loving and hating him could only end one way;

James Hook was going to die, and he was going to take anyone who loved him down with him. Sure, I might not be underground in a box beside him. But I might as well be, for what losing him would do to me if things went any further between us.

Which meant I needed to let go…for real this time.

Even if letting go broke my soft heart.

CHAPTER 11

The next morning started off with a cool breeze and a blast of sunshine. The type of day we got back in The Hollow maybe three times a year. I forced myself to take it in…to be grateful I was alive to enjoy it. But no matter how much I tried, last night's dream still lingered in the center of my chest.

Hook was yards behind me, but I didn't dare look back. Part of me wondered if there was some chance he'd had the dream too…I was fairly sure it wouldn't be the first time we'd shared the exact same dream. But then I saw his red-rimmed eyes and exhausted face, and I realized he hadn't even slept, never mind dreamt. Not that I'd be able to tell beyond his appearance. He had no trouble keeping up so far, and he'd been his usual, brooding self when we'd broken camp earlier.

I, on the other hand, had been quiet all morning. I knew the others had noticed, and even thought about trying to pretend all was well, but I couldn't muster the energy.

"You alright there, Princess?" Billy's voice interrupted my thoughts.

She tossed a glance over her shoulder my way, not slowing her pace as she guided us through yet another janky-ass trail that ran parallel to the Yellow Road.

"Yeah." I straightened my shoulders, attempting a smile. "Just a lot on my mind, that's all."

All true. Every step brought us closer to The Emerald City and I had no idea what we'd find when we got there. I had to trust in Gayelette and hope the fates had our backs.

Again.

Surely, even they were getting weary, though. And I couldn't help but wonder when we were going to run out of miracles…

"Word of advice." Billy shoved aside a supple branch that snapped back and hit me right in the throat. "Don't think too far past the here and now. It will only make the task seem more monumental. One foot in front of the other and take it in chunks. Today, we get to The Emerald City. That's it. One thing and when we do, we count the win and move on tomorrow."

I rubbed at the sting in my neck and nodded.

She was right. The big picture…the total sum of all we had to do to succeed? Was like contemplating a climb up the sheer side of an ice mountain with murderous monkeys and the most powerful being alive waiting at the top to kick us right back down it.

Keep your head down and climb.

It was noon by the time the forest began to thin, and the landscape changed over to grassy, rolling hills.

"High alert now, in case of scouts," Billy called back. "Without the tree cover, we're vulnerable."

The men were already ahead of her, hands on sword hilts. We crested the top of the steep hill we'd been slogging up, and I paused to stare down at the view.

"Oh, wow," I breathed.

The Emerald City shimmered in the distance below, its towers glittering like shards of polished gemstones. Delicate, green-tinted glass caught the sun's rays, sending tiny rainbows across the hills and valleys surrounding it.

Duncan stepped up beside me and let out a low whistle. "And I thought Alabaster was beautiful…"

Hook stood in silence, face unreadable, although his gaze lingered.

"Even fancier than the last time I was here just a few years ago." Billy's lips were flat as she turned away from the view. "Good news is, we're close. Once we get to low ground, it's maybe another hour walk, and we'll be standing at the gate."

It was a mix of dread and relief for me. Closer to answers meant closer to danger, too.

The first tremor rippled beneath my boots when we were about two thirds of the way down the hill. Billy and I both stumbled, catching each other's arms for balance.

"What was that?" I glanced around, looking for the cause.

The ground shuddered again, a low, steady rumble from deep inside the earth. We all stopped and widened our stances to stay on our feet.

I turned to Billy, my stomach going sour. "Do you have earthquakes here?"

"I don't know what that is, but—"

A deafening roar erupted as a ten-foot chunk of the ground in front of us exploded. Dirt and grass flew through the air, bits of it pelting my face. Instinct took over, and I reached for my whip.

Billy scuttled back as a monstrous, scaled worm surged up from the fresh hole in the ground, its gaping maw full of razor-sharp teeth snapping.

"Billy!" I shouted, flicking my whip. It wrapped around her wrist, and I pulled hard, yanking her safely out of the creature's reach just as it slammed into the earth again and disappeared.

She landed beside me, eyes wide. "What the bloody hell was that?"

Bookworm—albeit supersized this time—but I wasn't about to try to explain now. "They're a gift from Almira."

Hook and Duncan, who had been trailing behind, rushed to stand in front of us. Hook lifted his hand as Duncan surged past him, sword drawn.

"Run!" Hook shouted, throwing his arm out. An inky shadow snaked through the air as another massive worm burst from the ground. Dirt and rocks rained down on us and the creature lunged our way, but didn't get far. Hook's shadow blessing curled around it and tightened like a rope made by the devil himself.

His face was a mask of pure focus as he wrestled the beast to the ground, the noose around its neck tightening until its body twitched and dropped with enough force to shake the ground.

"Fucking hell, that's terrifying," Billy shouted, looping her arm with mine and dragging me in the opposite direction.

The next few minutes passed in a blur of adrenaline and panic as the area around us erupted with worm after worm, their enormous, segmented bodies surging through the ground like it was water.

Duncan whirled, leaping through the air and peppering one with a flurry of strikes as Hook sent gusts of wind crashing against the ones closing in behind us, knocking them off course for long enough that we had time to scramble forward.

Billy darted ahead, bow drawn, calling warnings over her shoulder as she fired. "Left!"

I dodged as another smaller worm breached just feet away from me. It let out a squeal as an arrow buried itself into the creature's side, and I came in behind it to deal the death blow with my dagger.

It was sheer chaos, but we managed to stay one step ahead of them, if barely. The ground around us was riddled with sinkholes, and I was just starting to wonder how we could continue to dodge the worms and still manage to keep ourselves from plummeting into one of the holes when, for one dizzying second, everything went still. Nothing but the ragged sound of our breathing and the creak of shifting dirt beneath our boots.

And then a new sound tore up from the depths of the earth, so deep it rattled my bones. It was like the ground itself was screaming. A huge swatch of ground twenty yards ahead of us split with a thunderous crack.

I stumbled back just in time to avoid a shower of rocks when a worm the size of the earl's mansion busted through the ground, its jaws snapping open wide enough to swallow a full-grown oak tree.

"We're dead," Billy breathed, her voice tiny and certain. "We're so dead."

That's when I saw her. Sitting on the creature's back, silver hair whipping in the updraft, black lightning sparking and cracking all around her. A living storm. Her cackle rang out, sharp and shrill.

Billy let out a howl of straight fury and burst into a sprint, firing five arrows in rapid succession, her hands a blur. Each one sliced through the air with deadly precision until the very last second when Almira flicked her wrist, sending a shimmering wall of black energy to block them... Each ricocheted off and plummeted, harmless, to the ground.

Billy cursed and nocked another arrow, but Duncan was already moving, a bellow tearing from his throat as he leapt for the beast's side, hacking with brutal strikes of his sword.

Hook moved opposite him, trying to create a shadow big enough to encompass the creature to no avail.

It wasn't enough.

I knew it in my gut. We couldn't win, not like this. I tossed the whip aside and shoved a shaking hand into my satchel, tugging out my jeweler's loupe, making quick work of finding the right lens.

The others were still fighting, and every second was one I couldn't spare, but the only way we had any chance at all was if—

There! As the worm reared back bearing its unarmored belly, a pale pink spot, dead center, came into view.

"Together!" I shouted, my voice hoarse. "Everything you have to the pink swatch of skin on its belly!"

Duncan charged, hurling his sword with both hands as he let out a war cry. Hook sent a lightning strike even as Billy loosed an arrow, all aimed dead center.

The attacks hit almost in tandem, and the creature let out a squeal as steaming green liquid rushed from its belly. It thrashed once, twice, and then came crashing down with an impact that sent my head snapping back and my loupe flying.

I caught myself just in time to see Almira leap free of the worm's back and float toward the ground, flickering in and out of view.

"Don't let her get away!" I shouted, diving for my whip as Billy and the boys ran toward me. We charged toward her when she flickered one last time and fizzled away.

"What the hell?" Billy shouted, skidding to a stop.

I slowed, heart hammering against my ribs as a pile of clothing fell to the ground with a thump. On the churned-up earth before us lay only a pair of pointed black boots, a tattered black cape, and two shriveled, striped socks.

No witch.

Just an eerie silence and an icy gust of wind that swept

over us, carrying a whisper that curled cold fingers down my spine…

"I'll be back for you, my pretty."

I searched the ground for any sign of rippling, my breath coming in ragged gasps. Another horse-sized worm poked its head from a mound of dirt a few feet away and I readied my whip only to stop short as it shrank back to the size of a normal earthworm. It writhed on the dirt for a second before slipping away into a hole and disappearing.

"What happened? Where did she go?"

"My guess? Even Almira can't sustain that level of magic for long. I bet she ran out of juice and was transported back from the realm she truly comes from."

"Which is?"

"A place called C'an Saas, far far away."

"So she's gone from Oz for good?" Billy actually looked disappointed at the prospect.

"No, we aren't that lucky. She goes back and forth. She's just regrouping, I imagine. I think we wore her out. Which is why I have to figure out how to get to her while she's still weak, and make sure we keep her on her back foot and fighting. Taking her on at full power would be a--"

We all shared a look, and I didn't have to say the word out loud.

Suicide mission.

The worms that had been killed topside started shrinking as we all watched.

"Let's hope that bitch saves us the trouble of having to hunt her down and dies of exhaustion, then." Billy's mouth tipped into a grim smile. "You did good out there, Princess. That was a neat trick with the whip, too. Thanks."

"No problem. Just returning the favor." I managed a smile in return, and for the first time in days, I felt like something other than dead weight.

A familiar shadow passed over us, catching my eye, and I tipped my head back as a bolt of excitement shot through me.

"Fetch?"

"Bonnie!" Duncan called at the same time.

I tamped down my disappointment as the falcon glided toward us, swooping down to drop a four-inch scroll into Duncan's outstretched hand.

Of course it was Bonnie. Fetch was still in Neverland, where he should be. Moll and The Lost Boys needed him more than I did. For now, at least…

Duncan unfurled the scroll quickly, his shoulders relaxing as he scanned its contents. "It's from Crispin. Alabaster is holding together. He and the rest of the guards are keeping the nobility in line and talks to establish a functional government are making progress."

In other words, things weren't imploding in his absence, which was great.

Bonnie circled again, dropping a second scroll I hadn't even noticed in her grasp on the ground in front of me. I bent to grab it and then tugged it open with trembling hands to find Druzilla's looping scrawl.

My stomach did a little flip as I read…

~~Dearest,~~

~~Dear,~~

Harmony,

I suppose you'll be pleased to know we're managing adequately here. The Hollow has improved in recent days, in large part thanks to your antics, I presume? Stay humble, keep yourself alive, and don't embarrass the family name. I do hope you're staying safe.

Warm~~est~~ regards,

Druzilla

P.S. If you do get a chance to speak to your Prince Duncan, please tell him that I've been keeping a list of things that could still use improvement and I'd be happy to take a meeting with him to discuss upon his return.

THE NOTE WAS BEYOND RIDICULOUS. This woman not only drew a line through anything that might sound too gushy. She went on to add insult to injury by making me read her crossed out words because she couldn't bring herself to waste another piece of parchment on little old me.

I should've been hurt or at least pissed off. Instead, I found myself grinning. When everything was fucked beyond all belief, with new and everchanging dangers lurking around every corner, one thing remained constant;

Druzilla Fallowell was going to be an asshole, every single day that ended in y.

Something about that felt real, almost normal. And fuck did I need a little normal right now…

"All is well?" Duncan cocked his head, studying my face.

"It's great, thanks. And thanks to Bonnie, too."

I glanced up to see the snowy falcon perched on a nearby branch, preening her feathers. I reached out with my magic, trying to touch her consciousness. Still nothing, but I forced the disappointment down.

"You're such a good smart bird, aren't you?" I cooed.

I'd still saved Billy. I'd used the lessons I'd learned and tools I'd been given and came up with a plan that worked. For now, it would have to be enough.

Hook appeared beside us, his onyx eyes softening as they met mine. "We need to move. If you're right, Almira's weakened again for now, but let's not test our luck."

"Agree. And good work out there." Duncan gave Hook's shoulder a firm clap.

Hook didn't glare at him, but he didn't return the compliment either. That was alright. Baby steps forward on all counts. Way better than getting rabbit-punched in the dick at every turn.

"Emerald City, here we come," Billy muttered.

We started forward again, my steps feeling lighter, the sparkling green towers before us a little closer.

All was well in Alabaster, confirmed. We'd survived our first face to face brush with Almira, and found out she wasn't invincible, and this time I'd actually been able to do something to help my team in the fight.

The fates better be careful. Another victory in the dance with death, and I might start thinking they were actually rooting for me…

CHAPTER 12

By the time we finally neared the gates of The Emerald City, my mood was still high, but my legs were like lead.

One foot in front of the other.

It was only when I'd gotten within fifty yards of it that I realized, the city wasn't just *named* after emeralds. It was carved from them. I knew my way around gemstones, and there was no jeweler in the world who could fake the lush green color, no matter how meticulously they cut and faceted. A massive emerald wall ringed the entire city, five or more stories high—nearly double the height of Alabaster's walls. I shook my head.

"How could they afford this? Surely, no one would ever go hungry if you hacked even ten feet off that wall."

Billy shrugged. "It looks fancy, which is part of why they like it. But the mines are bursting with them. You could get a copper a pound for emerald, maybe. Twice that for rubies. This place is worth far less than the road we took to get here."

Molly would curl up in a ball and die with excitement if she could see this right now.

And she's going to be on the edge of her seat when you see her again to tell her all about it.

I swallowed the tightness in my throat. No point in thinking about Molly when I needed to focus on the task in front of me.

We drew closer, and my steps faltered as we approached the gates to find our own faces staring back at us.

Wanted posters, plastered up and down the wall, cheapening the gleaming emerald, making it look like hard candy with bits of the wrapping still stuck to it.

My heart sank. The witch's reach was long…

Duncan scanned the posters, his expression grim. "Not exactly a warm welcome, is it?"

"Not to mention, whoever sketched these needs an art class." Billy leaned closer to one that had sharpened her features and added a madness to her eyes that made her look like a professional assassin. "Although, to be fair, I do look intimidating."

I glanced at Hook, who was busy glaring at a dark and pretty sinister version of himself that was pretty spot on except with a—

"A parrot?" he muttered. "Fucking ridiculous."

I pulled one of his posters down and pretended to inspect it. "I don't know what you're complaining about. Yours is actually an improvement. Maybe it would be better if they put a vulture on your shoulder to match your charming personality instead?"

"And we all still think this is the right move?" Duncan asked, cutting in before Hook could reply. "After what happened back with Jack, I'm wondering if we aren't walking right into another trap here…"

I lifted my chin and tried to look confident. "This is where I'm meant to be. Gayelette said my mother left the prophecy here for me, and that I needed to get it. She hasn't misled me yet, and think about it. Why would Almira blow all that magic trying to stop us from getting here if she could just come and snatch me once I was corralled behind these walls?" I paused, flicking a glance between them. "Look, I've said it before, but I'll say it again. This is my destiny. If I'm wrong, I'm prepared to pay the price. You guys got me here and I'm grateful for that, but you don't have to stay. I'll understand if you want to turn back."

Billy flashed a grin that was all teeth. "And miss all the fun? Nope. I have a score to settle, and I'm not walking away until it's done."

I turned to Hook and his dark gaze softened, if only a fraction. "Not a chance, Princess."

"Duncan?"

"Do you even have to ask?"

I released a breath I didn't know I'd been holding and nodded. "Okay, let's do this, then."

Billy stepped forward and rapped her fist against the massive gate.

"State your business!" barked a voice from somewhere above. A green-helmeted guard popped into view, peering suspiciously down from the top of the wall. "We don't allow foot travelers."

Hook's voice rumbled. "Do we look like we're here to sightsee?"

"A wise guy, hmmm? Off with you! Go on." The guard disappeared from view and Billy's brows caved into a scowl.

She raised her fist again, pounding even louder. "As a former citizen, I have the right to be here, damn it. We've come too far and gone through too much to turn around now. Get down here and let us in, or we're going to let ourselves in."

Diplomacy at its finest. I bit my lip but stayed silent.

"Go away, dagnabbit! You aren't welcome," the guard shouted back.

Other heads peaked above the wall, voices chiming in.

"Wait..is that her? Look at her boots—it's her!" a young woman gasped.

"The good witch has come?"

"It can't be!"

My heart lurched as more faces appeared above us, each more excited than the last. Within moments, the sounds of an argument broke out from behind the gates.

"They're wanted by the witch. We can't risk her wrath."

"But the prophecy! The Wizard should decide whether—"

"The Wizard isn't king here!" a bitter voice growled.

I held my breath, listening to the muffled argument, fingers flexed around my whip handle.

"He said if she ever came that we were to let her in."

"That was before the witch sent those posters…"

Finally, the first guard we'd spoken to popped his head over the gate to glare down at us again.

"You're causing a ruckus! I'll allow you inside the city walls while we go ask the Great Oz if he will see you. If he declines, you must agree to go without a fight. Do I have your word?"

It was only a problem if The Wizard said no, and I'd worry about that later.

"You do."

He disappeared again and the enormous doors swung open. Emerald towers were connected by sidewalks at ground level and hanging brass footbridges were two levels up. Mechanical birds whirred overhead, powered by tiny propellers, darting between buildings as they delivered letters and brown paper wrapped packages.

Bonnie let out a chortle and moved restlessly on Duncan's shoulder.

"And we thought our falcon chutes were impressive..." he murmured.

The citizens who rushed to greet us looked nothing like the brightly-clad Munsch Kin folk we'd met when we first got to Oz. These people wore bold, jewel-toned gowns, velvet waistcoats, shiny riding boots, and the wildest hats I'd ever seen. Most were human, but a handful were some sort of human-animal hybrids. A man walking on two legs with the face of a tortoise and a shell to boot. A woman who I'd never pick out of a crowd from the back had the face and ears of a rabbit when she turned around.

Billy didn't bat an eye, so I had to assume this was the norm in Emerald City.

"Keep it moving," one of the guards commanded as the others, also dressed in green from head to toe like him, formed a tight circle around us. "Straight to the palace."

The crowd only thickened as we headed deeper into the city, and they got braver with every step. Hands reached out, touching my hair, my shoulders, grasping at my sleeves, like they were trying to check if I was real or not.

More than one touched my boots which was...weird.

"It's her!"

"Thank the fates you've come!"

I forced a smile, praying that we'd made the right choice stepping through that gate, despite the posters.

We rounded a corner, and I froze mid-step. A mural in the distance featured a lean woman with dark, billowing hair, tall red boots, and lightning crackling from her fingertips, standing over the body of a dark-haired witch in striped stockings. One enterprising citizen had taken it upon themselves to draw a handlebar mustache on the woman's face, but there was no question.

She was me.

"That's flattering...ish?" Billy said.

"I look ridiculous," I muttered.

"Enough!"

The guard who'd been hesitant to allow us inside herded us toward a building that was even more incredible than the others. Massive columns framed doors of brass, each etched with a cheery scene. Hot air balloons skimming through puffy clouds, and people dancing in a town square.

The stairs seemed almost endless as we climbed, and by the time we reached the top, my legs shook with exhaustion. I could only imagine how Hook was feeling after doing everything I'd done today, except on zero sleep.

"Weapons," the guard stationed there demanded by way of greeting.

We reluctantly handed them over, though when he approached Hook, gesturing to the gleaming hardware at the end of his wrist, the pirate shook his head.

"Don't even think about it."

The guard opened his mouth, hesitated, then made the right decision, accepting Hook's offered sword with a frown. "Fine...but don't try anything. There are hundreds of us within shouting distance, so you won't get far."

Debatable, but I wasn't about to point that out.

Stepping into the palace was like tripping into a dream... Or a nightmare, depending.

"Good gods," Duncan muttered beside me. "Is it a carnival, then?"

It sure looked that way. A dozen multi-colored horses trotted in dizzying circles around a ring, their coats shifting from crimson to cobalt to lemony yellow right before our eyes.

"Weird," I murmured, shaking my head.

"I've seen way weirder stuff. Though it usually involves

more alcohol, and fewer horses." Hook eyed the mechanical birds gliding through the hall, their brass wings clicking as they moved.

Bonnie dipped and bobbed on Duncan's shoulder, eyes pinned on the birds as he stroked her feathers with a reassuring murmur. "Easy girl, they're just clockwork."

In another ring, acrobats and trapeze artists flew through the air, flipping like there was a featherbed waiting to catch them if they fell, which there most surely was not.

I looked away, my throat aching.

All it would take is one slip...

Hook nudged my elbow. "All right?"

I glanced at him, forcing a smile. "Don't love heights and just thinking I'm glad I'm down here."

A handsome woman dressed in gold from head to toe walked toward us. Of all the hats I'd seen, hers was the most spectacular. Perched atop her white-blond hair, it was covered in flowers made of turning gears, and a fat, mechanical bumblebee buzzed around them.

The guard whispered a few words into her ear, then strode away. If she was worried about being left to defend herself against strangers, she didn't show it as she flashed a set of pearly whites. "Welcome, weary travelers. I'm Olga, valet to The Great Oz himself. You stand within the halls of our own Emerald City Palace. A place of dreams and imagination."

"Whose imagination? Because I have suggestions…"

The woman gave Billy a patient smile. "All of Emerald City contributes to society here, one way or another. For some, it's coin; for others, it's ingenuity; and for others still, it's something more…spiritual."

Billy stiffened beside me at the cryptic words, but Olga was already turning away.

"Please, follow me."

We fell into step behind her, and I couldn't help but be a little on edge. I was going to feel really fucking stupid if I walked in to find Almira herself standing there waiting for us.

When we stopped in front of an ornate, carved door a minute later, Olga faced us again. "The Great Oz will see each of you. One at a time."

There was a heavy pause as we all looked at each other.

Hook stepped forward at the same time as Duncan. "Not a chance."

For the first time, Olga's pearly smile slipped.

"The Great Oz insists—"

"And we insist otherwise," Hook interrupted. "But you're welcome to try and separate us."

Billy cracked her knuckles. "We came together; we'll see him together."

The other woman seemed to weigh her options for a long moment before shrugging an elegant shoulder.

"He doesn't like having his authority questioned, so don't say I didn't warn you."

As she stepped back, the heavy door swung inward to reveal a pitch-black room. I hesitated, the chaos behind us suddenly far more appealing than the thought of going inside.

"After you, Princess," Billy urged.

I squared my shoulders and stepped into the gloom with the guys flanking me on either side and Billy bringing up the rear. The door swung closed behind us, the sudden silence heavy as a sodden cloak.

"This doesn't feel ominous at all." Duncan's low voice was thick with sarcasm.

A shiver rolled over me and I reached out, my fingers brushing Hook's arm. I couldn't see him, but I felt him flex beneath my fingertips, coiled and ready.

It was going to be fine, everything was going to be—

White light burst through the chamber, revealing the room to be a massive dome. Stars glittered overhead, and a massive, silvery moon glowed brightly.

The sight helped settle the roiling in my stomach. A reminder that we were all part of a universe and connected by something that could only be considered magic.

Gayelette had said it before, and I'd known it in my gut. As tough as this was, I was right where I was supposed to be, right *when* I was supposed to be here. This wasn't a mistake. Too many stars had to align to make it all happen for it to be anything short of destiny.

The comforting thought shattered as quickly as it had come as a roar of flames erupted around the chamber, exploding from a dozen torches set into the polished marble floor. I scrambled back as another light appeared, filling a quarter of the space. An enormous face surrounded by green smoke and fire glared down at us, lips drawn back in a fearsome scowl.

"I AM OZ, THE GREAT AND POWERFUL!" The voice boomed through the room as the face's eyes locked onto me. "YOU HAVE COME ALL THIS WAY TO MEET ME, YET YOU DEFY ME BEFORE WE EVEN MEET?"

Hook tensed beside me and my knees threatened to buckle, but I stiffened my spine, forcing myself to meet that gaze.

"TELL ME, WHY SHOULD I NOT STRIKE YOU DEAD WHERE YOU STAND?"

CHAPTER 13

could sense the tension in my companions…their readiness to fight and to protect me at all costs, even now. But the question hung in the air, waiting for me to answer.

Taking a deep breath to steady my nerves, I stepped forward.

"You allowed us in to see you for a reason. Because our destinies are intertwined somehow and—"

The flames near the floorboards crackled even higher, the heat blasting my face. "YOU SPEAK OF DESTINY BUT DESTINY IS NOT YOURS TO COMMAND!"

That voice...there was something about it that tugged at my memory. If I had even a hint of my power, I could sense his magic, gauge what we were up against, and maybe even figure out where I had heard that voice before. Instead, I was left fumbling in the dark across from a man who was supposed to help us and seemed to hate me already.

"And besides," he continued, less shouty now, "What could you possibly have to offer me, The Great and Powerful Oz?"

Time to lay it all out there and hope it was enough.

"Gayelette sent me to retrieve the prophecy my mother left for me. I hope to use it to free Oz from control of The Wicked Witch of the West. Surely, that would be a help to you and your people."

For a heartbeat, silence settled over the room again.

"You," he finally replied through mocking laughter, "and these three misfits want to take on The Wicked Witch? With what army? If four people alone could march into her territory and kill her, don't you think it would've been done by now?"

He was making a whole lot of sense. In fact, I'd thought the very same thing just yesterday. I opened my mouth to respond, but Duncan beat me to it.

"Maybe. But you've never known four people like us."

"Like *you*?" Oz replied, oozing contempt. "Step forward, Duncan Westerly, Final Prince of Alabaster."

That caught my attention, because he knew Duncan's full, given name and at least a little bit about Alabaster's recent coup.

Duncan's jaw tightened as he stepped into a harsh spotlight as the projection grew.

"You spent most of your life like a child hiding from monsters, covering your eyes to avoid seeing the ugliness all around you. Only you weren't a child, and haven't been for a very long time, have you? You stood in Relyk's shadow, watching in silence as he destroyed countless lives. Were you too stupid to see the suffering around you, or are you just too weak to fight for those who couldn't fight for themselves? Which is it, Your Highness?"

Duncan's shoulders quaked, and for a second, I thought he might charge straight at the projection. Then, he let out a growl and spun to punch the nearest wall. "I can't defend it."

"I'm sure the poor souls you 'saved' from The Hollow wouldn't have much to say in your defense either if they realized how long you watched them suffer from your castle window before acting."

My heart ached at Duncan's bowed head and the shame pouring off him.

"Maybe he could've acted sooner, but he's here now, ready to risk everything to defeat Almira. We all are," I said.

Oz tossed his head back and laughed, which made my vision go a hazy red. I knew I should shut my mouth, but I couldn't.

"You don't even know him! He's brave, loyal, and he'd do anything for the people he cares about. You hide behind fire and illusions, but—"

"Harmony." Duncan's tone was gentle but firm, cutting me off mid-sentence. "Stop. He's not wrong. When I started to see it, I ran. I spent most of my teen years travelling and sparring…doing anything I could to stay busy enough so that I didn't have to face the truth of what was happening in Alabaster. It's something that haunts me, but that doesn't make it less true." He stepped back next to Billy, staring hard at the floor.

I wanted to rush to his side, to remind him of all the good he'd done, but The Wizard was just getting started.

"And you, Billy O'Donnelly," the voice thundered again, the flames roaring higher. "Step forward."

Her teeth were clenched so tight she could've cracked rocks. She didn't step forward, but she didn't turn away, either.

"Fearless hunter, infamous thief. On the outside, you are tough as nails. Shooting monkeys from the sky, camouflaged in the trees. Perhaps that looks like courage to those who don't know better. But in the moment that mattered most, your courage failed you, didn't it? Tell me, do you have nightmares of their screams?"

She lunged at the projection, yanking a hidden dagger

from her vest and flinging it straight at the center of his fore-head. It passed through the hologram, bouncing off the wall before clattering to the floor.

"You dare raise a weapon against The Great and Powerful Oz?" His voice was deadly quiet, at odds with the bellows he'd started with.

But through the noise, a faint rustling snagged my attention. I squinted, searching the shadows at the edge of the room until I spotted a sliver of light near the floor.

Was there something else back there?

I tapped Duncan's arm. When he glanced my way, I held a finger to my lips, jerking my chin toward what I'd seen. He nodded and stepped forward so I could slip behind him.

The wizard was already at it again, directing his fury toward Hook this time.

"Captain James Tyler Hook!"

Hook stepped forward, a dark smile tugging at his firm mouth. "I'd tread carefully if I were you, Wizard. I'm not keen on your diplomatic relations tactics to this point, and I come armed with more than knives and fists."

"Of course you do! In fact, your name is synonymous with suffering, feared by friend and foe alike. Letter of blood, harbinger of pain, all in the name of vengeance for loved ones long dead. You've offered your sword, your hand, even your life, to settle the scores of the past. But what about your heart, pirate? Has your thirst for revenge stolen the very humanity you once fought to defend? Ask yourself this; Are you really any better than those you despise?"

I slowed to a stop, my mission stalled as the question hit me like a sucker punch.

Hook's voice was a lethal whisper. "Are you asking me if I'm better than a fairy who murdered countless children? Better than a man who kidnapped them to feed her dark, demonic needs? I'd say I am, sir. Infinitely. But you've spent a lot of time asking questions about us. Who are you, really?"

Hook lifted his hand, and I watched in terror as he conjured a vicious gust of wind that blasted toward the hologram. For a second, the emerald flames flickered and twisted, and a low muffled sound came from just a few feet from where I was standing.

Adrenaline shot through me as I caught sight of a velvet curtain.

"I AM THE ALL POWERFUL WIZARD OF OZ, AND YOU WILL BE BOW BEFORE ME OR THE WICKED WITCH WILL BE THE LEAST OF YOUR CONCERNS!"

Holy shit.

He was behind the curtain. The voice...the real voice, was coming from behind the curtain!

Blood rushed in my ears as I reached for the fabric and yanked it aside, exposing a tiny room filled with levers, copper tubing, and pulleys. In the center stood a man working the controls, his back going rigid as he realized he'd been discovered.

"Guards!" Two voices rang out at once; the wizard's booming one, and the frantic shout of the man behind the curtain.

Duncan was at my side an instant later, pushing past me to get to The Wizard. He dragged him back, as the man twisted and fought to escape. I moved aside to let them pass and then froze when our eyes collided.

Eyes I hadn't seen in years, and thought I'd never see again.

My voice cracked and I managed to croak the word...

"Pawpaw?"

CHAPTER 14

The man now sagging in Duncan's grasp was Willy Fallowell…

My *dead* father. But not him, surely not him but a doppelganger. Like Cissy had been. Like Billy was. Right?

He was older, his salt and pepper hair had gone almost completely white, and his face was lined with exhaustion, but there was no mistaking him.

I staggered backward as Duncan gripped him by the collar.

"The Great Wizard of Oz, I presume?" Duncan snarled.

I tapped Duncan on his bunched shoulder. "Be gentle."

He shot me an incredulous look, but loosened his hold. "He's a phony. And he shouldn't talk to people that way. Did you see Billy's face?"

But I barely heard him as I stared at Willy Fallowell. "Do you know me? Do you know who I am?"

He searched my face but there was zero recognition there. Just a mix of fear and blooming panic.

"Yes. N-no. I mean, I know you from the posters and such…"

"Someone's coming," Hook said as he and Billy stepped up, lip curling in disgust.

Duncan pinned the man in place as the heavy footsteps of guards rang from the hallway.

"Keep your mouth shut, old man, or I'll give you something to holler about."

"Let go of me," The Wizard hissed, squirming to free himself from Duncan's iron grip. "You have no idea of the trouble you'll cause! You don't understand what's at stake."

The sound of pounding rang through the room followed by a low voice calling through the doors. "Sir? Are you alright?"

Duncan gave him a warning glare and The Wizard cleared his throat. "I'm fine," he said, in a failed attempt to match the booming voice of the hologram. "Return to your posts!"

There was a tense pause as the guards on the other side murmured to one another, clearly unconvinced.

"Sir," another guard tried. "Your voice sounds…odd. Has an old woman taken you captive or something? Should we fetch the battering ram?"

"I'm telling you I'm fine," The Wizard replied, straining to drop his voice another octave. "There's nothing to see here. I-I command you to leave me be, this instant or there will be hell to pay!"

"Yes, sir."

Footsteps faded into the distance. They would be back, but I'd damned well have some answers before then.

Before I could start asking questions, though, Billy closed in, blue eyes glittering like chips of ice.

"How do you know all about us? You dug into my past like it was your damned bedtime reading. Explain yourself, you charlatan."

The Great and Powerful Oz shrank right before my eyes.

"Please." His eyes darted between us like he wasn't sure which one of us was liable to strike first. "Just don't hurt me."

It was tough, but I didn't try to reassure him. He *had* said some pretty awful things and, this world's version of my adopted father or not, he had to answer for them. Because so far, he wasn't giving me a whole lot of confidence in his ability to help us.

Billy must've been thinking the same thing, because she leaned in to poke him hard in the forehead, sending his head snapping back.

"Fuck this guy if he doesn't want to talk. He's a snake-oil salesman who's been conning innocent folks long enough. Let's just kill him and save ourselves some trouble. I don't see how we could possibly need him."

"Happy to help." Hook stepped up, hand raised. Darkness rippled as the shadows around us pooled toward his fingers. He manipulated them into inky ropes, wrapping them around his quarry until they had him in a tight hold from waist to throat.

"What is this?" The Wizard gasped, eyes bulging as he clawed at his neck.

"Talk or forever hold your piece." Hook's tone was flat, as if it didn't matter one way or another which he chose.

"James, please." I tugged on his arm. "That's enough. I know he's awful, but my mother wouldn't have sent me here if we didn't need him. There has to be more to him than we're seeing."

He held tight at first, then flicked his wrist, and the shadows dissolved into harmless wisps.

The Wizard slumped forward, hand to his throat as he fell into a coughing fit that had his whole body spasming.

"Your guards will be back soon, I'm sure, so there's no time to waste." My voice wasn't shaking, even though my hands were. It took all my willpower not to bend over him and pat his back while I murmured words of comfort.

Not your father. Just a stranger with his face.

"You owe us an explanation. How do you know so much about us?"

"Alright, alright," he began in a hoarse whisper. "Decades ago, a little more than two now, your mother Marin came to Oz. She brought with her a prophecy, one that could save Emerald City from a coming threat, and possibly even all of Oz," he continued, eyes locked on mine. "She spoke of an evil witch who would bring misery upon the land. It would be hellish, but there was a hope on the horizon. Her own daughter, Harmony, would come when she was ready and able. A good witch bearing magic beyond comprehension, destined to defeat The Wicked Witch of the West and return the land to peace again."

"Okay…and I'm here." I threw my hands up in disgust. "That's what I've come to try to do. So why are you treating us like the enemy?"

"That wasn't all, child!" His voice cracked as he pressed on. "She was terrified you would make it this far, but still not be strong enough to defeat the witch. Rather than have me give you the prophecy and send you off to a certain death, she made me promise, with a vow as binding as any magic, that I would only reveal it to you if I was absolutely certain you were ready and able to fulfill it. Worst case, she put some protective spells on The Emerald City and hoped that if you weren't able to grow into your power, you could live out your days here. Best case, you would save us and then return to your homeland."

I swallowed hard, pulse hammering in my throat as The Wizard's gaze shifted between us.

"Few believe in the old stories anymore, sure that Marin had been wrong, or even a false prophet, but some of us kept faith. When the wanted posters bearing your face began to appear, whispers spread. Believers, those who still remembered, began to hope again, praying that you were real." He ran a hand through thinning hair. "I'm sorry about what I said to each of you earlier, truly. Marin gave me enough tidbits of information to ask the questions, but everything I said is all that I know. She said Harmony would need to come to me with a trio of allies who would lay their lives down to protect her. She made it very clear that she would need every single one of you if there's any chance of succeeding. I had to make sure you were all committed."

Billy shifted from foot to foot. "Why the cruelty? You could've explained yourself instead of twisting the knife, digging at old wounds."

The Wizard shook his head. "If mere words were enough to break you...if you turned away at the first harsh truth, you wouldn't stand a chance against Almira." His lips lifted into a shaky smile. "Look on the bright side, though. You've already passed your first test!"

"Okay, then!" I stepped between them rather than waiting for Billy to punch him in the face. "You felt like that was the best way to test us to see if we were ready. I don't love the choice, but I guess it makes sense. The thing I'm still stuck on, though. You said, 'first test.' That implies that there's more to come."

Tell me I'm wrong. Please tell me I'm wrong...

He lowered his gaze and took a subtle step backward, maybe to get out of Billy's strike zone?

"You're not going to want to hear this, but in order for me to give you the full prophecy and the item Marin left behind for you, you must prove yourselves worthy through a series of trials." He held up both hands as Billy closed the gap between them with a grumble. "It's not my doing! It was Marin, I literally have no choice in the matter."

"What trials?" I demanded.

"Three challenges await you. Marin was adamant about keeping them secret, even from me. All I know is that they're meant to test the qualities she believed essential for defeating Almira."

"Sounds suspiciously vague to me, old man."

The Wizard sighed and raked a hand over his wrinkled face. "And still, it's the truth."

"So what now?" Duncan's voice was wary, but much more composed than before.

That was good. We needed level heads right now.

"I need two days to prepare, then you will complete the trials at midnight," The Wizard explained. "They're sealed by a powerful spell Marin put in place. Unlocking them is a task in and of itself, but I'll make sure you're well cared for here in the palace in the meantime. You're free to explore The Emerald City as well, of course."

Hook's expression darkened, the suspicion plain on his face. "And how exactly are you going to explain us wandering through your city after that display earlier? Half your people think we're heroes, the other half that we're villains. And they're all watching."

"Which is where The Great and Powerful Oz comes in handy. I'll tell them to leave you be and they'll listen."

"And what's stopping us from revealing exactly what you are instead?" Billy asked, eyes narrowed.

He shook his head. "Nothing. But understand this; without me, Harmony will never receive the prophecy, or the magical item Marin entrusted to me. Without them, you will fail. You might not trust me, but I'm all that stands between this city and chaos. They haven't had a king or queen in a century. Without The Great and Powerful Oz, they have no one to protect them from The Wicked Witch."

"So we're supposed to play along and hope for the best?"

The Wizard offered me a tired smile. "If you choose to expose me, I won't stop you. To be honest, it might even be a relief. I'm tired of hiding. But understand the consequences of your actions. This city needs a figurehead. Someone to handle diplomacy and hold Almira at bay. Because we give her enough of what she wants, she respects the current boundaries we've set. Once she learns you're here, even with Marin's protections in place, it would only be a matter of time before she battered through them to get to you. I can keep you safe…for a time. But you must trust me."

Trust.

That was the word of the day, wasn't it? And after us all getting fucked over six ways to Sunday, it was currently in very short supply.

The heavy, uncomfortable silence was broken by footsteps tapping on stone in the distance.

"May I?" He gestured toward the hidden room we'd dragged him from earlier. "I can call them in and have them bring you to your quarters if I can do the voice…"

Hook stepped aside with a warning frown. "Careful, Wizard. No more tricks."

Willy Fallowell's doppelganger slipped back behind the curtain with the rest of us close on his heels. A moment later, his voice boomed once more.

"Guards, to me!"

The doors burst open a few seconds later, armored soldiers pouring into the chamber, weapons ready.

"Bring our visitors to Fenwick. They are under my protection. Let all of Emerald City know, if they cause them any trouble, they will face my wrath!"

Hook rolled his eyes but said nothing.

"Of course, sir," one of the guards said with a nod.

The Wizard's voice thundered once more. "Good. Now get them out of my sight!"

Without another word, the soldiers lead us through the doors and out into the hallway. My thoughts were still racing as we marched through the palace.

The Wizard of Oz was not only a fraud, but he was also some version of my father. But even that paled in comparison to all the revelations about my mother. She'd come here to pave the way for me. She believed in me.

And then, there were the *trials…*

Two days.

I had two days to find my magic again and get strong enough to beat Almira. If I failed, I'd lose the prophecy my mother left for me and any chance to know her and connect with her in some way along with it.

"Oy." Billy must've noticed my expression, because she reached for my shoulder. "We'll figure it out. At least we're in, right?"

I nodded, but dread was already seeping through the numbness. Without magic, these trials could mean death. To me. To Billy and Duncan.

To Hook.

While he had a death wish, and the others were more than ready to roll the dice, the thought of losing any of them made me ill, and the thought of failing the mission my mother had entrusted to me was no better.

The solution was clear.

Failing was not an option.

CHAPTER 15

After returning our weapons to us, the guards led us to the other side of the palace down a wide marble hallway, polished to a high shine.

The guard at the front pulled to a stop in front of a door and knocked twice before a voice called out.

"Come in!"

He flung the door open, and we peered inside to find two young servants polishing silverware at a mahogany table, their heads bowed. I blinked as I caught sight of a fox standing on two legs, watching their every move. He was tall, nearly six feet, lean with auburn fur that was perfectly groomed, and he carried a decorative cane. The emerald brocade waistcoat he wore was so rich-looking, it would've had Molly drooling.

The fox's voice, smooth as velvet, commanded attention. "When I say I want it to shine, I mean SHINE!"

He looked up as we stepped into the room, his golden eyes sparkling. A smile spread across his narrow, white muzzle.

"Well, hello ladies…and gentlemen." He winked, glancing

toward Billy and me. I looked over to see Billy's nostrils flare with irritation, but the fox seemed oblivious.

He turned to the servants, tapping the floor with his cane. "You're dismissed, my dears. Good work. Keep up the attention to detail, and you'll make fine house managers one day yourselves."

They stood and slipped past us, out the door.

The fox straightened his waistcoat and dipped into a low bow. "My name is Fenwick, and I have the distinct honor of serving as your guide during your stay. The Wizard sent word we would have guests, but he failed to mention names, aside from yours, of course." Fenwick's gaze flicked toward me. "You've become something of a celebrity around here, Harmony. Please introduce me to your friends."

"I'm Duncan Westerly of Alabaster."

"Pleasure, Duncan. And you, sir?" He turned toward James.

"Hook." The response joined a glare so fierce, I half expected Fenwick to flinch.

"Charmed," he murmured instead, eyes flashing with something like a challenge. It was gone before I could be sure, though.

Interesting.

Fenwick was smooth, but there was something about that smile—something almost predatory...feral—that made me wonder if he might be capable of maintaining it while slitting your throat.

Smoothly.

Hook said nothing, but a little muscle at the base of his jaw jumped as Fenwick turned his attention to Billy.

"And you. Aren't you a fascinating creature." He licked his chops, not bothering to hide his attraction. "The Wizard did mention the Ozian in your midst. A former resident of Emerald City, even. So you must be—"

"Unimpressed," Billy interrupted flatly.

Fenwick's laugh was rich and deep, amused rather than offended. "Then I suppose I'll have to find some way to impress you. Tell me, what do you think of my view?"

He swept an arm toward the far wall at the back of the room. Other than the wooden frame around it, it was all window, showcasing lush, green hills and a seemingly endless sea of scarlet poppies.

Billy's eyes narrowed and she shrugged.

"Seen poppies before, but I guess it's alright. Nothing I'm writing home to my Ma about."

Fenwick winced. "Oof. Tough crowd. That's okay, I like a challenge, and we have a bit of time. The Wizard said that you'll be staying for a few days." He dipped his head and lowered his voice to a murmur. "He also mentioned that his...*wig* may have slipped a little during your meeting, hmmm? It's unfortunate, of course. Illusions can be delicate things. But I think we can all agree that a little theatre is a small price to pay for law and order, yes?"

When that was met with stony silence he clapped his paws together, unfazed.

"Enough chit-chat, then. You must be tired after your long journey. How about we get you four settled in, eh? I hope that you find our guest wing to your liking. Now, if you'll follow me?"

We trailed behind him as he led us deeper into the palace. Unlike Billy, I *was* super impressed. It was a feast for the eyes *and* the mind. Miniature mechanical creatures scuttled around cleaning walls and floors, lamps filled with tiny clockwork fireflies, and even a moving portrait made of gears and polished gemstones that played out a little garden scene on loop.

"Incredible," I murmured under my breath, glad for the distraction. I always did love a good invention, and this place was chock full of them. So many, in fact, that I was hardly even thinking about the fact that my mother had been in this palace…might've even walked down this very hallway.

And I super definitely wasn't thinking about my foster father, or how much my stomach still ached at having looked into his face without leaning into him for one of his bear hugs.

My eyes went hot, and I blinked hard, clearing my throat.

Nope. There'd be time for that later.

"The city has managed to get even swankier," Billy said, turning to Duncan, who slowed to examine a brass model of Emerald City, spinning in a glass display case. "It was always pretty fancy, but all this clockwork wizardry hadn't begun three years ago when I was here last."

Duncan flashed a smile. "Maybe they were just waiting until you left town. Afraid you'd break something valuable."

"Careful, Ox, or it'll be your face I'm breaking."

Duncan laughed, unbothered as Fenwick stopped in front of a large, brass door. "And here we are, friends. A private wing reserved for the most special of guests."

He swung open the door, revealing a massive common room with a picture window in the center. Sunshine poured in, lighting the thick, green carpet and gold-hued furniture. A fireplace took up the lion's share of one wall, with a long, thick cushion in front of the hearth.

Fenwick stepped toward a panel on the far wall, sliding it aside to reveal a compartment attached to a network of copper tubes. "Should you require anything at all, food, drink, you need only request it here." He demonstrated by pulling a lever that brought down a panel of labeled options. "Our chefs will have your meal prepared and delivered through this chute in a flash."

I stared, fascinated. It was like nothing I'd ever seen, even in the most magical places I'd visited. Hook, on the other hand, didn't even glance at it. His posture was stiff, his gaze still chilly.

"Enough of the luxury tour," he growled, eyeing Fenwick. "Tell us about the city. Does the witch trouble you here?"

Fenwick shook his head. "Things were…tense when she first arrived eight years ago or so. She came in like a tornado, full of piss and vinegar. And, at the risk of being rude, even that was mostly piss. She went on a rampage the second she arrived in Oz. Many were killed as she scoured the land looking for you. It was a dark time, but at least we had hope." He turned my way and inclined his head. "Your mother foretold all this, and she was right. Surely, that meant she was right about you too. But I don't think we realized how long it might take…" His furrowed brow smoothed, and he smiled. "Never mind all that. You're here now, aren't you? And, to answer your question, Hook, no. Right now, we're in a time of peace with The Wicked Witch. She keeps her distance, so long as we pay our tithes on time. We can go months without seeing or hearing from her at all."

"And you trust her to maintain this peace?"

Fenwick's eyes narrowed. "Trust is perhaps too strong a word. She is a complicated being and allows her emotions to get the better of her…usually anger. Luckily Marin's protection spells have kept her from doing too much damage so long as we stay inside the city walls. There are occasions that she punishes us seemingly for no reason. It's happened several times of late. We had to grapple with an infestation of locusts, and at one point the river water was making people ill."

Add another shovel full of guilt to the pile.

"I have to admit, that's probably on me." I thought back to Neverland, when she'd riddled the sea with wormholes that had nearly taken me and the entire Jolly Roger out for good. When she'd written my name in fire across the sky…

Surrender Harmony.

"She's not happy that we've managed to evade her."

"Well, you're here now, and many of us are glad for it."

But not all...

That tiny, uncomfortable nugget of truth made me distrust him a hair less.

"You shouldn't feel bad, Harmony. Emerald City is a dream most of the time. We're rich in resources, both natural and mechanical. The Witch benefits from our continued prosperity, just as we benefit from her absence. In the end, she's always backed off and we've worked something out."

Billy's expression was as lethal as I'd ever seen it. "Making deals with the devil, yeah? You city folk are as opportunistic as I remember."

Fenwick shrugged.

Mr. Unflappable.

"Perhaps. But it's allowed the citizens to live in peace most of the time, which makes it a good deal if you ask me. Now," he clapped his paws together and forced a bright smile, "I daresay you've all earned a moment of peace yourselves! These discussions are best suited to tomorrow, after you've rested from your long journey."

I hesitated, part of me desperate for more answers, but unable to deny the exhaustion closing over me. A glance at the others sealed the deal. Billy was flagging, Duncan's sun kissed skin was pale, his massive shoulders slumping, and even Hook's usually razor-sharp gaze seemed a little unfocused. It didn't take magic to see that my team needed to rest.

"Good idea," I said with a nod.

Fenwick pointed out the doors around the perimeter of the room. "Four bedrooms, each with its own bathroom. Please, make yourselves at home, and, as I said, feel free to have dinner sent up. I'll see you all tomorrow."

With a final bow, the fox-man slipped from the room, closing the door behind him.

Billy started pacing the second he was gone. "This might be comfy, but we're not learning a damn thing stuck inside here. We need to get boots on the ground and start poking around. I want to know where people's heads are at, and I want to know it before Oz the Great and Powerful has time to tell them what to think. There's got to be someone who can give us more information than he did. I'm sure I can tap some old connections…"

"She's right," Duncan said. "The palace machine is churning propaganda already, I'm sure. Soon enough, people will be spouting whatever nonsense they're being fed."

Hook was silent, but he didn't disagree.

I rubbed at my gritty eyes, wishing like hell I could argue with their logic, but I knew they were probably right.

"A couple hours, then. We need rest as much as we need information. Maybe even more, if these trials are as tough as I think they'll be."

Tougher than facing The Wicked Witch of the West riding a bookworm big as a house, with countless rows of teeth as long as me? I closed my eyes, trying not to relive that near-death experience in my mind.

CHAPTER 16

We didn't waste any time. Each of us grabbed a room at random and tucked our belongings away. Fifteen minutes later, we left our quarters with Bonnie holding down the fort.

And by holding down the fort, I meant perched on a curtain rod sleeping.

I couldn't even blame her. She'd had the longest journey of all, traveling between the pages, and it only seemed fair that at least *she* get some rest. She'd earned it.

Billy took the lead, retracing our path through the palace corridors until we reached the long flight of steps, we'd trudged up more than an hour before. We stepped out onto the pristine streets of Emerald City moments later. Metal gears hummed overhead as city folk rushed in and out of fancy shops. Several people stopped in their tracks to stare and murmur, but I followed Billy's example and avoided eye contact, barreling my way through. Someone could try to step in front of us and stop us for a chat, but they'd be risking life and limb to do it.

Still, when we came across a small crowd gathered near a

long metal structure that ran right through the gardens, I couldn't help but slow. Men and women in grease-smudged clothes bustled around, barking instructions and working on the strange contraption, a seemingly endless carriage, only with no horses to pull it.

Interesting...

"Do you know what's going on there?" I asked a short blonde woman standing a few feet in front of me.

"Trouble with the trolley." She eyed me like she wanted to say more but then tugged her shawl tighter around her shoulders.

"Is that what that's called? A trolley?"

Her brows shot high in surprise. "You've never seen it before? Steam-powered. Those gadgets there," she gestured toward a group of large metal cylinders, "heat water and the steam drives the engine forward on the rails. It hauls people and cargo across the city."

I stared at the enormous metal beast, fascinated. Workers shouted and hurried around, tightening bolts and looking at gauges.

"Clever, isn't it?"

"Amazing."

Damn. Why hadn't I thought of this back in The Hollow? How much easier would things have been for people? For a second, homesickness hit me in a rush. Me and Moll, walking through the streets of The Hollow, brainstorming inventions and her teasing me. We'd had plenty of struggles, but there was a lot to miss about it, too.

This wasn't The Hollow, though, and instead of sweating where our next meal would come from, I stood in The Emerald City, preparing to wage war against the most powerful being who ever lived. If it could even be called a war when one side consisted of three soldiers, a magicless tinker, and a bird...

"Are you...You're...her, aren't you?"

How was I supposed to answer that? My cheeks went hot, and I shrugged.

"I guess so?"

She took a furtive look around. "I know we aren't supposed to bother you, but me and my family are big fans. Good luck at the trials!"

I managed a smile. "Thanks." As much as I liked hearing *anyone* was on our side, the sense of being watched and recognized wasn't one I loved.

I turned my head, about to move on, when I caught sight of a massive sign that read "Ruby Reach". The letters were made from real rubies, inset into the wood.

Duncan squinted up at it. "Ruby Reach?"

"It's going to be so wonderful," came a smooth voice from behind us. We turned to see a well-dressed older woman with her hand resting on the shoulder of a teenage boy. "They've been working on it for a year and a half now. It's meant to be Emerald City's sister, only a day's journey by train."

The young, ginger-haired man at her side grinned, raising his broad shoulders. "I just got chosen to join the work crews myself. Headed there later this week."

Billy tilted her head. "Chosen?"

The woman nodded. "There's a drawing every fortnight. Pretty much anyone can apply, and they pick people through a lottery system to help keep things fair."

The boy beamed. "My pa went three months back. Can't wait to get out there and start working with him."

"Hope the trolley is fixed soon, then," I said. "Good luck."

Billy shifted nearby and glanced at her wrist as if it carried a watch. "It's getting late. We need to get a move on."

I spared a final glance at the trolley, taking in every detail I could, missing my magic more than ever. If I'd had it, it'd have read it like a blueprint in my mind. An image that I could recall any time I wanted. Instead, I was left doubting I could replicate this feat of engineering even if I wanted to.

"Right. Sorry."

We continued, but my thoughts stayed on the trolley.

As we made our way deeper into the heart of the city, the emerald spires and suspended bridges gave way to simpler structures. Some people stared as we passed, but looked away quickly. The Wizard had done his job well. He clearly held a lot of power and influence over the citizens of Emerald City. Strong motivators that made it hard not to wonder...

Even if he was telling the truth and had started the whole con to unite the city and help protect its people, had it gone to his head? Was he really looking out for them...or was he looking out for *him*?

I vowed to do my level best to find out before I left. The goal, as ever, was to return to C'an Saas. But somewhere along the way, it had become just as important to leave each story—and the people in it—better off than when I'd gotten there.

Two down, one to go...

Soon enough, we found ourselves in a section of town that reminded me of The Smudge back in Alabaster, except less grungy, and not hidden from sight by a magical shroud so that rich people didn't have to insult their eyes by looking at it.

Simple wooden houses dotted busy streets where children played and merchants shouted greetings, advertising their wares. Everything was a little aged and worn, but there was a warmth to it all, too. The same held true for the people. Still smartly dressed by Hollow standards, they were much less fussy than those closest to the city center. Regular citizens; mothers chasing little ones, shopkeepers, laborers, and craftsmen. Most of whom were too busy working and living their lives to spare us a second look.

The tight feeling in my chest unfurled and I took a deep breath as my steps slowed to something close to normal.

My kind of people. My kind of place.

I hadn't realized how being surrounded by fancy things and even fancier people affected me, both inside and out. My body had been in a constant state of fight or flight. It was exhausting.

And necessary, I admitted to myself. My "betters" had shown time and time again that they were anything *but* that, and I'd be insane if I didn't sleep with one eye open when on their turf.

Billy paused by a fountain carved from brass and waved us closer. "Alright," she said in a low voice, "Now we're far enough from prying eyes, it's time to make a plan."

This was a language I understood. Planning…strategy. I was already feeling a little less gloom and doom.

"Agreed." I stepped closer, adrenaline forcing the exhaustion away. "We only have a couple days to prepare, so we need to focus on three things. First priority is getting my magic unlocked. I'll almost certainly need it for the trials."

"Seems like." Hook nodded. "And the second?"

"We do as Billy said. Talk to people. Ferret out information…anything that could help us against the Witch," I continued, ticking off item two on my fingers. "I've only gotten this far by being out and about and keeping my eyes and ears open. No reason this place should be different."

"And the third thing?" Duncan asked.

"We train. We all need to be as sharp as possible in every discipline. Hand to hand combat, weapons, speed. We need to be ready for anything."

A smile momentarily softened Billy's features. "A woman after my own heart. You're growing on me, Princess."

Hook glanced at the sky and then back at us. "We've got a plan. Let's not waste any more daylight."

Billy took the lead again, and we headed toward a row of open-air stalls and merchants. She seemed at ease as she moved through the vendors and patrons, pointing out changes in the city she'd noticed since she'd been here last.

"That place there used to sell honey buns for two coppers," she said, nodding toward a busy shop with a display case bursting with baked goods. "But it seems the new owner prefers filling pockets over stomachs. Prices have doubled."

Duncan jerked a thumb at a guy selling skewered meats and vegetables. "What about that one?"

"You can, but I wouldn't. Word on the street was that mystery meat surprise he's always on about is actually rat."

"I'm hungry," Duncan said, "but I don't think I'm quite 'rat' hungry yet."

"I know a place. Food's good and cheap, and there's a guy I want to see over that way in any case."

We walked for another ten minutes or so before Billy stopped in front of another little bakery, and I let out a groan at the smell of yeasty bread and cinnamon.

"This is the place. Best baked goods in all of Oz, *and* the price is right," she announced.

"What should we get?"

Inside, we ordered exactly what Billy recommended. Golden pastry pockets stuffed with meat and gooey cheese, and half a dozen dumplings filled to splitting with goozle-berry jam. The owner, a sharp-featured woman with a dusting of flour on her apron named Connie, packed every-thing into parcels. Duncan fished out the coins to pay her, and then we were on our way.

"It's still warm," I murmured, tucking into one of the savory hand pies.

"Eat up. We've got another ten-minute walk. No point in waiting for it to get cold."

We ate lunch on the move, with me stuffing a couple of those jam-filled dumplings into my satchel for later. Billy led us to the outskirts of Emerald City, which was a breath of fresh air. Simple homes spaced much further apart than the more tightly packed city center and surrounded by wildflowers and gardens.

We followed a winding dirt path to a whitewashed cottage tucked in the middle of countless fruit trees. Herbs sprung from a garden that somehow looked both well-tended and wild at the same time.

As we approached, the mat on the front porch caught my eye.

Leave your boots and your bullshit at the door.

Duncan grinned. "I kind of like her already."

Billy raised a fist to knock, but the door swung open before she had the chance.

"Well, if it isn't Billy O'Donnelly in the flesh."

"Hello, Nora."

The woman stood framed in the doorway, hands coated in something dark brown and sticky. Long white hair hung down her back in a braid, framing a lined face that had seen some years, and had only grown better for them. She wore a beige crocheted dress that should've made her look frumpy, but instead lent her an earth mother appeal that had me glancing at the men to see if they noticed.

Hook was too busy scoping out the surrounding area for potential threats, but Duncan noticed, and Nora noticed him noticing.

"Who's this handsome young man you've brought me?"

"That's Duncan. But, uh..." Billy stared pointedly at the woman's messy hands, wrinkling her nose. "We could wait outside if we caught you at a bad time..."

The woman paused, then let out a belly laugh that warmed me from the inside out. "You are always with the jokes. I'm just throwing some clay, child. Come in and let me wash up. You can leave your shoes on if you like. Tomorrow is cleaning day."

Inside, the cottage's warmth matched its owner's. The parlor and kitchen were all one room, filled with shelves of mismatched crockery. Woven rugs and potted plants were scattered around, and the furniture was built for comfort over form.

"Sit where you like." She gestured with an elbow as she scrubbed her hands at the chipped basin. "I'll be right with you."

We took our seats around a worn walnut table, and a sleek black cat padded into the room, weaving itself between our legs. I reached down to pet her, but instead she leapt onto my shoulders, curling herself around my neck like a scarf made of fur.

I froze for a second, wishing I still had the magic to communicate with her. The cat didn't seem to mind, though. In fact, she was happily purring away.

The older woman returned, drying her hands on a towel. "I see you've met Brunhilda. She's a fickle one." She took a seat at the head of the table, giving us each a long look before stopping on Billy. "I heard you'd come back. Haven't seen the likes of you or your thieving brothers in years. You still owe me three silver pieces for that potion you bought before skipping town. Come to pay up—with interest—or are we done here?"

Billy's expression shuttered instantly. Without looking, she jabbed Duncan with an elbow. "Can you pay the lady for me?"

Ever the gentleman, Duncan didn't even mention the

shitload of silver she'd won at dice. He just tugged the coins from his pocket and slid them over wordlessly.

Nora tucked the coins down the front of her dress and sat back. She dipped her head in my direction. "I suppose you're here to talk about Marin's daughter, then?"

My hand stilled mid-stroke down the cat's silky back. "You knew my mother?"

She turned toward me with a soft smile. "I did. Quite well, in fact." Her voice was quiet, steady. "I helped Marin place the protection spells around Emerald City. Mind you, I'm nothing compared to your mother...small potatoes, really. Never had a coven of my own, but I've still got a few tricks up my sleeve."

She flicked a finger, and cups lifted themselves from one of the shelves, floating to the table as if carried by an unseen hand. Another gesture, and a steaming pot poured fragrant tea into each of them.

She sniffed the air, eyes narrowing. "Do I smell Connie's jammy dumplings?"

Reluctantly, I pulled out the pastries I'd squirreled away and set them on the table. She took them with a grateful nod, biting into one and closing her eyes in pleasure.

"Alright, then." She gestured with half a dumpling. "Ask what you've come to ask."

Billy leaned forward, pulling zero punches. "We're here to kill The Wicked Witch, but first, Harmony has to complete the trials in Emerald City. We figured you might know a thing or two about them."

The woman brushed crumbs from her dress and nodded. "Marin set the trials herself. This much I know for sure; the first is a test of wisdom, the second of heart, and the third of courage. She wanted to ensure her daughter had what she needed to face Almira at her strongest."

She fixed her gaze on me again, eyes serious. "Your

mother believed you could become the most powerful witch ever known, Harmony. But she worried you wouldn't survive the training it required. The magic you needed to harness would have lured Almira right to you, and she would've killed you long ago."

"So she hid me away instead." I swallowed hard, glancing down at the tea cooling in my hands. "Honestly, after our last couple of run-ins with Almira, I'm not sure hiding helped. She attacked me with some kind of black lightning…and I've barely been able to feel my magic since."

The room went quiet. Finally, the old woman let out a long sigh. "She can do that. Disable magic. Usually, it doesn't last long, but for those of us who have always felt the magic living inside us, the sensation can be jarring. Like a death, almost. And it can be hard to find your way back to it."

"But I will?" My pulse stuttered and I rubbed the cat a little harder, like it was good luck or something. "It's not gone forever?"

"Only you can answer that, Harmony."

A duck and weave. I tried another question. "Have you seen the prophecy my mother left for me? Maybe you could tell m-"

"I have not, and I cannot. The prophecy will be yours when you are ready to receive it."

Motherfucker. Gods save me from cryptic witches. Why couldn't any of them give me a straight answer about anything?

"I know that isn't what you want to hear, so I'll also tell you this. If anyone can defeat Almira, it's Marin's daughter." She stood abruptly and left the room, returning less than a minute later. She held out her hand and gestured for me to do the same.

"This belonged to your mother." She pressed a pearl ring into my palm and closed my fingers around it. "When your mother came here for the very last time, preparing for your eventual arrival, her magic was weakening. She'd been ill for some time and knew this would likely be her last trip. Rather than use the last of her power to get back to C'an Saas and die in your father's arms, she chose to save a little girl from a burning hut. It was her last deed of service. And when her spirit winked away, her wedding ring was all that was left behind. I know she'd have wanted you to have it."

I stared down at it, my vocal cords locked up tight.

Hook laid a hand on my back and murmured low words in my ear, but I could barely hear him as I slid the ring onto my finger.

It fit like a dream.

The woman straightened and offered me one last smile. "Now, you must take your leave. Once night falls, it's my job to go and unseal the magic that has bound the trials until now. Good luck to you all. I truly hope with all my heart that you succeed."

I stood and my feet carried me to the door, but it all felt surreal. Like I was in a dream.

"You stay back a moment, will you, Billy?"

Billy stiffened but nodded, slipping back into the cottage as the rest of us milled outside.

"You alright?" Duncan asked.

"I will be. I'm sad…but happy. It's just…a lot."

Hook's gaze was locked on the front door, mine was locked on my mother's ring.

My ring.

When Billy stepped out a few minutes later, her face was grim, but she didn't say a word as we made our way back toward the palace. That was fine by me. My mind was plenty busy.

Elated that I had this piece of the woman who made me—

a mother who loved me enough to do all this to guide me. To protect me and help me survive.

Fear trickled through me though, even with that hope. A deep terror sinking into my bones that, no matter how hard I tried, I'd never be the witch—or the daughter—she had hoped for, despite all she'd done.

Wishing I could've seen her face, just one time…

But wishes were for children, and there was no time to dwell on all that. I had to hang onto hope and aim for the stars as Pawpaw had told me, swinging my ladder for all I was worth.

I had a witch to kill.

CHAPTER 17

By the time we got back to the palace, I was dead on my feet. It had been a whirlwind of a day, and I still hadn't given myself time to process that the man who'd raised me was The Wizard of Oz. Kind of.

Never mind all that Nora had added to the mix.

And then there was that little moment at the end there where she'd called Billy back…

I winced, recalling the expression on the ranger's face when she'd walked out.

Something important had been discussed, but damned if I was going to be the one to ask what it was. How many times had I snooped, sneaked, picked, or prodded to find information only to wish I never found it out in the first place?

So many.

If I came up with one more thing to worry about, I was pretty sure my head was going to explode. All I wanted right now was to head straight for my bedroom, face plant onto the mattress, have a good come apart, and crash out for the night.

I paused to give sweet Bonnie a scratch on her head when she fluttered down to the table, and then faced the others with a stiff smile. "I'm exhausted and going to hit the sack. See everyone in the morning!" I turned on my heel to go, tears already prickling my eyes.

Walk fast, dummy.

Only I wound up walking right into Billy, who had used her preternatural stealth to get around me in a flash. I let out a grunt as she shoulder-checked me and I bounced off, stumbling back a couple feet.

"Not so fast, Princess," she drawled, her brogue deeper than I'd ever heard it as she crossed her arms over her chest. "You, me, Tall Dark and Cranky, and the ox here are going to play a little game before you go night night."

"A-a game?" I stuttered, the blood draining from my face at the dead serious look on her face.

"Yup. See, when we first met, I told you all I was a private person, which is true. In turn, I allowed you all to be private, too. Fair is fair. But now, things have taken a turn, and the time for secrets is done. So we're going to play a game," she repeated. "I'm calling it *Truth or Consequences*. It's where you all start giving me some truth, or I start dishing out some consequences." She raised her brows and glanced at each of us in turn. "Who wants to go first?"

Five minutes later, the four of us sat cross-legged around the low table, the silence thick and uncomfortable. The common room's plush couches stood unused a few feet behind us.

Billy had pulled a worn deck of playing cards from her bag and was now shuffling with a skill that bordered on hypnotic. The cards moved through her fingers with an ease that had me wondering if dice wasn't the only game she was especially skilled at.

I was about to ask her, but something in her stormy expression kept me silent.

"Here's the rules." Billy broke the silence without looking up from her cards. "High card asks low card a question. Low card answers truthfully, or else."

"Or else what?" Hook asked, raising an eyebrow.

Billy's gaze flicked to him. "Or else we are going to have a problem."

The tension ratcheted up one more notch, and I was about to enter the fray and try to diffuse the situation when Hook shrugged.

"Fair enough."

I glanced over at Duncan, who'd been staring down at the table. He lifted his head now, clearly reluctant, but he met Billy's stare.

"Are there limits on questions?" Duncan asked. "Subjects that are off the table?"

Billy cocked her head, eyes flinty. "Something to hide, Ox?"

He shrugged. "Nope. But I'm not the only one here, and I don't want anyone forced to share things they don't feel comfortable sharing."

"And I don't want to die on the battlefield next to a bunch of people with secret agendas," she shot back. "This is going to be a shitty few minutes, but it's a necessary evil if we want a chance in hell of getting Harmony through these trials so we can face Almira." She set her jaw, stubborn like a mule. "I've come this far, but I can't wholeheartedly pledge my bow to someone whose purpose doesn't line up with mine."

Hard to argue with that.

"We could just lie, though."

I shot my elbow out and it caught Duncan in the side. "What? We could..."

"You're absolutely right," she said, her smile downright terrifying. "But you've seen me shoot an arrow, and I'm a better lie detector than I am a shot. Do what you will with that information."

She riffled the cards one final time and then fanned them out face-down on the table.

"Grab a card."

Hook didn't hesitate. He reached out and pulled one free, flipping it up to show the group. The jack of hearts. He flicked it onto the table in front of him without a word.

Duncan picked next, drawing a nine of clubs.

My turn. My heart sped up just a little as I slid my hand across the smooth surface of the cards, third eye wide open for some clue as to which to pick but coming up blank. I grabbed one at random and turned over the three of spades.

Shit.

Billy went last, ending up with the King of diamonds.

"Looks like the princess is up first." Billy's expression softened for a second as she met my gaze before snapping back to all-business again.

I braced myself, expecting her to come out swinging, and she didn't disappoint.

"Nora Broomall knew your mother better than most. She said Marin was the most powerful witch she'd ever known, and the greatest clairvoyant." Billy rested her elbows on the table, her gaze boring straight through me. "Tell me something, Harmony. When you asked me to join you, did you already know your mother had read your tea leaves countless different ways, countless different times? And that, no matter how she turned the cup, no matter what path she tried to clear for you, every future ended the same?"

My vision went hazy, and I swayed in place. I was no clairvoyant, but I knew what came next, and the words hit like physical blows.

"It ends with Almira as the victor, and all of us dead." Her eyes blazed as she looked at the guys and then back to me. "Did you know we'd lost this fight a thousand times before it even started?"

"She didn't know." Hook's tone brooked no argument, and Duncan nodded in agreement.

"There's no way she knew that."

But Billy turned back to me and waited.

I had to stop thinking about what that revelation meant for me...for us. It would only send me spiraling. Instead, I had to deal with the problem at hand. Billy didn't trust me, and I could hardly blame her, but I needed to fix it.

So I launched into the story I probably should've told when we first met. About Molly and Heinrich, and The Speaker. About the storybook and finding the first Whisper of my magic in Alabaster. About Pan and Tink and Noru the Croc. I even explained about The Wizard of Oz, and how he was a dead ringer for my foster father. When I was done, I reached out and grabbed hold of her forearm.

"The most important thing I need you to know is...I wouldn't have put people I care about through all of that. I wouldn't have knowingly dragged you all into a battle we were destined to lose." I shook my head. "Never."

She seemed to process that for a second before leaning back. "I believe you. For what it's worth, that wasn't all your mother told Nora. She also said that destiny is like a river. Ever changing. One, tiny thing—the turn not taken, a kindness to a stranger, or a last second pivot—could alter it all."

It was a small comfort, and I looked around the table at the others. "We've all seen what we're up against. If we go in thinking we have no hope—"

Hook snorted. "I never go into a battle thinking that."

"I don't need any promises or guarantees," Billy tacked on.

"My concern was going into battle with a leader who lied to me. I know what the risks are, and I'm willing to take them."

"Same," Duncan added, tossing his card back into the pile as Bonnie lit onto his shoulder and nuzzled against his neck.

"Next round."

The room fell quiet as Billy gathered the cards again, shuffling them once more, the silence broken only by the click of the deck. She fanned them back out and we each drew again.

It was hard to concentrate after the news she'd dropped on me, but Billy was still on a mission, and the rest of us were along for the ride whether we wanted to be or not.

King of clubs for me, five of diamonds for Dunc, and another jack for Hook. Billy let out a triumphant whoop as she held out the ace of spades.

"Looks like my lucky day! So give it to me straight, Ox. What gives with all the—" she broke off and flexed, making the veins in her neck pop, "and the eyes and all."

Duncan settled back, using hands to brace himself. "In Alabaster, where Harmony and I met and her journey began, people who have magic are called Whispers. My Whisper is that I can harness anger and other emotions and channel them into physical strengths."

"But it hurts, yeah?"

He tipped his head in acknowledgement. "Let's say it doesn't tickle and leave it at that."

"Fair enough. I guess all I need to know is that it won't affect your judgement when we're in battle. So far, that's seemed to be true. I'd fight by your side any day, Ox."

I let out the breath that had been stuck in my chest since this whole thing started. It was actually going better than I expected.

Then it was Hook's turn as he drew an eight.

As luck would have it, Billy pulled high card again.

"I'm guessing you're a Whisper too, then?" Hook was about to answer but she held up a staying hand. "Nope. Hold on. That's not the question I want to ask."

She scratched at her chin, deep in thought, then she let her gaze travel over the tattoos barely visible above his shirt collar. The clock on the mantel ticked, loud in the silence, but she wouldn't be rushed.

When she finally spoke, her words were slow, deliberate, and sucked every molecule of air from the room.

"Why are you so sad?"

Duncan's eyes went wide, his gaze colliding with mine. There was a good chance our little fellowship was about to implode. The odds of Hook answering were—

"Smart." Hook interrupted my thought with the resigned look of a person strangely at peace with some terrible fate. "Because that's the heart of it, isn't it?"

She gave him a sad little smile in return. "I'm afraid it is, and I'm sorry for that."

He fixed his gaze on a spot behind her head somewhere as he spoke. "I've hurt a lot of people. Some intentionally, some by accident. I've tried to make amends for the latter, but the peace I hoped would come with that has eluded me. To complicate matters, the magic that you speak of isn't really mine. Most of my powers are ill-gotten gains earned from the terrible deeds I've done, and they come at a cost. Where I'm from, we don't call those with magic Whispers. We call them Tideblessed. When I take a life, I absorb that person's Tideblessing…along with all their memories."

Billy let out a low hiss and closed her eyes. "Fucking hell."

"On the nose. It's fucking hell." He stared at her long and hard. "Have I answered to your satisfaction?"

Duncan's throat worked, but he didn't comment. As for me, I sat on my hands to keep from throwing my arms around Hook and trying to comfort him. He'd made it very clear that wasn't my job anymore, if it ever was.

"I'm good," Billy replied finally. "My fear was that your disregard for death would make you reckless with not only your life, but with ours. Again, from what I've witnessed, I'm happy to fight at your side. Let's keep going." Billy picked up the cards again and shuffled.

If there was a less fun game than this, I couldn't think of it. I was about to say as much when a bell chimed merrily. We all turned to see the dumbwaiter door slide open to reveal a basket brimming with sandwiches half-wrapped in parchment that we hadn't ordered.

Fenwick, ever the perfect host.

"I think that's enough for tonight anyway," Billy said, setting the deck down with a sigh. "Let's try to get some sleep, shall we?"

The others agreed, but I stayed silent. The rest of us had been forced to answer a question, while Billy had not only managed to avoid the coals, but she'd also been the one with the high card each and every time. I'd suspected she was a card mechanic and respected the hustle. Enough was enough, though. Fair was fair, and if it wound up biting me in the ass, so be it.

"One more round," I said before I could talk myself out of it. Duncan winced, shaking his head but I pressed on. "Only this time, we'll pick for each other." I met Billy's gaze and held it. "Everyone select a card for the person to your right."

Billy's eyes narrowed but she must've sensed that I wasn't budging because she let out a resigned sigh. "Go ahead, then. It's fine by me."

Now was my chance. I just need to get super lucky...

"I'm out," Hook announced, pushing himself to his feet and taking a seat on the couch.

"Me too," Duncan said, a light in his eyes dawning as he followed suit.

It hit me like a bolt of lightning. They were trying to turn the odds in my favor. Now I had to get half as lucky, because the men were out of the game. It was me against Billy. Fifty fifty. Worst case, I'd have to reveal another secret, but what did I have left to hide?

"Hook, pick for me, Duncan, pick for Billy then."

Her eyes narrowed as if she were trying to think of a reason to deny my request, but after a brief moment, she shrugged. "Whatever."

Duncan went first, taking a long time to pick. He looked miserable, and I wondered if he was trying to pick high or low at this point, knowing he was in a no-win situation.

"Ten of diamonds," he announced as he set the card on the table.

Hook stood and leaned over me, but he didn't waiver. He stabbed the card closest to me with his hook and slid it under my trembling fingertips.

I gnawed on my bottom lip as I dug at the corner and flipped it over.

The queen of hearts.

I blew out a shuddering breath as relief rolled through me. I could finally ask about the fairytale book in her bag, find out exactly how she'd gotten it and when. My hands were trembling with anticipation at getting the answer I wanted, but when I opened my mouth, something else entirely came tumbling out.

"Where are your brothers?"

What the fuck?

It was the wrong question, no doubt about it. And still, as I waited, my whole body was on high alert.

She pinched her eyes closed, and went silent for so long, I was sure she was going to break her own rule and deny me my answer. Then, she pushed herself to her feet and stared down at me, her expression one that told of a heartache so keen, it cut me sure as a blade.

"You're right, Princess. I had four brothers, and they're not here with me now. My whole life, we were thick as… well…thieves." She let out a bitter laugh as she wrapped the pendant around her neck in her fist. "They were my only family. My best friends. And my mistake cost them their lives. They're dead because of me.…"

CHAPTER 18

BILLY

THE EMERALD CITY, THREE YEARS BEFORE...

My gaze flitted from person to person as I strode across the busy street. An older, bearded man with a gold-encrusted cane? I stepped right around him, pushing the thought aside.

Too worldly.

I eyed a nervous looking lad in a stylish turtleneck, a stack of books pulled tight to his chest. I edged toward him, biting back a curse as an older woman—likely his mother—stepped in beside him.

Disappointment gave way to a flash of excitement as I saw him. A bespectacled young man, jacket even deeper green than the city itself. And that ring on his finger...He clearly came from money. Seeing that he was too busy talking to a vendor to notice, I beelined toward him.

"But how much for two of them?" he asked as I moved into earshot.

"Eighty," the vendor answered, reaching out to grab a second of the tawny fur rugs. "Fine Virukian mink. Soft, yet sturdy."

It took all I had not to laugh out loud. Fine Virukian mink my ass. Knowing that shopkeeper, it was almost certainly muskrat fur. Hell, even if it was mink, I'd have decked the bastard for asking half that much.

But Pretty Boy had other ideas. He nodded, stuffing a hand into his pocket to pull out a small pile of coins.

I peered through the crowd to find that Paddy was doing such a good job blending in that it even took *me* a few seconds to spot him.

Not bad, little brudder.

He dipped his head in recognition, and I cracked my knuckles, stepping the last few feet forward.

My new mark accepted his rugs in exchange for coin, grinning as he swiped a hand across the fur. "Fine indeed," he marveled.

Ugh. This was going to be so easy it'd almost make me feel guilty.

Almost.

I made a show of peering down to inspect my fingernails, bumping into him just as he strode away from the vendor. I staggered back, glancing down at one of his rugs as he dropped it.

"Oh, what have I done this time? I'm so clumsy." I pitched my voice to make it high and breathy and then forced a giggle. "Please, accept my sincere apology." I moved as if to grab the rug, stopping short as he picked it up himself.

"No harm done." He smiled, wiping a bit of dirt from the fallen rug. "See? Good as new."

"I really should pay more attention to where I'm going." I

held my breath then, sending a red flush to my cheeks. "Are you new in town?"

"Is it that obvious?" he asked, chuckling. "Yes, my father and I just got here. Working on a new project."

We stepped out of the way, moving around the corner as a couple approached the shopkeeper. I spared the briefest of glances behind him, seeing that Paddy was still quite a distance away. I had to keep the conversation going. "Ooh, what kind of project?"

"We just opened up a new factory, just a few miles out of town."

"A factory that makes what?"

He paused, considering, and his voice went softer. "We've developed an amazing new medicine. It helps with all manner of things, from nausea to fevers. But it's tough to make, and demand is growing. We need loads of workers from the city."

"S—sounds like it'll be good for jobs," I said, faltering slightly. "What's your name, by the way?"

He straightened, extending a hand. "Emerson Jones. Nice to make your acquaintance, Miss—?"

"Albright," I answered, using my standard fake name for jobs like this. "Rachel Albright."

"Well, Miss Albright, I really ought to be going. I've got a lot of items on my list today as we try to outfit our home, but if you know anyone who might be interested in working at the factory, don't hesitate to send them my way. We hire every Saturday. The pay is ten gold per day, and they'll really be able to make a difference in people's lives."

"I'll do that." It was hard to smile through the pit forming in my stomach. It wasn't just guilt—The O'Donnellys did whatever it took to get by—but it'd been years since we'd given the straight life a go. Was I really going to rob a guy who was making medicine for people, and was also willing to pay a good wage to boot? Ten gold per day for each of the five of us was worth a hell of a lot more than whatever was in his pockets right now, no matter how rich he was.

I caught sight of Paddy just a few dozen feet away, but ignored him, catching hold of Emerson's arm before he turned to go.

"Sorry, but you said the factory is just outside the city. Are there any fears about...trouble?"

"Ah," he said, expression going grim. "The Wicked Witch, you mean? We have 'round-the-clock guards. Plus, she's been so quiet of late, I'm not even sure she's still around. Things have gone smoothly so far, I can tell you that."

I nodded, sucking in a long breath. He was right about that. There were times when she wreaked havoc, and other times we started to wonder if she'd died up in that tower of hers, she was quiet for so long.

This was bigger than paying for tonight's dinner—it was a chance. A chance to get out of this life, once and for all. I owed that to myself and to my brothers.

"Thank you very much for your time," I blurted as a figure appeared behind him.

"Of course. See you again soon, Miss Albright."

I stepped deftly around him, smacking my shoulder right into Paddy's and shooting him a pointed glare as I moved back toward the street. I glanced back a few seconds later, pleased to see that he had gotten the hint.

Emerson was on his way, his two overpriced rugs in hand, and, no doubt, his wallet still in his pocket.

I took a long arc through the street, searching halfheartedly for another mark while Paddy lurked in the crowd. Nothing too obvious came, though, and I found myself exiting the same way I'd come, striding down the little alley that led to the place we called home.

I loosened my corset as I walked, breathing in the sweet

smell of Mrs. Bradley's bread as I passed the little bakery on the corner. We'd have to go without today, unless I wanted to dip into our meager savings. Yesterday, maybe, but today wasn't the time for that. It was a time for new beginnings.

"What in the seven hells was that?"

I turned, frowning as Paddy strode up, emerging from a little side street. "Change of plans."

"I was this close!" He mimed a grabbing motion.

I raised an eyebrow. "You trust me, or no?"

He scowled for a moment, then sighed. "I trust ye."

"Then shut your trap 'til we get home. I'd rather let you all in on it at once."

"You sure we shouldn't just rob the place?" Scotty asked for the umpteenth time that morning.

I frowned, slowing down to let him catch up. I'd filled them in last night, but clearly, they hadn't taken it to heart. Annoying, since we were already nearly to the factory.

I cuffed him across the ear. "What'd I tell you? The O'Donnellys are going straight. If we put in a year of hard days at the factory, we'll have enough to buy our whole fuckin' block."

"And then we rob 'em," Andrew clapped. "Good thinkin', sister."

"We ain't gonna rob them at all." I scowled. "We'll save up a nest egg, then roll it into some kind of business. Never gonna have to risk our necks again."

Jacob nodded, chewing his thumbnail. "It really isn't a bad idea. Not as fun, though…"

"It's the plan, like it or not," I declared. "Keep your hands to yourselves in there and hush up from here on out. I don't want the guards hearing you talking like that."

Scotty dipped his head, resigned. "Understood."

The factory loomed into view minutes later, iron-and-stone amidst lush forest. As promised, patrols of guards circled the place, eyeing a crowd by the front doors.

We joined the line, my heart thumping with hope and dread. A chance—perhaps our last—to change everything.

"Remember your roles?"

Paddy sighed, flashing me an eye roll. "We get it, Billy. I'm Patrick Alton, Scotty's—"

"Albright," I corrected, staring daggers at him.

"You there!" called a guard from the top of the hill. "Line up behind the others. Someone'll be around shortly to speak with you about joining up."

As promised, the doors swung open, and nearly a dozen suits stepped out, weaving through the crowd and conducting quick, minute-or-less interviews.

A short, weaselly man reached us first. He wiped a streak of sweat from his brow as he approached, clipboard in hand. "Names and ages?"

"We're the Albright family." I dropped into a slight curtsy. "I'm Rachel. Nice to meet you."

I held my breath as my brothers rattled off their aliases, but luckily none of them screwed it up. So far, so good.

"What interests you about the company?" he asked, eyes flicking everywhere except at my face.

"It's a chance to do something that actually matters." *But the money don't hurt.*

The interviewer nodded, not bothering to write that down. "Any health issues we should know about?"

"Nothing comes to mind."

He finally met my gaze, teeth digging into his lower lip. He opened his mouth, snapped it shut, then gestured toward the side of the building. "You're in. Line up over there and wait for further instruction."

I stepped away to do as asked but paused as he called out to me. "Wait."

"Hmm?"

"It's hard work, you know? You sure you're up to it?"

I forced a grin, flexing a bicep at him. "More than up to it." *Asshole.*

The line grew by the second, with seemingly no one turned away. They were hiring this many in a single day? And now that I was closer, I could clearly see there were many more already hard at work inside.

"They really take anybody, huh?" Scotty muttered, elbowing Jacob in the ribs. "Lucky for you, skinny bastard."

A voice rang out before they could continue bickering. "Right this way! Wipe your shoes as you enter and move in an orderly fashion."

The crowd shuffled forward as one, stepping through the doors single-file. Hammers clanged, and squeaking wheels echoed around us, accompanied by the smell of grease.

The place was still under construction, wooden scaffolding everywhere, and sections blocked by flimsy fences—but it was like nothing I'd ever seen. Sturdy iron beams stretched high, floors and walls made of smooth stone. Sunlight filtered in from a small opening in the ceiling—some kind of chimney, perhaps?

I was so busy staring at the walls and ceiling that I hardly noticed the sound as the door slammed shut behind us.

"Stop."

The crowd halted. A single, robed figure appeared above, stepping onto a raised metal platform from a hidden door. "Welcome," a feminine voice rang out, sending a chill down my spine.

Just one word, and yet…

"Something's wrong," I hissed. That voice—regal yet

distorted somehow. Every muscle in my body screamed for me to run.

A second, larger figure emerged beside her as a yellowish mist began seeping upward from the floor.

Emerson?

But not quite. Was that—I leaned in, squinting—fur on him?

A scream erupted from the first row, snapping my head back.

"Move!" I shouted, charging toward the entrance.

My brothers leapt into action instantly, but a wicked cackle erupted behind us.

"No use running now, my pretties. I've already got you."

Searing pain shot up my legs, but I ignored it, leaping over a man crouched on the floor, screaming.

What the fuck was happening?

"Up!" Paddy shouted. "We have to go up!"

I scanned the massive space in front of me and nodded. He was right. That chimney—there was still a way out. I spun toward him, blinking tears away, holding back a scream of horror at what I saw.

Tufts of fur sprouted from his cheeks, his ears growing longer and more pointed. Jacob, Scotty, and Andrew looked the same. The yellow mist was changing them...

I snapped my mouth shut and plugged my nose as Scotty lunged forward, gripping my arm with inhuman strength. "GO!"

He yanked me upward, setting me atop Jacob's shoulders, easy as if I was a doll.

The witch cackled again, and lightning crackled in our direction. Scotty leapt forward, roaring with pain as the bolt caught him in the arm.

"Fucking go!"

Paddy hunched over, furred muscles rippling grotesquely,

tearing his shirt as he heaved Jacob onto his own shoulders, raising us both higher into the air.

I reached up desperately, my heart pounding as a breeze brushed my fingertips. The chimney…it was so close! I lunged, barely gripping its edge before another bolt of lightning streaked past, striking Paddy directly in the chest.

Tears blurred my vision as he howled, but didn't falter. Every fiber of my body screamed as I hoisted myself out, scraping my palms raw as I dragged myself onto the gravelly rooftop.

I sucked a breath into my burning lungs and then held it again before turning back and reaching down into the chimney hole.

"Come on!" I waved frantically. "Grab my fucking hand!"

But Paddy slumped backward, groaning as Jacob fell on top of him. Growing furrier by the second, Scotty let out a roar and grabbed Andrew by the scruff of his neck, hurling him upward in a last, desperate attempt to get our youngest brother's hand to reach mine.

I leaned in as far as I could, gripping the tin of the chimney so tight, it warped beneath my fingers. Time seemed to slow as Andrew sailed toward me, his furry face filled with terror as he reached out.

"Stop them! Obey your master!"

My fingertips brushed Andrew's and my shoulder screamed as I wrenched it out of the socket and managed to grab his hand.

"Don't let go!" I sobbed, bracing my knees against the chimney and throwing my weight backward. Agony made my vision go black, but I kept pulling. I managed to get his arm all the way out of the hole before I lost leverage and slammed back into the chimney again with a gasp.

It was only then that I realized he was pulling back. "Don't panic! Let me pull—"

The snarling, wild-eyed face that I saw as I peered down into the hole was no longer my brother. His face had changed into one of a feral beast. He tried in vain to unfurl what looked to be some sort of feathered, bony wings in the narrow space even as he snapped at me with razor sharp teeth.

And still I held on. A second hand swung up to join his first and he yanked with all his might, as desperate to kill me as I was to save him.

"Please, Andrew. You know it's me. Come on, we can-" I broke off as I met his gaze one last time. This wasn't my brother anymore. Andrew was gone. They were all…gone.

I snagged the dagger from the sheath at my belt and yanked it free. With tears streaming down my face, I plunged it into the hand of my baby brother. He let out an unholy screech and then released me, tumbling into the darkness.

Then, I ran.

But no matter how far or how fast, the anguished screams behind me never left my ears. It wasn't until I found myself half a mile away, lying on the ground, sobbing that I realized; My brothers knew we couldn't all make it out. In our darkest hour, without hesitation or discussion, they'd all chosen the same thing; To save me first.

By the time I crawled my way into bed that night in our silent little hut, I was blessedly numb. The only feeling left inside of me was hate.

The Wicked Witch of the West had taken my brothers and turned them into monsters. And now, I had to face a lifetime without them. But I knew one thing for sure;

Theirs' wouldn't be the only blood staining my hands…

CHAPTER 19

HARMONY

"That's where she got the monkeys from." I had imagined that they were monkeys of some kind, only enchanted by her magic. I'd never even considered that they were people to begin with.

"We didn't even put up a fight. We all just walked in there willingly." She touched a finger to her slightly pointed ear and shook her head. "Imagine me thinking I was conning Emerson Jones and the whole time he was conning me. I was so fucking arrogant. But he got his in the end."

"How?" The question came from Hook, who was looking at Billy as if seeing her for the first time.

If anyone could relate to what she'd gone through…

"The witch packed up and left with her new army, and the factory disappeared like it never existed. Emerson could've gone off and set up a sweet life with his newfound riches, but he was stupid enough to stay in the city so he could show off a little. And I was smart enough to wait for him. I caught him outside a tavern one night about four days later, and let's just say that there isn't enough of a body left to be found if anyone was looking."

Duncan's grim smile was tinged with something dark and furious. "Bastard."

"I couldn't stand the thought of staying in Emerald City, so I went off on my own to figure out what to do next. I saw what the change had done to my brothers, and I decided that, if it was me, I'd rather be dead. Under her control, outside of my own body. I had the smallest taste of it, and that was more than enough. Even now, my shoulders ache where my wings would be, my tailbone throbs. I have a feeling that's why they are so enraged. They're in constant pain. I made it my job to relieve that pain."

"So you hunt for them," I finished, heart aching for my friend. It explained so much. The preternatural speed, the secrecy, the sadness…

She tipped her head in a clipped nod. "I do. My brothers and several of the others from the factory became her first team of scouts. I managed to set up an ambush for them." She looked off into space, gnawing on her lower lip. "Freed all of them from her that day…except Paddy. Wily fucker he is… He got away. That's why I needed to stay with the corpses and had you all leave to bathe in the river. Once they're dead and the enchantment fades, they turn back to human again. I needed to see—" she broke off suddenly, the despair in her eyes disappearing as if on command. "Anyway, there's my story, Princess. You wanted it, you got it. Anything else?"

I shook my head miserably.

What would she do if she knew there was a version of her in another dimension? Another version of *them*? Could she even exist in the same story if a Billy already existed there? Until I knew the answer, telling her would only be a cruelty, and she has suffered enough.

But maybe someday…

Another reason we couldn't fail in our mission, no matter what it took.

I shook my head, feeling sick to my stomach. "No. Nothing else."

"I have one more question," Hook said, his expression grim but determined. "I believe you have a book in your possession that might be of interest to us all. Care to share why you never mentioned it?"

The room went silent, but if a glare could make a sound, Duncan would be ripping Hook a new asshole right now.

Billy's jaw went tense as she bent and picked up her bag, holding it close to her chest. "I'm afraid that one is classified, Captain. If that means you want me to go it alone from here on out, that's fine. This is an either you trust me, or you don't moment here. I'm choosing to trust you all. What's the verdict on me?"

Duncan didn't hesitate. "With all my heart."

I tried to think clearly, past all the heavy emotions clogging my thoughts. If I was hanging off the edge of a cliff, would I want Billy O'Donnelly at the summit, trying to pull me up?

I would. "I do."

"And that's enough for me," Hook said.

"Excellent. I'll see myself to bed, then." With that, she headed toward her bedroom.

"Billy, wait," Duncan called, rising to follow her.

Now that she'd gone, I allowed my muscles to relax, and I slumped forward as grief threatened to swallow me whole.

Scotty. Andrew. Jacob. All dead. Part of me already knew it…so why the fuck did I ask that? What did it have to do with anything at all?

Nice job, Harmony. Because nothing said "great leader" like making a person relive the worst thing that ever happened to them.

The queen on the table in front of me blurred, and a fat tear plopped onto her face as we both wept.

I sensed Hook moving but didn't look up until a gentle hand took my wrist. He swept me up into his arms, and instead of fighting it, I nestled closer. Bad idea or not, I needed him more than I've ever needed anyone in my life.

So when he yanked back the blanket, laid me gently on the bed, and tried to straighten, I held tight.

"Please...don't go." I swallowed hard and met his gaze in the moonlight. "Not yet."

A muscle in his jaw flickered as he sucked in a breath.

"You're not yourself tonight, Princess, and frankly, neither am I. It's not the time to be making decisions like this."

My laugh came out more like a strangled sob. "For such a ruthless pirate, you're quite the gentleman. What was it you used to tell the crew? 'Make sure anytime someone asks, you tell them my soul is as black as night' or something?"

His eyes widened just a little. "Figured that out, did you?"

"I did. They listened *too* well...repeated it nearly word for word. I heard it from both Tom and Xander, just a day or so apart, and put two and two together." I traced my fingers along his stubbly jaw. "The question is, why? Why did you want the world to think you're so evil?"

His lean throat worked as he looked away. "Easier to kill a few and rely on reputation than having every pirate on the seas trying to test their luck. I had one goal; find the clock and kill Pan and Bell. Every other job was to make sure my crew was paid fairly until I achieved it."

"Meaning you're not as bad as you like to pretend," I said, running the pad of my thumb over his lips.

He nipped the very tip just hard enough to make me gasp.

"I'm bad enough, Princess." His onyx eyes gleamed with something dangerous that had my skin breaking out in goosebumps. "Ask the men who *did* try to test me. If they're alive to tell the tale..."

I wet my lips and pushed myself up to sit. "What if I just want to take my chances?"

Our faces were close enough that his musky scent wrapped around me like a magic spell.

"I don't want to be alone tonight. I don't want to think of all the ways I've hurt people to get myself here. I just want—" I broke off and shrugged helplessly. "I just want you."

He let out a low growl and pressed his forehead to mine.

"Ah, you're well and truly killing me, love."

But this time, he didn't pull away. He thrust his hand into my hair and tipped me back, crushing his lips to mine.

Instantly, all thought fled. The pain, the fear, the despair, sizzling away under the heat of his mouth. His tongue swept along my bottom lip and then teased its way inside. I moved, grabbing at his shirt with both hands, gripping it like it was a lifeline.

Then he was urging me back, until my head rested on the pillow even as he stretched over me, covering my body with his, the heat of his skin warming me from the inside out. He pulled back far too soon and stared down at me, his weight resting on his elbow. With painstaking care, he began to undo my shirt, fingers deftly flicking open each button. When he was done, he tugged the shirt open, baring me to the waist.

I shivered, nipples pebbling, but not from the cold. No, it was the look on his face. Like he wanted to drop low and devour me then and there. But he didn't. Instead he rolled away and moved to the bottom of the bed.

"What are you doing?" I breathed, terrified he was going to leave, but just as determined not to beg him to stay.

"Taking care of you," he replied simply. He began unlacing the tops of my boots and then tugged them off, one by one. My socks came next, and then he reached for the buttons of my pants. I could hardly breathe as he worked them over my hips, his face a mask of concentration. When he tossed them onto a chair against the wall, he spared a glance at my face.

"I'm...I'm going to leave the underwear on. A man can only take so much." His expression bordered on pain as he took one last look at my near-naked body and then pulled the blankets over me.

Before I could protest, he was making his way to the other side of the bed. Wordlessly, he climbed in and then tugged me against his chest.

"One day...if we make it through all this alive?" His voice was a low rumble in my ear. "If you decide this is still what you want. You can have it, Princess. But for tonight, just let me hold you. Can you do that?"

I wanted to answer, but the knot in my throat made it impossible as his tenderness unlocked all the grief and guilt I'd been holding inside. It came out in an agonizing rush, a storm that couldn't be stopped.

And through it all, he never let go...

WHEN I WOKE up the next morning, dawn had just broken, I was alone and my pillow was damp. I pressed a hand to my eyes, blinking away the last remnants of a dream.

This time, it wasn't about Hook. It was a wild mix of people and worlds. Me with my Pawpaw at the forge, making shoes for his mule. Me with the O'Donnelly family, Paddy fastened to a wheel in the center of the room, spinning as we threw knives at him. Me with Moll and Fetch at our table in

The Hollow, laughing over our meager dinner…happy just to be together.

My friends who'd become family. Chosen and sealed in our willingness to fight for one another.

I rubbed at my tear-streaked face, doing my best to put it out of my head as I turned to my side. Hook's scent rolled over me and butterflies fluttered in my belly. He'd been so gentle. So sweet. How could he not see that he was deserving of love and forgiveness? How could he not want—

Nope. Shut it down, dummy.

He had taken care of me the same as any friend would. No more, no less.

The memory of his lips on mine had me clenching my thighs together and I gritted my teeth. Okay, so maybe a little more than a simple friend. But we both knew he'd been doing me a kindness. Nothing had changed, not one lick. If anything, I had a dozen new reasons to put the man out of my head…

I sat up and let the rest of yesterday's events come rushing back.

The battle with Almira and her worms. Seeing my father in the face of the Wizard. Billy's confession. Finding out about my mother's role here in this place.

Finding out she never saw a way for us to win.

Destiny is like a river, everchanging…

"Damn right. And we are about to change the course of this one, starting right fucking now."

I looked down at the gleaming pearl on my finger and pressed it to my lips.

"I won't let you down, Mother."

With that, I rolled out of bed and headed into the common room, surprised to find myself alone. Hook wasn't much of a sleeper…

The sound of approaching footsteps pulled me from my

thoughts. A knock followed, and I made my way to the door. "Yes?"

Fenwick pulled it open, poking his head inside. "Good morning, Miss Harmony. Hope you slept well," he said, pulling the door open further.

"Well enough, thanks. You're up early."

"Always. The palace is an exacting mistress! Apologies if I've disturbed you, but breakfast is almost ready downstairs and it's a rather fine spread, if I do say so myself. Fresh pastries, eggs, braided bread with nuts and currants with some truly delicious marmalades…"

My stomach growled and Fenwick's sharp ears perked at the sound. "I'll take that as a yes?"

We'd left the sandwiches untouched after last night's gut-churning game of Truth or Consequences and I was famished. "I'll check with the others."

"Excellent. I'll have your place settings and tea waiting," he replied as Hook, Duncan and Bonnie made their way into the room with Billy trailing in behind them. "I've also taken the liberty of arranging a little something extra for you and your companions. Our palace spa is excellent, and we'd love for you to pay them a visit. Complimentary, of course, at The Wizard's insistence."

We hadn't exactly ended on friendly terms with The Great and Powerful Oz—more like a reluctant truce—so I couldn't contain my surprise. "Really?"

"Indeed. After your long journey and all that is left to come, he thought you could all use some time to relax and recover."

"That's very kind—"

"We'll see what happens after we train," Hook cut in. "We've got work to do."

Fenwick straightened, smoothing the front of his immaculate coat. "Understood."

"And we've still got provisions left from our travels, so no need for breakfast either," Billy added. "Too much to do and too little time to do it in."

Fenwick lingered at the door, leaning on his cane, but made no move to step out.

"Sooo…" Billy paused and then shuffled her feet. "Thank you for your hospitality, though."

"My pleasure. Might I ask what your plans are for the day? Perhaps I can help with those in some way?"

I glanced at Duncan and Hook. "We *will* need a place to spar…and maybe access to the armory and some additional weapons if possible?"

"I've got you covered there." He pulled a map of the palace from a deep pocket inside his vest, then pulled it open and pressed it against the wall. "The training courtyard is mainly used by the palace guards here." He tapped a gleaming, black claw against a large rectangular symbol not far from the palace." He whipped out a pencil, drawing a quick circle around it. "I shall inform them that you'll be coming. They can assist you with whatever you need."

"Thanks again." Fenwick was annoying, but he did seem eager to help. "We'll head down there now."

"If you require anything else, grab hold of any of our little birdies in the palace. Whisper my name, and they'll fly right over to fetch me." He handed me the map and swept from the room, closing the door quietly behind him.

Billy let out an audible sigh. "That guy's exhausting."

I spared a glance at Billy; it was clear that Fenwick wasn't the only thing exhausting her. Her skin was nearly translucent, it was so pale, and the hollows under her eyes could've been two bruises if I didn't know better. All in all, it looked like someone had beat the shit out of her—which I might as well have—and I was so sorry for it. It took everything I had not to throw my arms around her and squeeze. The only thing that stopped me was the knowledge that she would hate every second of it.

All I could do now was try my best to make it up to her by leading us to victory against Almira.

No problem.

By the time we dressed, scarfed down some stale crumpets and stepped outside a short while later, the sun had fully risen. Another beautiful day in Oz…

Which, given the previous days of sunshine followed by utter chaos, meant absolutely nothing.

Hook walked a few feet away from me but other than a quick search of my face that seemed to pass muster, he kept his attention face front and opted out of idle chatter.

That was good.

Eyes on the prize, Harm.

We walked through the palace gardens a couple minutes later, following our map as Bonnie flew overhead, eyes peeled for some critter or other. The training grounds came into view, and they were already buzzing with activity. My jaw dropped as I took it all in. Dozens of guards trained and sparred, fists flying, swords clanging, morning stars whirring. Those not armored wore vibrant uniforms of every color imaginable, from deep violet to emerald green.

Duncan cracked his knuckles, grinning. "Now this is more like it."

"Looks more like a festival than training if you ask me," Hook muttered.

"There's something strange about it though, don't you think?" Billy turned, waving to an older guard in a crimson uniform, who was standing right by the entrance. "Why is everyone wearing all those different colors?"

He turned, running a hand through his thick, graying beard. "We're privately contracted."

I frowned. "Privately contracted? You mean mercenaries?"

"Something like that," he said with a shrug.

"And the ones dressed in green?" Duncan interjected.

The guard cocked an eyebrow. "The greencoats work for the Wizard, but they're no different from the rest of us. He's the most powerful, but our city has no king and other houses choose to protect themselves as well."

"You all seem well trained," Duncan said, seeming unbothered. "I'm looking for some very hearty sparring partners. Any recommendations?"

The grizzled veteran looked him up and down, standing up a little straighter. "Give me a few minutes, and I'll come work with you myself."

"You might want to bring some friends." Duncan softened the words with a wink and a smile, and the guard let out a hearty laugh.

"We'll see if you're still saying that once I'm done with you. I'll be right over; I'll grab some training swords."

The old guard headed toward a building that was marked as the armory on our map.

As we crossed into the training yard, soldiers watched and whispered as we approached, but I just rolled up my sleeves and kept my gaze forward. This was no time to get self-conscious. We had a witch to kill.

"Billy and I can work with Harm while you burn off some of that energy," Hook said, turning to Duncan.

Duncan sized up each group of soldiers as we passed, stretching his arms high over his head until his shoulders cracked. "Should be fun."

Hook let out a low hiss. "We're here to work, not play, Pretty Boy."

"I don't know. Watching the ox beat some cocky sellswords sounds like a damn good time to me," Billy said with a smirk.

Duncan bent into a deep bow. "Always happy to entertain."

"Just try not to embarrass us out there," Billy said. "After running your mouth to that guard, it would be pretty humiliating for me to have to come and clean up your messes."

"Not going to happen," Duncan said, his jaw flexing.

He might seem lighthearted on the outside, but he was taking this as seriously as any of us. I had no doubt these men were in for a very rough day.

He turned to me. "Once I'm done, we can do some more hand to hand combat training."

"Sounds good to me."

"Ready for us, big fellow?" We all turned to see the barrel-chested guard from before coming toward us with three other men, each of them built like the side of a barn. "Ask and you shall receive!"

Duncan's dimple flashed as he strode toward them and reached for a sword.

"Let's do this."

CHAPTER 20

The sun beat down on me as I snapped my whip through the air, getting more frustrated with every crack. Hook stood nearby, watching intently.

"Loosen your wrist," he advised, stepping closer. "You're fighting it."

"I'm trying," I said, gritting my teeth. "I know what I'm supposed to do, but without my magic it's like—"

"Forget that! And forget everything else, too. You didn't need magic to figure out how to defeat the bookworm, and you don't need magic now. It's just you and that whip."

I sucked in a breath, pushing away all thoughts of the trials, the witch, and my lost magic.

Just me and the whip.

Slowly, my muscles began to relax. Then, I snapped my arm forward, using more elbow than wrist as I yanked it back. The force rattled through the whip, and a thunderous crack split the air a heartbeat later, cleaner and sharper than I'd managed in days.

Hook flashed a rare smile. "Better," he said. "Now let's take five then try it again."

I swiped the sweat off my brow and took a deep breath. It was slow going, but it was going.

Across the courtyard, Duncan had drawn a crowd. Billy, who had drifted away a short while earlier to watch, had apparently decided that the time to spectate had ended, and they'd clearly been at it for a while. Admiring guards gathered all around them, hooting and hollering as the two of them squared up.

Duncan looked like he was enjoying every second of it.

He'd stripped down to a loose tunic, his practice sword in constant motion as Billy circled him like a gladiator who'd found herself tossed into the ring with a lion.

Duncan lunged first, his blade arcing toward her, but Billy didn't break stride. The blade passed inches over her head as she ducked, lashing out with an attack of her own in the same, fluid motion. Duncan made a slick move of his own, though, and my breath caught as he dropped his sword mid-swing and feinted to one side, neatly avoiding her blade, and tackling her at the waist. The crowd erupted into a mix of cheers and grumbles as Duncan pinned her to the ground.

Duncan grinned and pushed himself onto his forearms to gaze down at her. "Almost had me."

Just as coins were about to exchange hands, though, Billy grinned back. "*Almost?* You're far too cavalier with your soft bits, Ox."

Duncan's brows flew up, and Hook and I stepped closer, craning our necks to see how his fortune had changed.

"Perfect." Hook barked out a laugh.

Billy had Duncan's bait and tackle in a firm hold, a maniacal grin on her face as the men around them let out a collective, "Ooohhhh…"

His lean throat worked as he swallowed hard. "Draw?"

"Sure." Billy's eyes twinkled and she shrugged. "Draw it

is." She released him and he leapt off her like she'd been dipped in acid.

He shook his head and blew out a breath. "Gods, you're fast. You're terrifying." He reached down to offer her a hand.

Billy let him help her and patted his shoulder before releasing his hand. "Next time I'm gonna get you to use that weird, meathead magic of yours to see if I still have a chance."

"I'll look forward to it…and make sure I wear a codpiece."

The old guard stepped forward again with two fresh victims. The first round of them had gotten a sound whooping last time, and I couldn't help but respect the guy for coming back for another helping.

Duncan grinned and picked up his sword. "Do your worst."

The small crowd roared, but Hook couldn't have looked less impressed. "He seems to be enjoying himself."

"You should try it sometime." If I could've kicked myself, I would've. Why did I keep beating my head against the same stone wall?

His inky eyes stopped looking through me for a second and locked in. "You of all people should know I'm capable of enjoying myself."

Oh, fuck youuu...

I could feel my cheeks flushing, and I glared at him. "Look, I get it. You're jealous." I should've left it there, because it was true, but I was having regrets about bringing it up before I even finished the sentence, so I kept going. "Duncan is a great fighter and deserves some admiration. Deal with it."

There. Let him think I didn't mean something else entirely when I called out the jealousy.

Hook snorted. "Admiration, maybe. Hero worship? Not

so much. And the fact that he seems to crave it is pathetic. Now let's go again."

I wavered, still inclined to argue, because he was wrong. Duncan was just blowing off steam…making the best of a terrible situation. We could all be a little more like him. But arguing when Hook wasn't going to change his mind was a waste of very precious time, so I nodded, getting back into position.

We did a few dozen more reps, and each one felt smoother than the last. The movements were finally beginning to flow as I fell into a rhythm.

"Good," Hook said, breaking my focus. I glanced at him, surprised by the sincerity in his voice. "Your reflexes are getting sharper. It's rather uncanny."

As I was about to go back for another try, I noticed movement in the previously empty stands that overlooked the courtyard. Fenwick sat in one of the carved seats, watching. He caught my gaze and raised his hand in a quick wave.

I nodded in acknowledgement before turning away. Nearby, Billy had stepped away from the sparring circle, coming to lean against the stone wall next to Hook. She folded her arms, watching Duncan as he continued cutting through the competition like a hot knife through fresh churned butter.

"Your prince is winning both fights and hearts. That's hard to do."

"He's not my prince," I mumbled, feeling Hook's eyes on my face.

I turned away just in time to see Duncan reaching out a hand, pulling yet another beaten man to his feet. "You had me scared for a second," he said, patting his opponent on the back with an encouraging smile.

The young soldier beamed, obviously thrilled at the praise.

Hook let out a low growl and stepped away from the wall. "Tell me something, Westerly. Do you ever get tired of swinging your dick around?"

Silence fell over the soldiers in a flash as Duncan turned to face Hook, the smile slipping from his face. My fingers dug into my palm as I realized his eyes were already showing a hint of preternatural silver.

"What did you say?" His voice was calm, but cold as ice.

Hook's posture remained relaxed as he held the other man's gaze. "I asked if you ever tire of all this—" he waved dismissively toward the circle of guards, "self-congratulatory circle-jerking."

Gods, was he really going to do this?

Yeah, yeah he was. I groaned inwardly. It had been inevitable, so maybe it was better to deal with it now, before we went into battle?

Duncan took a slow step toward us, every muscle standing in sharp relief against his shirt that was looking smaller by the second.

"I'm training. Isn't that what we came here to do?"

"You're showing off," Hook corrected. "I've known enough men like you to recognize dick-swinging when I see it."

Duncan spat on the ground, and when he smiled this time, there was no dimple in sight. It was all challenge.

"If you've got it, why not swing it, pirate?" He flicked a glance to the spot just below Hook's belt. "But I guess if you don't…"

This had gone too far. My eyes darted between them as blood rushed to my head.

"Guys, we don't have to do this."

But Hook didn't seem to hear me. His expression darkened, and he rolled his shoulders. "It's been brewing from the start anyway. You want to fight, come and get it. But leave the toy behind."

Duncan let his training sword clatter to the ground, his hand straying toward the handle of his massive broadsword as Hook drew his saber. The boisterous crowd went dead silent as they faced off across the yard, the afternoon sunlight glinting off their deadly blades.

And then it began.

Duncan pumped his powerful thighs, sprinting at Hook in a blur of speed and power, his sword smashing into Hook's with a spray of sparks. I flinched, expecting Hook to go flying backward, but he didn't. Instead, he batted Duncan's sword with a swirl of his hand, letting out a low growl as they leapt apart.

"You'll need to do a whole lot better than that, Pretty Boy."

Hook pivoted around Duncan's next attack and unleashed a flurry of his own. His saber snaked in and out of view, striking faster than I could keep up with. But Duncan?

That was another question entirely.

He roared, not only keeping up with the pirate, but matching him blow for blow. Where Hook relied on speed and technique, Duncan got by on brute force, his sword cleaving through the air with enough force that one clean shot would mean certain death. His muscles rippled with every movement, and the sound of the metal clashing put my whip cracks to shame.

The fight was brutal, but Hook matched Duncan's ferocity with precise movements, never moving further than he had to. The message was clear; no ranged magic was needed.

"Unreal," Billy murmured, shaking her head in awe.

They were getting more serious with each passing moment, their feet sending up puffs of dirt each time they clashed. Hook stepped around a particularly nasty looking overhand from Duncan, and the former prince's eyes narrowed, the silver sheen growing deeper.

My stomach dropped and I stepped forward to intervene, but Billy's firm grip landed on my shoulder.

"Not yet."

"What do you mean? When, then?" I demanded, my voice shrill. "They're going to kill each other!"

She never took her eyes off the fight. "I have…had four brothers. If you really want them to get past their problems, let them work the testosterone and stupid out of their systems. This would be way scarier if they weren't both masters of their craft, because accidents happen. But right now, as good as they are, they're still toeing the line between fighting and an all-out deathmatch. Let it play out a little longer to see if they can come to an understanding."

I turned back toward them, unable to find the words to respond. If *this* was toeing the line, then I'd hate to see if they were going all out. Would we even be able to stop them if it got to that point?

But, deep down, I knew she was right. The tension between them had been brewing for way too long for them to just end this here and move on like nothing happened. Watching it was agony, though. Fear for them both had my throat in a vise.

Bonnie chose that moment to swoop down and land on my shoulder, and I couldn't help but hope that maybe I'd called her to me somehow. But as I reached for her mind, the connection was still nowhere to be found.

Across the yard, Duncan swung low, and Hook leapt smoothly over his blade, already thrusting out with a counter as he landed. Duncan's torn tunic bloomed with red from a nasty slice to his shoulder and he let out a growl.

"Is that all you've got?"

"You wish." Hook flashed a lethal grin as he lifted his arm. His black coattails waved like twin black flags, as if he stood in the eye of a storm. The next flurry of attacks seemed twice as fast as he harnessed the wind and used it to add speed behind every strike. Duncan's berserker power kicked into high gear as he took a dozen tiny cuts from Hook's whirlwind blade.

Nearby guards whispered nervously, backing away even further as he charged like a raging bull. Hook sidestepped the full swing of his broadsword that cleaved straight through a nearby training dummy, sending splinters spraying across the yard.

While Duncan tried to stop his momentum, Hook took full advantage of the opening, lunging forward as he recovered from his overzealous swing. Hook reared back, blade on a direct path to Duncan's unprotected torso, only to flick his wrist at the last second, slamming the hilt of his saber directly into Duncan's ribs with a resounding crunch.

The larger man flew backward, sending up a cloud of dust and debris as he crashed into the stone wall behind him.

Silence fell over the yard once again, only broken by both men's ragged breathing. Blood dripped from Duncan's forehead as he snarled, his eyes flashing brighter than I'd ever seen. His berserker magic had consumed him entirely, and he looked more beast than man as he leapt to his feet and let out a feral roar.

I charged forward as he and Hook faced off again, my pulse hammering in my ears. And this time, Billy didn't even try to stop me.

"James! Duncan! Stop this, now!"

Thunder seemed to crack overhead as swords clashed, the deafening crack ringing through the air loud. The two men stood frozen mid-strike, their blades still locked together as they trembled with exertion. For a long, agonizing second, nobody moved. Then, with a metallic snap, Duncan's broadsword snapped in half, the pointed end dropping to pierce the ground between them.

Duncan let out a groan and sank to his knees, pressing a hand to his surely shattered ribs. I'd been there myself, after falling off the crow's nest of The Jolly Roger running the Devil's Gauntlet. It was excruciating, each breath feeling as though a hot blade jabbed through the bones.

Bonnie let out a low, mournful squawk as I shot Hook a pleading look. He grunted as he stepped forward, thrusting his saber back into its sheath. Duncan didn't—or couldn't—muster the will to lift his head as Hook hovered his hand over Duncan's.

I held my breath, only letting it go when the agony on Duncan's face faded and Hook pulled away. He spared a final glance toward me, then turned away without a word, striding across the courtyard.

As much as part of me wanted to go after him, now wasn't the time. I shifted my attention back to Duncan and began to head his way, but Billy got there first, strolling up like it was another random day.

She snatched a cloth from her quiver and pressed it against his still bleeding shoulder, unbothered by the lingering glow in his eyes or the rumbling breaths of his fading fury.

"Looks like you're gonna need a new sword there, handsome."

CHAPTER 21

The tension from the courtyard stayed with me, buzzing beneath my skin as me, Billy, and Duncan with Bonnie on his bloodied shoulder headed back to the palace a short while later.

I'd never seen two people fight like that before. Never mind two people who were supposed to be on the same side. The memory kept replaying in my mind. From the unchecked fury I'd seen in Duncan, to the way Hook had cut through his broadsword like it was paper made it impossible to think of anything else.

What would've happened if we hadn't been watching?

A chill rolled through me as I asked myself the question for the dozenth time. Would he and Duncan even be able to work together after what had happened? I could only pray Billy was right about them needing to get it out of their system.

But I couldn't stop the little voice inside my head that wondered if *"fighting it out"* wound up actually being the solution, then what did that say for her *other* little nugget of wisdom when it came to me and Hook?

I shook my head furiously to shake the thought loose and glanced over at Duncan.

"How are the ribs?"

Duncan blinked and squinted my way, as if he was just waking up from a fitful sleep. "Fucker is as good of a Whisper as he is a swordsman. I'll be fine."

His whole demeanor had changed, like someone had blown out the candle inside him, so I was far from convinced that he was truly fine, but now wasn't the time to push. As much as my heart hurt for him, his pride needed a chance to recover. I only hoped that was the worst of his injuries.

"It's lunch time anyway. Let's grab something to eat. Food always helps, right?"

"Always," Billy agreed as she yanked off her headscarf to run a hand through her tawny curls.

Duncan didn't argue, so we ducked into the palace kitchens, grabbing some fresh fruit and sandwiches from the cook, and then headed back to our quarters.

As we neared the doors, Fenwick came into view. He broke into soft applause as we approached, a smile curving his lips.

"Bravo, Sir Duncan. I know it didn't end how you would've liked, but it was a truly thrilling performance by both you and your pirate comrade. Impressive."

Duncan's jaw tightened, but he dipped his head. "Glad you enjoyed the show."

"I hope I didn't offend," Fenwick said, raising a hand. He glanced at our spoils from the kitchen and frowned. "Enjoy your lunch but please don't eat too much, my friends. You'll want to save room for tonight's formal supper."

I held back a groan. While I did want to see The Wizard again for reasons I didn't feel like exploring, a fancy party was about the last thing any of us needed right now.

"I wouldn't normally, but I must insist on a couple hours

of your time to satisfy The Wizard's request," he continued, practically reading my mind. "He has put out the edict that all should treat you as revered guests here in Oz, but he's sticking his neck out to do so. When The Wicked Witch finds out he's openly defying her, and she *will* find out, there will be hell to pay. He's rightfully concerned and wants to make sure you all understand the delicate balance of life here in The City. I think he could use some reassurances."

"What kind of reassurances?"

"That you believe you can defeat Almira." He swiped a nonexistent piece of dust from his lapel. "That, if you don't pass the trials, you have a plan in place to help protect The Emerald City going forward. And that, no matter what happens, you don't intend to…upset the applecart as one would say, in regards to his true identity. The Wizard *does* want to help you, Harmony."

The unspoken "but" was clear; An alliance was a two-way street.

After my time in Alabaster, I was no stranger to politics, and we were in no position to be turning away a powerful ally. *Especially* if I didn't pass the trials. We could be stuck here for…ever.

The thought nearly sent me into a spiral. I'd never see Molly or Fetch again. I'd never get to read the prophecy my mother left for me. Billy would never avenge her brothers.

I twisted the pearl ring on my finger and pushed those dark thoughts away, turning my attention back to Fenwick.

"What time do we need to be there?"

Fenwick took a glance at his pocket watch. "I'll make sure to have a selection of appropriate attire in your closets. Be downstairs at six o'clock sharp. See you then." He wriggled his fingers in a wave and a long look in Billy's direction, then he strode off without another word.

Duncan sighed as we stepped into the common room.

"Damn. I was hoping I'd have time to go into town and commission a new sword."

I craned my neck to peer into Hook's room, but there was no sign of him. "Let's wash up and all three of us can go."

He hesitated for a moment, then nodded.

Billy, on the other hand, was shaking her head. "I'm going to stay here with Bonnie and take a nap. I didn't get much sleep and it's probably good if one of us stays behind anyway, in case tall, dark, and cranky comes back looking for us."

The three of us scarfed down some lunch and then bathed. The engineers of Emerald City had figured a way to carry water all through the palace and distribute it through these amazing nozzles that shot streams of it hard enough to take the paint off a wall. As I stood beneath the steamy spray, it felt like no less than a miracle on my aching muscles.

I didn't enjoy it for nearly long enough. I could have stayed for hours, but we had shit to handle.

Duncan and I were headed down the palace steps less than half an hour later, marching toward the bustling streets. We had some cleaning up to do in our proverbial house, and it needed to happen fast. The trials loomed ahead, barely a day out, and I had a feeling we'd need each other more than ever if we were going to pass. Especially since I had yet to regain even a lick of my magic.

I shot a look at my companion, who was silent as we walked, his steps heavy and his eyes distant as the tension radiated off him.

"How are you feeling for real?"

He shrugged. "Honestly? Not great. I don't remember the last time I lost like that. Or…lost ever, really."

"Lost like *what?*" I asked, incredulous. "You were still amazing. I've seen you defeat a bear once, remember. No one else in the world—this or any other—could've done what you did."

He let out a dry laugh. "You don't get it, Harm. Straight up brawls like that are my specialty, and he beat me anyway."

"By a hair." But Duncan knew as well as I did that Hook had tricks up his sleeve that he hadn't even used. He could've used lightning or those shadow chains or who knew what else, but he'd wanted to beat Duncan fair and square.

"I'm not looking forward to having to see him again. Not after losing control like that. It's humiliating, and beneath me. But he pissed me off, pressuring Billy last night when she was in a bad way, and then today…it's like he knows exactly how to yank my chain. Something inside me snapped. This was exactly what Billy asked me about at her little card game. When I was under the most pressure, I cracked. I failed her. I failed you," he paused to rake a hand through his hair with a growl, "And I met every low expectation that bastard had of me."

"You're wrong. I think he's got more respect for you than you think. He wouldn't have used his mending blessing on you if he didn't. Have you noticed he's quick to use some, and less to use others?"

Duncan shrugged. "I guess so."

"That one in particular was gifted to him by a friend. He uses it sparingly. If he thought as little of you as you're saying, he'd have walked away and let you suffer."

Duncan seemed to chew on that for a moment and then let out a sigh. "Either way, that fight showed me I still have work to do."

"Don't we all? But we're getting better and better. We're helping each other grow, even though it might not feel that way." I shuddered as I gave his forearm a gentle squeeze. "If you two fight half that hard against Almira, we might actually have a shot at winning."

He groaned, a hint of a smile creeping onto his lips. "I don't even want to think about using my Whisper right now.

Pretty sure I tore half the muscles in my body. I'm lucky the bastard managed the worst of it."

"I really need to get my magic back, then find a way to step up and match you guys. I don't think I can take it if I have to play the helpless damsel for another fight."

"You'll get there," he said, laying a hand on my shoulder. "And once you do, Almira will *really* be in for it."

I was half listening as I caught sight of something that stopped me in my tracks.

"No way!" I stared at a quaint, wooden shop on the left side of the street. It was a bit shoddier than its neighbors, but that wasn't what made it stand out to me. Instead, my eyes were on the wooden sign hanging out front, which read, "Smithson and Smitty's Smithery." A plume of smoke curled from the stone chimney, and I could smell the faint tang of hot metal in the air.

"What?"

"I know those names…"

Duncan cocked an eyebrow. "From Alabaster?"

"The Smudge, and in a little town near Neverland. I wonder if they're the same guys."

Only one way to find out.

The door creaked softly as I pushed it open. In most ways, it was a normal blacksmithing shop, complete with iron in various lengths lined up against the walls, massive anvils, and sturdy bellows. But, like everything in Emerald City, it had a little something extra. Ornate clockwork gears ticked gently next to the iron length, with long copper pipes that connected them to a variety of instruments and gauges.

And, sure enough, Smitty was standing over the forge, pulling on a chain that pumped the bellows as he pulled a glowing, orange blade from the heart of the forge. He was sturdy and broad as ever but looked a little older than I remembered him.

On the other side of the room, the older Smithson stood behind the counter, polishing a dagger.

Smitty glanced up as we entered. "Afternoon. What can we do for you?"

I knew that I could have made Duncan his sword, but I didn't think that was where I needed to be putting my time. Practicing, building my magic, not a weapon for Duncan was what I had to do.

We stepped up and Duncan leaned on the counter. "Looking to have a new sword forged. Preferably as sturdy as you can make it."

"Size?"

Smithson's eyes bulged as Duncan pulled the bottom half of the broken weapon from its sheath, setting it on the counter.

"Hellfire…Never seen anything like it. And to see it cut clean through like this…" He sucked in a breath, examining the hilt more closely. "Yeah, we can definitely make you a sturdy blade. Want us to fix it to the same hilt?"

He shrugged. "Whatever works best. As long as it won't break on me."

I leaned forward, suddenly inspired. "What is that stone on the Yellow Brick Road made out of? It almost seemed kind of metallic. Wonder if you could incorporate something like that."

The older blacksmith, Smithson, stepped up behind me.

"You've got a good eye, miss. But the stuff is notoriously hard to work with. The forge doesn't get quite hot enough to fully melt the bricks, so while it's easy enough to punch out into blocks, it takes ages to hammer it out and shape it into a blade. We can try, but it'll cost you a pretty penny."

"Money won't be an issue," I said, "but there is a small catch."

Smitty raised a soot-stained eyebrow.

"We need it by tomorrow night." I pasted a bright smile on my face, hoping to trick them into feeling good about my declaration.

The two exchanged a look, and the younger was first to speak. "You're asking us to forge you an unbreakable sword, that size, in one day?"

Duncan shrugged, a slight smile on his lips. "More or less. But we can pay you handsomely for it."

Smitty cut in, "Ain't a matter of money. It just can't be done. Not with our setup here."

"Because of the forge?"

The blacksmith nodded. "It'd take us *a week* to get a clean edge on that kind of blade at the heat we can manage here."

"Okay, so do you have any already made that I could buy that are close to fitting the bill?"

"Citizens don't really have a need for anything like that, and even the ones the guards at the palace use are half that size."

Duncan slumped, then looked over at me, clearly ready to call it quits. But the gears in my mind were already turning.

Just like everything else that had gotten me here, this problem was put before me for a reason. I had to put my head down and press on, no matter what obstacles we faced.

Destiny is like a river...

"I—I'll make the forge work for you, so it will get hot enough," I said, startling even myself by how confident I sounded. Making a sword, or the tip of my whip was one thing, but a forge?

Smitty folded his arms across his chest, amusement sparking in his eyes. "And what makes you think you can manage that? You don't think we've tried, or is it that you just think you'll figure out something that we haven't?"

"I've got a knack for finding creative solutions to tricky

problems." I stuffed my hand into my pouch, fishing out my easy lockpick and presenting it for their inspection.

It was a spectacular specimen of precision engineering, and it had saved my skin more times than I cared to count. I turned it slowly to show them the delicate gears and switches on the side.

Smitty took it from my hand, more intrigued with each passing second. "You made this, eh?"

"I did," I confirmed. "And I'm not just a tinker; my pa was a smith like yourself, so I know my way around a forge. I really think I can come up with a way to do this if you give me a chance."

Smitty passed the lockpick back, looking me up and down, as if seeing me for the first time. "Hope you realize that we'll need it done fast. Even if we can work it as easily as steel, a sword that size will still take a good six hours to make even with both of us working on it, assuming you want it done right."

The challenge of the forge was something to focus on outside of the trials ahead of us and it gave me a spur of excitement. "We do. Give me until tomorrow morning, first thing, to bring you a solution. If I can get it done with at least eight hours left to work, do you think you can pull it off?"

A grin spread across his wrinkled face. "You get me a hotter forge, and we'll make you the greatest sword this city's ever seen."

My thoughts drifted to the whip tied to my side. I'd known in my gut when I made the tip at Smithson's place, it was missing an element. Hopefully I'd have a little extra time to rectify that while we were here with a forge hot enough to…do whatever it was I still needed to do.

The younger smith nodded, already grabbing his parchment and charcoal. "I'll start sketching out a design for the hilt and grip. We'll want to make a whole new one for something like this."

With that settled, Duncan and I took our stuff and left the shop, back out into the bustling streets of the market district. We were halfway back to the palace, each lost in our own thoughts, when he slowed his steps and glanced my way.

"Hook *can* be an asshole, but I get why you picked him…"

My steps faltered and he slowed to a stop. A riot of emotions rushed over me all at once. Embarrassment, relief, sadness. I opened my mouth to deny it, because he'd said out loud what I didn't even want to admit to myself, never mind to him. But when I looked into his soft, gray eyes, I couldn't form the words.

His smile was gentle. "It's okay. I'm not mad. We made no promises to each other." He looked off in the distance and let out a low, bittersweet chuckle. "That's not to say I didn't have high hopes. But as soon as I saw the two of you together, I knew. I didn't want to believe it. Fought it every step of the way, but the way you look at him? You never looked at me that way. And he…he looks at you like I wish I could."

I folded my arms around myself, suddenly chilly despite the heat in my cheeks. "It's not like that. We aren't together." *Mostly*? "And even if I wanted to be, I don't see a way that we ever could. Not really."

Not when I knew the guilt he held to his chest in a death grip made every day on this earth a fair bit of torture and freeing him of it was beyond my power…it was a task only he could tackle, if he even wanted to.

"This isn't jealousy talking—I've come to terms with it now," Duncan continued, "but I'm glad to hear you say that."

I winced. "And why is that?"

His face was grim as he considered his answer. "Because he isn't whole, Harm. Something inside him is broken. And while I do think, despite his outward nature, he's a good man and cares deeply for you, I don't think he can give you what you need."

It was nothing I didn't already know…So why did it feel like I'd been kicked by a mule right in the chest? He must've seen my expression because he cupped my chin and gave me a reassuring smile.

"That doesn't mean you won't find it one day. The thing you're looking for."

But we both know it won't be with me. He didn't say the words, yet they couldn't have been clearer if he'd shouted it, then spelled it out on a piece of paper.

A piece of me mourned the loss of what we'd had in Alabaster at a time that we'd both needed that connection so much—a gentle affection that had burned slow and careful. But the bigger part of me was proud of him. Duncan deserved more than being some woman's second choice, and he knew it.

"We should probably get back," I murmured, managing a smile in return. "It's getting late, and I want to get a head start on the plans for Smitty and Smithson before the banquet."

"Shit. I almost forgot about that."

He broke into long strides, and I lurched into motion after him, jogging to keep pace.

Since we were clearing the air, I might as well go whole hog with it…

"Duncan, there is one little thing I should also probably mention before we get back to the palace."

He turned, cocking his head at me. "What's that?"

I scratched my chin and let out a sigh.

"I don't have the faintest clue how to fix that forge."

CHAPTER 22

I rubbed my eyes, blinking down at the scribbled notes and sketches I'd spent the last hour on. The paper was full to the margins, but I had yet to come up with anything of substance, just half-formed good ideas, and an equal number of really bad ones that wouldn't come close to solving the forge's problems.

I squeezed the pencil tight enough to nearly snap it.

You can do this, I told myself, for the dozenth time, but the words felt hollow.

I was in over my head. In the past, getting stuck had meant I needed to relax and trust in my subconscious to step in and solve the problem for me. Even before I'd known I was a Whisper, my magic had been a tiny ember inside that helped guide me. And, now that it was gone, I was grasping at straws, frantic and making mistakes where normally I wouldn't.

I snatched up the loupe again, pressing it to my eye. The lens still magnified the tiny lines and curves in my drawing, but the little threads of magic I'd once been able to see were nowhere to be found.

A curse slipped past my lips as I tossed it down, shoving it to the other side of the desk. My chair squeaked as I pushed away from my workstation and stood, stretching my aching back. Dinnertime was quickly approaching. I let out a long sigh, glancing into the hall, where Hook had appeared an hour earlier before disappearing again into his room.

Where had he been all afternoon?

"Did you look in your closet yet?"

I jerked back, surprised to see Billy suddenly standing in the doorway.

"Boy, you're stealthy."

"Yeah. It's my thing." She crossed her arms and leaned on the door jam. "So did you?"

I frowned. "Look in the closet? No, not yet."

"Well I have, and this is looking like it's shaping up to be a fancy event we gotta attend. You want to start getting ready? You can help me pick a dress, and maybe I can help you with that hair?" One winged brow shot up, and I couldn't hold back a laugh.

"That bad, huh?"

"Not great," she admitted with a grin.

I was glad to see that she looked far more rested and at ease than she had before the nap. In fact, she seemed lighter...freer somehow. Maybe telling her story had helped her some after all?

"Come on, Princess. Stalling isn't going to make it any easier."

I gave the notes on my desk one last longing look and pushed myself to stand. A couple hours away from it might be good. Maybe it all needed a little time to brew inside my head.

Somehow, it never occurred to me that this Billy O'Don-nelly would have any clue about hair *or* clothes, but just like every other version of the woman, she was full of surprises. Forty-five minutes later, she'd stuffed me into an emerald green column of silk that skimmed my modest curves in the most flattering way. Better yet, with a little water, a dab of hair cream, and a lot of muscle, she'd managed to style my chin-length chestnut locks into a sexy side-swept tousle.

"Wow. You're a genius." I turned left and right, admiring myself in the mirror.

"Damn right I am. Now get out so I can finish dressing myself."

We'd picked a gown for her as well, but I knew she didn't feel comfortable with me seeing her get dressed, so I didn't resist as she herded me toward the door like I was a reluctant cow.

"Be out in a few."

She closed the door in my face, and I wheeled around just as Hook stepped out of his room.

I froze in place, the breath in my chest stilling as I stared. He was painfully handsome in the tailored waistcoat, the black velvet hugging his broad shoulders, silver accents curling around his collar to create the perfect foil for those onyx eyes. Clean-shaven, the angle of his jaw was even more pronounced. Despite the distance between us, the sandal-wood and spice of his skin reached me.

My breath caught in my throat as his gaze turned molten, sliding slowly from my face to my feet and back up again. His attention was almost physical, sending heat flooding through my cheeks and my heart into a frantic stutter. It was a relief when Duncan's door swung open, shattering the tension between us.

He stepped out, glancing between us as he straightened the sleeves of his fitted jacket. "Am I interrupting some-thing?" His eyes seemed even brighter than usual, practically glowing in contrast to his dove gray waistcoat. He looked every bit the second son of a king raised in privilege, and the difference between the two men had never been starker than it was now. As sharp and refined as Hook appeared in those clothes, there was still an untamed wildness to him that no suit could hide.

I shook my head in response, still not trusting myself to speak.

Duncan's eyes traveled appreciatively over my gown, and he smiled. "You look great."

"What am I, chopped liver?" Hook deadpanned.

I whipped my head toward him in surprise and Duncan barked out a laugh.

"Sure, you look good too."

It was their first time in the same room together since the fight and, so far, so good. I could only pray that Billy had it right, and this fragile truce would stick and maybe even grow stronger.

As if I'd wished her into existence, her door swung open, and she stepped into view. If the deep blue gown had looked lovely when I'd pulled it off the hanger, on Billy, it was a dream. Her headscarf was gone, revealing a tumble of tawny-colored hair that framed her face in soft, feminine curls. Her dress was covered in a million beads, cut low to reveal award-worthy cleavage, and clung to her in all the right places on its way down over her waist and hips.

The rough and tumble ranger we all knew was nowhere to be found.

She chewed on her bottom lip for a second, then threw her shoulders back and popped one hip to reveal a slit that bared a swath of skin from ankle to thigh, vamping it up.

"What do you think?"

It didn't take a witch to know what Duncan thought. He

was staring at her, eyes wide, looking like someone just slapped him with a fish.

"You look like a goddess, Billy." He breathed the words, choking a bit on her name.

"Yeah, well, don't get used to it," she snorted, her cheeks flushing.

I shook my head in awe. "If we're supposed to charm them tonight—honey versus vinegar—then you're a whole damned pot of honey."

"Agreed," Duncan added.

She waved us off with a *harumph,* but not before I noticed the sparkle in her gaze. "Eyes up here, Ox."

Bonnie let out a squawk as she lit onto Duncan's shoulder and preened herself.

"Bonnie wants to look her best too," Billy added with a chuckle.

The morning's tension seemed to have vanished by the time we made our way toward the dining hall a few minutes later. As we got closer, I couldn't shake the anxious feeling in my gut.

We were still woefully unprepared for tomorrow night's trials, and what little we'd learned hadn't told us much. Wisdom. Heart. Courage.

And while tonight wasn't a physical battle, the stakes felt just as high as they had at the training grounds this morning. At least you could see a fist or a sword coming. The people of Emerald City didn't need a blade to stab you in the back. As much as The Wizard of Oz might need reassurances from me, I could use some myself. He might be a fraud, but his influence was all too real. If we *did* find a way to succeed in the trials, we'd need the folks of Emerald City on our side if we wanted a chance in hell at marching on Almira's fortress in Oz and taking her down.

And if we didn't pass my mother's tests?

We'd need them even more. Which meant I had to show Willy Fallowell, The Great and Powerful Wizard of Oz, exactly why his doppelganger loved me so much.

I squared my shoulders and prepared to play the most dangerous game of all.

CHAPTER 23

We stepped into the formal dining room, and as much as I missed my pants and boots, I could've kissed Fenwick for sending us clothes to wear because I'd have felt foolish in anything less.

"Fenwick's house budget must be outrageous," Billy shook her head. "If I'd known, we should have asked for more options."

The place was decked out in gold and green from floor to ceiling. The tile floors were patterned squares alternating colors, glittering under the multitude of hanging golden ornate chandeliers.

Wall hangings and floor to ceiling mirrors decked the walls so that if you looked in one, you could see the reflection going on and on behind you. Chairs and settees were strewn about seemingly at random and yet the plush cushioned seats were put together so people could gather and chat at leisure.

I had to hand it to those servants Fenwick had been training when we'd first met, I could've found a lash in my eye from the reflection off that goldenware.

A golden food-covered tray whirred slowly past, flying on tiny propellers, and Duncan reached over to snag some kind of miniature puff.

He popped it into his mouth and groaned. "Delicious."

Before I could grab one myself, Fenwick appeared, looking us up and down with a wide grin.

"You've all cleaned up beautifully. Well done." His gaze lingered on Billy a little too long.

Her eyes narrowed. "Enjoying the view?"

"Absolutely. Though it seems I have yet again failed to impress you…" He let out a dramatic sigh. "Tell me, is it because I'm not fully human? I wouldn't have expected that to be a problem…"

I drew back and shot a glance at Billy, whose face had gone bone white. Surely, he didn't know the truth about her. If so, how? Duncan and Hook had both stiffened, and I knew they were wondering the same.

"We're quite progressive here in Emerald City, you know," he continued. "Some of our happiest couples are a bit of this, a dash of that. Variety is the spice of life, after all."

Some of the color returned to her cheeks and she shrugged. "I feel like booze is the only spice I need in my life right now. You want to impress? Buy me a drink."

Fenwick bowed. "Your wish is my command. Have a seat next to your name cards and I'll be right back."

The fox walked off, heading toward the far side of the room as I made my way toward my seat at the long, oval table in the center of the room, doing my best to control the storm of emotions raging inside me.

"You alright?" Hook whispered.

"All good," I lied. I was a wreck. Now that we were here, I felt the weight of wasting time on my shoulders. I wanted to run back to our rooms and try to figure out the forge, wanted to train, anything but be here. Even though *here* was where the prophecy waited.

I'd barely made any progress on the forge problem, and now I had to stare into the face of my beloved father, and put aside years of trust to see through to the man behind the curtain.

"Do we think we're getting the man or the massive talking head tonight?" Billy glanced around the room as if to check that she hadn't missed him.

"I hope he realizes that would be ridiculous," Hook replied, settling into his chair to my right as I took my seat.

As big as the table was, his delicious scent still curled around me like an embrace, and I forced myself to breathe through my mouth. The last thing I needed was another distraction.

Duncan nodded. "It certainly wouldn't endear him to me any. Although I'm not sure there is much that would at this point..."

I glanced around the rest of the table to see only two more place settings but no name cards.

"Only one way to find out."

Olga stepped into the room with one of the maids, gesturing to a bouquet of flowers with a frown. As the maid scooped up the vase and scurried away with it, the taller, elegant blond headed in our direction toward the doors of the kitchen.

"Excuse me, Olga?" I called out to her.

She slowed, arching a brow at me. "Yes?"

Her tone was cool, and it was clear she was still miffed at us for bullying our way into the solarium together the day before.

"Will The Wizard of Oz be joining us for dinner this evening?"

Her eyes went wide, and a surprised laugh shot out of her

mouth. "Oh, my, no. He doesn't leave the solarium. He's far too busy..." she rolled her hands, "wizarding as wizards do, to spend time socializing and the like. No matter how... *important* our guests believe themselves to be. Now if you'll excuse me, I must see about the duck." Her smile was a little slice of winter as she turned and swept away.

"I guess we won't be adding her to our list of fans any time soon," Billy murmured.

I was about to agree when Fenwick stepped back through the arched doorway with a nattily dressed Willy Fallowell by his side, balancing a gleaming copper tray laden with glass goblets filled with deep violet liquid.

The fox set it carefully before Billy, a triumphant smile on his lips as he tried not to drool on her dress. "Ask and you shall receive, my lady."

Billy took a careful sip, eyes narrowed before widening in surprise. "Blackberry mead," she murmured, raising her glass in a grudging salute in Fenwick's direction. "Maybe this honey pot thing isn't so bad after all," she murmured under her breath.

"You all remember *Lord* Fallowell," Fenwick said. Ah, so that's how it would be played? He was Lord Fallowell now.

Willy smiled mostly in my direction, avoiding even a glance over at Hook and the others.

"He's agreed to take time from his busy day to break bread with you all on the eve of the trials. Excuse me if you would while I check on dinner." Fenwick bowed and backed away.

Lord Fallowell wore a fitted waistcoat in a green so dark it was nearly black, and his hair was combed back away from his face. My heart gave a squeeze as he took his seat to my left.

"Good to see you all again," he said.

The others were silent, so I made sure to lay it on thick with a wide smile and all.

"Good to see you as well! I'm so glad you could make it, what with your busy schedule."

"How does it work, exactly?" Hook's gaze was intense as he studied the older man like he was trying to drill directly into his brain. "The Wizard runs the city, and you act as his eyes and ears?"

"Oh no," the older man said with a cough and a forced chuckle. "The Great Wizard sees all. I act as a sort of an emissary on his behalf. I travel outside the palace to gather information about any disputes or problems and bring the information back to The Wizard to rule upon. Fenwick makes sure that both I and The," he cleared his throat, "Wizard have everything we need to do our jobs effectively, handles our work calendars, and oversees all the employees in the house. Olga works under Fenwick, delegating various tasks, and manages most of the day-to-day scheduling and maintenance issues. We run a tight ship, and it works. But enough about me. How has your stay been?" he asked. "People in the city bothering you much?"

"We've been busy, and though people are curious, they haven't bothered us much." I said.

He shook out his napkin and laid it over his lap. "That's good."

I dropped my voice low. "Do you think Almira knows you allowed us in and are helping us?"

He glanced around surreptitiously and then leaned closer.

"Be careful what you say. While I do trust the staff within these walls, Almira does seem to have eyes and ears in the city. That said, I have my own eyes and ears, and I know she's not returned to Oz yet. I think you're safe for now."

"Likely replenishing her strength for another attack," I whispered.

"More likely, preparing for your arrival in C'an Saas. Now that you've made it and are within these walls behind your mother's protection, she might not bother coming back here."

He looked so hopeful, and I didn't want to dash that fragile belief so I stayed quiet. Maybe he was right. But something told me that Almira wasn't the type to forgive a slight so easily.

Lord Fallowell clapped his hands, startling me. "Ooh, here comes the first course now! We had the chef pull out all the stops for you."

A whirring sound had my hand going to my hip, but my whip wasn't there. I half expected some sort of attack. Instead, a neat row of miniature hot air balloons, each with a wicker basket hanging below it, came from the kitchen about three feet apart, gears clicking as they flitted through the air.

Hot air balloons. Like those in Alabaster.

Each was a different color, one the most royal of blues, another vibrant, rich purple. I couldn't help but smile as they each veered off toward a specific guest around the table. The deep blue one headed straight for Billy. I watched in delight as the basket detached from the balloon and dropped to her plate. Inside the basket sat a colored egg in a matching shade. She craned her head to peer down at it as the top sprung open to reveal the appetizer inside.

She leaned closer to sniff.

"Savory egg custard," Lord Fallowell said, his chest puffing with pride as if he'd baked it himself. "The idea for the delivery system was mine."

Still unwilling to forgive their first meeting, Billy shrugged and dug the spoon in. "As long as you feed me, I don't care how the food gets here, or how pretty it is."

The rest of the balloons found their diner, a black one heading for Hook, and a crimson one for me.

"To match your boots," Fallowell said with a smile that took me back to my childhood and squeezed at my heart. As much as I wanted to stay angry at the detached cruelty of his words that night in the solarium, it was hard to separate the two.

I tucked the thought into a dark corner of my brain and focused on the food.

It didn't hurt that the custard was delicious. Thick and rich, loaded with butter and pepper that slid easy down my throat. I let out a little moan of pleasure. Beside me, Hook stiffened, and goosebumps broke out on my arms as I did my best to ignore him and enjoy my custard.

The food just got better with each course. Crisp, roasted duck glazed with honey and sprinkled with toasted walnuts. Fluffy potatoes whipped with cream, garnished with sprigs of fresh herbs. Colorful vegetables, perfectly sautéed, and baskets of warm, crusty bread with thyme olive oil for dipping.

All the while, conversation flowed, made easier with wine and mead as the evening wore on.

"Thank you so much for hosting us," I said, setting down my fork with a sigh. "But I give up. I can't eat any more."

Lord Fallowell beamed and beckoned for me with one hand. "Then come for a walk with me. There's something I'd like to show you while the chef finishes up dessert."

"I'll ask the others if they'd like to join us."

"I don't mean to offend, but all three of them are rather scary. The woman, most of all, and I would like to speak with you alone."

This could be my chance to get the prophecy and I was going to take it with both hands if I could.

I leaned toward Hook, ignoring the rush of heat that shot through me as our thighs pressed together.

"Lord Fallowell would like to show me something. I'll be back shortly."

Hook scowled and pushed back his chair, but I laid a hand on his forearm and shook my head as I leaned closer to whisper in his ear.

"I'll be fine. I think he wants to tell me something important and can't in front of everyone. This is the moment I've been waiting for. If I'm not back in fifteen minutes, you can come find me."

He grunted in agreement, but he wasn't happy about it.

Fallowell and I stood, and he held out his arm. I slipped mine through it, and tried not to let the rush of memories flood in.

Me and my Pawpaw, skipping down the cobbled streets of The Hollow, arm in arm, just like this as he made up a silly song about the baker and his stale pies.

Me and my Pawpaw, standing at the edge of the woods, holding hands and our breath as we waited to see if Fetch managed to catch us something for the soup pot after a bad day of bow hunting.

I pushed my shoulders back and lifted my chin, reminding myself to stay strong. I was on a mission to get some assurances from the most powerful person in Oz that, whether we passed or failed tomorrow, he could be counted on as an ally against The Wicked Witch going forward. A man who held the prophecy my mother left for me.

He led me up a grand, spiral staircase to the third floor in silence, only speaking once we'd rounded the corner and made our way down another long hallway. Even then, his voice was for my ears only, hushed low.

"I do fear speaking in front of Fenwick at times. He's a worry wart, and I think he's concerned that you and your friends know something so damning about me. Something that could turn this whole city upside down. I told him I believed you would keep my secret." He glanced down at me to study my face. "Am I right about that, Harmony?"

Fenwick had claimed it was the wizard who had concerns, but I wasn't about to pick nits.

I considered my words carefully before replying. "I have a question for you first, Lord Fallowell; If I don't complete the trials so that I can return to C'an Saas to face Almira there… then what? Will you cast us out of the city and into her hands, or will you counsel the people to stand with us against her and help us fight?"

His neck waddle trembled as he shook his head. "I made a vow to your mother, and I would keep it. You and yours would be welcome to stay in Emerald City for as long as you chose. We would figure out how to deal with The Wicked Witch when the time came. Together."

That was the answer I was looking for. I only wished I was as good at detecting bullshit as Billy…

"Is there anything I can say that will convince you to give me the prophecy now if I vow to complete the trials?"

He shook his head ruefully, dashing my hopes before he spoke another word. "Forgive me for not making it clearer. It's magically bound. I can't access the safe she locked it in until the trials have been completed. No one can. That was your mother's choice, not mine, and she had her reasons. I know that isn't what you hoped to hear tonight…" He shifted uncomfortably and then sighed. "So where does this leave us, Harmony? Can I consider you my ally?"

I stared at him for a long moment and then nodded. "As long as you're not abusing your power, and you honor the promises you made to my mother, your secret is safe with me."

"Good." He blew out a shuddering breath. "That's good. He will surely sleep better knowing, and so will I, quite frankly."

We slowed to a stop as we reached a massive set of doors. The tension seemed to melt away and his sudden, almost childlike smile of anticipation hit me right in the heart.

So familiar, it brought me back to a very clear memory of me and my father. The first time he'd ever taken me to work in the forge with him. When I stepped inside it was to see a little workstation, complete with a tiny stool, and my own set of tongs and small hammer, and even a miniature leather apron he'd sloppily sewn an "H" onto. I'd worked on my first set of shoes for a neighbor's pony.

"Wait until you see this…"

I blinked hard and forced a wobbly smile as he tugged the doors open. "I'm excited!"

He led me into a room—not. Not a room. A soaring, glass-ceilinged sanctuary, full of trees, and ferns, and most of all?

Birds. Birds singing and flying and filling the air with their variety of noises, the whoosh of their wings.

"Aren't they magnificent?" he breathed.

They were. And they were *everywhere*.

I picked my way over the mossy ground, watching a pair of robins flit past, both chasing the same dragonfly. A bold blue jay cried out from its perch on the branch of a silvery willow tree. Red-winged blackbirds dipped and weaved through lower branches, as if they were practicing some sort of obstacle course.

I paused, watching as a swallow-tailed kite dropped from the trees above, doing a neat little twirl before using its tail like a rudder to straighten and swoop back high into the air.

"It's beautiful." I closed my eyes for a second and sucked in a lung full of air, lovely and cool from the mist pouring off a waterfall across from the entrance.

He sighed. "There are koi fish in the water, although I have to replenish them. The osprey just won't leave them alone no matter how much I feed them."

We made our way over to the water pooling off the rock-face that made up the back wall of the space. Ripples flowed across the pond as shimmering gold, orange, and white fish swam lazily around the floating lily pads.

At the heart of the space, a lush canopy of trees formed and as I searched it, I realized there were far more birds than the ones I'd seen, and many I didn't recognize.

"What's that?" I pointed to one with shimmering emerald and gold feathers as it glided by.

"That's a duskwhisper. One of my favorites."

Willy Fallowell had loved birds too. Whenever we found one injured, or kicked from the nest, we always brought it to the forge to try and save it. It didn't work often, but when it did, there was no better feeling than setting them free again.

I shot Lord Fallowell a look from beneath my lashes and tried my hardest to remember…

This man is not your father.

"Why?" I blurted. I wanted to know, but I also wanted to get him talking so I could stop fantasizing about throwing my arms around him and telling him how much I fucking missed him. "Why did you make this place?"

The joy in his eyes dimmed and he pressed two fingers against his temples as if a headache had come on suddenly.

"When Almira's army of flying monkeys came, they wiped out three quarters of the area's bird population within weeks. The worst part was the monkeys rarely even ate the birds they killed. They took pleasure in the killing, hunting them out of the sky. It's sport for them, bloodthirsty bastards. At first, I tried to figure a way to keep the birds from leaving the protection of the city, but birds by nature don't like to be caged. I knew if I wanted to save them, I needed to find a place to hide them until she was gone." His expression was soft, his face serene as he turned and took in the paradise before us. "This is what I came up with. A sanctuary. Of course, I called on Nora to help me build it. And then there was the matter of capturing the birds and collecting eggs. It was a process. But I think it came out well, don't you?"

His expression was hopeful, so earnest…

My throat was tight, knowing that *my* Willy Fallowell would have loved this place. "It's amazing. Truly, I can't imagine it being better."

He beamed at that for a moment, nodding, and then his face grew serious. "There are so few things I've done that I can be proud of during my time presiding over The Emerald City. This is one of them." He met and held my gaze for a long moment. "I couldn't save them all, Harmony. But I did my best to save as many as I could. Please know that."

And as I stared into his eyes…the eyes of my father, I believed him.

We headed back downstairs, and while my heart was full of bittersweet memories, my head light from the drink, and my belly content with good food, I also felt like something important had been accomplished tonight. In spite of our rocky start, I truly felt like we had an ally in Lord Fallowell.

Fenwick breezed back to the table, carrying another pitcher brimming with that delicious blackberry mead.

"Refills?" He waggled his furry brows and leaned forward to fill my cup before I could answer.

Not that I was going to say no. My time with Lord Fallowell had been an emotional ride, and I was left feeling shaken and elated at the same time.

I took the glass gratefully, nearly downing it in a few swift gulps.

"How did it go?" Hook murmured as Lord Fallowell tried to lure Duncan into a chat about the ins and out of sword fighting.

"It went well. I believe he's on our side." I couldn't explain further with everyone around, but Hook seemed satisfied with my answer, or at least too relaxed with food and drink himself that he sat back in his seat.

As dessert was served, the last of my tension drained away. I glanced over at Hook to see that he and Fenwick were talking, and Hook was smiling. A little smile, to be sure, but it was something.

I reached for the pitcher to refill my cup one more time before heading back upstairs to work when suddenly a white blur streaked over the table, knocking it from my hand. It hit the table with a crash, spilling purple mead all over the white, linen tablecloth and onto the marble floor.

"What the hell was that?"

Bonnie squawked as if in answer, zooming after one of the tiny mechanical birds zipping through the hall.

"Oh, Bonnie!" Duncan groaned.

We both apologized and began swiping at the spreading purple stain with our napkins.

Fenwick raised a hand, chuckling. "Please, no harm done. She's just having fun. I'll fetch another pitcher from the kitchen and send a maid to clean this up."

As he hurried off, Billy nudged my foot under the table. "Maybe this is our cue to head out. I need sleep and I'm so full I could burst." She let out a low burp and I giggled.

Hook nodded, his inky eyes slightly unfocused. "Agreed. We can't be here all night. You've work to do."

I turned to Lord Fallowell and offered an apologetic smile. "I'm afraid my comrades are right. Thank you for a lovely evening, and especially for showing me the sanctuary. We really have to prepare for tomorrow, so we're going to go, but thank Fenwick for us, and please give our compliments to the chef."

He stood and bowed his head. "Thank you all for giving me a chance to show you that I'm not all bad. I wish you good luck in your preparation, and I'll see you tomorrow night."

Back in our quarters a few minutes later, I made a swerving beeline for my room, dragging out my hastily scribbled notes on the forge issue and spreading them across a low table. Hook followed me in as the others drifted into their own spaces, clearly as exhausted as I felt.

"Anything I can do to help?"

"I don't think so, but if you want to hang out for a little while and lend moral support, I won't say no."

He sat on the edge of the bed as I bent over the papers, squinting at sketches and figures, each attempt to visualize a solution slipping through my mental fingers like grains of sand.

"So frustrating. I feel like, even before I got my magic, I could've come up with three ways to tackle this issue, and would've had no problem creating a—"

A low snore cut me off and I turned to see Hook flat on his back, dead asleep on my bed.

I could hardly blame him. Besides, I wasn't sure he'd had a good night's sleep since we'd met. Rest was probably the best thing for him right now. For all of us...

"No rest for the wicked," I muttered under my breath, turning my attention back to the paper in front of me that seemed to twist and blur into an unreadable mess as I tried to focus.

"Grrr!"

Maybe I just needed a little fresh air to clear my head. I pushed myself to my feet and made my way to the window. I pushed it open a crack and leaned heavily against the frame, pressing my forehead to the cool glass, staring outside when a puff of steam billowed into the air. I watched it drift lazily upward.

I blinked several times as a thought began to build. Cranking the window open, I leaned out so I could see beyond the city and the glittering golden path that had brought us here.

Steam. Gold pavers.

A bolt of clarity cut through the weary haze.

The sharp cool air followed me as I shut the window. Pressing my palms flat against the window, my breath fogged the glass as my thoughts raced. I could harness steam to boost the bellows, cranking them faster than humanly possible. Not unlike the first forge I'd worked in for Smitty in Alabaster.

"The gold pavers," I tapped my fingers against the window…the warmth of the room stealing my thoughts, "They could be…I could use them…"

My brain buzzed with possibilities, each piece falling into place. But even as the adrenaline hummed through my veins, a bone-deep exhaustion tugged at me, dragging me down as sure as if weights were tied to my limbs.

I blinked, eyes drooping despite my efforts to stay alert. My legs felt unsteady, my head unbearably heavy.

You'll wake up early in the morning and get it down on paper.

I barely made it back to my bed, fumbling to crawl in, eyes closing as I curled onto my side.

Before I completely passed out, a blanket was pulled up over me, and I was pulled tight into the crook of James's embrace. He buried his face against the back of my neck, lips brushing against the sensitive skin behind my ear.

His deep rumble was like the purr of an overlarge cat, sinking through my bones. "Sleep, Harmony."

A sigh slid through me as I rolled to face him, wrapping my arms around him, as he did the same to me. A place of safety, and in our exhausted states…we sunk into each other.

If only…

If only we could find this place when we were wide awake, and not in the in-between of sleep and dreams.

CHAPTER 24

"Harmony?" Hook's usually gruff voice was nearing panic, penetrating through the fog blanketing my brain. "Wake up, damn it."

It was like my eyelids had been weighed down with rocks, but I forced them open anyway.

"James?" I blinked in confusion as I looked up at his concerned face. My temples throbbed with every beat of my heart as I pushed myself to sit up. "What's going on? Why do I feel like someone hit me upside the head with a bag of potatoes?"

He stepped back a little, blowing out a heavy sigh of relief. "Too much mead plus exhaustion, I imagine. Billy and Duncan—"

"Both feel like shit. They need to put a warning label on that stuff," Billy finished for him, stepping through the door.

I turned toward the window, wincing as the bright morning sunlight attacked my eyes.

"Wait…what time is it?" I demanded, scrambling to swing my legs off the side of the bed.

Duncan grunted. "Maybe eight-thirty?"

The forge. I was going to be late!

I leapt up, ignoring the shooting pain in my skull. "I'm supposed to bring my design to Smitty's! I haven't even finished—"

Hook grabbed me by the elbow, holding me steady. "Take it easy, Harm. If you don't have a solution, we'll buy Duncan another sword. It's not the end of the world."

"No," I snapped back, feeling it in my gut that I had to do this. "It really might be." I speared a hand through my hair as I headed toward the wardrobe for my clothes. "It's more than just the sword. It's…if I go into these trials feeling this help-less, we're screwed. I know it doesn't seem like a big deal, but I have to figure this out."

Not just for Duncan but for me too.

Hook went silent for a moment, then nodded. "Okay, just tell us what we can do to help."

I pushed the others out. "Let me change." *Let me think.*

Formal attire ditched, I grabbed my notes from the night before, and met the others in the common room. The steam idea from the night before definitely had potential, but it was still a seed…

If I still had my magic I could—

Nope. We work with what we've got. Sit down and get it done, damn it.

I waved the others over, pulling a crumpled napkin from my pocket as I sat down at the desk. We were all out of paper, so it would have to do. My fingers trembled as I flat-tened it out, looking for something to write with.

Duncan stepped up from behind me, handing me a foun-tain pen. "Here."

"Thanks," I whispered, already beginning to scribble.

"Tea?"

I nodded, too focused to meet Billy's gaze. When Hook

placed a steaming cup and a scone near my elbow a few minutes later, I handed him the napkin.

"We'll need these items, as fast as you can manage. If you can't find something, think of an alternative that might work, and I'll try to make do."

Duncan eyed the list over Hook's shoulder with a frown. "You sure about this?"

I shook my head. "Not even a little. But that's what we've got, and I have to trust myself to make it work. I'm going to draw the blueprint for the improvements while you're gone."

A knock sounded at the door, but I didn't look up as Fenwick's voice rang through the room.

"Ah, good morning, my friends! Not coming down for breakfast, then? I was worried when I didn't see you all."

"Too much mead," Billy replied, her tone short. "We've got work to do today in the city, so we won't be back until after supper."

"Alright, then. But make sure you aren't late for the trials. The Wizard needs-"

"The Wizard will wait and administer the trials no matter how late we get back, unless he wants everyone to know he's just a dotty old man hiding behind a curtain, yeah?" Billy snapped.

I did glance up at that and wasn't surprised to see Fenwick's grin. I still wasn't sure if he wanted to sleep with Billy, or if he just enjoyed her sass and wanted to spend more time verbally sparring with her, but there was no doubt that he had a thing for her. The meaner she was to him, the more charming he seemed to find her.

"You *are* the quick wit, aren't you? But I can't argue with you there. I will make sure he knows you'll be back…sometime tonight for the trials. Have a fruitful day in the meantime!"

Billy closed the door in his face with a slam and looked at

me with a shrug. "I know you said honey, but vinegar may buy us another hour or so."

"Can't hurt," Duncan agreed.

I'd already agreed not to share his secret, but there was no time to argue about it. I glanced at the grandfather clock in the corner of the room and groaned. Here I was, in a city full of steam-driven technology beyond anything I'd even dreamt of, trying to create something that no one else had thought of. And I was cocky enough that I expected to finish designing it, get it there and build it by the end of lunchtime so they'd still have enough time to make Duncan his sword before the trials started.

The thought was almost laughable.

Except...except I wasn't laughing.

I stared down at my notes with renewed determination. Emerald City was amazing, but they didn't have a tinker like me. And I was about to prove it. I fell into a near trance as I struggled to refine the scribbles, ignoring the trickle of sweat trickling down my temples.

At some point, I reached the end of the page, then filled up the back with another elaborate drawing. My invention would be made up of two parts; one to make the steam that would power the bellows. The other for how to lay the gold pavers to tighten the space of the forge, increasing the heat. My plan was to layer them in, using them to hold and increase the heat. Like they had on the road.

I hoped I was right and that the properties of the road weren't restricted to when they were placed on the road.

The first part of the piece was done, the twisting pipes, the lines that would take heat in and out of the bellows. I just had to figure out how to put the rest together—where would it all come from? How would it be powered? I glanced around, my mind still buzzing with ideas, but there wasn't a piece of paper or napkin in sight, so I started sketching right on my hand, drawing a diagram that snaked all the way up my wrist. The further the lines and design went, the more excited I got.

Once I got to my elbow, I grinned. This might actually fucking work.

I pressed a hand to my chest, startled as the others burst back through the door, arms laden with supplies.

"Did you get it all?" I asked, rushing toward them and examining their haul. A huge cast iron pot with matching lid, coils of copper wire, metal piping that had clearly already been used for something else…and four large gold pavers with dirt still hanging on the edge of them, clutched in Billy's arms.

The items were a mismatched hodgepodge, but my list looked to have been filled.

"Everything you asked for," Hook confirmed. "Are you ready?"

"I don't know, but we've got no choice. It's now or never."

THE SOUND of the heavy forge hammer stopped as we burst into the shop, breathless and disheveled.

"You're late," Smithson grumbled, wiping his hands on his apron. "Look, lass, I've got other orders to take care of. If you got here an hour ago, maybe—"

"Wait," I gasped, holding up an ink-covered hand. "Just hear me out."

He eyed me, folding his arms across his chest. "I'm listening."

"We're going to use steam to increase the bellows to start, but that's just half my plan." My breath came in short bursts, and I fished the wrinkled paper out of my pocket. "Take a look." I strode over to the counter, smoothing it out. The ink had blurred during the trip, making it even more illegible, but I jabbed my finger at it anyway, praying he'd understand.

He squinted, his brow furrowing in confusion, turning the paper over and over. "What am I even looking at?"

Billy stepped up next to me, jabbing me in the side with an elbow. "Show him the other part."

My cheeks flushed as I extended my hand, doing my best to stop the trembling as I showed him the drawings that wound up my wrist and forearm. His eyes widened, and he scratched at his scruffy chin.

"You alright in the head, lass?"

My stomach sank. It was a miracle he hadn't thrown me out already, given how insane I must've seemed.

"Smitty, get in here," he called, leaning in even further to get a better look. "Can't make out a damn thing. Maybe he'll have better luck."

"It looks messy, but it makes sense, I swear." I swiped a sweaty lock of hair away from my forehead.

The back door creaked open, and Smitty stepped into the room. "Yeah?"

"Need you to look at these drawings for me. She thinks that she can increase the bellows."

I bent over the paper, poking my finger at the water reservoir.

"Let's start here…The forge isn't getting hot enough on its own, like you said. But if we steam power the bellows, the amount of air that could be pumped in…it more than triples." I pointed to the forge itself. "We'll open the wall behind the forge and install a vat of water. The heat that would normally be wasted can be used to boil it, creating steam."

Smitty narrowed his eyes, still silent as the back door creaked open. "Still not hot enough."

"And *then*," I continued, pointing to one of the sketches on my arm, "we pipe that steam down here, harnessing it to drive the bellows. As long as you refill the water every couple of hours or so, you'll never have to pump them again. With the increased airflow, you'll easily be able to hit the higher sustained temperatures you need."

Smithson squinted, nodding his head slowly. "Like Smitty said, that still won't be hot enough."

Smitty didn't seem as convinced. "I get how it could work, but how do you even expect us to install something like this in such a short time? I'd have to start working on the sword in a few hours, if you want it tonight. And that's *if* it works as well as you said it would. Which, I don't mean to be rude but, I still have my doubts about it."

"I have a new brick and flux too." I pulled one of the gold pavers out of the bag at my feet. "These capture and create heat from the sun, if we use them as the bricks in the bottom of the forge..."

Smithson frowned, taking the paver from my hand. "But we're trying to melt one of these for the sword."

"Right, which is why I'm going to make a flux that will take the forging to a heat above even these."

I hoped. "It will work just...." The resolve in my voice surprised, even me. "Give me three hours. That's all I'm asking."

Smitty glanced at Smithson, looking conflicted. "We'd have to reschedule a few jobs...What d'ya think?"

The other man shrugged. "If she has a chance in hell at making it work, it'll be worth it. We'd be the only ones in the city able to bend that gold."

Smithson straightened, turning back toward me. Then, after a long moment, he nodded. "Alright, then. The forge is yours."

"Thank you!" I shouted, a fresh wave of energy pumping through my veins. "I won't let you down."

"We'll get out of your way for now. We can use this time to clear out that back room like we're always talking about."

The younger smith nodded, sparing a final glance at us. "Good luck. Let us know if you need anything. And don't screw up my forge."

The two vanished into the back room, their voices fading as they left me alone with Hook, Duncan, and Billy.

"Alright, let's lay out our supplies," I said, gesturing toward the table.

Duncan emptied the sack, piling up gears, copper tubing, valves, the cast iron pot, and a larger, metal reservoir. Each one was like a little makeshift puzzle piece, and it was my job to turn them into a masterpiece.

"Damn," I muttered, my heart sinking. I'd been so focused on convincing them to let me try that I'd almost forgotten that the hardest part was still ahead of me. "I'm still short a couple of copper attachments for the pipes. Do you think you could go grab them for me?"

Billy let out a dramatic sigh, "If you keep sending us out for errands, I'm gonna have to start charging you."

I swatted at her arm. "Just a few things this time, I swear. I'll also need something to insulate the copper pipes. Maybe some kind of wool or cotton from a vendor?"

"Florbax wool would work really well for that," Billy cut in. "Super coarse and near indestructible. Shoring them is a nightmare. I know just the guy."

"Okay, then for Duncan…" I scanned the pile of junk a second time. There were plenty of things I could use, but, given how little time I had, I had to focus on bare necessities. "I need some good rope, as well as some little wheels or similar sized gears. I want to make a little pulley for part of it."

And with that, the two of them were out the door, Billy

already bossing Duncan about where to go and the fastest way to make it back.

"No marching orders for me?" Hook asked.

"Actually…I need you for something else. Something important."

He crossed his arms, raising an eyebrow. "Why do I have the feeling I'm not going to like it?"

"For this whole thing to work in the time we have left, we'd have to use one of your Tideblessings."

He stared at me, unblinking. "You want me to use my magic to help that meathead get a fancier sword than the one he broke while trying to kill me?"

Well, when he said it like that…

"That's about the gist, yep."

He scowled, but dipped his head. "What do you need?"

CHAPTER 25

I hefted two of the pavers up. "These already have some sort of magic going on in them, right?"

Hook nodded. "The heat induction you mentioned."

"Right. So I need to dig out all that coal," I motioned to the pile of steaming black rocks in the bottom of the forge, "take out the bricks that are probably welded into the bottom of the forge, and then set these in."

"What if they don't fit?"

Question of the day. "They have to," I whispered.

Hook stepped up and lifted his hands, calling the Tideblessing he'd taken from the old pirate leader, Davey. The wind was controlled as he lifted the coal still steaming from the forge, and set it down behind us. "Figured faster is better yes?"

"And easier on our hands." I leaned over the forge, grabbed a bucket of water and poured it in. The blackened bricks sizzled and hissed. The steam rose up fast and hot and I jerked back, stumbling into Hook.

His arms went around me, holding me tight. His good

hand was nestled just under my breast, pressing against my ribcage. A single move and he'd be cupping me.

Fucking hell.

My body reacted and I fought not to shake in his arms.

"You're trembling, are you hurt?" His voice was at my ear like the night before. I turned my head, laying a hand over his. My eyes travelled up over his lips to his eyes.

"Not hurt."

Was that a whisper? Yes, yes it was.

His throat bobbed and his lips parted. "We should hurry."

A boom from the backroom had us jumping like teenagers caught holding hands.

"I'll go see what's going on back there." He wheeled around and headed off, which gave me a blessed moment to gain my composure. One that I sorely needed.

My lady bits were out of control.

"Get it together, woman," I muttered under my breath.

I had my pulse close to normal and my hands on the old bricks in the forge when Hook came back. "The old codgers dropped a bin of tools. Nearly knocked themselves out."

"Here," I motioned with my head. "Can you help me pry these out?"

The bits of metal and slag that had slipped below the coal had spent years building up along the bottom, welding the fire bricks together.

With much sweating and no small amount of cursing, and fighting not to touch each other, we got the bricks out.

Now for the real test. I swallowed hard and lifted the pavers into the bottom, settling them in as if they'd been meant to lay there. "Perfect."

"Coal back in?" he asked.

"Yes, thank you."

Look at us, so proper…like we were both doing our

damnedest not to wind up tearing each other's clothes off when we were supposed to be trying to save the world.

Hook used his Tideblessing again, lifting the coal back into the forge.

Next was the piping and small reservoir for the steam.

Moving on instinct and with as much speed as possible I put the copper pipe together, feeding it from the bellows, to the cast iron pot at my feet, to more piping, all the way to the back side of the wall.

Lighting the forge I had a good heat going in moments, the gold pavers cranking the heat way up. I melted down some metal to liquid form, and used it to seal the cast iron lid tight around the pipe going in and out of it.

I panted, wiping sweat from my brow as I stepped back over to the forge, jabbing my finger toward the wall. "Okay, this is the last thing we need you to do with your magic. I need a rectangular hole, big enough for this." I gestured toward our makeshift reservoir.

He lifted his hand, and I winced as the stone began to tremble and crack under the power of a wind like no other. But the lines appeared a moment later, carving out the perfect little brick of stone, just large enough to do what we needed. He dug in with his hook and wedged it out, dropping to the floor below with a *thunk*.

I leaned over to slide the water tank into the little hollow. We'd shut off the forge a good hour earlier, but the wall was still blasting me with heat. Experience told me that it'd be a solid day before it cooled. "That was pretty amazing."

"You didn't do too bad yourself." He flashed a rare smile.

I slid the tubes into place, connecting them to the ones we'd fastened to the ceiling. "When we close this, try to seal the hole *around* these pipes. If we crush them, we'll have to try again."

He watched in silence as I slid the rest into place. If we

did this right, Smitty would be able to refill the water using a tube on the other side of the room. Sweat poured down my face, but I kept moving anyway, the anticipation was almost too much to handle as it came together, piece by piece.

Finally, I stepped back, giving Hook a nod. "Okay. Do your thing."

He put his hand out toward the opening once again, closing his hand little by little. The stone responded in kind, warping and stretching from the edges to cover the middle like it was made out of rubber. I glanced over, worried, as he let out a grunt.

His progress slowed to a crawl, as if the stone was straining against him. But he pushed through, seeming to find a second wave as it slid the rest of the way shut, sealing the water reservoir inside.

"Good as new," I said, glancing at the smooth section of wall where the hole had been just a moment earlier. "Now let's hope it worked."

"It better've worked," he grunted, pulling his sleeve up to glance at his inner bicep.

"Hmm?" I cocked my head.

"Tattoo's gone. We'll have to find another way if we need to do more of that."

I chewed at my lower lip, "That was the last of that kind of magic?"

"Unlike the memories I absorb when I kill a Tideblessed, the magic eventually runs out."

"I'm so sorry, I didn't mean for you to use up all your—"

He held up his hand to stop me short. "If we get through those trials in one piece, it'll be worth it."

"Thank you," I mouthed, leaning closer to him as we eyed the nearly finished contraption. He would've known how close he was to using up the rock magic, and it meant a lot that he was willing to do it for something like this.

"Glad I could help. You did most of the work, anyway."

I sucked in a breath, walking over toward the back door and rapping on it twice. *And now for the moment of truth.*

The two Smiths stepped back in, pulling a cart full of yellowish rock. Billy and Duncan followed just behind them, copper fittings and wool in hand.

"Well, young witch, think it's ready for a test?" Smitty asked, eyeing the cluster of tubes and gauges next to the bellows.

I nodded, as excited as I was anxious. "Light it up. Let's see how hot this thing can get."

The next few minutes seemed to stretch on for hours as Smitty reignited the forge. Little wisps of steam rose from the pipe, currently funneled right into the chimney where it blended with smoke and disappeared into the sky. All that was left was to flip the switch.

Smitty wiped his hands on a rag, joining me by the controls. "Well? Are you just gonna stare at it, or do you plan on showing us what it can do?"

I swallowed, glancing at Duncan, Hook, and Billy. There was a lot riding on this. But no one but Hook knew how much of my own confidence was riding on this...how desperately I needed it to work.

"Okay," I muttered, resting my hand on the lever. "Here goes nothing."

I pulled it, setting the steam in motion toward the bellows.

And nothing happened. The gears stayed silent, and the bellows didn't budge. Panic bubbled up in my chest, and I froze, too worried to even look at anyone else.

The groan that came from the pipes sounded like a beast of Almira's making, and my stomach did a flip flop. A second later, steam hissed through the pipes, rattling them and sending the gears spinning. With an audible *woosh*, the bellows expanded, pumping a fresh gust of air directly into the heart of the forge.

Sparks danced, coals glowed, and the bellows were already pumping again before the fire could truly flare. Better yet, it seemed to be pumping faster with each passing second, blasting more air into it than any human could've managed. If working the bellows by hand was like breathing, my contraption was full on hyperventilating.

As the fire roared to life in a blinding flash, hotter and more intense than I'd even dared to hope for, I felt a little spark of that magic inside me now. Faint…just a flicker, but it was there. As if responding to my efforts here in the forge…where my magic had first woke all those years ago.

"Fucking hell, lass." Smitty spun on me, his eyes wide with shock. "You did it!"

Billy and Duncan whooped and cheered from the back of the room, and Hook tipped his head in approval.

"Think it's hot enough to make the sword?" I asked, turning back to Smitty.

"And then some," he grunted, already pulling on his apron. "Good work, lass. I wasn't sure you had it in you. It's a little later than I would've liked, but we'll drop everything and get it done. You have my word."

"If the fire stays this hot, it will take half the time," Smithson chimed in, striding up to get to work.

"Told you she'd do it." Smitty strode up to me as his father went to work.

While we could have left them to it, I felt compelled to stay. Near the forge, the heat searing my skin, the glow of the metal as it morphed and changed…this was my safe place. The place I felt most at home in the world. So, I stayed and helped where I could, handing them tools, sweating alongside them, working in tandem as they used a pair of hammers while I held the sword steady with oversized tongs.

The time flew by, I barely felt the hours slip and when the sword was done it glimmered with a deep vein of gold that slid from hilt to tip.

I took a step back to admire it.

"And in half the time we figured!" Smitty grinned.

I blinked. Three hours had gone by, and I'd barely felt them.

Yet I wasn't done here. My fingers went to my pouch and the coins there. One from Alabaster. One from Neverland.

One from Oz.

"I…can I use the forge? I need to…fix something."

The pull to the coins and to my whip that had cracked fighting Noru, had me moving, not even sure if the two blacksmiths had given permission or not.

I just went to work.

The three coins went into a crucible—the fire hotter than anything I'd worked with before—and melted them down. Poured them into a rough shape and with only a little more sweat had a new tip built for the whip.

"Holy sheep shit," Smithson breathed. "I never seen a blacksmith work that fast! Like magic!"

My head jerked up and I snapped out of my second trance of the day. "I'm sorry…I…" I looked to my friends and two were dozing, only Hook still had eyes on me.

He smiled. "Good job."

Smithson rubbed at his chin. "You gonna use the sword, and that whip against the witch?"

I pursed my lips, the thrill of victory dimming, making way for a rush of fresh nerves. "We'll need every advantage we can get."

"Are the trials tonight, then? The Wizard's been cagey about it. Doesn't want anyone interfering or distracting you."

"That's why we're in such a hurry," I confirmed. "It's supposed to be late, sometime around midnight."

"No blackberry mead for us at dinner this time, then," Duncan cut in with a wince.

Smithson cocked his head, "What's wrong with blackberry mead? It's a local favorite."

"It's delicious, but it knocked us out cold last night. That's why we got here so late, and we've had raging headaches all day."

His frown deepened further, and his voice went deadly quiet. "How much did you drink?"

"Three cups, maybe?" I shrugged, glancing at the others for confirmation. The memory of it was still fuzzy.

Smitty and his partner exchanged a long look, and Smitty turned his amber gaze on me. "There's only one place in the city that makes it, and part of the reason it's so popular is that it barely has any alcohol in it. They give it to teething babes. Hell, I was practically raised on the stuff. You could drink half a barrel of it and hardly feel a buzz. Certainly, it wouldn't affect you the next day."

Billy, Hook, Duncan, and I all exchanged a look and there was no question in my mind that we were thinking the exact same thing.

The drink had been laced with something.

My mind raced as I replayed the events of the day before: Fenwick, coming to the courtyard to watch us spar. His disappointment when we'd skipped breakfast. His insistence that we attend dinner that night. The drinks that he'd personally brought to our table. Then that second pitcher…

Bonnie, the beautiful, brilliant falcon that she was, had swooped in, knocking it over before any of us could drink from it.

"That bastard tried to poison us," Billy blurted, sounding more offended than angry.

"He sure as hell did," Duncan replied through gritted teeth.

But I was already past that. Because, to my mind, the far bigger question…

Had he been working alone, or had The Wizard of Oz, this story's version of my own father, been behind a plot to kill us all?

CHAPTER 26

Thirty minutes later, we headed up the walkway to Nora's cottage for the second time in two days. We'd all agreed it wasn't safe to go back to the palace. Who knew if or when Fenwick would make his next move? In a slick city full of people we couldn't trust, Nora stood out as the exception.

At least, that's what my gut told me. I just hoped it was right.

The cottage door swung open before we knocked, and Brunhilda the cat leapt straight into my arms from the threshold. I caught her and held her close, feeling some of the rising panic fade at her warmth.

Bonnie bent close to inspect the cat from her perch on Duncan's shoulder, and Brunhilda let out a hiss.

"She sensed you coming before I did," Nora said, arching one brow as she patted the falcon's head tenderly. "She's all hiss and no fight. Don't let her scare you, snowy one."

"Sorry to bother you again, but can we come in?" I asked.

"Of course." She stepped away from the door and waved us inside. "I didn't expect to see you until tonight."

"Yeah, well, we didn't expect Fenwick to try to poison us before we even got to the trials, but here we are."

Nora made *snick*ing sound with her tongue as she closed the door behind us and led us into her living room. We settled onto mismatched but cozy chairs gathered around a low coffee table.

"Poison, hmmm?" she muttered.

Duncan cocked his head as he studied her. "You don't sound the least bit surprised."

"Not surprised that he did it, no. Maybe a bit surprised that he didn't succeed—or at least manage to cover his tracks better."

"Do you think he did it to protect The Wizard, or you think he's working for Almira?" Hook asked, eyes narrowed.

Nora tucked a loose lock of white hair behind one ear. "I can't say for sure. Although I never fully trusted Fenwick, I often questioned where his loyalties lay over the years. I knew he was wily, though. Always has been." She moved toward a roughly hewn table in the back corner of the room, its surface covered with bowls of herbs and vials of various potions. She paused briefly to peer into a tiny cauldron, roughly the size of a mixing bowl, before turning back to us. "I'm still finishing up the spell to unlock the trials. Forgive me if I seem distracted. Back to the poison, though. I'm assuming it was milk of the poppy?"

"How would we know?" Billy asked.

"He loves them. Obsessed with his garden. Tell me, how did it feel when you drank it? It makes you feel quite good at first. It's only later that you begin feeling bad if you have too much."

We all shared a look and nodded. We had felt pretty damn good last night. I thought back to Fennwick's pride when he showed us the crimson field of flowers through the window the first time we met. Had that been a boast or even him subtly taunting us?

I'm showing you exactly how I'm going to kill you, and you fools don't even know it.

Anger flared in my chest, and I fisted both hands.

"That first morning he was very pushy about getting us to come to breakfast," Duncan said.

"And then when we were playing cards," Billy added. "He sent up sandwiches in the mechanical dumbwaiter, but we didn't eat them."

"If he is working for Almira, I imagine seeing you on the training grounds only made his mission even more of a priority. Word travelled very quickly that you all," Nora flicked a glance between the men, "were rather impressive. That's both good and bad. He got desperate and rather than be able to point a finger at the kitchen staff or servant, he gave you the drink himself to get the job done. The fact that he was willing to risk getting caught if his attempt failed this time tells me that whatever he saw while you were sparring made him think you had a chance of passing the trials."

It was a dicey silver lining, but I supposed being seen as a credible threat was at least a bit of a morale booster.

Nora's expression darkened. "Where does Fenwick think you are now?"

"We told him we had business in the city." Hook shook his head, leaning forward to brace his elbows on his knees. "He could have spies watching for us. In fact, he could know we're here and be on his way right now. What do you think?"

He held Nora's gaze for a long moment, and she broke into a wide grin.

"I like this one," she said, looking my way and shaking a finger at Hook. "He puts his duty above social niceties and politeness. Your mother would be pleased."

Heat flared along the back of my neck but before I could

protest that there was nothing to be pleased about, Nora turned back to Hook. "To answer your poorly concealed accusation, no. I am certainly not one of Fenwick's spies. I'm on the side of The Emerald City, and the people of Oz. Not to mention that I respected and very much liked Harmony's mother. Which is why I must counsel you not to return to the palace." She sighed, shaking her head. "If Fenwick's goal was to stop you from completing the trials, there's no time or need for subtlety. The next one will be a full-blown attack."

"Let him come," Duncan growled, his gray eyes spitting fire.

"Unfortunately," Nora countered, "he wouldn't come alone. The witch has supporters scattered throughout the city here, though I can't say exactly how many. Not to mention, the palace guards will fight for whoever pays most. I'm not suggesting that you couldn't win if it came to it, but I'd rather spare you the battle, if possible. Especially when you'll need your strength to face Almira herself."

"And what about the wizard?" I asked, finally finding my voice and posing the question that had haunted me since we uncovered Fenwick's plot. "Do you think he was in on it? He didn't drink the mead we drank…said it was too sweet for his taste."

She crossed her arms over her chest and leaned a hip against the table, considering for a long moment before answering. "You know, of course, that The Wizard is Lord Fallowell, yes?"

"We do," Billy said with a clipped nod. "We figured it out the day we met him."

"Then you know he's weak. In a perfect world, he would push for Emerald City to be rid of Almira for good, but he's never had the backbone to make it happen. However, I do know he was fond of your mother, and Marin of him. I don't believe he could stomach betraying her, especially after protecting her secrets all these years. He has done a lot of good for the city...or as much as he could without rattling too many cages. I can't say for sure, but if you ask me, my bet is that he didn't know what Fenwick planned to do."

Relief washed over me, and I released a shuddering breath. I didn't know why it mattered so much—it wasn't as if he was actually *the* Willy Fallowell who raised me—but still, it did.

"You know," she stared thoughtfully at the tiny cauldron as she moved closer to the table again, "If you help me, I'm sure I could finish preparing the spell early. Then I can administer the trials myself, without Oz or anyone else present, before Fenwick is any wiser."

Billy and I exchanged a quick glance, then I looked to Hook and Duncan, who both nodded.

"Okay. Put us to work."

A few hours later, after clipping herbs, melting wax, burning hair, and scanning spellbooks, we stood around the table staring down at a truly disgusting-looking potion. Thick, viscous, and black, it bubbled and writhed like a living sludge monster.

Billy leaned closer, nose wrinkled. "So...now what? Do we have to smear this stuff on the ground into the shape of a pentacle or something?"

Nora's eyes twinkled. "No, child. Now that night has fallen, I take you to the graveyard, do the incantation, and then you drink it."

"No, ma'am." Billy raised both hands and shook her head. "I have a hard and fast rule not to drink anything that looks like it might try to drink me back."

Hook took a decisive step forward to peer down at the cauldron's contents, his expression blank. "We're going to drink it, and we're not going to complain about it. Let's get to the cemetery and be done, before Fenwick realizes we're onto him, if he hasn't already."

Minutes later, we moved along the wooded path parallel to the main street. Nora had provided cloaks, and we'd split into groups to attract less attention. Duncan and Billy walked ahead, close enough to pass as a couple, while Nora, Hook, and I trailed behind as a trio. Bonnie had already flown off scouting the path.

Nora assured us the streets would be emptier at this hour, with people home for supper. Once we left the path, the cemetery would only be half a kilometer away.

I squeezed down on my pouch, feeling the coiled whip inside. With the new and improved tip, fusing the coin from Oz with the Alabaster gold piece and the pirate's coin Hook had given me...I knew that the weapon was as ready as it was going to be. A formidable combination, and one that would be a game changer if I got my magic back.

Not if, I reminded myself. *When.*

As silly as it was, my success at the forge had me feeling hopeful. The spark had been there, although faint. Maybe once I got the prophecy and the final magical item, every-thing would fall back into place...

As we neared the city market area, Billy stopped and sniffed the air.

"I smell smoke. And not cooking smoke. Like big fire smoke."

A cold feeling settled in the pit of my stomach as we all picked up our pace, moving closer to the street to peek out from behind a copse of trees.

Twenty yards away, Smitty and Smithson's forge was nothing but a smoldering black skeleton of a building, black smoke still rising from the scorched roof.

"No!" I lurched forward, but Hook caught my arm and yanked me back.

"There's already a whole crowd of people there assisting. Fire looks like it's down to just embers now. I know you want to help, but we can't risk someone spotting you."

Nora stepped forward, drawing her hood tighter around her hair.

"Stay here on the path while I go see what's happened."

I sank down onto a tree stump, guilt churning in my gut. Had I done this? Were the bellows I'd created faulty somehow? Maybe I'd overlooked something, rushed the work—

"This isn't on you, Princess," Hook murmured, seeming to read my thoughts.

That was easy enough to say, but the next few minutes dragged on like an eternity as I imagined every scenario, each more awful than the last.

When Nora returned, her face was grim as she tugged back her hood.

"Apparently, there was some sort of explosion."

I leapt to my feet, pulse hammering. "Are they…are they alright?"

"The younger one is fine. He managed to drag Smithson clear right before it blew. Just a twisted ankle between them and a few superficial burns. They got lucky."

Thank Gods. But it was starting to feel like luck was a requirement to survive helping me, and that wasn't good.

"I think it might've been my fault," I blurted.

"No, it wasn't," Nora cut in. "When Smitty tried to escape through the front door, it wouldn't budge. He had to use an ax to hack it open. Someone had barred it from the outside with a metal stake. This was intentional."

"Fenwick."

That motherfucker…

"Even more reason to get the trials done immediately. The gloves are off. But maybe him thinking you're dead will buy us some time." She dipped her head toward Duncan,

"Smithson said, and I quote, 'make sure you use the sword to cut that bastard fox's head off.'"

Duncan put his hand to the hilt of the blade, his jaw set tight.

"With pleasure."

Hook stepped forward, pulled a small bag of gold from his belt, and pressed it into Nora's hand. "Can you get this to the smiths after the trials? Just in case we don't—"

He let the words die.

Good of him not to say it, because after two close calls with Fenwick, we all knew the truth. We were on borrowed time.

We needed to get out of Oz, and fast. Or failing the trials would be the least of our worries…

CHAPTER 27

Clouds drifted in front of the moon overhead, sending shadows across our path, and the cool night air prickled at my skin as we walked.

A rusted iron gate stood at the far end of the gardens, and Nora paused as we reached it, sparing a final glance behind us to make sure we hadn't been followed.

"Not far now. Stay close."

She pushed the gate open, and a chill rolled through me as I scanned the winding path ahead. Weathered gravestones flanked us, and fog rose from the ground, swirling around our ankles as we stepped into the cemetery.

"Good thing this isn't creepy," Billy murmured, taking a step closer to me until our elbows brushed.

Nora ignored her and pointed toward a hulking, marble mausoleum a few dozen feet away. "That's the place." It stood apart from the rest of the graves and looked as if time hadn't touched it. The iron door was already partially open, squeaking gently as a breeze came through.

"You four will go inside. Get to the bottom of the stairs and I'll close the door behind you. Drink your potion, and I'll say the incantation from here that will bring the trials within to life. Beware that, while you know right now in your minds that this is magic and the trials are a test, once you drink the potion, the consequences will become very real to you." She glanced at the night sky and then back to us. "Take your time and be deliberate, but don't dawdle. Especially in between. Go from one to the next. We don't have time to fool around."

Bonnie had been flying high above us and Nora whistled softly, calling to her. "I'll keep watch and take care of the falcon until you come out."

I reached out and took her hand in mine, giving it a squeeze. "If someone comes, make sure you protect yourself. Run, hide, whatever it takes. You've done so much for us already."

"Your mother was like the sister I never had. I don't know what my life would've been if she hadn't shared her knowledge with me." She squeezed my hand back and held my gaze. "So, I *will* be here when you get back."

I recognized the mulish set of her chin and the determination in her eyes. I'd seen it in Molly countless times, and I knew there was no point in arguing.

"See you on the other side." I sucked in a final breath of the chill night air as I pressed the door open, revealing a stairway that stretched into the darkness. Hook moved to continue ahead but I tugged him back so we could take the first step side by side. If I was leading my team into trouble, I was going to be on the front lines.

My pulse hammered in my ears as we neared the bottom of the stairs. It wasn't that deep, but the air here was stale, and a musty dampness seemed to cling to the walls.

With that, the iron door swung shut with a clang. Billy let out a muffled curse. "Can't see a damn thing."

"Take out your vials," I instructed, reaching into my pouch and retrieving mine. I tried not to think about what was inside as I tugged the stopper free and held it a few inches from my lips.

"Ready…set…go."

I snapped my head back and dumped it down the hatch. The look of it had been bad, the smell, awful, but nothing could've prepared me for the taste. Like if someone took a dead body and soaked it in rancid sausage water for a month, then blended it together into a sticky, chunky soup.

Tasty.

I couldn't see my friends, but I could hear their feet stomping and the choking sounds that let me know we were all in the same boat. In that moment, I channeled Moll's voice in my head.

Harmony Marie Fallowell! Stop being so dramatic and get it done, this instant!

I bent at the waist, braced my hand on my thigh, and used every muscle in my body to force it the rest of the way down. The only saving grace? Since it was a single mass, once it was down, the torture was over.

"Done." Billy paused, gagging one last time for good measure. "The good news is," she croaked, "nothing that happens from here could be worse than that, so…"

"Bloody hells, that was foul," Duncan agreed.

I waited for Hook to chime in, but he was silent.

"James? You alright?"

My pulse was rising when he finally answered with a cough. "I've been better."

The grim but flat reply eased the tension in the dark space for an instant and the three of us chuckled.

"Step one, potion down. What's—"

Before I could finish, a faint humming filled the space, and a pinprick of golden light flickered into view from above, shining down the passage in a tight beam. I felt for my whip, suppressing a shudder as we walked gingerly after it,

Hook at my side, with Duncan and Billy bringing up the rear. The light danced all around, illuminating just enough of the darkness that we could see where we were stepping. After a minute of walking, it pulsed, growing suddenly brighter to illuminate a carved stone archway just ahead.

"Guess we're supposed to go through," I murmured, taking the first step through the opening.

The moment I did, a rush of air whipped up behind me. Hook growled and I spun, whip ready, to see him staggering back from the entrance, as if he'd hit some kind of invisible barrier.

"I can't get through." His voice was oddly distorted.

Billy lifted a hand to try but was stopped in mid-air.

Duncan went next, but after expecting to be stopped as well, he wound up stumbling right through it, grunting with surprise as he gripped the wall for support.

Relief flooded through me as he approached. At least I wasn't alone. Still, I'd rather all four of us be together…

I turned to look at the others, only to find their images going fuzzy. A moment later, the entrance solidified into solid rock.

I blinked, trying not to panic about the fact that we were now in a sealed room with no visible way out.

"It must be my mother's magic."

I did my best to focus on that fact. The trials were sure to be scary and maybe even dangerous, but she wasn't trying to kill us.

Right?

I shoved aside the nerves and turned my attention to the golden orb that poked through the wall and began floating to the center of the room.

The space was large, a thirty or forty foot square. Not only was there no exit, but there also wasn't even a single window.

Duncan pulled up beside me and we both stopped to stare at the massive, brass scale at the room's center. On either side of it lay a pile of emeralds as tall as me, with gems of all sizes, from tiny pebbles to chunks the size of boulders.

The orb of light lowered, dropping to the floor a few yards away. A chill rolled through me as it pulsed again, beginning to shimmer and warp. It grew, taking on the shape of a massive lion. Its face, on the other hand, was human, but ever-changing. The features shifted, making it impossible to get a clear idea of what it looked like. What was clear, though, was the creature's glowing, golden eyes, which were fixed right on me.

Duncan's hand went to the hilt of his sword. "What the hell is that thing?"

A *sphinx*. I couldn't form the words, but although I'd never seen one, I knew it to be true.

The creature's lips tipped into a strange smile.

"Harmony MacInnes…daughter, tinker, pirate, mage. But not queen. Yet." Its voice shifted from masculine to feminine, and from deep to high, unsettling and impossible to place.

A chill crept up my spine as it echoed the words of the last prophecy.

"MacInnes? Is that my true last name?"

"It is. A proud name inherited from your father, Alistair MacInnes. You are the only remaining soul of his bloodline. Will you be the last? Time will tell."

Its face grew serious, those golden eyes seeming to stare right into my soul.

"In emerald hues, *two piles lay,*
 Upon these scales, your fates now sway.
 Match the sides and be precise,
 Balance calls; heed its advice.

Judge not by eye alone, beware,
The truth concealed is waiting there.
Find harmony of heaviness,
Or suffer grave unpleasantness.
Think sharp, think swift, your time draws thin,
For soon the walls come pressing in."

As soon as the final words left its mouth, the ground began to tremble beneath our feet. A low groan echoed through the room, stone scraping against stone.

I turned, my fingernails digging into my palm. "The walls."

Clouds of stone dust filled the air at the edges of the room as the grinding sound continued, and the walls began inching toward us, at a snail's pace, but there was no question.

"Hell," Duncan hissed, lurching toward the gem piles. "Quick. We need to balance the scales."

I followed him to the center of the room, each of us taking position on one side of the scale. The two plates were already imbalanced, with Duncan's side sitting a good deal higher than mine. He hefted a large emerald onto his hip and slid it onto the plate. The scale began to wobble, shifting back and forth for a long moment before shifting toward him.

My heart pounded in my chest as I took another look at the walls. Their progress was still slow, but steady, and based on the square footage we'd lost, I doubted we had more than ten minutes before they flattened us out like pancakes.

I scooped up an armful of smaller emeralds, piling them onto my side. It teetered, as if it was just about to balance, then lurched back down, crashing into the ground with a clang. "What the fuck is going on?" I asked, wiping sweat from my forehead.

Duncan grabbed his side of the scale, pulling the large emerald off and replacing it with a slightly smaller one, but it didn't budge. "I don't get it. Yours should be way heavier…"

To test it, I grabbed the biggest emerald I could lift, sliding the others out of the way before plopping it down on the plate. It still didn't budge.

"Okay," I muttered, slapping my hands to the side of my face. "We need to think… Maybe it's working backwards?"

We removed several emeralds from my side, but again, the scale hardly responded. "Maybe it's not about weight at all," Duncan suggested, speaking through clenched teeth as he glanced at the walls.

"Balance calls, heed its advice…"

We stared at each other in silence, because what the hell did that even mean?

We were going to fucking die here.

The walls grinded closer with each passing second, seemingly moving even faster than before. Duncan let out a grunt, staggering back from his side of the scale.

"Did you just do something? This side just got way heavier."

I stared back at him, desperately searching for an answer. None of this made any sense. The scale was reacting as if the weight of the emeralds were completely irrelevant.

"Take them all off," I blurted, swiping the ones off of my side and sending them toppling to the ground.

I blinked, catching a bit of stone dust right in my eye. The walls were closing in faster than ever now, and were just a few feet away on either side.

Duncan swiped the emeralds from his side as well, his cheeks going pale as the scale didn't move an inch.

"If it has nothing to do with the emeralds, then what's moving the scale?"

My heart hammered in my chest as the walls crept even closer, and I mentally ran through the riddle for the thousandth time.

In emerald hues, two piles lay,
Upon these scales, your fates now sway.
Match the sides and be precise,
Balance calls; heed its advice.
Judge not by eye alone, beware,
The truth concealed is waiting there.
Find harmony of heaviness,
Or suffer grave unpleasantness.
Think sharp, think swift, your time draws thin,
For soon the walls come pressing in.

DUNCAN GRUNTED, his eyes flashing with silver berserker fury as he threw his arms out to either side, physically holding the wall back from crushing us.

"I'll hold it back for as long as I can," he roared, his eyes going even brighter. But that only seemed to make the walls move faster.

Why?

Judge not by eye alone, beware,
The truth concealed is waiting there.

And then it clicked. This wasn't a test of brawn. It was a test of brains.

"Wait," I whispered. "Stop fighting it."

"What the hell are you talking about?" he shouted, his Whisper beginning to take over.

"The emeralds don't matter to this at all. The balance isn't about that, it's about *us*!"

His arms trembled as he pushed back against the wall, his muscles looking ready to tear free from his shirt. "Us?"

I dropped, sitting cross-legged onto the ground despite the dire situation. "We need to find a way to relax. The scale is responding to our emotions."

He stared back at me, dumbfounded.

"You have to try. We were meant to use our heads here. The balance we need to achieve is inside us."

He nodded and relaxed his arms, sucking in a deep breath. "I'll try," he whispered, taking a seat right across from me.

I closed my eyes, focusing on my breath and trying to block out the grinding all around us. All my instincts screamed for me to stand and find some way to fight back. To push and struggle against them, even if we didn't have a chance.

A faint memory fought its way to the surface. Me, in Little Alabaster's palace, trapped in a falcon chute with no way out, this same, horrible feeling of being confined. I'd overcome it then, and I'd overcome it now. Not by kicking and screaming, but by calming the fuck down. The only way to beat it was to stop resisting.

I willed my heartbeat to slow, even as the first wall pressed up against my arm. Duncan groaned across from me, and I risked a look at him. The walls had him firmly in their grip, squeezing like a vise from both sides, threatening to crush him from shoulder to shoulder.

I reached out to him, grabbing him gently by the wrist. "You can do this," I said, knowing how much I was asking. It was hard enough for me to stay calm, and I wasn't the one with magical rage running through my veins, and on the verge of being crushed.

"You taught me to predict, not just react," I whispered. "How to move *beyond* instincts, Duncan. You're so much more than brute strength. It was your brilliant mind that allowed you to stage a coup and save an empire."

He took in another, shuddering breath. For a second, his jaw clenched so tight that the veins bulged on his neck, but, gradually, he began to relax.

"Hi," I murmured, forcing a smile to my trembling lips.

His mouth tipped at the corner and his dimple flashed for an instant. "Hi yourself."

We stayed like that for a long moment, and suddenly, the groaning around us grew quieter.

We both turned and watched as the brass scale shook and shimmied before slowly righting itself, the plates lining up in perfect balance.

"Excellent."

"We did it." Duncan exhaled slowly and slumped as the walls pulled away. His face was slick with sweat and we were both still shaking, but I was shocked to see that his eyes were still molten silver. Rather than suppressing his magic, he'd managed to use his mind to control it.

"Holy shit," I whispered, covering my mouth with my trembling hand. We'd prepared for battle, and I thought I was mentally ready for whatever the trials threw at us; lions, tigers, bears…but this?

This was a different beast entirely, pure psychological torture.

The walls around us dissolved into wisps of smoke and we were back in the room with Hook and Billy a few feet away, as if we'd never left.

They turned, staring down at us, backlit by the golden orb of light.

"You two alright?" Hook asked, stepping closer and

cupping the back of my head gently in one hand to study my face. "Are you hurt?"

I glanced at Duncan, and he met my eyes with a slow nod. "We're good," I said, realizing with a start that it was true.

We'd made it past the first trial, and now, I could see the light at the end of the tunnel.

Or—I corrected as the orb blinked and began to move— *the light in the mausoleum.*

Before I could even celebrate the win, though, the voice of the sphinx rang out again.

"You have the wisdom of a queen," it said, slipping strangely from one voice to another. "But do you have the heart of one?"

Billy, James, and Duncan all exchanged a worried look and my stomach sank.

Shit.

CHAPTER 28

Dread washed over me and I reached toward Hook, fingers brushing against his arm as the ground trembled beneath our feet.

"No, wait! I need a second to—"

Billy and Duncan went up in curls of smoke, their startled faces disappearing as the mausoleum itself warped and stretched. The stone walls faded, and the darkness gave way to a riot of color, swirling around Hook and me.

My stomach lurched as the colors went solid, and I stumbled forward, struggling to find footing as swampy earth squelched beneath my boots. The chilly night air had gone humid and wet, and the world had gone deathly quiet.

I was alone.

My chest tightened as I caught sight of the glinting saber in my right hand. Where my other hand should've been, there was only an iron hook.

I swallowed hard as I looked down at my clothes, mud stained and dark. Gone were my sweater and gray britches, replaced by a pirate's coat that hung loose on my small frame. I was still me, but somehow, I was also Hook.

I looked up to take stock of my surroundings. Massive cypress trees loomed overhead, their branches tangled with ropes of moss. It was a place I knew all too well;

The Weeping Fen. Noru's lair.

And, as I looked forward, the rest of the scene flooded into view. The massive crocodile was there, jaws open as if lunging at me, but frozen in time. Until he wasn't.

He lurched forward, those crimson eyes shining in the dark cavern. My pulse hammered, but I reacted instantaneously, leaping out of the way faster than I'd ever moved. Those jaws snapped shut on nothing but air, and I shot forward, swinging my saber with skills that I knew weren't entirely my own.

Tendrils of magic arced up my back, wind swirling around the blade as I sliced into the beast. Noru roared as blood spurted from the wound, and I danced effortlessly around his next attack, scoring another slice on my way out.

A whip snaked out from the side, smashing into the beast's skull before it could recover, and I turned to see Xander yanking it back, leaping out of range as the monster lashed at him with its tail.

Another whip flashed into view a moment later, and Hook let out a feral roar as he pulled it back, readying himself for another attack.

I was Hook. Hook was me. Somehow, the sphinx had sent us back to the moment we'd tracked down and killed Noru, only we'd swapped places. But why?

I looked past Hook, my blood freezing as I caught sight of the person behind him.

"Take that, you ugly bastard!" Moll loosed a bolt from her crossbow, her hand already whipping down to grab another as it slammed into the croc.

Why is Moll holding a crossbow?

And why was she dressed in a full-on pirate uniform? It

was only when she lowered her bow that I caught sight of a patch over one eye. It wasn't only Hook and I who'd been swapped. Molly had taken on the guise of Trick-Eyed Tom, the crew's Mend…

Horror rocked me to my soul, and I let out a feral scream as Noru whirled, surging right past me to launch itself at Hook. I sprinted after him, closing the distance in a heartbeat. I leapt over the beast and held out an arm, blasting as much wind and lightning as I could manage, right into the monster's face.

A figure appeared on both sides of me, Hook on one and Xander on the other, and I realized a moment too late what was coming. Xander hooked his whip around Noru's eye, tearing it free with a squelch, but the beast was too fast on the follow-up, sending the first mate hurtling backward with a swipe of its massive tail.

I leapt back into the fray, wielding sword and magic in tandem. Lightning crackled around my hook, slamming into the monster's side, and my sword never stopped moving, even as my reserves of magic began to run low. Noru lunged at me, snapping wildly and lashing out with tail and claw. I avoided each attack, but I could feel myself slowing with every passing second. Not that it would matter—I already knew what was coming next.

Not this. Anything but this.

Noru snapped sideways, charging toward Hook instead of me, and I pushed my body to the limit, trying to keep up, but he was too fast. Molly hurled herself forward, sliding under Hook's arm as he moved to block her, and leapt right at the beast, just like Trick-Eyed Tom had done that fateful day.

"Moll, no!" my voice tore through my throat, and I forced out another bolt of lightning as Noru closed in on her.

"Come on, you overgrown lizard!" she shouted, and it

took everything I had not clap my hands over my ears and snap my eyes shut for what came next.

Noru's jaws snapped shut around her, crunching her near in half in a spray of blood. Hook let out a roar, and his magic was like a physical force on the air as he slammed into the croc a moment too late, same as I had.

Noru went still, and I caught up a heartbeat later, slashing the monster across the throat as tears poured from my eyes. Blood soaked my shoes, but it hardly even registered. The croc's jaws swung open, and my vision started to darken, a loud ringing drowning out everything around me as Moll's mangled body tumbled out.

I dropped to my knees beside her as she let out a ragged breath.

"Moll, please," I choked, voice shaking as I looked down at her. "No, no no."

She threw her hand to the side, the last of her—Tom's—healing magic rushing toward Xander's fallen form. "End it, Harm," she gasped.

"I can't," I whispered, choking on grief. "Please, Moll. I—"

"You have to," she rasped. "Let me…go on my terms."

I held back a sob, my hand trembling as I lifted my saber. Footsteps splashed through the swamp behind me as Hook approached, his face a mask of sorrow and understanding.

"Let me do it for you," he begged, voice hoarse as he held out a hand for the sword that rightfully belonged to him.

For a weak moment, I considered it. But it had to be me, in the same way it had to be him the first time.

Hook stopped short, and I kept my eyes pinned on Moll as I brought my sword to her neck. "I love you, Moll. Always."

"Love you too, Harm." She managed a weak smile, her cheeks so pale, she looked like a doll. "Me and you are like bangers and mash. I'll be with you forever, no matter what."

The swamp faded, mist curling around me until Molly's face was all I could see. With a final, wrenching sob, I pulled back and drove the blade straight into her heart. She gasped once and then stilled.

I collapsed against her, the weight of what I'd had to do crushing me.

I barely heard the sphinx's voice when it echoed through the space.

"I'm sorry for your pain, but you did well, young Harmony…"

I was still sobbing when Hook wrapped his arms around me, pulling me against his body as if he could shield me from my own pain.

"Are you guys okay?"

Billy.

I pulled my face from Hook's shirt and realized that we'd been transported back to the mausoleum. The golden orb darted around us impatiently, and James lashed out at it with his hook, barely missing, his voice low and dangerous.

"That's it. She's done. We're done."

The sphinx's voice echoed all around us, calm but firm. "You give up, then?"

"No!" Billy snapped, her voice edged with desperation. "Harm, I know it's hard, but you've got to get up. If we stop now, Almira wins."

Duncan knelt beside me, laying a hand on my shoulder. "Whatever happened in there, it's not real, Harm. Remember that. None of it was real."

But damn if it didn't seem like it was. I could still feel Molly's weight in my arms, still see the pain in her eyes as I ended her suffering.

Real or not, I would never forget how it felt to watch the life drain from her eyes.

Before I could fall even deeper into darkness, a stinging

slap pulled me back. My cheek burned, and I jerked upright, staring in shock at Billy's stern face, which was hovering inches from mine.

"Sorry, but you'll thank me later. Now get your shit together, woman."

Her tone, and that no-nonsense glare…

Moll would've done the exact same thing. And she could again, if I could pass this last test and get us out of here. Because the real Molly was out there and alive. I just needed to find my way back to her.

"She's right. We must keep going."

Hook drew back, studying my face. I saw the resistance there and could almost *feel* how badly he wanted to shield me from this. But, after a long moment, he nodded, helping me to my feet.

Billy slipped her arm through mine, flashing a tight smile.

"Guess it's you and me, toots."

Whatever the sphinx would throw at us, we would face it together.

But as the orb darted toward us and the room began to shift, I couldn't shake one, terrifying thought…

Had she saved the worst for last?

CHAPTER 29

The mausoleum melted away, and in its place stood a single podium carved from gray stone. On it sat two crystal balls, each glowing softly. A delicate hourglass stood between them, grains of sand already trickling down.

"This is a test of courage. Not leading with head or heart but being brave enough to make the hard decision when it matters most." The sphinx's voice rang out, its strange, shifting tones filling me with unease as it spoke a single word of direction. "Choose."

My chest tightened as I stepped closer. In front of the first crystal ball, there was a detailed depiction of a human heart, complete with veins and arteries, etched into the stone podium. In front of the other, a brain, its grooves and folds so lifelike I could almost see it pulsing.

"What do you see?" Billy murmured from a little way behind me.

I took a shuddering breath and peered into the first crystal ball. Fog swirled, but then images appeared, sharp and clear.

Me, standing on a battlefield, magic roaring around me in

waves. Almira's forces lay scattered and broken. Almira herself knelt before me, defeated, eyes wide with fear. The others—Hook, Duncan, Billy—all standing strong and safe at my side. All of C'an Saas free, the world restored. I felt a surge of triumph, tasting the victory I'd fought long and hard for. It was everything I'd dreamed of all within my grasp.

Heart pounding, I forced myself to step away and peer into the second sphere. The foggy images shifted and then became clear.

Billy stood laughing, her face lit with pure joy. Four men surrounded her, eyes alight with mischief. Paddy, Scotty, Jacob, and Andrew. Her brothers were whole and human again, alive and free of Almira's cruel spell.

Tears filled her eyes as she embraced them, the pain she'd carried for years finally lifting.

My stomach twisted into a knot as nausea threatened to overwhelm me. I wanted to scream, to throw the spheres to the ground and shatter them both into a million pieces.

A sure victory over Almira, or give Billy back the family she'd lost?

Choose.

Bile rose in my throat as the sand in the hourglass continued to trickle, the sound growing louder with each grain.

"What is it?" Billy called again. "What do you see?"

My throat was dry, my tongue like a wad of cotton as I tried to force the words out.

"A choice," I finally managed as I turned to face her. "The one on the right is sentimental. Saving a few lives, and letting the chips fall where they may. The other is logical. The power to defeat Almira and save thousands."

Billy exhaled, shoulders relaxing. "Great. This one's easy, Princess. I've said it from the start; your soft heart will get you killed if you don't toughen up. Grab the left orb and let's get the hell out of here." She turned away, already walking toward the spot where we'd entered. "Honestly, I don't even know why I'm here for this one. It's a no brainer."

I shook my head, unable to move as surely as if my feet were rooted in place. "It's not so simple."

Billy stopped mid-step, then turned, the confusion plain on her face. "Sure it is."

"These lives might be few, but they are precious." My voice wavered and broke as I choked back tears.

Billy froze, eyes widening, dread creeping over her face. "H-how many lives, exactly?"

I forced myself to hold her gaze even as my stomach churned.

"Four."

I saw the second the truth penetrated. Her face crumpled as she shouldered past me to the podium and stared down into the glass sphere.

"I don't see them. I don't see anything…"

The sound of the trickling sand grew louder…faster, and she wheeled around and held up both hands.

"No. No, wait! Let's think for a second here. Nora said not to be hasty." Panic rose in her voice, and she pressed her hands together as if in prayer. "I know it sounds bad—but if I have my brothers back," she swallowed, choking back sobs, "if Paddy and Scotty and the others are with me, nothing can stop us. You won't just have me at your side. You'll have all the O'Donnellys fighting for you! And you've never seen fighters like us. Please, Harmony…"

I stood in silence, swaying on my feet, tears spilling silently down my cheeks.

Billy let out a cry as she wheeled around and made a dive for the sphere, only to pass straight through it and crash to the stone floor.

She rolled and leapt back to her feet, nose bloodied, wild-eyed as I shot a glance to the hourglass.

We were out of time. I'd let my heart lead us before, nearly killing us all in the process. Billy had said it herself. This was a war, and a soft heart wouldn't win it.

"No!" Billy pleaded, stumbling to intercept me. "Please don't—"

Black threads appeared from nowhere, piercing her lips and stitching them shut. She clawed at her face, eyes wide in panic, tearing the stitches away. Blood trickled down her chin, but the stitches returned before she could speak again, only made of wire this time.

And still, she pleaded, a muffled cry, eyes burning with desperation as she dropped to her knees before me.

I reached out, my fingers outstretched, every nerve in my body screaming at me to be brave, and make the hard choice. The right choice…

And yet—

As the final grain of sand fell, my hand changed course.

Billy's stitches vanished and she gasped, opening her mouth to speak. Before a single word could escape, she disappeared like smoke, leaving me utterly alone.

A golden glow filled the air, and the sphinx's form writhed and shifted until a woman stood before me. Tall and graceful, with black hair tumbling over her shoulders, and eyes the color of warm honey. I knew her instantly, even though I'd never seen her before in my life.

My voice trembled. "Mother?"

Her gentle smile warmed me, and she reached toward my cheek. I leaned in, desperate to feel the touch I'd dreamed of forever, but her fingertips passed through me, no more solid than mist.

"My beautiful daughter, you've finally come," she whispered, her voice rich and full of emotion. "I'm so sorry for the pain I've caused, though it was a necessary evil. I wish I had more time to explain, but the last of my stored magic needed to be used to start the trials. With it, the protective wards around Emerald City are gone. Almira knows you're here and she is surely coming. You need to get to the palace and retrieve the prophecy."

I drew back, swaying in place.

"I…I passed?"

Marin's eyes dimmed as a shadow passed over her face. "No. You failed the third trial. You were meant to choose the win. Instead, you chose Billy over the greater good." Before I could speak, she shook her head, eyes softening. "But your heart might be the very thing that changes the course of every path I've seen. Besides, courage is forged in the heat of battle. Remember that lesson when the moment comes again. And it will come again."

I swallowed hard, her words sinking in. "I won't forget."

"And remember, you aren't alone. You have your guardians to help. Don't judge Billy too harshly. The test was yours and yours alone, and she will prove to be invaluable in battle. They all have a part to play…especially James." Sadness clouded her face, and I wanted desperately to ask why, but her form was already blurring at the edges, going hazy. "I'm proud of you, my daughter. Proud of the witch you've become, and of the woman before me. I will see you again someday, but not too soon, Gods willing."

She placed her palm flat against my chest and while I couldn't feel the weight of her hand, something warm surged within me, filling every cell. Magic rippled through my veins, a tidal wave of power and possibility.

"My magic. You're giving it back to me," I whispered, voice breaking.

"No, child. It was within you all along. I just removed the doubt and fear in your heart so you could see it clearly again." Marin's eyes shimmered with unshed tears, determination hardening her face. "Go to the wizard now. He has the prophecy, and a gift that will help you get to C'an Saas. Go now. I can already sense her coming!"

Her words echoed in the mausoleum as she vanished, leaving only the faint golden glow of magic behind.

CHAPTER 30

My knees wobbled, nearly giving out as we surged back to reality. Hook caught my elbow, steadying me, his eyes dark with concern.

"Are you alright?"

I shook my head, searching for Billy. I was still reeling from seeing my mother, and that paled in comparison to what Billy must be going through.

She stood a few feet away, scowling and rubbing at her cheeks with the back of her hand. The second test had been cruel, but the last had taken it to a whole different level. To tease her with the thought of her brothers coming back, and then snatch it away…

I reached out, voice gentle. "Billy—"

She threw up a hand, pulling away. "It's okay, Princess…I remember it all…the choice…what was promised, but the pain isn't there. It's almost like I was a bystander, or it was a memory of the distant past."

I nodded, a rush of relief rolling through me. They didn't call my mother the "good witch" for nothing.

"What happened in there?" Duncan asked, concern furrowing his brows.

"We'll talk about it later," I said, my mother's warning fresh in my mind. "But…" I raised a hand, somehow willing an orange flame into existence, right in the palm of my hand, "My magic is back, and stronger than ever."

I reached inside, sensing the massive wall of energy inside me, pulsing. Something told me I'd need every ounce of it to defeat Almira.

Hook reached for me as the others pumped their fists, but I held up a hand. "No time to celebrate. The trials are over, and Emerald City is no longer protected. Almira is coming. We have to go, now."

I led the way toward the mausoleum door, our footsteps echoing against stone as Marin's words replayed in my head.

You're out of time.

As we reached the top of the stairs, Hook stopped in his tracks, grabbing my wrist as he went completely rigid.

"What's wrong?" I whispered.

"Listen," he said, gesturing toward the door. "Someone's out there,and it isn't Nora."

"We have to keep moving." I set my hand on the hilt of my whip. "We'll have to face it head on."

I probed the space in front of us, and now that he said it, I could sense a presence out there. Or maybe more than one?

I pushed harder, then drew back. "Three men. Strong with some sort of magic I'm not familiar with."

Hook unsheathed his saber, then held it up, raising three fingers in the air.

3

2

1

He threw open the mausoleum door, and we shot out,

weapons at the ready. Rather than the chaos I'd been expecting, we were greeted by total silence.

Moonlight spilled across the graveyard, lighting tombstones and statues, but nothing else.

"I don't like this," Billy muttered under her breath, scanning the darkness.

Then, something shifted at the edge of my vision, a flicker of movement too fast to track. I whirled in time to see the cluster of shapes darting behind a thatch of shrubs on silent feet.

"Ambush," Duncan warned, pushing past me so he could stand at the front of the group with Hook.

A blade appeared as if out of nowhere, slicing Duncan across the forearm before he could react. He hissed, and wheeled around, holding his sword at the ready as blood dripped onto his pants.

"Damn it! Where—"

Another strike, as if on cue, slashing Billy's cloak at the shoulder. She snarled, drawing back her bow, but whoever it was had already melted back into shadow.

"Keep close," Hook growled, maneuvering so I was in the middle of the group as they formed a wall around me.

I caught sight of another figure in my periphery and cried out as it lashed out at Duncan again. This time he parried, lunging forward with a strike of his own as a dagger came hurtling toward his side. James intercepted it, throwing the blade off course with his hook, and letting loose a bolt of lightning in that enemy's direction for good measure.

The would-be assassin yelped in pain as the strike connected. Were those...*ears?*

I filled my whip with magic right as Billy loosed her arrow. But a second, taller figure shot into view between us, sparks flying as he deflected both attacks.

Fenwick's teeth caught the moonlight as he flashed a

wicked grin. His cloak was pulsing and dark, and it emanated a strange magic. He let his cane-sword fall to his side, then dropped into a bow.

"We meet again, my dear guests."

Hook lunged at him immediately, but the fox-man batted the strike aside in a shower of sparks. Wind kicked up all around us as Hook charged forward with a follow up, but Fenwick hardly seemed to notice. Instead, he threw caution to the wind as he charged forward to meet him. Two blades emerged from the shadows in unison, one from either side, knocking Hook's sword off course at the last second.

But rather than seizing the chance to stab him, Fenwick changed directions, narrowly avoiding a kick, then slapped the top of his cane-sword right into Hook's back.

Duncan was dashing forward to help, but one of the shadows appeared in front of him, keeping him at bay as Hook roared, lashing out with a spray of lightning. But Fenwick didn't even move. Instead, he sat there and laughed as it sputtered out into nothing.

"Remarkable, isn't it? A gift from Almira. A brief pause on magic, nothing permanent. But *so* effective."

Any question of who he worked for faded as Hook growled, squaring off with him as he regained his footing. "I don't need magic to best you."

Fenwick grinned, surging forward in a flurry of slashes. Their swords clashed over and over, sending up sparks, with neither of them gaining an upper hand.

I wanted desperately to help him, but Duncan was dealing with one of the foxes…so where was the third?

My magic.

I reached out mentally, tentative at first, searching for energy that felt like…fox. Only the second I sensed it, a black void snapped down, severing the connection.

What the hell? I felt the power inside me so strongly. Had I been wrong?

The shape fuzzed into view at exactly that moment, slashing Hook in his exposed side. Fenwick roared in delight, easily sidestepping an arrow from Billy as he continued his onslaught.

"We need to get to him!" I shouted, dashing forward.

A loud screech sounded overhead, and Billy cursed. "Monkeys, three of 'em. Fucking scouts, too," she grunted, shooting an arrow into the sky. "Keep moving, Princess."

I would…as soon as I tried, one more time. Again, I opened my mind and reached out for the energy of the nearest monkey. And again, I was shut out. Almost as if—

Almira.

She didn't just have a hold of the army she'd created. She'd also placed a spell on them that kept them cleaved only to her.

Fucking hell.

"Hold them off. We'll finish up fast," I shouted to Billy, praying that she could manage without my help. The three monkeys were surging toward us, but her bowstring snapped yet again, and I watched as the arrow caught one of them in the head, sending the creature hurtling toward the ground.

Two scouts would still be a tall task, but she was in her element, and I had no choice but to put my trust in her. Not when Hook was magic-less and fighting two even more dangerous enemies on the ground.

"On your right!" I shouted, alerting Hook in time for him to dip out of the way of the second fox.

If only it wasn't so dark, it'd be a lot easier to keep track of them…

I threw my hand up at the thought, calling on my newfound power with a single, focused thought.

Give me light.

I slammed my eyes shut as the sky practically exploded with it, illuminating the entire graveyard. Hook roared, seizing the opportunity as Fenwick and the other fox-man came into full view, their shadowy cloaks melting away in the piercing light.

But Fenwick was still unfazed, grinning ear to ear as he blocked. "Excellent. I do enjoy a fair fight."

I sucked in a breath, remembering Duncan's advice as I lashed out at the other fox with my whip. He leapt backward, trying to dodge, but I'd been ready for that.

I tore my arm backward, sending out a thunderous crack as the tip smashed into his chest. "If you wanted a fair fight, why resort to poison?" I spat, but I kept my gaze trained on his comrade, who was wounded but rising.

"Poor form, I'll admit. Almira insisted. After I told her about your little sparring match and the power I sensed in you, she grew...concerned. She insisted on nipping it in the bud rather than letting you complete the trials."

"And you obeyed her?" I shot him a cold smile. "Being the witch's errand boy seems beneath you, Fenwick."

"Careful, Harmony," he snarled, skipping out of Hook's range as the other fox recovered, taking his place. "I am Almira's most trusted advisor, her closest confidant. She places more value on me than you could ever understand."

"Sorry that you won't be alive to see me kill her."

Hook was fighting wildly, trying to move toward me, but the other fox stayed entirely on the defensive, parrying and keeping him at bay as Fenwick closed in on me. My pulse thrummed in my neck, but I met Fenwick's gaze. "Bring it, fox."

Fenwick's smile widened, flashing rows of sharp teeth. "As you wish."

He seemed to disappear, as he flashed toward me, far

faster than the scout that had almost killed me a few days earlier.

But, this time, I was ready.

I forced magic into both my eyes and whip at once, focusing in on him then snapping forward with an attack. His cane flashed toward me, the crystal tip slicing through the air. I snapped my whip forward, meeting his attack. Leather wrapped around steel, and we strained against each other.

"Where is Nora?" I shouted, yanking the whip back, trying to wrench the cane from his grasp. "Did you hurt her?"

"Hurt her? She wasn't even here." Fenwick's lips curled into a sneer. "Guess she abandoned you exactly like your parents."

"Shut up!" I growled, yanking my whip sideways and throwing my other hand forward in a single motion. Raw magical energy surged to my fingertips, blasting out at him in a bubbling orange mass.

Fenwick's eyes lit up with surprise for a half second, but he dipped right under it, grinning as he tore his sword free. "Oh, come now. You can't be that naive to think any of these people care about you. I'll bet you think The Wizard is a good guy, too."

I snapped my whip forward, but, this time, he deflected it easily. My pulse raced, anger clouding my vision even as I reminded myself that the phony wizard wasn't *truly* my father. "Stop talking."

He lunged forward yet again, then cut back as I sent out another blast of energy. "You've heard about Ruby Reach, yes? Why don't I let you in on a little secret…"

I hesitated, my heart sinking as his smile widened.

"It doesn't even exist, my dear." Fenwick's voice was practically dripping with satisfaction. "It never did. The noble Lord Fallowell made a deal with Almira. The good citizens he sends off by trolley are nothing but tributes. Warm bodies to add to her army."

My stomach twisted into a knot as a memory flitted through my mind. The young man at the railway station, so excited as he told us how he'd be joining his father soon...

"No," I breathed. "You're lying."

"Am I?"

Rage burned through me like wildfire, my whip cutting through the air as I struck, harder and faster, but Fenwick anticipated me each time, laughing all the while.

A flash of anger seared through me and faded, giving way to a deadly calm. He was mocking me for a reason. He wanted me angry.

I thought back to the first trial, settling my mind even as he closed in on me. I needed to use my head…

I spared a quick glance at Hook, walking backwards to bait Fenwick in even closer. He danced toward me, dipping and weaving as I searched for an opening, but I stayed patient. When he was a few feet away, he drew back his sword, ready to strike.

And that was the only opening I needed. I switched directions on a dime, leaping forward to meet him. His sword hissed through the air, passing right over my head, and I slammed, headfirst, right into his gut.

He leapt sideways, trying to create some distance but my whip was already there, swinging around his back like a snare trap. I yanked on it with everything I had, throwing him to the ground, then leapt out of the way. My part in this was done.

Hook appeared right on time, driving his saber straight through Fenwick's chest. "You…" Fenwick sputtered, blood trickling from the corner of his mouth. "You think you've won? She will—" Hook twisted the blade sharply, silencing him for good.

"How'd you know I was coming right then?" Hook asked, staring down at me. "You shouldn't take that kind of risk."

There wasn't time to explain how my magic worked now that it was, finally, truly free. That I'd been able to look at the scene before me and see not only what was happening, but what was likely to happen next.

"I saw you about to kill the other fox and I knew you'd be coming to help. No risk involved. Now let's move. Billy's in trouble."

I jabbed my finger in the direction I'd come from, focusing in on a group of figures in the distance. Duncan had joined her, now, but the two Scouts were putting up a hell of a fight. Hook and I charged toward them, and I couldn't help but wince as we passed the body of the third fox-man. Duncan had sheared him in half at the belly, and the grass around it was soaked in red.

"Fenwick's dead!" I shouted, staying on high alert as we approached. These flying monkeys weren't as dangerous as Fenwick or his assassins, but I knew what could happen if they caught me off guard.

But rather than charging at me, they leapt backward, letting out a guttural screech.

What the—

"Don't let them escape!" Billy dropped her arrow and charged at them, throwing caution to the wind. Their feathered wings extended from their backs, and they let their weapons clatter to the ground as they leapt upward, preparing to flee. But Billy wasn't having any of it. She bent her knees, then shot upward like an arrow, clawing at the legs of the larger monkey.

He kicked and fought, but she clung to it with everything she had, wrapping her arms and legs around it. "Billy!" Duncan yelled, lunging to grasp the monkey's tail, but his fingers closed around empty air.

"Hold still!" I shouted, readying my whip.

But before I could do anything, Billy got hold of its wing, slashing straight through it with her dagger. The monkey shrieked, then went into a wild spin, and they plummeted to the earth as one. They landed with a heavy thunk, and the monkey immediately got on top of her, pinning her against the dirt.

"No!" I yelled, horrified as it pulled its arm back, ready to swing.

Billy let out a grunt and rammed a knife straight into the monkey's throat. It jerked once, twice, then slumped down on top of her, lifeless.

I had only taken two steps toward her when a low gurgle caught my attention. I turned, my breath catching in my throat as Fenwick's lifeless body jerked upward, limbs bending at impossible angles as he rose to his feet. His head lolled to one side, the hole in his chest still gushing with blood.

He turned to face me, eyes empty and lifeless, then opened his mouth, but it wasn't his voice that came out—it was hers.

"My sisters did well to bring you this far," Almira's voice said, speaking through Fenwick's dead lips. "But you haven't seen anything yet. My true power lies in C'an Saas. And don't even think about hiding. Nowhere is safe for you now, and I will destroy any world you try to hide in. See you soon, my pretty!"

Fenwick's corpse jerked again, as though caught in a seizure. Flames erupted from his skin, then exploded into a massive pillar of fire.

I turned as Duncan helped Billy to her feet. She stood and looked down into the face of the flying monkey she'd killed as we all waited with bated breath.

"Not him," she murmured. "And it doesn't matter

anymore if it was. I always knew that if we killed the witch, her magic would die, and my brother would die with it. Before tonight, I wasn't sure if you could do it…if *we* could do it. And now, I know we can. I believe in you, Harmony. More than I've ever believed in anything."

She lifted her gaze to meet mine and moved closer. Then, she dropped before me, only this time, to just one knee.

"I have one last secret to share. James asked about a book. I did have it. I still do…in some fashion. And I should've told you about it. Should've told you that, my whole life, I knew it was my destiny to protect you. My mother was given a tome of fairytales by an old bookseller when I was a child. And in it, the beginning of our story was told. I waited for you…we all did…me and my brothers. But as time passed, we started to think it was all the rantings of some crazy old man or someone playing a prank. Then, the worst thing that could happen happened. My brothers were as good as dead, and I wanted to die myself. I nearly managed it, too. Went to a pub and drank myself into oblivion. Then, packed my satchel and pockets full of stones and hurled myself off the side of a cliff into the sea." She shook her head and let out a low laugh. "I wanted to die, but something inside me wouldn't allow it. Against my own will, my body started to fight. I kicked my feet and emptied my pockets. I wriggled the bag off me and swam to the surface. By the time I was strong enough physically and mentally to swim back out and find it days later, the book was ruined. Inked smeared and useless." She met my eyes and hers were filled with tears. "Princess, I'm so sorry…"

"You don't need to apologize." I gripped her hand tight. "I don't care about the book. I'm just glad *you're* still here. You did nothing wrong, Billy."

She shook her head furiously. "I couldn't let go of the past. That's why I was too ashamed to tell you about it. I'd shirked my responsibility. Put revenge above duty." Under the despair, resolve shone in her eyes. "I pledged my bow to you, but it was at half-measure. I need you to know that you have it fully now. Forgive me, Princess. I know I let you down back in that room, but it will never happen again."

I pulled her up to stand beside me.

"You didn't let me down, my friend. You never could. I do accept your offer, though. Your pledge to me means everything. In fact, I can't imagine a better army than the one we have right here."

And it was a good thing. Because it was now or never…

I looked at each of their faces in turn, trying not to let my gratitude and the host of other emotions get the better of me.

"Now let's get the prophecy, and go kill that bitch, shall we?"

CHAPTER 31

The walk back to the palace was a painful one. About a hundred yards away from the mausoleum, we found Nora's body. She'd been stabbed by a cane-sword, but judging by the blood and still burning embers around her, she'd put up quite a fight. I paused to lay a hand on her chest and say a little prayer before continuing.

My mother's friend wouldn't be the only loss we would suffer, and when it was all over, I would take the time to mourn each and every one. But for now, we had to carry on.

It wasn't until we were nearly to our destination that I realized we were gathering a small stream of followers. A handful of men and women, giving us a wide berth but moving toward the palace with us.

"We saw the lights. We heard the fighting. Did you kill all the monkeys or are there more?"

"Did you defeat The Wicked Witch, then?"

"Are we still safe?"

"Did you pass the trials, miss?"

I didn't answer, focusing instead on the cluster of guards,

who'd moved into our path, blocking us from entering the palace.

"The Wizard isn't taking visitors at this time." The old, grizzled guard Duncan had sparred with stared down at us, arms crossed over his barrel chest.

Fenwick's words came back to me as I stepped up, rolling onto my tiptoes until we were nose to nose. Nothing was going to stop me from seeing The Wizard.

Nothing.

"Out of the way."

His fingers twitched toward his blade and then stilled as he looked over my shoulder, catching sight of Hook.

"Bah," he said, "let them through."

"What? Boss, he said not to."

"We couldn't stop them if we tried. Let them through. We don't get paid enough for this."

The guards shoved the doors open, and I stalked through, fury driving every step I took until I reached the solarium.

At the far end of the grand chamber, the gigantic green face flickered to life on the wall, and the braziers ignited, painting the room in red and green.

"You dare disturb the Great and Powerful—"

"Save it." I waved a hand, cutting him short and sending my whip through the air with a violent slash. The braziers hissed and then went out, plunging the room into darkness. The enormous image began to ripple like water. "Is it true that the trolley to Ruby Reach is a lie? That it brings people to the witch so she can turn them into monkeys?"

The gasps exploded all around me, but this wasn't time for subtlety. I needed answers, and I needed them now.

"Send everyone from this room and close the door so we may talk privately!" Oz thundered.

The fact that he didn't even try to deny it instantly told me all I needed to know.

"I'm done with these games." I strode toward the curtain at the side of the room, magic burning hot beneath my skin. Hook moved to my side, hand on the hilt of his saber as he shot the guards a warning look and shook his head.

"Step out and show yourself!" I demanded.

The crowd had gathered right by the open doors to watch, and the curtain flapped but didn't open.

"Go away. Come back later, when you've calmed down!" The Wizard boomed.

But the time for calm had passed.

I let the full force of my magic loose, aiming straight at The Wizard's image. It flickered and disappeared even as the bolt of power smacked into the wall, leaving a scorched hole in its wake.

"Open. The. Curtain. Or your real face is next."

The fabric shifted and this time, it opened. Lord Fallowell stepped into view, shoulders slumped, looking like the scared, weak man he was. The crowd's murmurs exploded into cries of outrage.

"Behold, your Great and Powerful Wizard," Billy shouted, her voice trembling with rage.

"He's been lying to you this whole time. Tell them the truth, *Lord Fallowell*," I pressed. "Tell them about Ruby Reach."

The crowd raged, their whispers turning to full on shouts, but Hook turned, holding up an arm, "Stay back. Let's hear what he has to say for himself."

"It's true." Lord Fallowell closed his eyes and nodded. "I didn't have a choice. She swore she would stop trying to break through Marin's protections as long as we kept sending them. If you could've seen her power...It was only a matter of time, and then the whole city would've fallen. It wasn't meant to be forever. I thought you would've come sooner..."

"My uncle took that trolley!" a man shouted.

"I swore to my son going would give him a better life!" another woman sobbed.

Duncan, Hook, and Billy joined arms and created a human wall to keep the swelling crowd from coming for him, but it was all background noise as I stepped closer and held his gaze.

"And if I couldn't complete the trials? Would you have done as you swore to me last night and fought by my side when Almira came for us?"

His nostrils flared as he lifted his chin. "I'd have done whatever I could to protect this city, as I've always done. As I told you in the sanctuary. If I couldn't save them all, I'd do my best to save as many as I could."

Meaning he'd have turned us over to her and gone back to being a flesh peddler for Almira, and in that moment, it was as if I saw him for exactly who he was for the first time. Willy Fallowell was a small, weak man.

Not just this version of him—but my father too.

All those years of Druzilla and her idiot sons treating me like garbage, and he'd let it happen. All those years of me loving him anyway. Worshipping him, even. Defending him to anyone who'd listen. But he didn't deserve it then, and this even more pitiful version of him damn sure didn't deserve it now.

I moved closer, unable to stop my voice from rising. "You traded their lives for your own comfort and ease. So you wouldn't have to lead when a leader was so desperately needed. So you didn't have to fight a battle that desperately needed fighting."

Rage rose hot again in my gut. Most reserved for the people behind me who had lost someone they loved…a bit for the child that was me, who'd never known a living parent who would take a stand for her.

"Sometimes, a deal cannot be struck, Willy. Sometimes

you have to draw a line in the sand for the people counting on you. Instead, you didn't even give them the choice or the truth. You betrayed them all."

Us all…

His Adam's apple bobbed. "For what it's worth, when I saw you, I felt hope again after years of hopelessness. You have no idea how badly I wanted you to pass those trials. I prayed for it, and despite all this," he gestured at the seething crowd and the remnants of his reign, "I wouldn't change it. Take what you've come for and draw your line in the sand, Harmony."

He reached into his jacket and pulled out a box, worn smooth from age.

"The safe was unlocked, and this is what was inside. From your mother." He held it out toward me. "I hope it brings you some peace."

I accepted the wooden box, anger still burning beneath the surface. Duncan had made his way over, positioning himself between us and the increasingly rowdy crowd.

What happened to Lord Fallowell from here?

His fate was in my hands. If I left him to the mob, they'd tear him to pieces. I wasn't even sure if they'd be wrong to do it, either. But I couldn't let that happen. As deeply flawed as he was, there was also good in him, too. He'd saved the birds of Emerald City, as well as many of its people from the witch's wrath. Just as my own father had saved me in the woods that fateful day he found me.

And I couldn't bring myself to hate either one of them.

"Guards, come get Lord Fallowell and escort him out," I called, then turned my attention to the crowd. "Anyone who harms him will answer to me. He'll be tried in court like anyone else. Who is next in the line of power?"

Olga stepped forward, her eyes damp with tears that she swiped away. "I am."

She'd been chilly to me in deference to her boss, but she seemed both smart and capable. "Put together a team of advisors. Include the guard there." I jerked my chin toward the older guard from the training grounds, and she nodded.

"Warwick."

"And three others of your choosing. Lead with honesty and integrity, and be aware, I will be watching you." I threw my hand sideways, sending the braziers roaring back to life for effect as the crowd gasped. "Do not take this opportunity for granted."

She bowed and stepped back as I turned to Hook, who had broken away from the chain as Fallowell was led away by the guards.

"I need a few minutes alone here. The three of you pack up and gather some provisions and as many weapons as you can carry." I made my voice as sure and Queen-like as possible. "Tonight, we leave for C'an Saas."

It wasn't until I was alone that I dropped to the floor, legs trembling as I wondered how the fuck we were going to get there.

I just had to hope the answer was in the final prophecy. The last words my mother left for me...

I reached into my pouch and pulled out the other items I'd collected in my travels—the jeweler's loupe and the magical clock— and I arranged them side by side. Then, I stared down at the wooden box in my lap.

It seemed impossible that something so small could hold answers so monumental.

With shaking hands, I lifted the lid and peered down to see a package wrapped in brown paper and a small scroll of parchment tied shut with a thin, red ribbon. Tugging out the scroll, I set the box aside. I held my breath as I untied the knot and unrolled the parchment...only to find that it was blank.

"Blank?"

I flipped it over, and then bent closer, illuminating the space around me with a flick of my hand.

"No. No no no no!"

I closed my hand over the parchment and let out a broken howl. All this time, all these lives, all the pain and sacrifice of so many, and my mother's final words were…

Nothing?

The tears I'd been holding in for days came out in a rush, along with a grief so deep it pierced my soul.

Grief for the mother I'd met for the first time and lost, nearly in the same breath.

Grief for Nora Broomall, the witch who had given her life to give *us* a chance.

Grief for all the bright lights Almira had snuffed out here in Emerald City in her quest for power.

It was only when I heard the sounds of nails scratching against stone that I stopped and cocked my head.

Rats?

I stiffened, but then realized it wasn't rats at all. It was the rhythmic scraping of a quill. I lifted my head to follow the sound only to find the wall already half-covered in black writing.

The same phrase in the same looping scrawl, repeated over and over.

There's no place like home.

There's no place like home.

There's no place like home. There's no place like home There's no place like home There's no place like home There's no place like home There's no place like home There's no place like home There's no place like home There's no place like home…

I leapt to my feet and wheeled around, heart hammering. Was it Gayelette sending me a message from C'an Saas?

Hairs on the back of my neck prickled as I stepped closer,

squinting through shadows as I caught sight of it…the quill bobbing as it scratched away at light speed. I turned to look back at the open box on the floor. The wrapped gift inside was gone. The box was empty, except for the torn swatch of brown paper.

This was the gift from my mother. The quill and ink. Had she enchanted it to deliver this message to me before she died?

It was only when I was nearly touching the wall that I saw it in the dim light. The thin filaments of magic—silky, living threads that spilled from my fingertips, wrapping around the quill, guiding it into a familiar script.

It wasn't Gayelette or my mother doing this.

It was me.

I staggered backward as I stared down at my hands. I'd sensed it growing inside me since my mother had helped me free it. It had gone from feeling like a dying ember to a rising sun.

Fear of the unknown…doubts about what I knew was supposed to come next, made me want to wait for the others. Ask them if it felt right. But I knew this was my choice, and mine alone.

Breathing slow and deep, I reached out, capturing the quill and inkpot from midair. Their magic thrummed softly against my palm, warm and comforting. A sense of certainty filled me—my path clear for the first time.

I sat back down on the stone floor and stuffed everything back into my pouch before smoothing the wrinkled, blank parchment out in front of me. Then, I dipped the quill, pressed pen to paper, and closed my eyes as the prophecy flowed out of me.

It played like a familiar song in my mind even as I wrote…

The time has come to leave the story,

And return C'an Saas to its former glory,
With her she brings the Guardians three,
Sister in spirit, found family,
A charming prince, a captain's crew,
A band of rogues, to name a few,
And once, ding dong, the witch is dead,
They'll restore the blood this land has bled,
Dawn will rise, a blossom's kiss,
A hunter's bounty, nature's bliss,
No place like home, a sight unseen,
Daughter, tinker, good witch, queen.

THE MOMENT that last word poured from my hand, I dropped the quill and ink, and a bolt of something that felt like lightning shot through me, and my back arched as I tried to absorb it in vain.

Then I was floating, to the ceiling and beyond. Hurtling through the sky, through time and space itself. I looked down to see The Emerald City winking far below me, and I could've screamed.

Instead, I lifted my arms to the heavens, tapped my crimson boots together, and whispered the words beating in my heart.

"There's no place like home…"

CHAPTER 32

The breath left me in a whoosh as I dropped into a throne carved from pale marble. My fingers tightened, and I looked around, trying not to let panic set in.

I'd never been here before, but I knew for sure that I was home.

The throne room had seen better days. Char marks snaked up the walls, remnants of fire and magic etched into the stone. Tattered banners hung in ragged strips that fluttered in the draft that flowed in through broken windows. The throne itself, though, was perfectly preserved, down to the gemstones inlaid in the armrests.

I laid my hand onto the hilt of my whip and then paused as golden, glowing script appeared on the stone floor below, pulsing with so much magic that I could see it without trying. Words appeared…words I had penned myself a few minutes earlier.

Guardians three.

My brain stuttered for a second. Duncan, Hook, and Billy?

299

A soft pop echoed through the chamber, and a familiar form burst into existence before my eyes.

Fetch.

"Hey there, boy," I whispered, my throat tightening at the sudden reunion.

He burst forward in a mess of feathers, landing awkwardly on my arm. He pressed his beak to my cheek, and my heart soared with relief. It'd been right to leave him behind to watch over Molly and the kids, but that hadn't made me miss him any less.

Guardians three. I'd assumed Duncan, but the truth was that Fetch *had* been my very first guardian. The brave falcon was with me from the very start, from the day I left C'an Saas and my Pawpaw had found me in the woods.

Another pop sounded, and Hook appeared, landing on the golden letters. He staggered slightly, disoriented, before locking eyes with me, the relief plain on his face.

"Well done, Princess." He glanced around, taking in the room. "Not half bad."

Before I could reply, Billy burst into view. Her hand went instantly to her bow, but she relaxed as she spotted me.

"What in the seven hells happened?" She shook herself, then scanned the chamber. "And where's the ox?"

"I—I don't know. Somehow I…wrote you into this world with me."

Hook took a step closer, narrowing his eyes as he looked at the throne. "Is this your home?"

I nodded. As unreal as this all felt, there could be no doubt. "My parents' throne room. I've seen it in dreams."

The ground shimmered again, this time a few feet to the left of the first set.

"Sister in spirit, found family," Billy murmured the words, flicking a glance my way. She let out a short shriek as Molly popped into the room.

Her copper hair stood out in the dreary room, but not as much as her smile when she caught sight of me.

I sprinted toward her, unable to find my voice as she called out to me.

"There she is. I knew you could do it!"

Fetch took to the air as I moved to pull her into a hug, but she stopped me short with a raised hand as her eyes narrowed.

"What's the secret handshake?"

I blinked, mind still reeling with excitement at seeing her, so it took me a second to put it together.

The secret handshake she'd created for the two of us so we'd know that neither of us were doppelgangers.

I waggled my brows and held out my hand. "Two firm shakes, slide up, grip the wrist, then pull back down until we're almost not touching…and sizzle fingers!"

She wriggled her fingertips against mine and tossed her hand in the air with a flourish and then dragged me into a bear hug. My arms locked tight around her, squeezing until she gasped with laughter, hugging me back just as tight.

"I missed you so fucking much," I whispered.

The joy in her expression dimmed slightly as she pulled back, scanning the room. "I-is this everyone?" she asked, sounding nervous as she flicked a glance between Hook and Billy.

"No." But I cursed myself for not knowing the answer to the question she was asking. Had I brought Xander and the kids along? And if I hadn't, was it even possible to send people back to where I'd gotten them from? I tried to remember all the words of the prophecy as I put on my bravest face, for Moll's sake. "It's going to be okay. Whatever happens, I'll make it right."

"Already replacing me, eh?" Billy cut in, flashing a smile as she eyed Moll. "Who's this?"

"Billy O'Donnelly?" Molly asked, eyeing her dubiously. "But not *our* Billy?"

"I promise, there is only one Billy O'Donnelly, and it's me," Billy said with a smirk.

I wanted to correct her, but Duncan materialized right behind her, with Bonnie perched on his shoulder.

A charming prince, a captain's crew...

He glanced around, mildly confused, then grinned. "Glad to see you're all safe. Good work, Harm." He stepped up to Billy and gave her an affectionate shove.

A sudden commotion broke the quiet as Hook's entire crew *fwipped* into existence in the room's center. They were clearly in the middle of something, gripping mugs of rum and playing cards. A look of shock flashed across their faces as they took in the throne room, but the confusion quickly turned to relief as their eyes landed on Hook. The crew murmured with excitement, and Xander pushed through from the back.

The first mate towered over the rest, his brilliant red hair glowing even in the dim firelight. Unlike the others, he was dressed in casual clothing, and the crew seemed surprised to see him. His eyes instantly found Molly, and his expression softened. He closed the gap in two strides, wrapping an arm around her waist.

"Hey, Cap!" He looked toward Hook, eyebrows raised. "Are we preparing for battle, then?"

Hook gave him a grim smile, a sparkle in his eye as he reunited with his friend. "Aye. If you're game."

"Always."

The crew echoed Xander, those with mugs raising them high in spite of their confusion. "Always!"

A band of rogues, to name a few...

Oh, Gods...Billy!

I lunged toward her, and yanked her around to face me.

"I need you to listen and listen carefully. Something is about to happen that's going to rock your world, but I need you to understand that while they might look like your brothers and sort of are, they're from another—"

"What the hell is going on here?" Paddy O'Donnelly demanded, his hand shooting to the hilt of his dagger as he took in his surroundings.

Scotty, as broad and imposing as I remembered, towered over the rest, scratching his head in confusion. "Where the fuck are we?"

"I summoned you here," I blurted, a pit forming in my gut as I looked at Billy.

Andrew stood perfectly still, his eyes darting from Hook to Duncan. Jacob straightened his thin glasses, relaxing a bit as his eyes settled on me.

"Oh, it's you again."

Billy's bow slipped from her grasp, clattering against the stone floor as she broke into a full on sprint toward her brothers. She collided into the pile of them a second later, nearly bowling over Jacob as she wrapped her arms around Paddy first.

The four of them stood there, stunned for a beat. Then laughter erupted from Paddy, who squeezed her tight.

"Well, hello to you too, lass. But what's all this? We were talkin' with you a moment ago…"

"Not me," Billy murmured, clearly putting the rest of the pieces together herself. "I'm a different Billy. But I'm your sister just the same."

Paddy raised an eyebrow as he leaned back and studied her. "I guess you do look a little different. Skinny. We'll never say no to another Billy, though, will we boys?"

"Depends how many more we're talking, and if this one's as bossy as the other," Scotty cut in, not bothering to dodge as Billy cuffed him lightly upside the head.

Through it all, the smile never left her lips as she stared at each one, as if memorizing every line of their faces.

Warmth spread through my chest as I caught Molly's eye, jabbing my finger toward the three glowing sets of words that lit the floor.

Dawn will rise, a blossom's kiss,

A hunter's bounty, nature's bliss...

Her face lit up as Caleb, Cissy, and Tristan shimmered into view at once. Their expressions shifted from confusion to wide-eyed excitement as they caught sight of us.

"Harmony!" Cissy cried out. "Moll!"

Fetch sprang from my shoulder, shooting right toward Tristan and landing on the boy's outstretched arm. His shoulders sagged in relief as he leaned in, nuzzling the bird. I couldn't deny that it hurt a little bit to see, but he wasn't only my bird anymore, and it was good to see that the boy had been taking good care of him. I stepped back as Caleb and Cissy made their way over to Moll.

"What the heck is happening?" Cissy asked, burrowing against her as Caleb took her hand.

Already, he looked like a different boy. Cheeks pink and plumper. Eyes gleaming with love as he looked up at Molly.

"Harm." Hook's low voice had me turning to face him. "Were those braziers lit when you got here?"

I flicked a glance at the lights set into the stone floor. "Yes, why?"

Molly swept up the kids in another tight embrace, but a loud crash cut their reunion short. Every head snapped toward the entrance at once, weapons drawn.

"We're not alone," Hook murmured, padding slowly toward the door as it creaked slowly open.

Dread pooled in my stomach as I waited for Almira's face to materialize there. Instead, a stooped, elderly woman inched into the throne room, her jaw dropping halfway to the floor the moment she laid eyes on me.

She stumbled back, nearly collapsing against the whip-thin boy who strode in behind her, catching her by the elbow. She lifted a single, shaking finger toward me, tears streaming from her eyes.

"I told you she'd be back! Our Queen has returned!"

CHAPTER 33

An hour later, we gathered around a long, battered dining table. It was loaded with whatever the old woman—called Freya, I'd learned—and the handful of other survivors could scrounge. Old bread, dried meats, and a few casks of ale. We'd added the provisions the others had packed before leaving Oz, and while it wasn't much for as many people as we had, it felt like a feast to every one of us.

Introductions had been chaotic, but Freya had somehow managed to set some order. Then, she rallied everyone into the dining hall, assigning tasks and getting everything set up.

The hall around us was much like the throne room, with cracks running through the stone walls and soot blackening the ceiling beams. But there were signs of care, too; swept floors, sheets as makeshift tablecloths, and candles burning all around in makeshift holders.

Freya and the others had clearly been looking after the place, waiting for this day.

Waiting for *me*.

I'd taken so damned long, it was a wonder they didn't hate me...

I looked across the table at her as she beamed at Cissy, who handed her a juicy plum we'd brought from Oz.

Moll and Xander sat nearby, huddled together with an ease and comfort that spoke to the difference in the passage of time. They were happy, and they were in love.

Hook's fingers brushed mine beneath the table, grounding me.

"You look joyful and terrified all at once. It's going to take a little time, but we're all exactly where we're meant to be."

Things had changed for so many of us since we'd parted ways. There was a lot to catch up on.

At the next table over, Paddy was howling with laughter at something Billy said, nearly choking on his ale as Scotty slapped him between the shoulders, breaking into a laugh of his own. The pirates sat across from them as they played cards together and chugged pints of ale.

I'd pulled Paddy aside, wanting to explain what'd happened with Billy, but he'd waved me off. She was theirs now, no questions asked.

Family.

The word swelled inside me as I glanced around. It was great to see everyone getting along and accepting this new reality so easily, but I couldn't stop thinking about what was to come. Every person in this room was here because of me, and, as much as I knew deep down that I needed them if we were to succeed, some would not survive the coming battle.

Which meant I'd basically brought them here to die.

Hook leaned in close, his voice for my ears only. "Tonight, they need to see the queen they've been fighting for and celebrate all we've accomplished to get you back here. Tomorrow, we'll prepare them for the realities of war. There was no choice to be made. Almira said it herself. Nowhere is safe. At least together, we have a chance."

I knew he was right, but that didn't make it any easier to

swallow. Was I more like Lord Fallowell…more like my father than I'd thought?

Good witch, bad witch. Good witch, bad witch.

"How many people are still living outside these walls?" I asked, forcing my attention back to Freya, who swallowed her last bite of plum with a wistful sigh.

She paused, cloudy eyes drifting upward as she considered the question. "Perhaps a thousand total, scattered across C'an Saas. But here in the palace, we're all that remain—around thirty of us. We've learned to survive in the shadows, scavenging what little we can and not calling too much attention our way."

"How have you managed it for so long?"

She smiled, the lines around her mouth creasing deeper into her skin. "Faith. We knew your mother and Gayelette well. We never forgot Marin's promise that, one day, you'd return and put things right. Many lost hope and ventured out on their own over the years, but those who stayed behind are true believers. We waited, and now you're here. And it was all worth it."

She glanced toward the throne room and then back to me.

"May I ask, my Queen, why you haven't put on your crown yet?"

I shook my head, bile rising in my throat as I glanced over at the brilliant gold crown she'd brought out at the start of our dinner.

"I haven't earned it."

I wondered if anyone truly could. Even if Almira fell tomorrow, the damage done to C'an Saas would take time to repair. This place would need leadership, and I wasn't about to shirk my duty the way Lord Fallowell had.

"It will be ready when you are."

Across the table, one of the older girls under Freya's care,

Essie, watched me carefully, her eyes wide and curious. Beside her was Logan, a boy about the same age. They both leaned in whenever I spoke. Behind them, two younger children whispered and watched my every move.

"The orphans of C'an Saas," she said, reading my thoughts. "Most of the adults you see around you started as children under my care. When Almira seized power over two decades ago, they lost everything. Their parents, their homes. I took them in as my own." Her gaze drifted toward the children, the pride evident on her face. "They've never had much reason to hope, and this last year was the hardest yet. We were beginning to think you'd never come."

She turned back to me, staring at me so hard I could barely keep from squirming. "Then, when things seemed darkest, you returned to save us, exactly as Marin promised."

No pressure at all.

I took her frail hand, giving it a squeeze. "I—I'm going to do everything I can. I hope that your faith hasn't been misplaced."

Freya's voice dropped low, and she leaned in. "We've been training for this moment, Your Highness. Even the youngest among us knows how to wield a blade, at least well enough to defend themselves."

My chest tightened as I glanced at the thin faces of my people, scattered around the hall. "I hope it doesn't come to that."

"We've already sent word beyond the palace. We must move carefully, but I think we'll be able to get some able-bodied volunteers to join us in the battle."

Hook's expression darkened as he leaned toward Freya. "What can you tell us about Almira's forces?"

She frowned. "She has a hundred or so men and women from C'an Saas who've sided with her. Traitors, betraying their kin to fill their own bellies. They serve as officers to keep her hordes of flying monkeys in line."

I grimaced, wishing more than anything that those fuckers had stayed trapped in the pages of Oz.

"Do they cause you trouble here?"

"It depends on her mood. Months will go by without an attack. Then we'll have two in one day. It used to be that they only struck at night, but there is no day here, now. Not truly. It's like her magic has blotted out the sun itself." Someone called her name from the side of the room, and she offered me a weary smile. "I have some matters to attend to, if that's alright, Your Highness."

"Of course."

She rose from her seat, patting my shoulder before making her way to the cluster of men and women near the doors.

Across the hall, Paddy O'Donnelly was already acting up, as he had Scotty setting a stale loaf of bread onto his head before launching a knife at it with practiced ease. Billy stood off to the side, arms crossed as she shook her head, but there was no hiding that smile as she took in every moment.

"Damn it, Paddy!" Scotty bellowed as crumbs showered over his hair. "You're aiming a bit low there, aren't ya?"

Paddy cocked an eyebrow. "Seems to me that I'm aiming exactly right, seeing as you're still alive to whine about it."

The stuck loaf tumbled off his head and he caught it, pulling the knife free and tossing it to a laughing Caleb before charging right at his brother.

Paddy laughed as he feinted right, sidestepping Scotty and patting him on the ass before sprinting away. Scotty lunged at him, grabbing him by the back of the shirt, and Paddy threw up his arms in surrender.

"Okay, okay! I yield. New game?"

Scotty grinned, tossing him toward a nearby table and yanking up his sleeve. "Arm wrestling it is, then."

Billy was riveted, chuckling in delight as she nudged Duncan. "Think you can beat him?" she asked, arching an eyebrow.

He faked a yawn, stretching out his arms. "Blindfolded."

Scotty spun on him, cracking his knuckles.

"Excellent. Been meaning to get back at you for ruining our smuggling hustle in The Smudge, anyways. Let's see what you got, Your Highness."

Ah, so these were the Alabaster O'Donnelly's. I wondered what the Billy from their world was thinking. She was probably worried sick but hiding it by swearing up a storm as she tried to figure out where they'd gone.

Gods willing, I'd return each one to her, whole and hearty. I shot a glance at my Billy and bit my lower lip. Maybe with a spare O'Donnelly for good measure…

"You've got to stop. Don't borrow trouble." Hook's voice pulled my attention back. "Let them enjoy each other. Tomorrow will come soon enough."

Duncan slammed Scotty's arm down, sending the hall into peals of laughter and cheers. I smiled and raised my cup, determined to be in the moment.

As the laughter quieted, I rose from my seat, the movement pulling all eyes toward me. The hall fell silent as I glanced at the faces of all my favorite people in the world, my anxiety fading.

"I know all of you must be confused, some more than others. To the people of C'an Saas, your loyalty makes me believe in the goodness of people again. I am humbled by your faith in me and will do everything I can to make sure I'm worthy of it. To those I brought here…" I let my gaze travel the room again, committing each to memory. "Each one of you was selected because you're special. Some may bring a skill or talent to this war against evil that just may be the very thing we need to defeat it. Others might have a gift that can help us rebuild in the aftermath. But that doesn't mean we're lost without you. If you'd rather go back to the world as you remember it, now is the time to say so. Know that if you choose to stay, it could cost you your life."

"And if we go?" Xander asked, his smile telling me he already knew the answer, but wanted to make sure all the others did as well.

"It could cost you your life," I said with a nod. "The witch that is our enemy will rain her fury down on every world. This one, yours, and all those in between. There are no guarantees either way. But the choice is yours. All those who would like to go back to where they came from, raise your hands now. I'll do my best to return you there with only love in my heart for each of you."

Feet shuffled, chairs creaked, but not a single hand was raised.

"Last call," I murmured, my throat already going tight with emotion.

"Going, going, gone!" Xander leapt from his seat, yanking a half-empty bottle of rum from one of his crewmate's hands. "You can't make a proper toast without rum though, Your Highness!" He flashed a grin and handed the bottle up to me with a theatrical bow.

I lofted it high in the air and tried not to let them see my tears of gratitude. "To those we've lost, and to those who remain. May our sacrifices not be in vain!"

A chorus of cheers echoed through the hall and pirates thumped their fists against tables, drowning out the last of my insecurity...for the moment.

The chant started softly at first, rising louder with every

repetition. The hall shook with their voices, and I tilted the bottle, rum burning down my throat as tears welled up in my eyes…

"Long live the queen!"

CHAPTER 34

"Much better, if I do say so myself."

Molly stood back and admired her handiwork, her fingers tugging my chin this way and that to get the full view before she let out a low whistle.

"Damn, I'm good."

I pulled away and turned to look in the last remaining shard of the broken mirror behind me.

"You really are," I agreed.

Once we'd eaten all there was to eat, and celebrated our reunions, reality had begun to set in with exhaustion hot on its heels.

Freya and some of her people helped each group find a place to lay their heads for the night while her wards, Logan and Essie, led me and my crew to the Queen's quarters. Most of the furniture had been destroyed, but they'd salvaged what they could, and it was more than enough. A room fitted out for each of us to have a pallet to sleep on, swept clean and free of vermin, as far as I could tell. Duncan, Billy, and Hook had gone to their rooms to take advantage of the basins full of rainwater so they could wash up, and I'd finished doing the same when there had been a knock on my door.

I'd been thrilled to see Moll standing there.

"You have the bone structure to carry off the shorter hair, but I'll be glad when it grows out."

I couldn't agree more, although she'd done a fine job trimming the uneven tufts and making the best of a bad situation. Especially given the fact that she'd used my dagger to do it.

"Maybe you should see if some of that fresh magic works on hair?"

I grinned at her and stood, flipping my head upside down to shake off the trimmings. "As much as I'd love to try, I'm doing my best to store it all up for Almira. When we battled her and the bookworms in Oz, I watched her get weaker and weaker the more magic she used, until she couldn't even anchor herself to the page anymore. She just…disappeared. I need to conserve, at least until I know what I'm doing."

She scrunched her face and nodded. "Yeah, I mean, I guess if you think that's the priority…"

We both broke into a fit of laughter and she handed me back my dagger before dragging me in for another hug.

"Part of me wanted to kill you when I saw the Jolly Roger pulling away without me on it," she whispered. "But…thank you." She stepped back with a sniffle. "Taking care of these kids has been the joy of my life. If I hadn't been so worried about you, it would've been like paradise. And Xander…"

Her cheeks went pink and I grinned. "He's a real peach. I can see why you love him."

She drew back like I'd cuffed her upside the head but then she nodded slowly. "Yeah. Yeah, I guess I do love him. And he loves me, too. Harm…" She gripped my hands, her cornflower eyes alight with sudden urgency, "This has to work.

We have to figure out a way to defeat Almira and save these people. They deserve a little happiness. We all do…"

The sour taste of fear flooded my mouth, and I let out a low groan. "I know, Moll, and I'm going to do my best—"

"Including you," she interrupted, lifting her hands to cup my face. "Most of all, you. I'm not telling you this to add to the burden. I'm telling you this, so you don't lose sight of the fact that you have something to fight for, too. Not just for me, Xander, and the kids. Not for the O'Donnellys. Not even for C'an Saas. That's all amazing, and you're my hero for putting everyone else above yourself. But don't lose sight of what you have to gain here. Bringing this beautiful palace back to its former glory. Getting to know your mother and father through your people. Maybe even taking a chance on love. It's not selfish to want those things. Instead of thinking about everything you have to lose if you fail, focus on everything you will win when you succeed and let that drive you."

I blinked at her, mind spinning like a top.

"Who are you and what have you done with my Molly?" I asked when I finally found my voice.

She let out a snort-laugh and gave my shoulder a shove. "Right here, dummy. Having other people to take care of has given me a new perspective, is all." She narrowed her eyes at me suspiciously. "Why, did that sound real good and mature and stuff?"

"It did. It sounded perfect, actually. Exactly what I needed to hear."

"Yeah, well, luckily, I decided to give up on the whole 'vow of silence' thing, or I might've had to take those nuggets of wisdom to the grave with me."

I winced at the very mention of graves and was about to tell her to strike the word from her vocabulary until after the battle with Almira when there was a knock at the door.

"Yes?"

The door opened and Hook stepped inside. "Can I have ten minutes of your time when you two are finished?"

"We're finished now." Molly released me and stepped back, shooting him a quick smile. "I have to go tell the kids a story or they'll never go to sleep. See you tomorrow?"

"See you tomorrow."

She headed out of the room, patting Hook on the shoulder as she passed him and then closing the door.

"You look pretty."

Heat crept up my neck as I lifted a hand to my hair. "Molly gave me a little touch up."

"You always look pretty." He padded towards me, his gaze never leaving mine.

I wanted so badly to make a joke to break the sudden tension in the room, but with him looking at me like that, all I could manage was a whispered, "Thank you."

"I came to tell you that the pretty boy, Billy, and I had some ideas for the battle."

He was on me now, we were toe to toe.

"O-okay."

He lifted his hand and ran a fingertip over my jaw in a featherlight touch that left me breathless.

His voice was low and gruff when he spoke again. "I came to tell you that we deployed the falcons as you said, and they're already bringing word of your return to the furthest reaches of C'an Saas in hopes of getting more fighters here in time."

I wet my suddenly dry lips and nodded "Perfect."

"I came to give you support, and words of encouragement." He shook his head slowly as I melted into the silky darkness of those onyx eyes. "But now that I'm here…all I want to do is touch you."

My nipples pebbled and it took everything I had not to abandon all thought and plaster myself against him.

"Is it because you think we're going to die and you want to go out with a bang?"

His mouth twitched as he shook his head. "Nope. It's because I've been dreaming of you since I can remember, and I can't live one more day without knowing what it feels like to be inside you."

A low ache settled between my thighs. "That's a decent answer," I croaked, suddenly lightheaded.

He closed the last of the distance between us and rested his hand on my hip. "In fact, for the first time ever, the thought of dying doesn't seem like a reward."

"W-why is that?"

He shrugged, his gaze holding mine. "Because I'd never get to see your face again."

I let out a shuddering breath and laid my hands on his shoulders, as much to feel those glorious muscles as to steady myself. "For a guy who's usually short on words, you're doing pretty good right now."

"Yeah, well, I've spent a lot of time fighting it, and tomorrow is promised to no one. If you still want this—"

I mashed my lips against his on a groan.

That was enough talking. If tonight was our last, I didn't want to waste another second of it. His tongue swept out to meet mine as he dragged me even closer, until I could feel the thick, hard weight of his cock against my belly that left no room for doubt. He wanted this as badly as I did. My heart hammered like a wild bird in my chest. It was finally happening, after countless nights spent dreaming of this very moment.

His mouth never left mine as he guided me backward until the back of my knees hit the wooden bedframe. I sat as he pulled away and began to undress me.

He lifted the hem of my shirt inch by inch and I hissed as the cool air brushed my skin, making me shiver. When the shirt finally slipped over my head, his eyes roamed over my exposed flesh reverently.

"Beautiful," he murmured, his voice gruff.

My cheeks burned, white-hot as I fought the urge to cover myself. He was the only man who'd ever seen me this way. I wasn't buxom like Moll, or—

A gasp exploded from my lips as the tip of his tongue found the sensitive hollow at the base of my throat, leaving a trail of searing kisses lower...lower...

"James, I—"

He cupped one breast gently, his thumb brushing over my nipple until my back bowed. I plunged my fingers into his hair and pinned him against me as his mouth closed over my nipple, sending sparks of pleasure skittering through me. My hips bounced as heat pooled low, the ache between my thighs growing with every passing second.

"James, please..."

"Ah, Princess," he whispered huskily against my skin, "I'll do anything for you, but I won't be rushed. Not this first time." He sucked and nipped, pinched and teased until I was trembling like a leaf in a storm.

When his deft fingers finally drifted to the waistband of my britches, they traced patterns on the soft skin of my belly before slipping beneath the fabric. My breath caught on a hiss as he tugged my pants and underwear down my thighs in one motion, the anticipation nearly driving me mad.

He pressed me onto my back against the bed, spreading my legs and then standing back for a moment to stare down at me.

"I'll not forget this sight for as long as I live," he vowed, his face a mask of something between pleasure and pain as he took in every inch of me, from head to toe, before meeting my gaze. "No matter what happens tomorrow, know this. I love you, Harmony Fallowell MacInnes, Princess turned Queen, and I've loved you always."

My heart sang and my vision blurred as I tried to give voice to the emotions rioting inside me.

He loved me. James Tyler Hook fucking loved me...

I was about to tell him I loved him too, but then he was settling between my thighs, head bent, mouth inches from where I needed him most. The warmth of his breath sending a delicious shiver racing through me. When the very tip of his tongue finally touched my sensitive flesh, every nerve ending flared to life. I clawed at the blankets, desperate for something to anchor me as he sucked my clit into his mouth and began to draw on it with soft, insistent pressure.

Oh, gods.

It was pure torture. His mouth was so hot. His tongue so soft...

My breath went harsh as blood roared in my ears. I was going to—

"No!" I managed, tugging his hair hard in one fist. "No. Not this time. This time I want to taste *you*."

If it was our last night together, I vowed to make it a night full of firsts.

He didn't fight me as I rolled to my side and tugged him up the bed until he was lying flat. He was still fully dressed, but I was ready for the challenge. I threw one leg over his hips and set to unbuttoning his shirt.

"This is better than any of the dreams. Fuck, you're beautiful," he growled, skimming the tip of his hook up my thigh.

His hard length bucked against me and I groaned, barely resisting the urge to grind against him to relieve the ache building like a bonfire. With my shaking hands, it took me far longer than it should've to finally yank his shirt free. Damn, was it worth it, though. His chest was a gorgeous tapestry of tattoo and muscle, and I could've traced every inch of it for hours if not for the sudden rolling of his hips distracting the fuck out of me.

"You're incorrigible."

I launched myself off him with a growl and went to work on his pants, trying not to think about what was waiting beneath them in hopes of making quicker time that I had with his shirt. But when I pulled them down over his hips, the world screeched to a halt.

I wanted desperately to make him feel the way I felt. Like there was nothing but the two of us...

Or the three of us...

I stared down at his heavy length, mesmerized. "Is that going to...will that...fit?"

His pained laugh broke the spell and he nodded slowly. "It will, love. Promise. We could try right now, if you're game?"

But I wouldn't be dissuaded. I closed my fingers around his shaft squeezing lightly, and was instantly rewarded with a snarled string of curses.

"You've got two minutes of this, maybe three, so do your worst."

I bent closer and flicked out my tongue to taste him, drawing back in surprise as his cock jerked at my touch. His stomach was clenched so tight I could count every muscle as I tried again, this time drawing him lightly into my mouth. The head was so smooth, so warm. I tightened my grip and let out a low moan as he arched into me.

"Fucking hell!"

His reaction only fanned the flames higher and I ground my pelvis against his thigh as I sucked harder, pulled him deeper. He drove a hand into my hair, but let me control the pace as I moved up and down, sucking him in and then expelling him, almost until his cock was free before pulled deep again.

I was so lost in him—his taste, his scent, his soft skin, like velvet stretched over a length of steel—that I let out a cry of surprise when he grabbed me at the waist and yanked me up until we were face to face.

"That's enough of that, woman, or it'll be the end of me."

In one smooth motion, he rolled me to my back and rose above me. My heart skipped at the sight of his hard, powerful body over mine. I was here...with the man of my dreams, only this time, it was about to become a reality.

He pressed the swollen head against entrance, and I held my breath. I probably should've been afraid, but all I could think was how long I'd waited for this moment. How much I needed to feel him filling me up...

He pressed forward, the broad tip of his cock probing and then sliding in. Stretching me as he flexed his hips, bent low to touch his forehead to mine.

It was only when I let out a low gasp of pain that he slowed to a stop.

"Harmony?"

"It-it's okay. It's my first time, so it's bound to hurt a little."

His eyes widened and tried to pull away, but I would have none of it. I sank my nails into the muscles of his back and wrapped my legs around his hips.

His forearms trembled as I lifted my hips up to force him deeper, and deeper still. The pain was a mere twinge compared to the relief at finally feeling him wedged inside me.

"My love," I whispered, peppering his jaw with desperate kisses. My body was begging me to move. To take what was needed, and so I did, bouncing slowly at first, and then faster. Riding that thick, hard cock, savoring every drag of his flesh against mine.

He let out a groan and yanked one of my hands high over

my head and thrust his hips in rythmn with mine. Driving into me with bone-melting, sure strokes.

Each rock of his hips pressed the head of his cock against some spot hidden deep within me that had me chanting his name. It was almost too much. Like if he didn't stop, I was going to hurl straight off the earth and…

"James, I—"

He bent his head low to suck my nipple into his mouth and it was done. My body shattered into a million pieces as I clenched over him again and again. I wanted to watch him, but stars exploded behind my eyelids as waves of pleasure crashed over me.

"You feel so good. Ah, Princess…Fuck!" He drove deep one last time and held there, quaking as he spurted inside me.

CHAPTER 35

knock rattled the door, jolting me from sleep. Duncan's voice filtered through, muffled but clear enough.

"Hey, you two awake? Need you down in the throne room. The birds are back."

"Be right down!" I called, raising a hand and using my magic to light the lamp beside the bed. "They know we were…together."

Hook stretched beside me, clearly unbothered at having been caught sharing my bed, and as I caught sight of his muscular chest covered in Tideblessing tattoos, I was feeling less bothered by the second myself.

"Unless you plan on making them all wait on us another twenty minutes, you better get that look off of your face," Hook growled, his eyes locked on my mouth.

"Right. Going!"

I swung my legs out from the covers, grabbing yesterday's clothes from the floor and dressing fast, my eyes pinned to the floor. Hook did the same as he buttoned his shirt.

As I settled my whip on my hip and moved for the door,

though, his fingers closed around my wrist. He spun me around, yanking me flush against him and kissed me hard on the mouth.

"Once we have a few minutes," he said, voice rough, "we need to have a talk about us."

"I thought…" I cleared my tight throat, heart suddenly hammering as I tried again, "I thought there was no us?"

A grim smile curved his lips. "Liar." He brushed past me and called over his shoulder. "Better run a brush through that hair before you come down or Moll's going to be pissed."

Was it me, or did he seem lighter, somehow? Did I dare hope that our night together had changed something between us…something *inside* him?

Later.

There would be time to think all this through later, when an entire empire wasn't relying on me.

When I got to the throne room, Freya handed me a steaming mug of black coffee and a crust of bread. Hook was there shortly after drinking his, watching my every move over the rim. I took a long sip, not caring that it burned my mouth. It was bitter, but it would do the job, and that was what I needed after only a few hours rest.

"Bless you," I murmured to Freya with a smile.

Fetch perched quietly on the arm of my throne, his feathers looking bedraggled. I reached out, brushing his wings gently to right them. Exhaustion radiated from him in waves, and I winced. He was getting older. I needed to keep that in mind before I sent him out on long flights like that.

I'm sorry, old friend. Rest now.

He ducked his head in acknowledgment as Billy stepped forward.

"Bonnie's first," she said, handing over a tiny scroll.

I blew out a breath as I opened it and scanned the contents, instant relief easing the tightness in my chest.

"They're coming. The Eastern faction is on its way. Forty men, twelve women fighters, and several elders and mothers with young ones that can help behind the lines."

The room buzzed with murmurs of excitement.

"Fetch's, from the North." Billy handed me the second scroll, and I took it, hoping for similar news.

My stomach sank as I read the first few lines.

"They aren't coming." I lowered the note, glancing up at the anxious faces around me. "They would need to pass Almira's territory to get here in any reasonable amount of time, and the monkey population is too thick. If they leave en masse, they'll be slaughtered before they ever reach us."

I found myself wishing I hadn't accidentally dropped the quill and ink before getting sucked out of Oz, but who knew if it would've even worked in this case? Pulling people from the book into C'an Saas wasn't the same as moving them around in a story, and something told me that the quill and ink was meant to create the prophecy and the prophecy only. Once all the players were in place, it was up to us to write our story, and we didn't need a quill and ink to do it.

I read on, frowning as I took in the rest. "There's something else…a spy in Almira's kitchen staff says she returned yesterday and hasn't left her quarters since."

"That's good, isn't it?" Duncan said. "Means she's weak."

I nodded slowly. "Projecting herself into Oz and the attacks outside and in Emerald City would've drained her. This might be our chance."

More fighters would've been good news, but there was one in particular that we needed more than any other. In fact, more than a hundred others.

I turned to Freya. "Gayelette, the witch…do you know where she's being held?"

"Aye." Freya pursed her lips. "She's imprisoned in a cave to the north, about two miles from Almira's keep."

I paused, an ember of hope blooming in my chest. "You mean she isn't being kept somewhere in the lair itself?"

"No, Your Highness. According to our spies, Almira wanted her to suffer in solitude as she herself did when your father sent her to the Dreadkeep for all those years."

And there it was. Through it all, I'd sensed it was more than just a quest for power. There had been a hatred in her eye when we'd locked gazes through the glass bubble back in Munsch Kin Land. One that went deep. Now I finally knew why.

"She had long since lost her way," Freya continued. "Gone from mischievous to cruel and was only getting worse. Your father had no choice. But it stoked the flames of rage, and she spent her time in the Dreadkeep growing stronger, preparing for revenge."

I nodded, trying to think with my head and not with my heart. "Let's take advantage of her emotional choice and use it to our benefit then. Before we march on Almira, we rescue Gayelette. Let's come up with a plan. There are no bad ideas, so if you have something to say, speak."

Before anyone could, the door burst open and one of Freya's men rushed in, his face pale. "Your Highness, you need to see this!"

Freya was already pushing herself up from her seat, and Duncan paused to help her stand as the rest of us rushed after the guard. He led us down a ruined corridor that led to the palace doors.

He shoved them open, and I squinted as light flooded into the chamber. The full, radiant sun had just crept over the horizon. Something that Freya and her people hadn't seen in months. She let out a choked gasp, gripping my arm to keep from stumbling.

I held her up, but it was a task as my own knees buckled. The palace grounds and everything I could see beyond them were a blackened wasteland. Ruined buildings as far as the eyes could see were a grim reminder of the kingdom my father had lost. Twisted, long-dead trees littered the grounds, and there wasn't a speck of green in sight. Not even a blade of grass had survived, as if Almira had been intent on stamping out every sign of life.

"It's a miracle," Freya breathed. "Our Queen has returned and brought the sun back with her!"

I could hear the ripple of excitement around me, but it couldn't touch the block of ice that had formed in my chest. How could something this broken ever be fixed?

"It's a lot, I know, but you just need to breathe."

Hook's low voice in my ear had me searching for some crumb of calm.

"Don't look at it as a problem. Use that big brain of yours and figure out how to use this as an opportunity."

I sucked in some air and nodded.

Think positive. Think opportunity.

It's not a wasteland. It's a...Fucking hell, it's a wasteland.

I scrubbed a hand over my face and tried again.

It used to be dark, and now it's light again. Old burnt up buildings and dead trees don't matter. With time, we could rebuild. So long as the sun is shining—

"So long as the sun is shining, most of the monkeys can't come out," I mumbled, turning to face Hook as my heart pounded with excitement. "So long as the sun is shining, we can make a play to rescue Gayelette!"

CHAPTER 36

The sun was directly overhead, but it sure didn't feel like it as the icy wind bit at my skin, cold seeping through the woolen cloak Freya had given me. It had belonged to my mother, and she'd packed it away in a cedar chest to keep it from the moths. I couldn't have been more grateful for it as I pulled it tighter around me.

This move was a gamble. The biggest we'd taken so far, and judging by the eerie silence as we traveled, all of us knew it. But we'd all agreed that two witches were exponentially better than one, and we'd all agreed we had to try.

That didn't make the march toward the world's most evil-looking castle any less terrifying. We could see it now, clearly in the distance. The hulking, black eyesore, emanating dread.

But that wasn't our destination. Not today, at least.

Today, we had only one goal and one goal only;

Rescue Gayelette.

I shot a glance at Hook as we moved through the charred remains of what had once been a forest. Billy had taken the lead, keeping watch for signs of Almira's scouts while Duncan brought up the rear to watch our backs. The barren tree branches offered *some* cover, but if any came flying directly overhead, it was open season.

We'd set off a few hours earlier, leaving Freya and a handful of her people behind to watch the children and those who were too old to fight. Between the others from C'an Saas, Hook's crew, the O'Donnellys—minus young Andrew —and all the others I'd brought in, we numbered around fifty. Not exactly an army, but with mine and Hook's magic combined, plus the skills of our fighters, it was hopefully enough for a successful extraction mission.

As much as my heart wanted to leave many behind in the relative safety of the ruins of the palace, including Moll, I needed them with me, and as ragtag of a group as it was, I had to remind myself that we all knew the stakes. If we failed, Almira would ruin everything anyway, same as she'd done to my father's kingdom.

The only way out was through, and Gayelette was our best bet.

As the others had prepared for the journey, I'd brought Xander in to assist as I tried to think of how to make the best use of what I had. He'd helped me mount my jeweler's loupe to a leather strip that I now wore around my head. With a flick of my wrist, I could drop a lens in front of my eye and see whatever it and my magic needed me to see. The magical clock was stuffed in my pouch, ready if or when I needed it.

But even with all that, I couldn't help but think of that single strike of black lightning…through glass…from another world. A strike that had been enough to sideline my magic for a week.

As strong as I was, Almira was far, far stronger. Gayelette's magic could be the great equalizer. I just hoped that there was enough of her left—both mentally and physically—to save.

"We're close, now," Hook said, falling into step beside me. I could feel his gaze searching my face. "You ready?"

As I'd ever be.

"I am."

Billy glanced over her shoulder, slowing down to let us catch up. "And when we find her? Are you certain Gayelette will help us?"

I grimaced, thinking back to how frail she'd been. How tortured...

"It will take time for her to recover, but she'll help." I looked out over the crumbling remains of a village just off the path we walked. "If we don't do this now, we may never get another chance. Almira could restore her powers and plunge this place into darkness again any minute."

We all glanced up, as if to check that it hadn't happened yet.

Billy lifted a hand, signaling for those behind us to stop. "The cave's just ahead. Once we step into the clearing, we'll be completely exposed, so keep your guard up."

I took a steadying breath, magic already at my fingertips as I stepped forward, probing with my magic. I don't know what I'd been expecting, but an instant connection wasn't it. Sure enough, though, there it was; Gayelette's energy, flickering weakly from deep inside the cave.

And, better yet, Almira's magic was nowhere to be found.

"We were right," I murmured, momentary relief washing over me. "I don't sense Almira here. Just Gayelette. This is our chance."

Hook stepped up beside me, drawing his saber. "Let's not waste it."

I gave the signal, and we marched in, weapons drawn. The cavern opened up even further, revealing a massive, sloping chamber. Stalactites hung from the ceilings, and the stench of rot hung in the air.

Red eyes burst into view as a dozen flying monkeys awoke at once, unfurling their wings as they prepared to charge. They were nothing like the larger, fierce scouts we'd faced, and they hardly seemed ready for a fight, startled from their sleep.

"Attack!" Hook shouted, a gale of wind surging right out of his hand. The blast slammed into the first two monkeys that came for us, splattering them against the cave wall with a sickening squelch.

I sent my whip out with a crack, stunning one of them mid-air with a strike to the forehead before letting the whip curl around its neck and yanking.

Snap.

Billy's arrows whistled through the air, finding their marks back-to-back with brutal efficiency, as Duncan charged to the front, cleaving right through an oncoming attacker with his broadsword.

The battle was quick and violent, ending almost before it even started. Freya's men and Hook's crew hadn't even stepped into the chamber by the time Hook and Duncan were sheathing their swords.

I scanned the cave, sucking in a breath as I took in the monkey corpses. We'd taken out every one of them and hadn't suffered a single loss or injury.

It was a good start.

I narrowed back in on the glow of Gayelette's magic, on high alert as I guided us toward her. We'd ventured another twenty yards into the cave when a heavy wooden door came into view. Reinforced with iron bands and a sturdy padlock, I didn't need magic to know that Gayelette was behind it.

I pressed my finger to the lock, sending out a pulse of magic that shattered it instantly. "Gayelette?" I called softly as I tugged the door open, stepping in with Hook at my side.

The second we walked into the damp, dark room, we saw

her. She was chained against the wall in a standing position, that same strange jacket in place, a rusty cage locked around her hips and shoulders giving her hardly any room to move. A filthy, threadbare dress hung from her bony frame.

Horror flicked through me, sending a shiver down my spine. I was cold, and I was wearing a coat and had meat on my bones. She must be chilled to the core.

I rushed to her side and her eyes flitted open, settling on me for a long moment before lighting with recognition.

"How are you here?" A wracking cough seized her, rattling the chains at her ankles. "Is my sister finally dead, then?"

Her gaze shifted behind me, landing on Hook, and her face twisted in confusion.

I lifted a hand to the bars and sensed the magic there as I tried to work out how to get around it and free her.

"Almira returned from Oz too weakened to keep the sun at bay. We knew it was our chance to come and—"

"No!" Her eyes went wild with panic. "Oh, child, what have you done?!" She strained at her bonds, leaning forward. "Run! Get out now, all of you!"

A low rumble echoed beneath my feet, and I spun toward the open door. A presence filled the air…one I'd only felt at a distance. Dark, oozing with pure, unmistakable hatred. Dread hit me like a physical blow.

Almira was here. And she was waiting…for me.

The sound of beating wings filled the chamber, but it wasn't coming from the outside. It rose from somewhere below as well.

"Oh, gods." Gayelette shrank against the wall. "There's an underground passage that leads from here to her tower. She's coming through the tunnel."

Almira's dark presence grew closer, along with that of her monkeys. Hundreds of them.

"Weapons at the ready!" Billy shouted.

Duncan leapt into action, drawing his sword and preparing for battle, but everyone else in the room seemed focused on me, waiting for my orders.

Of course they are. You're their leader.

Lead!

I forced myself to breathe, remembering my training. Deal with the now first, worry about the rest later.

"We have to free Gayelette," I called out firmly.

Hook nodded and nudged me aside, magic crackling in his palm as he aimed it at the locks around the bars caging her in. They didn't even budge.

"Don't bother," Gayelette rasped. "She's put a spell on them. They can't be opened by magic."

Plan B.

The sounds below us grew louder as I stuffed my hand into my pouch and yanked out my auto lock pick, tossing it to Paddy O'Donnelly.

"Go!" I urged him. "Start working on that lock. I'll be right back to help."

I spun to face the others. "I'm going to stay here and guard Paddy and Gayelette. I'll send Bonnie out the way we came to scout our exit. Hook, Duncan, Billy, Xander, Moll… take all the others to the opening of the passageway and hold those monkeys off. These will be her best scouts, so pull out all the stops. Seal it off if you can, maybe it will hold long enough for us to free Gayelette and get out."

Hook nodded, already moving, but Billy hesitated for a split second, sparing a long look at Paddy.

"You heard her, let's move!"

Billy stiffened her chin and nodded, nocking an arrow and stepping beside Hook. "Let's go."

"You got this, Harm." Molly readied her trusty incapacitator, eyes hard with determination as she took a position beside Xander before rushing out with the rest.

"Hold the line!" I shouted, making my way back to Paddy to help him with the lock. "Do not let them through!"

The first shackle clicked open, and he passed me the pick, producing a more rudimentary one of his own as he moved to the other side. The sounds of the fighting, monkeys screeching, war cries echoing, had the pick trembling in my fingers.

He glanced over, his easy smile winking to life even in the direst of circumstances. "Take it easy, lass. We can do this, yeah?"

"Yeah," I managed.

I got my fingers moving almost of their own accord, my instincts kicking in as I reached out to Bonnie, channeling magic through our bond to send her out the mouth of the cave. No one was better with a lock than me, but right now, with all these lives hanging in the balance, I felt clumsy and slow. I flicked a magnifying lens from my loupe into place, and the path became much clearer as I got to work.

The floor rumbled, stone and dust falling from the walls. Almira wasn't far now.

Bonnie's conscience tickled mine, and I channeled my energy into her, seeing the world through her eyes as she flew over the cave. The sun seemed to have set, because I could barely see. It was only when Bonnie turned her gaze to the sky that I understood.

It wasn't dark out. The mass of monkeys—tens of thousands it seemed, headed our way—had blotted out the sun.

My throat closed as I tried to stay calm. A few dozen fighters, no matter their skill, could never withstand that horde.

The next lock clicked open, but it hardly even registered as the lockpick clattered from my shaking fingers.

"I thought only a few monkeys could bear the sun?" I said to Gayelette as Paddy worked to free her from the strange jacket next.

"There is no sun, child," Gayelette said, sounding as defeated as I felt. "She just let you think there was. A simple glamour spell."

The world spun as I thought back to our journey here. That was why it had been so cold, even when I turned my face to the sky, there had been no hint of warmth. It had been a false sun all along, and giving it warmth would've used up too much power.

With the horde on its way and Almira closing in from below, we were trapped.

"There's no way out."

I left Paddy with Gayelette and bolted into the hall, nearly tripping over the dead monkeys as I went. Hook was ripping his saber from the chest of one of Almira's human foot soldiers as Billy and Duncan finished off the last of the monkeys in sight.

"James, Billy, Duncan!"

I rushed back to Gayelette's side, catching her as Paddy finished the job of freeing her completely. She rubbed at her raw, bloody wrists and pushed the greasy mass of hair from her face.

"We have to move." Behind us, the stone floor began to shudder and crack, like some kind of earthquake.

Gods damn it. This couldn't be how it ended, not after everything we'd been through.

I dug frantically through my bag, fingers closing around the smooth surface of the clock just as Hook, Duncan, and Billy rushed into the room behind me.

"We're in trouble." My voice cracked as I turned to face them. "She's got us boxed in. We need a new plan, and we need it now."

"There's only one way out," Gayelette called weakly. "Surely you know what it is…"

"No more of your cryptic bullshit!" I snapped. "Just spit it out!"

"Use your magic. You already have what you need."

I squeezed my eyes shut, gripping the clock until its edges bit into my palm, and willed with every fiber of my being for it to do something. *Anything* that could stop this or give us a moment of reprieve to think.

Then, everything went silent.

I opened my eyes, breath hitching in confusion. Hook, Duncan, Billy, Paddy, and Gayelette were staring at me, looking just as shocked. The hall behind them was still, monkeys frozen mid-air, their faces twisted into snarls. Scotty and Jacob stood immobilized just beyond Billy, frozen mid-stride like stone statues.

A faint, shimmering blue barrier surrounded us in a circle about ten feet in diameter. Beyond it, the world had simply… stopped.

"What the—" Billy reached out, poking her finger at the edge of the barrier. The field shimmered as it sank into it, and she yanked it back, eyes going wide as she stared down at it. She poked at it a few more times. "Oh, that's a good one."

"We're frozen in time," Duncan said, letting out a sigh of relief.

"We aren't," I corrected. "Everything else is. But it won't last long. We need answers." I turned sharply to Gayelette. "Tell me what you want me to do."

"You still haven't figured it out…Either one of you?" Her gaze softened, as she turned her gaze toward Hook. "You weren't the only child of C'an Saas to be sent into the fairy-tale book that day. I sent James first. But not before half of your magic was placed into him for safekeeping. The darker half. The half that I feared would be too hard for you to control without guidance…too dark for you to bear without driving you mad. It was always meant to return to you once you were ready."

My mind tripped over the words even as my soul absorbed them.

Hook's suffering…all that he'd gone through, had never belonged to him.

It was meant to be mine.

The implications weren't lost on anyone else either, and the room felt as heavy as a blanket made of lead.

"You're ready now, and you must take it. Whatever he can do with his Tideblessings, you, as the original witch of that magic, can do tenfold."

"T-take it, how?" I croaked.

Gayelette hesitated. "The only way magic like that can ever be taken, Harmony. By dealing the death blow."

My vision blurred, bile rising in my throat. "No. No, that can't be right."

I could sense Hook's movement beside me as he went to his knees. He'd been silent so far, and stayed that way as he flipped his blood-stained saber, grabbing it by the blade, holding the handle in my direction. His gaze locked with mine as he pulled his hook across his shirt, tearing it open to bear his chest.

"Do it, Harmony, and don't argue. It's the only way."

I batted the sword to the ground and grabbed at his wrist, yanking hard. "Stand up. Stop this, right now. You're wasting time!"

"You've had my heart from the start, now take it. It's yours."

Gayelette clicked her tongue, her voice harsher than before. "Look at these people! Think of your subjects! Their lives are in your hands now. This is your destiny…and his. One life for many; it's an easy choice."

My heart seized, memories of the trial flooding my brain. I'd failed before, choosing the few over the many. I didn't have the courage to make the hard decision then.

As Queen, the choice was clear.

My fingers curled around the dagger at my hip, drawing it out in a shaking fist. I met Hook's steady gaze and reared back, plunging the blade deep…into the wall behind him.

"No!" I spun toward Gayelette, grabbing a fistful of her dress and dragging her closer, until we were nose-to-nose. "Fuck you, and fuck Almira. We win together or we lose together. You can join us or you can stay here alone. What's it going to be, Gayelette?"

CHAPTER 37

Time rushed forward before Gayelette could answer, and noise slammed into me from all sides. The clanging of swords, shrieking of monkeys, all resuming at once as the clock began to tick again.

Gayelette stumbled, and I latched onto her, holding her steady.

"We'll need a way out," she said, her expression grim.

"They'll be at the mouth of the cave in minutes," I whispered. "Thousands of them."

Gayelette drew a shaky breath. "Better to face the monkeys than her. Collapse the tunnel and buy us a bit of time."

I turned to Duncan, jabbing my finger toward Gayelette. "Help her into the hall. We need you ready to go once this is done."

I charged back out of the chamber to see piles of dead monkeys now clogging the space, with our forces finishing off the final few of that wave, but the break in the action was just the chance we needed.

Hook stepped out beside me, laying a hand on his shoul-

340

der, "What're we thinking?"

"We've gotta cave in the passageway."

He nodded, his magic bubbling to life. "There were too many monkeys to manage before, but I'm on it as soon as we get everyone clear."

"Retreat!" I called, watching as our small band of fighters pulled back.

"On three," Hook grunted.

I matched his stance, letting my own magic flow. I had no idea what Tideblessing he planned to use, but, somehow, I didn't need to. Instead, I tapped into something far deeper. The very essence of his magic, letting my energy meld into his. They swirled together in a single, palpable mass, ready to be unleashed.

And, even as the next wave of monkeys charged into view from the passageway, I had no doubt that we could do it.

"Now!"

The blast slammed into the ceiling, cracking the wooden support beams. The tunnel shuddered violently, bringing down more and more rubble. The screeches of the monkeys beyond turned to screams, then faded beneath tons of stone.

I spun, chest heaving as we sprinted toward the cave's mouth. "Outside, quickly!"

Duncan hefted Gayelette into his arms, charging into the hall in step with Hook and I. Collapsing the passageway had been a small victory, but we weren't in the clear yet. Not when there were legions of monkeys outside even now, waiting for our exit.

The tunnel behind shook, sending fresh debris skittering across the floor, and Almira's cold, taunting laughter seemed to roll right through it, like she was inches away despite the layers of stone between us.

"Did you actually expect that to stop me, little witch?"

My gut twisted into knots as we burst out of the cave, our

ragged, battle-worn fighters stumbling all around. The monkeys were still a good distance overhead, but their attention shifted to us almost immediately, and they came swooping down in droves.

"What do we do?"

I looked over to see Molly standing beside me. There was no fear in her eyes, just grim determination on her blood-spattered face as she awaited my orders.

I was about to give them when the world exploded.

A deafening blast shattered the cave, spraying stone and rubble in every direction. The force sent me hurtling and I struggled for footing, my vision going dark around the edges.

"Moll?!" My voice sounded muffled and distant even to my own ears as I searched through the settling dust.

A sick feeling settled over me until I caught sight of Molly sprawled in the dirt a few yards away, dazed but alive.

She scrambled toward me and linked arms as the shrieks grew closer. Our fighters were only beginning to find their feet, looking dazed and confused from the blast as shadows descended from above.

The monkeys were closing in, but it was a sizzle of energy at the now-obliterated cave that had my attention. There, from the rubble rose Almira in the flesh, her black cloak billowing, hair cascading behind her like quicksilver as she rose into the sky.

Her gaze locked on me, and she smiled.

"Such a simple girl," she called, shaking her head. "Naive, like your mother, running headlong into trouble time and time again, and not seeing the trap until it's sprung. All to help a feeble, starving old witch."

I stared into the face of the woman who had killed my father. Who had ruined my life and that of all the people in

C'an Saas. Instead of blasting her to pieces, I stood there. Frozen.

Billy grabbed me by the shoulder, jolting me out of my paralysis. "Snap out of it, Harm. We need you!"

Her words sliced through the mental fog like a slap.

"A shame you didn't take after Gayelette instead..." Almira continued. "That might've made this more interesting."

The first of the monkeys were touching down, and a few of our men were already fighting.

"I think the fact that you spent the past twenty years following me around, trying to stop me from getting here and failing is actually *super* interesting."

The words hit their mark, and she snarled and whipped off a blast of magic just like I knew she would. The second it came, I lifted a hand, deflecting it right back at her, superspeed.

She reeled back to dodge it, flew back, dropping closer to the ground as she tried to regain her composure.

"Hook, Duncan, Billy...You're with me," I called, more confident by the moment. "We're going to focus on Almira. Everyone else, hold those monkeys off for as long as you can! If we kill the witch, the monkeys go down with her."

The group surged forward, but Almira had recovered and cackled louder as she floated closer, hovering only a few feet above the ground now.

I saw a figure moving toward her out of the corner of my eye and tried not to react. It was Gayelette.

And she was making a move.

"It was a waste of time to come here. Gayelette was never a match for me, even at her strongest. Always weak, always trailing behind Marin and me. But at least she wasn't a damned fool. You, on the other hand, are barely more than a child. All your mother's faults, with none of her strength."

She lifted a hand and hurled a ball of flames our way, but Hook was ready for her, hitting it with a blast of water. It connected with a sizzle and disappeared into a harmless puff of steam.

That sent Almira into a fury, and she fired off a flurry of attacks, each more deadly than the last.

Black lightning came straight for my forehead, but I managed to catch it with my whip tip right on time, wrestling it to the scorched earth where it fizzled and died.

I looked over to seeing Billy tucking and rolling to dodge a dagger made of ice.

And Almira didn't stop, so busy trying to kill us that she didn't see her sister coming.

"Ahhhh!"

Gayelette launched herself onto Almira's back, wrapping her legs around the other witch's waist, putting her into a chokehold and dragging her to the ground in a tangle of limbs.

Almira let out a snarl, reaching for the knife at her waist and blindly stabbing behind her.

One, two, three quick strikes before she was able to flip her attacker off her back and onto the ground beside her.

"Did you really think you'd be able to kill me like that? Who dares—"

Her words died, sneer shifting to a look of shock as she stared down at Gayelette crumpled on the ground before her.

Gayelette's breath came in harsh gasps as she searched for me.

"I…wish your mother could have seen. She'd have been proud of me, I think." She let out a final cough, then went limp, her blood pooling in the dirt around her.

Almira threw her head back as agony gripped her face.

Her scream cut through the battlefield as she stumbled back, her hand going to her chest.

Blood pounded in my ears as I forced my feet into action, sprinting at her with Billy and Hook at my side as a monkey swooped down to tackle Duncan.

Killing her coven sister hadn't killed her, but it had dealt Almira a major blow. It was up to us to finish it.

"Now!" I shouted, channeling every bit of magic I could summon as Hook surged to my side. The air trembled with power as we blasted right into her defenses with twin streams of energy. She tried to shield herself with magic, throwing up her arms, but either she was too weakened or we were too strong. I could smell the burning flesh and cloth.

"Don't let up!" I shouted, watching as Billy sprinted past us, firing an arrow at Almira's exposed chest with a feral roar.

A second later, a monkey fell from the sky. Then two. Screeches filled the air and what had been a battle now became a game of dodging the bodies as they dropped from the sky.

Hook and I lowered our hands in stunned surprise.

Had Billy's arrow hit its mark?

But a low cackle had the hairs on the back of my neck rising, and it grew louder as Almira shot into the sky.

I yanked a lens of the loupe over my eye and watched in horror as all the dark energy flowing out of the dying beasts in the sky flowed in a straight path, right into Almira's outstretched palms.

"You could have done the same, you know," she snarled. "Killed your one-armed guardian and reclaimed the magic you loaned him all at once. Might've had a chance then, especially with that stunt my fool of a sister pulled. Did you know that Gayelette bought your pirate for a sack of potatoes? Though I'm starting to think she should've haggled more."

The words were cruel, and rage shot through me, but I tried to think past that to the meat of things.

The monkeys weren't dying because we'd cut the proverbial head off the snake. They were dying because she was draining her "vessels" of magic for herself.

"I missed," Billy rasped as she moved in beside me. "We were so fucking close, and I missed."

"We'll get another shot," I said, my throat like sandpaper as I gave one last look to poor Gayelette.

Billy grunted, and I turned, watching her face contort with pain.

"Hellfire…she's calling my magic back to her as well," she managed through clenched teeth. "It's faint, like a dull ache, but I feel it."

Almira let out a howl, then spun in the air, her power thick and sparkling behind my lens, like a suffocating wave.

"You have my thanks, dear sister," she called, gesturing toward Gayelette's body with a flourish. "I was too afraid to try it, but now I know. I have transcended our lowly coven, entering the realm of the gods. Fear me!"

With a flick of her fingers, Gayelette's fallen body exploded into a visceral mess of guts and bone. And then her attention shifted to me, her lip curling with contempt.

"You're next, my pretty."

She disappeared, then shimmered back into existence right in front of us. Her entire body glowed as she twirled, lashing out at us with raw magic. "I'm done playing."

Her first shot veered toward Duncan as he and the others formed a wall in front of me. He brought his sword up in the nick of time, his feet gouging trenches in the dirt as he skidded back. The blind fury he'd used to rely on was gone, and replaced with cool, calculated rage.

In the same, fluid motion, she turned her energy on Hook, blasting him with a torrent of flame like nothing I'd ever seen. He reacted with his water blessing just in time, but her fire ate right through it and would've struck him if I hadn't thrown up a quick shield.

The battle continued at a breakneck pace, but I was beginning to grasp the patterns. If I focused hard, I could see it. Each shift in Almira's posture, the subtle flares of magic gathering at her fingertips, just like Duncan taught me. The battle felt less chaotic and more choreographed with each passing second.

Each time she attacked, I was there just in time, throwing up a shield or knocking her off course at the last possible second. All the while, Billy kept firing. I used every ounce of magic I could muster to shield them, throwing out an occasional crack of my whip as Xander stepped in beside me.

Almira snarled, finally forced onto defense with her attention flickering between too many of us.

I risked a glance around me as I realized the last of the monkeys had fallen and the others were headed our way. If we were near to overwhelming her, with the rest of us, we could finish this! Raw power was on her side, sure, but our teamwork was too much for her to handle now that she'd gotten rid of all her allies.

"We've almost got her! Attack. Attack!"

For a moment, I allowed myself to hope. The O'Donnellys rushed into the fray, Paddy roaring as he hurled a sharpened stone at her, striking her in the side of the head. I threw up a shield before she could counter, letting him dip away free from a returning blow.

Molly and Hook's crew came sprinting forward, raining daggers and knives upon her like a hailstorm. She was distracted, shielding herself from them, when Duncan and Hook lunged at her in unison, but she skipped away at the last second, her lips twisting into a cruel smile as energy gathered in her fingertips.

I focused, trying and failing to see who she was aiming at. The bolt of magic streaked from her finger a moment later, hurtling toward Xander, faster than I could follow with my eyes. I strained, muscles tensing as I threw up a hasty shield, praying it'd be enough.

Relief started washing over me, then twisted to dread as the attack shifted in midair as if moved by an unseen hand and headed directly at Hook's exposed back as he turned to face me. I opened my mouth to scream, willing my magic to protect him, but it was too late.

The projectile slammed through his back, punching straight out the other side in a spray of blood. He staggered, his cloak of shadow and wind dissipating.

Almira's laughter pierced the ringing in my ears, shrill and victorious as I rushed to Hook's side and dropped beside him just in time to see the light go out in the those inky black eyes

"No…no!!!"

CHAPTER 38

"James?"

But I knew it was already too late. I'd sensed it the moment she'd struck him. His life force flooding out of him, his heartbeat slowing to a stop…

"Being Queen means sacrifice, Harmony. Your mother never understood that." Almira's voice sounded distant and far away, dampened by the fog of sadness and pain. "Are you going to be as naive as she was?"

I struggled to breathe, hardly registering her words as I stared down at the man I loved, and she wasn't done. I tore my eyes off him as she stalked forward yet again, power bleeding from her fingertips as she advanced on me.

Xander and Duncan stepped up in front of me in unison, ready to hold her off.

"No!" I gasped, horrified as Almira broke into a charge that they met head on.

The clock.

I yanked it from my pouch and stared down at it, willing it to stop with everything I had. If I just had a second, maybe I could gather my strength and—

The second hand froze, and time halted around me, freezing Almira mid-swing, along with all the others.

"That's not enough. That's not nearly enough!" I sobbed. Even if we could find some way to beat her, what did it all mean, without James?

The lives of many...

A Queen needs to make sacrifices...

"Fuck you and your many. Fuck you and your sacrifices!" I snarled, pinching the clock's brass hand, grunting as the metal fought back against me, resisting my magic with its own. "Just a few minutes," I begged, pulling with all my strength. *"Please."*

The metal ground, but held tight, and a scream tore from my throat as I blasted it with everything I had, using my pain as fuel.

Click.

The hand gave way, reversing just a scant bit, and the world exploded into a blur of color and sound as time began flowing backwards. Almira pulled away from Duncan and Xander, and my body moved against my will, surging back in the direction I'd come from, and Captain James Tyler Hook rose to his feet, his broken body whole again.

The relief kept me shaking and on my knees. While I was down there, I prayed for another moment to gather my thoughts, but the clock had other plans, ticking right back into motion as time began to flow.

"We've almost got her! Attack. Attack!"

The O'Donnellys rushed into the fray, Paddy roaring as he hurled a sharpened stone at her, striking her in the side of the head. I threw up a shield before she could counter, letting him dip away scott free.

Molly and Hook's crew came sprinting forward, raining daggers and knives upon her like a hailstorm.

She was distracted, shielding herself from them, when

Duncan and Hook lunged at her in unison, but she skipped away at the last second, her lips twisting into a cruel smile as energy gathered in her fingertips.

"Xander, back!" I shouted, spotting the shift in her demeanor.

Just as expected, Almira pushed herself into the air, letting loose a blast of energy, and I gritted my teeth, splitting my magic into two shields at once. One for Xander, one for Hook.

And this time, when she tried the same trick, turning the attack on Hook, and I let out a triumphant roar as it bounced uselessly off my shield. But it didn't last.

Almira flicked out of view, appearing at Molly's side with impossible speed. She lashed out with a blade of pure magic, severing her head before she even had time to cry out.

My scream tore through the air once again, raw and broken, and yet again, Almira laughed.

"No…Not this either! Fucking hell, come on!"

My fingers closed around the clock again, tears streaming from my face as I pulled it back once again, sending my surroundings into a blur. I couldn't lose her.

Not Molly.

Again and again, I tried. Again and again, I watched those I loved most perish, and it only got worse. Hook and Billy. Molly and Duncan. Paddy and Scotty. And then, everyone except me…

Each reset grew more taxing. Each time, the clock fought harder. Each time, the moment grew closer. I was running out of tries and I knew it.

Had my mother been right? Was I destined to lose, no matter how many ways I tried? In choosing Hook, had I doomed us all?

But somehow, even as I spiraled into despair, I wouldn't have changed it. There had to be another way.

One. More. Try.

I yanked with the last of my strength, and reality snapped back into view, and I fell to my knees.

My fingers shook around the clock, my heart twisting painfully in my chest. "This time, it'll be different."

"This time??" Billy asked, eyes filled with confusion as she looked at me. Her gaze drifted down to the clock, her eyes widening in recognition.

I leapt up as Almira charged, wiping my tears as I barked orders, moving my friends around the battlefield like pieces on a chessboard. "Hook, stay right! Xander, Paddy, stay on her. Don't give her a second to breathe!"

The battle shifted in our favor, as always, this time even faster than usual. Almira staggered back, hardly able to get an attack off.

We would be ready this time.

Almira reeled, dashing away a solid minute before expected, magic gathering in her finger.

Fuck, fuck fuck. What had changed now?

"Duncan, Paddy, get back!"

They hesitated, eyes wide with confusion, and my heart sank. She was far too close to them, and they weren't nearly ready for the counter that would come when I blocked her first attack. Panic clawed at my throat, knowing what came next.

I threw magic forward in a frantic wave, shields bursting into existence to cover Xander and Hook. My strength burned away as I strained to shield Duncan and Paddy, too, but Almira was already on them, a blade of magic forming in her hand.

My magic shimmered into view in front of them, but it was too little and too late. Her blade sliced clean through it, hurtling toward their exposed necks.

Then a blur of motion flashed at her side, smashing into

her the instant before her sword would've landed. I blinked in confusion, already gathering my magic for an attack as I realized what'd happened.

Billy had slammed into her at the last possible second, knocking her back and plunging her dagger deep into the witch's neck. Blood spurted into the air as if from a fountain, and an agonized scream tore from Almira's throat as she flailed.

"Not today, you evil bitch," Billy snarled, tearing her knife free only to plunge it in again, this time right into the side of her head.

Almira shrieked, her arm shooting out to grab Billy by the throat.

"You worthless defect," she spat, her voice shaking with rage.

I tried to manifest a shield around her, but Almira was ready, batting the spell away with a flick of her wrist. Almira slammed Billy onto the ground. The sickening snap of bone cracked through the air. Billy gasped once, pain etched on her face, then Almira unleashed a torrent of dark energy directly into her chest standing above her, relishing in her screams.

"No!"

Hook lifted his hand, taking advantage of her distraction, creating a funnel of swirling wind in his palm. A second later, a tornado surged from his fingertips forming a storm unlike anything I'd ever seen.

Miguel's tornado Tideblessing, I realized. The magic Hook had sworn to never use.

The storm slammed into Almira, breaking her dark hold on Billy and sending her skittering back, water battering her from every direction.

I screamed, pouring every bit of energy I had left into one, desperate strike. The sky itself opened at my command, a lightning bolt cracking downward and smacking right into her. The tornado pulled in on itself and then exploded outward in a flash of light, sending raindrops spattering to the dirt below.

Silence reigned as we all stepped forward, waiting for the steam to clear.

Please, gads…please let it be over.

And then there it was. Almira's rigid, carbonized body, mouth frozen open for eternity in a final scream. I could hardly believe what was right in front of me. The truth settled in the sudden silence. We'd done it.

She was dead.

I rushed to Billy's side. She let out a wheeze, sending a trickle of blood from the corner of her mouth. She managed a weak smile when she saw me.

"Did we get that bitch, Princess? We got the bitch, didn't we?"

"We did," I said, trying to quell the terror closing over me as I fell to my knees beside her.

Could I do it one more time? Surely, I had enough power to do it once more. I'd do exactly as we'd done, except for shield Billy as she mounted her attack. It would work out the exact same way this time.

It had to.

My hand flew to my pocket and a sense of dread closed over me. Had I dropped it in the battle? I searched the ground frantically as Duncan, James, and Paddy reached us. And then it hit me.

"What did you do!?" I demanded, covering the sucking wound in Billy's chest with my hand, watching in horror as the blood spread, soaking the front of her shirt in seconds. "Answer me, Billy! What the fuck did you do?"

Her head had lolled to the side and she met my gaze.

"Sorry, Princess. I need this to be the version that sticks."

Her arms flexed against my knee, and I looked down as her closed fist unfurled, revealing the shattered remains of my clock resting in her palm.

Clever girl. She'd seen me. She'd realized what I was doing and then decided to take matters into her own hands to save her brothers this time.

To save us all.

The lives of one for the lives of many.

"No!" Duncan cheeks were chalk white and his eyes filled with panic as he wheeled around. "No, fuck this! Hook?"

I swiped the river of tears from my eyes and turned to James. "Can you?"

But I already knew the answer before he shook his head. Even if he hadn't expended most of his energy during the fight, the Mend Tideblessing wasn't meant for mortal wounds. He could heal broken bones, help with pain, or stitch a gash.

Billy's heart was beyond repair.

"Please don't cry, Princess. I got everything I ever wanted." She sucked in a rattling breath as she focused on something just over my shoulder. I turned to see Paddy and the rest of her brothers just a few yards away. She yanked me closer and pressed my ear to her lips.

"When you write my story, will you tell them I was brave?"

"The bravest." I choked the words out as I cupped her cheek.

She nodded and pulled away as Paddy, Andrew, and the others all gathered around her.

"I'm here, love," Paddy murmured, taking her hand and squeezing. "We're all here."

"Perfect." A peaceful smile spread across her lips as she held his gaze for a long moment before her eyes drifted shut. "That's perfect."

CHAPTER 39

One Year Later...

"You better tell them rabbits to stop eating my lettuce!"

I whipped my head around to see Cissy marching toward Tristan, blonde curls flying like streamers behind her. She didn't stop until she was toe-to-toe with the older boy, neck craned as she glared up at him.

"You know how long it took me to figure out lettuce, Tristan?" she demanded, perching one hand on her hip. "Now I can barely get a couple heads of the stuff growing enough to pick before one of your ten million bunnies decides it's dinner and chomps through it all—a whole row!"

"So?" Tristan fed Fetch the last morsel of boar meat in his hand before swiping his palm on his pants and bending low enough to meet Cissy's gaze. "You weren't complaining about all my rabbits last night when we were eating that delicious stew, were you?"

He snicked his tongue and shook his head in disappointment.

Molly rolled up beside me and glanced my way. "Did we ever fight like this growing up?"

I shook my head. "Nope. Waste of time. You'd have badgered me to death until you got your way, so I learned fast to just give you what you wanted."

"And now look at us. You're Queen, and I'm one of your lowly subjects." She let out a sigh. "What a kick in the lady bits."

"You live in a palace with me and are about to be married to my Master at Arms. I think you'll be okay."

"Somebody's got to do it." She admired her gleaming engagement ring again and shot me a wink.

When Xander had come and asked me if it was too soon for a second C'an Saas wedding a few months back, I'd not only given my blessing. I'd also handed over the massive chunk of emerald I'd squirreled away in my pocket for Molly from the mausoleum in Emerald City. He'd come up with a gorgeous design and even asked me to facet it for him. The result had been the second most beautiful ring I'd ever laid eyes on.

I spared a glance to the pearl on my finger. A keepsake of my mother's that I would forever be grateful for.

"I'd better squash this." Tristan and Cissy had ramped up to a shouting match and Molly crossed her arms and headed into the fray.

"Let's not fight, children. Why don't we come to a compromise, alright? We've got two rows of cabbage that look perfect, so let's pick those for supper tonight. And maybe tomorrow Harmony can work out a contraption or a charm that will keep those rabbits out of your lettuce for next time. Sound good?"

Cissy shrugged and swiped the back of her hand over her

nose. "I guess so." She was about to walk away when Tristan tugged at one of her white-blonde curls.

"Wanna see something cool?" he asked.

She scowled at him but didn't say no. "What is it?"

"I think my Tideblessing finally worked on that pair of robins," he said. "I peeked in the nest the other day, and there was a clutch of tiny blue eggs. Want to check them out with me?"

Her eyes shined as she nodded.

"You guys go. I'll catch up when I'm done!" Caleb called. He was looking up from his snack of grapes and cheese. It was hard to even see the boy I'd first met in the robust, energetic kid that sprinted over to join the others. That's what a year of sunshine, nourishment, and love could do for a body.

In fact, C'an Saas on the whole was thriving. Largely due to the children. Their Tideblessings had been our saving grace. Caleb had chased away the darkness with his Dawn Tideblessing, harnessing the power of the *real* sun in his little hand.

Cissy, our Blossom, could make nearly anything grow. Xander and Moll worked with her tirelessly to improve and learn, and it hadn't taken long before she was able to bring the trees and meadows back to life.

And Tristan, our Hunter, had been a welcome surprise. His magic gave him a deep connection to the animals. Within months, the forest had been teeming with life again. Lives that nourished our people, but lives that he valued and cherished, and taught our citizens to do the same.

It hadn't all come easy, though. My heart gave a squeeze. We'd lost some of our people in the fight. Three from Hook's crew, four from our C'an Saas loyalists, and of course, our beloved Billy.

Losing her had been a blow we still hadn't recovered from, and I knew we never fully would. She'd had the courage to do what I couldn't, and her sacrifice would never be forgotten. We made sure of it by creating a fountain of her in front of the palace. Billy with her bow, arrow nocked and ready to fly.

I swallowed the knot in my throat and blinked back the tear as a warm hand on the small of my back had me turning my head.

"You've been on your feet for hours now. I think it's time to get in the shade and take a little rest."

I could see the worry in James's eyes as they dropped lower to my ever-growing belly. He wasn't wrong, although as I looked out over the endless fields, I winced, because there was still so much to do—a bounty of vegetables that needed harvesting, grains that needed processing, and animals that needed feeding.

Still, my lips tipped into a wide grin. Our harvest was too bountiful?

What a problem to have.

"If you have a lie-down on a blanket in the clearing, I'll have Freya make you a glass of lemonade and a peach-and-goat-cheese daintique."

I narrowed my eyes at him and laughed. "Oh, you really know how to bribe a girl, don't you?"

He dipped his head to steal a kiss and I wrapped my arms tight around his waist. Sometimes, I just needed to make sure he was real. I'd dreamed of him for so long, and then, when I finally had him, it always felt like he'd be snatched away. I was just getting used to the fact that he wasn't going anywhere. And better yet? He didn't want to.

There were times that he still woke up, bathed in sweat, from a terrible nightmare. But those times grew further and further apart. He was healing. We were healing each other, and while it wasn't magic, it was a blessing to be sure.

"Harmony, Harmony, you're not going to believe it!"

Cissy's voice echoed through the trees and James pulled away, heat swirling in his eyes as he gazed down at my lips and let out a sigh. "Be back with snacks."

With that, he stalked away, and I grinned as I watched him go.

Cissy and Tristan came running my way a few seconds later, both breathless.

"We found those robin's eggs...and guess what else?" Cissy whispered.

"What?"

"Another nest. A bigger one, on the side of the cliff face." She lowered her voice and looked around. "Bonnie was there, and Fetch flew up to join her. I think they got married like you and Hook!"

"I was able to see the eggs. Four of them, speckled and brown," Tristan confirmed with a wide smile.

"I'm going to be a grandmother!" I said with a delighted laugh.

Fetch was getting on in years, and the thought that a part of him would always be with me was like a balm to my soul.

"I was thinking, if all four hatch, we might want to think about building a mew...I could sort of run it. If you wanted, that is." Tristan's cheeks flushed, and I nodded enthusiastically.

"That's a great idea. Let's work out a good spot and we'll make a blueprint together and hopefully get it built before the baby comes."

"Let's get Caleb and show him!"

The two scampered off, and a few minutes later, I was stretched out on a blanket, waiting for my husband to come with my promised treats. His black edged book of fairytales was spread open on my lap, and I gently turned the page. The harvest had been a whirlwind, even with magic to help, and I hadn't had a chance to check on my friends all week, but I knew a big day was coming...

I tugged open the cover of the book and flipped the pages until I got to something new; A picture that had my heart singing.

Duncan Westerly, former Second Prince of Alabaster, stood hand in hand with smuggler in chief, Billy O'Donnelly. He was dapper in his dove gray waistcoat and pants, and she looked like the badass bitch she was in her crimson corseted wedding dress complete with a dagger at her hip...just in case.

This version of Billy was different. No pointed ears, not lean and rangy like the Billy we'd lost, but that spirit remained. The brash confidence, the wicked smile when she chose to wield it. Alabaster Billy was a less wounded version of Oz Billy. It wasn't hard to see why Duncan had fallen in love with her...again.

Flanking the happy couple were the O'Donnelly brothers. Paddy was making devil ears behind Scotty as Andrew stared down at some gadget in his hand.

The day was a beautiful one. The sun shone bright as the people of Alabaster gathered to celebrate the happy couple.

I turned the page with a sigh and leafed to the very back of the book. A huge picture took up most of the page, and I settled back to admire it for a second.

C'an Saas.

Rivers flowing, flowers blooming, the palace banners flying high, and beneath it, some new text that hadn't been there a few weeks before...

The Queen of C'an Saas and her pirate-turned-king had so much to live for, and even more on the way.

Soon enough they'll add to their family...

. . .

I PAUSED, finger poised to turn the page. Instead, I closed the book gently and laid it down beside me. More than anything, I wanted to know how much more had been written… whether we would have a boy or a girl. To read more about our happily ever after, and find out if he or she would have black hair like their father, or eyes like mine.

But then I remembered what my old friend Gayelette had told me long ago;

"The answers to our questions don't matter half as much as the journey we take to find them…"

And she was right.

THE END

Soon they'll add to their family,
Triplets, a blessing…and a new prophecy

All of them girls, to their father's delight
Lyric and Melody, love at first sight

Then little Billy to round out the three
A perfect, three-part harmony.

The grayest gray, the brightest light
And bringer of balance, the darkest night

No good witch, bad witch, wars within,
The three must unite to conquer sin

Seer, healer, hand of death
A coven's oath, a new realm's breath

But something's coming, a threat that's grown,
For they escaped the pages, but not alone…

CONNECT WITH ME

Email me at Shannon@shannonmayer.com or find me on social media.
FACEBOOK READER GROUP
INSTAGRAM
TIKTOK

Join my newsletter for updates on upcoming books, behind the scenes info, and exclusive content.